THE OATH

Michael Jecks gave up a career in the computer industry to concentrate on writing and the study of medieval history. A regular speaker at library and literary events, he is a past Chairman of the Crime Writers' Association. He lives with his wife, children and dogs in northern Dartmoor.

Also by Michael Jecks

The Last Templar
The Merchant's Partner
A Moorland Hanging
The Crediton Killings
The Abbot's Gibbet
The Leper's Return
Squire Throwleigh's Heir
Belladonna at Belstone
The Traitor of St Giles
The Boy Bishop's Glovemaker
The Tournament of Blood
The Sticklepath Strangler
The Devil's Acolyte
The Mad Monk of Gidleigh
The Templar's Penance
The Outlaws of Ennor
The Tolls of Death
The Chapel of Bones
The Butcher of St Peter's
A Friar's Bloodfeud
The Death Ship of Dartmouth
The Malice of Unnatural Death
Dispensation of Death
The Templar, the Queen and Her Lover
The Prophecy of Death
The King of Thieves
The Bishop Must Die

THE OATH

MICHAEL JECKS

**SIMON &
SCHUSTER**

London · New York · Sydney · Toronto

A CBS COMPANY

First published in Great Britain by Simon & Schuster UK Ltd, 2010
A CBS COMPANY

Copyright © Michael Jecks, 2010

3 5 7 9 10 8 6 4 2

Simon & Schuster UK Ltd
1st Floor
222 Gray's Inn Road
London WC1X 8HB

www.simonandschuster.co.uk

Simon & Schuster Australia
Sydney

A CIP catalogue record for this book is available from the British Library

Hardback ISBN 978-1-84737-900-9
Trade Paperback ISBN 978-0-85720-034-1

Typeset by M Rules
Printed in the UK by CPI Mackays, Chatham ME5 8TD

For
Beryl and Peter
The best parents possible!
With much love

GLOSSARY

Aketon a thick tunic, originally padded or quilted, that was worn over the shirt but underneath a man-at-arms' **hauberk**.

Alaunt a hunting dog, like a greyhound but larger, with a broad head and shorter snout. Known for their ferocity, these dogs were used to hunt big game, even bears.

Ambler horses for gentle riding were trained to 'amble', swinging both left legs together, then both right legs.

Amerce a financial penalty that was a type of bond. For example, a man would be 'amerced' to attend court, and if he failed to appear, the sum was his fine.

Attach to secure a man's attendance at court by means of sureties.

Berner the attendant in charge of hounds.

Centaine a unit of men-at-arms in the King's host: a hundred men.

Chevauchée a technical military term, generally meaning to ride out and pillage an area.

Deodand a tax, based on the value of a murder weapon, payable as a fine. This tax remained in force until the nineteenth century, when railway companies complained at the value of entire trains being levied for accidental homicides!

Fosser the sexton, a gravedigger.

Garbage animal offal used for food.

Guyenne that part of France still ruled by the British King: Aquitaine, Anjou, etc.

Hainaulter man from Hainault in Flanders.

Hauberk the mail shirt that was worn over the **aketon** but beneath the **pair of plates**.

Heriot a fine of the best beast, rendered to a serf's lord when the serf died.

Hobelar armed man who rode upon a 'hobby', a small riding horse.

Kennel the central gulley or gutter in a medieval street.

Leyrwite this was the fine imposed on women for adultery or sexual incontinence.

Lurdan a term of opprobrium – a sluggard, a laggard, a dimwit.

Mastiff a large dog, used as a guard and sometimes for baiting.

Murdrum the fine imposed on a **vill** when none could prove 'Englishry' for a corpse. It had been a means of fining the English rebels after the Norman invasion, and was imposed when a body was thought to be Norman, as a way of punishing the community.

Pair of Plates a form of body armour made by fixing overlapping plates of steel to the inside of a cloth or leather tunic. It was worn over the mail **hauberk**.

Palfrey   a small to medium-sized horse noted for its comfort.

Posse Comitatus   the force of the county, available to keep the peace or help hunt down felons.

Rache   a running dog, which we would probably call a greyhound today.

Rounsey   the common horse for general use: also used as a warhorse by men-at-arms, and as a packhorse.

Schiltrom   troops drawn up in battle order.

Vill   a territorial unit, comprising a number of houses and the land adjacent, which was the basic unit of administration under feudal law.

Vingtaine   a military unit of twenty men.

CAST OF CHARACTERS

Sir Baldwin de Furnshill	Keeper of the King's Peace, Baldwin was once a Templar, but now seeks a quiet life in Devon.
Simon Puttock	Baldwin's closest friend, Simon has worked with him on many murder investigations.
Margaret (Meg)	Simon's wife.
Peterkin (Perkin)	Simon and Margaret's son.
Hugh	Simon's long-suffering servant.
Rob	son of a prostitute in Dartmouth, Rob has become Simon's servant too.
Jack	a young fellow accompanying Baldwin.

Nobles

King Edward II	King of England.
Edward, Duke of Aquitaine, (also Earl of Chester)	the King's eldest son, the future Edward III, who was never made a prince.

Sir Hugh le Despenser	Sir Hugh 'The Younger', the closest adviser to the King, his best friend, and alleged lover. Known for his outrageous greed and ambition.

Earl Hugh of Winchester	Sir Hugh's father, known as 'The Elder', a loyal servant of King Edward I, but a man keen to enrich himself.

Queen Isabella	wife to the King, and figurehead of the rebellion against him.

Sir Roger Mortimer	lover to Queen Isabella and, with her, leader of the rebels.

Sir Ralph of Evesham	a knight in the service of the King.

Sir Charles of Lancaster	formerly a loyal servant of Earl Thomas of Lancaster, now he is in the service of the King.

Bristol

Arthur Capon	a wealthy burgess in Bristol.

Madame Capon	wife to Arthur.

Petronilla	Arthur's daughter.

Cecily	maidservant to the Capon family.

Squire William de Bar	husband of Petronilla.

Father Paul	priest who became Petronilla's lover.

Emma Wrey	widow of a successful merchant in Bristol.

Sir Stephen Siward	Coroner in Bristol.

Sir Laurence Ashby	the Constable of Bristol Castle.

Thomas Redcliffe	a merchant of Bristol ruined by pirates.

Roisea Redcliffe	Thomas's wife.

Soldiers

Robert Vyke	a serf brought into the King's host.
Otho	Sergeant from Vyke's vill.
Herv Tyrel	a friend to Vyke.
Walerand of Guildford	also Walerand the Tranter, a carter pressed into the King's service to help transport goods for the troops.

AUTHOR'S NOTE

The idea for this book has had a lengthy gestation. It all began when I picked up an Everyman edition of *The Old Yellow Book*, which was the source for Robert Browning's *The Ring and the Book*. It is not an easy book to read, because it revolves around a series of legal documents, but for a novelist it is sheer gold dust!

Browning's piece is a poetic reworking of a story he discovered while staying in Florence in 1860. As he tells it, he was wandering round the Piazza of San Lorenzo, past a bookseller in a booth, when the soiled old yellow tome caught his eye. He bought it and took it home, where he devoured it, translating the full story over a number of days.

The book gave the record of an astonishing murder case from 1698 – the assassination of an entire family. The vile behaviour of both groom and father-in-law, set beside the misery of the poor girl-bride and her pathetic lover, were as absorbing as any Shakespearean tragedy, and I could not put it out of my mind, trying to figure out how best to use it in one of my novels.

However, it was only when looking at that other wonderfully dysfunctional family – that of King Edward II and his wife Queen Isabella – that the comparison between the two families struck a chord, and I had to go and look up Browning's source again. Pretty soon it was clear to me that this was the book I wanted to write. There are changes, however, so anyone familiar with Browning's work can relax – there is no way they will guess how my story ends!

While I have tried, as usual, to be as true to history as I possibly can be, it's always the small details that give me the biggest headaches. For example, we know that the King set off from London in October 1326 with a small force of men, on the run from Sir Roger Mortimer and the Queen. He may have only had a few men with him, but he had barrels of money, somewhere in the region of £20,000. That was more than the income of England's king in a year, so he must have had guards. How many? Don't know.

Likewise, he set off towards Cardiff with even fewer men. He still had his money, but we know that his men were going AWOL and that no one was coming to replace them and fill the ranks. But when he quitted Caerphilly, he left behind a garrison, and still had a force of men about him with whom to travel to Margam and Neath Abbey. How many? Again, I don't know.

The tale of Despenser's decline and death is pretty well documented. I am especially grateful to Jules Frusher for the pointer on Edward being, perhaps, at Hereford during Despenser's execution. No one else has spotted this, but the King's journey was to Kenilworth Castle, with Lancaster guarding him. Yet Lancaster was present at Hugh Despenser's hearing and execution. If so, where was the King? It's perfectly logical to think that Lancaster came with the King and Despenser to Hereford, and at the time, it would have been thought perfectly acceptable to force the King to watch his favourite being executed.

I refer in this book to Edward's son as the Duke of Aquitaine, which may confuse some readers. Why don't I call him Prince Edward and be done with it? Well, young Edward had been made Earl of Chester by the King only a short while after his birth, and he was known as such throughout his childhood. Later, at the age of almost thirteen, he was sent to France to pay homage to the French King, in his father's place, for the English territories in France. For that, he received the gift of Aquitaine, and became a duke. However, he was never actually made Prince of the Realm. To become a prince was not automatic, it was an honour that the King alone could grant. So I use the most senior title that Edward was given.

For that last detail, I am grateful to Ian Mortimer. His *The Greatest Traitor: The Life of Sir Roger Mortimer*, and *The Perfect King: The Life of Edward III*, and also his excellent *The Time Traveller's Guide to Medieval England* have been regularly referred to. I often have to flick through Harold F. Hutchinson's *Edward II*, as well as Mary Saaler's book, and that of Roy Martin Haines – all with the same title! Among my more esoteric sources, Terry Brown's *English Martial Arts* ranks highly, as does *The Medieval Coroner* by R.F. Hunnisett, and *John Leland's Itinerary*, which is wonderful for those who want to see a landscape through the eyes of someone who was alive 500 years ago. I am also hugely indebted to Jules Frusher for her website 'Lady Despenser's Scribery' at http://despenser.blogspot.com. Jules has given me enormous help.

Which is why I have to quickly add that no matter how good all these, and other individuals are, the errors are sadly still all my own.

But errors and omissions aside, I hope that this tale, which is still thrilling to me, nearly 700 years after the events I describe, will take you back in time to a period when life was undoubtedly nastier, colder, wetter, more painful and more dangerous. And in so many ways, still extremely attractive.

Michael Jecks
North Dartmoor
November 2009

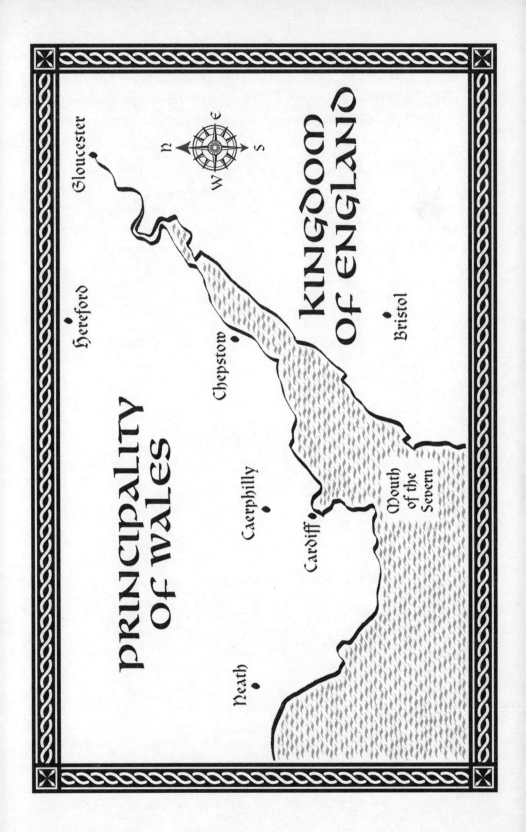

CHAPTER ONE

Bristol

Her nightmare always began in the same way.

It started with the urgent cry.

'Cecily? Cecily, help me!'

Cecily hurried to her mistress's door as soon as she heard the summons. A maid of almost thirty, short and mousy-haired under her wimple, she had an oval-shaped face and smiling green eyes. She walked in to find Petronilla Capon sitting on her bed's edge, waving a hand in the direction of the cot, from which all the screaming emanated.

'Good Cecily, can *you* do anything with him?'

Her mistress was almost eighteen years old. Quite tall, she had the sort of figure that men eyed with unconcealed lust, their wives with simple jealousy. Her face was unmarked with fear or sadness, which was a miracle after the last four years, but now there was an expression of mild panic on it which did not so much mar her beauty as add to it.

'Let me, mistress,' Cecily said comfortably, crossing the floor. Cecily had been her maid for years now and was as much a

1

part of Petronilla's life as the cross which hung from the silver chain about her neck. Everyone who knew Petronilla knew how devoted Cecily was to her and, since the birth of Little Harry, the maid had grown still more attentive.

Little Harry looked up at Cecily with his blue-black eyes still fogged with despair. 'Hush, little one,' Cecily said, beginning to wipe away the worst of the vomit with his slavering clout[1].

'I did what you said,' Petronilla stated with weary conviction. 'He had finished feeding, and I just had him over my shoulder . . .'

'You should have stopped feeding him a little earlier, mistress. Then, perhaps, you could have burped him *before* he was sick.'

Petronilla gave her a wretched smile. 'I don't understand the boy. He cries all night, sleeps all day, and when he whimpers and I try to feed him, he does this to me. Ungrateful little monster, aren't you? Oh no, what now? Why is he crying *now*, Cecily?'

In answer, her maid picked him up and sniffed at his backside before pulling a face. 'Why do you think?'

Her mistress often behaved as though she was a child herself still, thought Cecily. When she had married and moved to her husband's house near Hanham, despite the fact that it was only some three miles outside Bristol, the girl had reacted as if it were the edge of the world. Cecily had looked after Petronilla from her eighth year, and when the girl had married Squire William de Bar nearly four years ago, Cecily had gone to Hanham with her. When Petronilla's husband had evicted Cecily, forcing her from his young bride's side, the maid had been distraught.

It had been an awful time. When Cecily was dismissed and

---

[1] bib

sent back to Bristol, Arthur Capon was reluctant to give her house room, seeing her as a waste of space.

Cecily carefully unwrapped the boy, taking off the swaddling-bands then cleaning him with the old tail-clout[1]. The soiled bands were dropped into the bucket ready for soaking and washing, and then she massaged his limbs tenderly with a little oil of myrtle. It was hideously expensive, but there was nothing too costly for the young master. She wrapped him in fresh swaddling bands, then, cooing and shushing, she cuddled him close.

Petronilla watched her with a wan smile. The birth had been easy enough, but like so many new mothers, she was exhausted after too little sleep in the last two weeks.

'Mistress, sit and rest. I can look after the little master for you. He just wants company, I'll be bound.'

'All *I* want is my sleep,' Petronilla said with some acid. 'Harry keeps me awake all night.'

Cecily said nothing. There was no need – both knew that it was Cecily who most often went to the baby in the watches of the night.

Taking the little mite with her as she left her mistress, Cecily quietly closed the door. Petronilla was already on her bed, her eyes closed, and young master Harry snuffled and nuzzled against Cecily's breast. He seemed happy to accept her as a surrogate mother.

She murmured to him as she walked through the passageway to the hall. Little Harry looked up at her with those wide, trusting eyes, and she smiled as he burped.

Cecily had sworn to serve his mother and protect Harry, and she would not break that vow.

*

[1] nappy

That part of her dream was always so happy. She had been content, then, easy in her mind. Before that, while Petronilla was
away in Hanham, her life had been empty, her existence anxious,
because unnecessary servants were easily discarded. Now, with
Petronilla back once more, it seemed that Cecily could count on
a secure future.

Later that same morning, Cecily respectfully ducked her head to
Petronilla's parents as she passed through the hall on her way
towards the screens.

Arthur Capon sat near the fire, ignoring Cecily as he spoke
with his wife who was sitting in the light near the window's bars
and working on a fine cap for her grandson, peering closely with
her poor eyesight.

Cecily went to the little pantry near the front door. Here she
could dandle the boy on her knee while chatting to the bottler.
It was always best to keep a child busy. Just as he needed his
arms and legs restrained so that they might grow firm and
straight, there were other risks: a child might stare too long at a
single bright light, and that would produce a squint in later years.
Or a babe set to sleep in a hanging cot might wriggle free of the
bindings, and fall and hang himself. There were so many dangers. But at least people tried to protect children. No one would
hurt a child on purpose, would they? That would be wicked.

So she had believed, in her innocence.

In her dream, she remembered the knocking at the door,
reminding her of her failure, her dishonour.

She had sworn to protect Harry. And instead . . .

The rapping was insistent. Cecily had remained sitting while the
bottler rose from his stool and walked to the screens. There was
nothing unusual in visitors coming to the house, for Arthur

Capon was a successful merchant, and also a money-lender. Men often called by to speak with him, and so, as the bottler opened the door, Cecily did not look up. It was just a normal morning.

Except then it ceased to be normal.

There was a shout: full of malice, it was enough to startle Cecily and make her look up. The door was suddenly thrust wide, and the bottler remonstrated, only to make a strange noise, a watery, gurgling sound like Little Harry, and then he stepped back, falling hard on his rump. Seeing him, Cecily almost laughed aloud. He was so proud of himself and his position in the world, that to stumble like that would mortify him. But the smile was struck from her face as she saw the blood.

And then the men entered.

She told the jury at the inquest, held that same afternoon, that first inside was the squire, Petronilla's husband.

Squire William de Bar was like a man made of steel that day, she said. His blue eyes were cold and uncaring, and as he strode over the threshold, his sword was already dripping with the bottler's gore. He kicked the body aside before marching into the hall towards Arthur Capon and, as the older man demanded to know what he was doing in the house unannounced, he thrust his sword into his father-in-law's breast. Capon stared at the man disbelievingly, his mouth working, but no words came. He tried to stand, but that merely forced his body further onto the blade, and the blood gushed from his nostrils and mouth as he attempted to cry for help.

The only voice Cecily heard in her dreams was that of Madame Capon. Cecily told the jurors that, as Madame Capon's husband slumped back in his chair, his arms thrashing, legs beating a staccato rhythm as his soul fled, his wife gave a shrill little cry: the despairing whimper of a creature in the extremity of distress.

5

The jurors drew in a collective hiss of breath – like a snake's curse – as Cecily told that part.

Madame Capon's little wail had been enough for the murderer to turn to her. Pulling his sword free from Arthur Capon's jerking body, he said in a voice low with rage. 'You, you lousy old whore, *you* did this. You and him, you robbed me of my name, you took my honour and shamed me! Are you satisfied now, *you bitch?*' Cecily could remember each word with absolute precision. With that, he punched the woman with his free hand, and she lay sobbing, her hand at her face. It was not sufficient to save her. She was stabbed three times in the breast and throat.

Cecily stood clutching the baby to her, staring in horror. Now she darted to the side of the screens in the pantry, concealing herself and hushing the baby as more men ran inside, through the hall out to the solar and Petronilla's bedchamber, their boots thundering on the boards. Soon the hall was empty but for the two corpses and the dying bottler. So far, her quick thinking had saved her and the child from attack.

As the steps faded, she darted to the bottler. He was lying on his side, gripping his belly, and she saw between his hands the bulge of blue and pink intestines, the slow seeping of blood through his fingers as he began to shake, speechless with agony. 'Go!' he whispered.

With that, Cecily roused herself into action. She ran to her master and took his dagger from the sheath at his belt, turned, and began to run, Harry gripped tightly in her arms. She had sworn to protect him. Not that she repeated that to the jurors. They all knew her, they had seen her with her charge. No one could doubt her love for the mite.

Outside, in the paved court before the house, she heard another woman's shriek, a rising ululation of torment that gradually faded as Cecily ran farther from that house of horror, clutching the baby to her breast like a woman possessed, hurtling to the gate that led to the road outside.

Yes. She had told the jury all that. Sometimes, when she was fortunate, that was when she woke from the dream, out near the gate before the house. Better that, than to remain asleep and remember the rest.

At other times, she continued in her dream, reliving what happened next.

And always aware of her lies.

First Wednesday after the Feast of St Michael, twentieth year of the reign of King Edward II [1]

Near Barnwell Priory

There was a chill in the air as the men of the Queen's host moved down the broad roadway towards the next town, and young Edward, Duke of Aquitaine and Earl of Chester, shivered miserably. He was tired and feeling more than a little sick. Even with the aketon over his shirt, the hauberk and the pair of plates over that, the dampness seemed to soak into his very soul, making the nausea worse.

He was the son of the King, and the idea that he might shame himself and his father by puking in public was not to be con-sidered. Except he was shamed already.

Always in the past the English King had travelled to Paris to pay homage for the lands owned by him in France. Guyenne was crucial to the English Crown, after all. The money from those great wine-producing regions brought in more to the exchequer

---

[1] 1 October 1326

than England and Wales together. It was inconceivable that the King could allow those lands to be lost.

However, the worst had happened. King Edward II had allowed the French to occupy the whole of his estates in France, and King Charles had declared them forfeit *purely because King Edward had refused to pay homage*. Edward was in an impossible situation. Were he to leave England, his barons would overthrow his Regent, Sir Hugh le Despenser, son of the Earl of Winchester, just as the Earl of Warwick had done ten or more years ago when he captured Piers Gaveston and had him beheaded. The King dared not leave another close friend to the mercy of his barons.

Queen Isabella, the Duke's mother, was sister to King Charles, and had travelled to Paris to negotiate a truce and try to win back the English lands. Success seemed close at hand when she wrote to ask that her son be given the English lands in France. That way, she explained, he could travel to Paris, pay homage in his own right, and thereby satisfy the English King's need to remain in England, while also giving the French King the gratification of knowing that he had procured the confirmation of his subject's loyalty. It was the ideal compromise.

So the young Earl had been elevated to Duke and sent to France, but when he arrived, a year ago, he was thrown into a maelstrom of politicking. His mother had been recalled to England but refused to obey her husband, declaring that there was a third person in her marriage, and until her husband threw out Sir Hugh le Despenser, she would hold herself to be widowed. And then, although the King wrote to Edward to command him to return and not allow himself to be forced into a marriage contract or to remain under the control of his mother or the French King, he had been forced to do both.

He had not willingly disobeyed his father. He loved him – no son more; but he adored his mother too, and Isabella had made it clear that she could not return to Edward while Despenser remained at court.

'Do not worry, he will see sense,' she cooed to her son when he told her how anxious the separation made him. Not yet four-teen, he was a pawn in the battle between King and Queen; he feared he was the cause of their antagonism.

At first, to be in France was glorious. He had thought it a frolic, away from the stresses of life in England. But as the days grew into weeks, the weeks into months, he became aware of the influence the other man had on his mother: the witty, charming, shrewd and devious Sir Roger Mortimer.

Sir Roger, who had led the men of the Borders against the King, and who had escaped from the Tower of London when his death sentence was signed, was in France pouring acid into the Queen's ears. Edward knew it – he had seen them together often enough. And it was clear that his mother's relationship with this man was more than mere friendship. She was flaunting her affection for Sir Roger before all at the French court, and humil-iating her son into the bargain. Duke Edward heard the whispers and gossip as courtiers discussed his mother and her adulterous affair. An affair that was not only against her marriage vows but also a terrible felony. A man committing adultery with a queen was putting the bloodline of the royal family at risk, as Queen Isabella well knew. Her brothers' wives had committed adultery twelve years before, and their lovers had been executed, while the women languished horribly, dying in foul captivity. She *knew* she was causing mortification to her husband and heaping dis-grace upon the family.

Unable to intervene, Duke Edward could only watch and listen as opprobrium was heaped upon his mother and her lover.

And he felt that the same was his due, as he betrayed his father the King in all that he did. Now, here he was, back in England to fulfil his mother's desire to see his father forced to lose his adviser, Sir Hugh le Despenser. And then, to lose his throne.

Edward almost despaired. All close to him were placed there by his mother or Mortimer. His life was hedged about with 'protection' at every turn, so that for the first time in his life, he had no independence. At almost fourteen, he was a man now, and yet the responsibilities he had assumed were taken from him and managed for him – and there was nothing he could do about it.

No. That was not quite true, he told himself as he watched Mortimer talking to a pasty-faced churl with greying hair and sallow complexion. Behind them a short way was his own fellow. Not even a knight, this, but a guard who had proved himself more loyal to Edward's interests than any other: Sam Fletcher.

He was the one man whom the young Duke trusted.

CHAPTER TWO

First Thursday after the Feast of St Michael[1]

London

All about London, there was an air of expectation as the King finally rode out through the gates of his castle, the Tower of London, and past the great crowd of men and women watching silently in the streets outside. There was no fanfare.

From his vantage point, Thomas Redcliffe watched most intently, eyeing the King himself, the man riding at his side – Sir Hugh le Despenser – and then the other knights all riding in a knot. Behind them came the men-at-arms of all degrees, the group of Welsh knifemen whom the King honoured so highly, the pikemen with their long weapons shouldered ready for the march. And all about was the slow clank and rattle of chains and harnesses, the leaden rumble of cartwheels turning on the cobbles as wagons and carts passed by.

The King looked furious, Redcliffe thought. He rode

---

[1] 2 October 1326

upright, stiffly ignoring the stares from all sides. The whole world could have been here, and his disdain would have passed magnificently over it, noting nothing worth seeing, for this King was being forced to ride from his own capital by his Queen.

Those with him looked fearful of their own shadows, the marching men-at-arms ready to take up their weapons at the slightest provocation. They had been bottled up in the Tower for too long as the city began to fall apart. Law and order were collapsing as the King's authority waned, and the men in the King's guard knew it. It would take very little for the crowd to launch themselves on them, knowing that Edward's son and wife were only a few leagues away. The hated Sir Hugh le Despenser would die in moments, and all those who committed such a crime would be pardoned in an instant by the Queen. There was a rich reward offered for his head.

The entourage was still passing when Redcliffe dropped from the side of the building where he had been waiting, and in a moment he was gone, invisible amongst the restless hordes about the streets.

It was something he had always regretted, this ability to disappear in the midst of a throng. In the past he was sure that it had cost him membership of the Freedom of his city, and yet now he hoped it would help him to regain his lost fortune. He had much to win back.

All because of pirates and a thieving banker.

On the Road to Baldock, Hertfordshire
That evening, when they all settled in the next town, the Duke of Aquitaine was eating a solitary meal when his door opened and Sam Fletcher walked in.

'My lord, I have messages from Sir Roger for you.' He waved

at the Duke's steward to leave, and the man bowed his way from the room.

Fletcher was a heavily-built man, but all was muscle, not fat. His face was square, with an unfashionable moustache and beard, and his leathery skin was burned dark by the wind and the sun. He was not a restful companion, because he rarely relaxed. His grey eyes tended to be ever-watchful for danger. Now, they were fixed unblinkingly on the Duke.

Duke Edward sighed. 'Is there never to be any peace? Put them down and let me alone.'

'Yes, my lord. Shall I fetch you some wine first?' Sam said, closing the door behind him.

Duke Edward threw down his spoon and glared at Sam. The seething resentment which had been brewing for months was ready to spill over, and he felt as his grandsire must have done, when he was frustrated in his ambitions. Tales of King Edward I's rages were numerous in the household, especially over his son, Duke Edward's father, who once, so it was said, was grasped by King Edward I and shaken so firmly that handfuls of his hair had been pulled free. Now the Duke could feel a similar vexation even with his most loyal guard.

'You son of a hog – do you never listen to me?' he raged. 'No one else does, I know, but I'd hoped you at least would pay me some attention, man! Why does—'

He broke off as Sam Fletcher held a finger to his lips, then pointed at the door. Others were outside, listening.

'Oh, bring me some wine, Fletcher, if you insist I must read these things,' Duke Edward muttered, slumping in his seat. There was no point in arguing.

There were so many notes and orders for him to read and sign each day, so much to approve. He suspected that he was being deliberately given work to do, to maintain the feeling that he was important, while others went ahead and did just as they wished. He was caged here, a prince without the title, without the freedom to pursue his own ambitions, tied to his mother's apron-strings and forced to trail after her and her lover, always taking second place.

'Here, my lord.'

Still scowling, he took the goblet and drank off a half in one gulp. When he looked up at Sam Fletcher, he saw something in the man's eyes. 'What?'

Speaking very quietly, Sam Fletcher walked around until his back was to the door. No one could see his face through the keyhole or gaps in the planks. 'My lord, you must listen carefully,' he whispered. 'I dare not speak loudly in case we are overheard. Do not shout or exclaim, I beg. It would bring you trouble, and cost me my life.'

The Duke nodded slowly.

'I have a friend in Sir Roger's household. He tells me there is a plot to seek out the King your father and see him murdered. A man has been hired to assassinate him.'

First Saturday after the Feast of St Michael[1]

Marshfield near Bristol

Father Paul stepped back towards his church as the light began to fade, the old spade in his hand.

Today he had been out in the little strip fields with the other villagers. It was a long way away, but the walk did him good. Anything that could help him forget was good.

He had been fortunate, or so he had thought, to be given the

---

[1] 4 October 1326

job a few weeks ago of priest here in the little vill near Marshfield. It offered him that element of freedom from the Bishop
that a little distance conferred. Marvellous to wake in the morning and hear only the wind in the trees rather than the rattle and
clatter of the city. Not that he disliked Bristol itself, but he did
not see how the city could ever give a man enough peace in
order to consider the more important issues of life. The idea that
a man would be able to find his place in the world while living
in so hectic and febrile an environment was laughable.

And then there was the loss which he had suffered.

The wind was cold, a gust of pure ice that seemed to shear
through his jack and chemise to the very marrow in his bones,
as though his flesh and blood were no protection whatever. He
stood a moment, feeling the weight of the wooden spade, a piece
of carved wood with a strip of metal at the bottom of the wooden
paddle to help it cut into soil, and the exhaustion that came from
a day's hard work. Exhaustion both mental and physical.

It was hard to think of her and their babe. The little one should
be four or five months old now, and yet Paul had not seen it.
Never would, knowingly. That had been made quite clear to him.
He had besmirched himself with the sins of the flesh but, what
was worse, his Bishop said, he had also tempted a young and
immature married woman into adultery. That was unforgivable.

Yes, it was. He knew that. He knew it as he first met her and
felt that magical lurch in his breast at the sight of her smile. That
she felt the same was written there in her eyes. He could not
have been mistaken. She came alive at the sight of him.

And it was hardly surprising, after a look at the Squire. A
more cruel and inflexible sinner it was difficult to imagine. The
man did not deserve to own poor little Petronilla, as he proved
that day when he took hold of her wrists and beat her across the
back and buttocks. That was why Paul had to save her.

15

About him, a few beech trees were hissing in the wind, their little bronze-coloured leaves dancing, and he shuddered as he returned to the present.

The ferns were all turning, too. Their fronds golden and umber, they had begun to collapse on top of each other, while behind them the dark purple sloes were showing in the blackthorns. It was a lovely time of year, he always felt, but terrifying too, because it was the onset of the death of nature, the beginning of winter. He only prayed that his stock of food would last him. At least now, he thought with a small sigh, all memories of that other life were fading. He was a soul at rest, more or less, once more.

Continuing to the small single-bay cottage, he set the spade beside the chest where he kept his belongings, and pulled off his thick, fustian overtunic, hanging it on a hook near the fire to dry while he shrugged on a thick robe.

It was cold in the chamber. He would have to survive without heat for now, for he hadn't managed to keep his little fire going while he was out. The sticks and logs were still there on the clay hearth, but there was no warmth in the room. It was a miserable reminder of the way that the weather had turned in the last month.

He blew on his hands and set off for his chapel, crossing himself with some holy water from the stoup at the door and walking towards the altar, bending to his knees on the hard-packed soil of the floor.

The simple wooden cross was enough. He had made it himself out of two pieces of roughly squared wood, their faces cut and shaped so that they could slot together. It had been the first thing he had done when he arrived here, a kind of penance for the grave crime he had committed.

Petronilla had been his test, the trial of his faith. And to his undying shame, he had succumbed and failed.

Still, he reflected, at least he was here now in the peace of the countryside, where all memories of that crime could be forgotten. He was far enough away for his crime to be unremarked. As for the husband, cruel and vengeful as he was, Squire William wouldn't seek for him here; and Petronilla herself would be safe in her father's house.

He was safe; she was safe.

And that, he hoped, was the end of their story. The woman whom he had adored would live out her life with the joy of her freedom and their child to remind her of their brief time together.

Second Tuesday after the Feast of St Michael[1]

Bristol

Sir Stephen Siward thrust his thumbs into his sword belt as he left the castle by the great gates, strolling past the carters and sumptermen bringing in additional supplies, and out into the city itself.

To the city folk who met him, he was an amiable fellow, dark-haired, with blue eyes in a square face that was prone to smiling even when he stood before them in his new position as Coroner of the city. For a knight it was a post of some importance. There was no money in it, true, but a shrewd man could always turn a position like this to his advantage.

Yes, there was much to smile about. The city suited him well; he had been here only a little while, but there was an atmosphere of opulence about it that he liked, and he could still live well and be comfortable, despite his straitened circumstances.

Money was not so plentiful as once it had been. His two

[1] 7 October 1326

17

manors, on which he depended for his livelihood, had each suffered a catastrophe. The barn had caught fire, destroying the stocks of hay and the building itself, and in his panic, his favourite horse had tried to escape from the stables next door. Damned creature broke a foreleg attempting to free himself and had to be killed.

To add insult to injury, as well as the fire, there had been an outbreak of murrain in his flocks, and his sheep continued to die. He had needed a loan to survive the winter, at ruinous interest. Still, he had just won a small wager with the castellan's clerk, and with three shillings in his purse, Sir Stephen felt as though life was improving.

Seeing Emma Wrey, he bowed slightly. The widow was rather beneath his standing as a King's Coroner, and he had no desire to have other people seeing him show her respect as though she was the widow of an equal. Her husband had been merely a goldsmith and merchant, who had built a profitable business by loaning money, ignoring the Gospels' strictures against usury.

There were some other bold fellows in the city who were money-lenders too, not only Wrey. Such men had their uses: there were occasions, such as during tournaments, when a knight needed to ransom his horse and armour from a more successful opponent – or when a man's manors failed – but in the general run of things, it was better to avoid them. And it was best to avoid this widow, because Cecily worked for her, and Sir Stephen had no desire to meet that maid again. He knew she had held an infatuation for him. It was a relief that his involvement with her was ended, he reflected.

The widow gave him a gracious little duck of her head just then, honouring him with the correct amount of esteem, no more. It was enough to send him on his way smiling, his blue eyes glinting in the sun.

Yes, this city was a good one, although for how much longer it was hard to tell. He had only been away for a couple of days, but the change in atmosphere was marked: the place had a defeated air about it. The King had passed by, but it was the Queen whom all truly feared. She was a matter of days away, if the reports were accurate, and she had with her enough men to encompass this little city. Unless the King managed to magically summon up a host from somewhere, he could not hope to stand against her in a fight.

There was little to be gained by worrying about such things. Sir Stephen was a professional knight, and a professional politician. He kept his feet on the ground, and a foot in each camp wherever possible. So far he had successfully held on to his position with the King by regular doses of flattery aimed at that devious shit, Sir Hugh le Despenser, while at the same time assuring others who sought to give succour to the Queen that he was entirely on her side.

Here at Bristol it was easy to keep in contact with both sides of the debate. The city was, in theory, the Queen's own, a part of the gift to her on her marriage to the King. The Queen of England must be permitted her own resources and finance to maintain her household and allow her to support those whom she wished from her largesse. And yet the King had chosen to grant the city to his friend and adviser, the ever-acquisitive Sir Hugh. The Despenser would steal the milk from a mother's breast if he could sell it, Sir Stephen reckoned.

In recent years Sir Hugh had taken over almost all of Wales, robbing some, threatening others, capturing and beating a few. There was no need to wonder why the Marcher Lords, living in the lawless borderlands between England and Wales, had grown to detest him. Well, now he was being chased across the kingdom by those same men whom he had dispossessed.

Sir Stephen had reached the end of the roadway, and was in the middle of the market. Here, he wandered idly among the stalls. There was not a huge amount on display, he noticed. As the threat of war increased, farmers outside the city were keeping their food stores against the day when their price had risen. Those who manufactured goods were staying away from the markets. It was a shocking proof of how the locals felt. There would be a war here, they believed. And the city could go to the Queen in the blink of an eye, even though the castle at the eastern edge of the city was held by the King's garrison.

From now, things would get tight, and that in itself was a concern. Sir Stephen looked at the rows of stalls selling food. He bought a cold pigeon and pulled the carcass apart in the road, tossing the bones to a hopeful-looking dog.

Yes, money was a problem. He had enough to last a week or two, but after that, he wasn't sure what he could do. Still, the castle had food, and more came in each day. The barrels of salted meat and fish were already beginning to fill the castle's undercrofts, but Sir Stephen had no wish to be held there and forced to eat rations of badly salted food.

Well, there was no need to worry. Sir Stephen would not remain inside, waiting to be starved or killed. As soon as he knew which side was likely to win, he would make his move and join them.

CHAPTER THREE

Second Thursday after the Feast of St Michael[1]

Approaching Gloucester

In the mist of the October morning, Sir Ralph of Evesham walked from his tent as the men mounted their horses and prepared for the day's march. It was late already. If he could have had his own way, they would already be moving. They had need of speed, yet the wagons and carts restricted the entire column to the pace of the slowest among them.

He was a strongly-made man, a little above the average height, and with the thick arm and neck muscles that denoted a man of his rank. Grey eyes that rarely blinked gave him the appearance of perpetual concentration, while his square jaw showed his pugnacity. But there was kindness in his eyes too, and a series of creases at each eye showed that he could be an amiable companion.

Pulling on thick gauntlets, he watched as his squire and two

[1] 9 October 1326

21

pages packed his armour into a chest and locked it securely. He wore only his tunic, a padded jack stuffed with lambswool, and on his belt, a small riding sword. There would surely be no need to worry about an attack today. His armour would be a pointless weight for his rounsey.

'Hurry yourselves,' he said. There was no need to shout at these fellows. He knew Squire Bernard would cajole and berate Alexander and Pagan until they had all the goods packed away, his tent folded and stored on the little cart, and were themselves already moving with the King's host.

There were so few. So very few – the men about here, and some who had been sent on further west to prepare the way. That was all. Out of the King's entourage of thousands, only a few hundred had responded to his call.

To Sir Ralph, it had felt a great honour when the King had asked him to join the household. To become one of the King's own bodyguard was a source of immense pride, for it meant that Sir Ralph's loyalty was acknowledged. Not that it should need to be – he was old-fashioned enough to think that once sworn to protect the King and his lands, he was bound by his oaths. He was grounded firmly in the feudal tradition. There should be nothing unique in that.

But many were forsworn. They gave different reasons for their dishonour: distrust of the King's advisers, fear of the King's jealousy, dread of being asked to fight against the Queen and her son, the Duke of Aquitaine – but, as so often, the truth was more mundane. They wanted money.

In the past, life had been so much easier. A man gave his word to his lord and served him. That was enough.

Sir Ralph felt his rounsey stir beneath him and patted his neck gently. 'Easy, my friend, easy.'

'What do you think, Sir Ralph?' Bernard said.

Bernard was a younger man, of some five-and-twenty years, with long, flaxen hair and blue eyes. He always said that his family were knights from some strange country to the east of the Holy Roman Empire, but that they had lived in England since the days of King John, and from his looks it was easy to believe. He was looking at the older man now with exasperation.

'Think about what?' Sir Ralph asked.

'How far must we keep running?'

'You shouldn't speak of such things,' the knight reprimanded him.

'Everyone else in the camp is,' Bernard said reasonably. 'The ones who don't are leaving in the night. Look about you!'

'They are false, then.'

'Sir Ralph, I don't care whether they're false or honourable, I just want them to remain here so that it's not you, me, Alex and Pagan who have to defend the King on our own.'

'There're bound to be more men who come to our aid,' Sir Ralph said stoutly.

'In truth? Well, that's good to hear at least,' Bernard said. 'Sir Ralph, you know me well enough. I am not the man to moan and bleat at every twist of a sour fate. But even now, I can sense the men around us leaching into the woods. There are very few who'll stay for honour's sake.'

'Go and help the pages,' Sir Ralph said shortly.

He watched his squire stride off, bellowing at the two as they tried to take down the tent, and sighed.

There was little he would prefer more than to disappear into the woods himself, but the oath he had given the King had been made before God and was binding. A man was defined by how he behaved: whether he stood by his word or broke it. There might be cowards who were prepared to forswear themselves, but he was not one of them. He had never broken a vow in his life, and if it now cost him even that much, at least he would have lived honourably.

To distract himself, he urged his rounsey into a slow walk across from their tent so that he could look out over the men in the camp.

In the past he had ridden with the King's host from Leeds in Kent up to Scotland, and over all the lands between. He had seen enthusiastic forces gathered; he had seen the shattered remnants of all-but-destroyed ones. The cheery, the furious, he had seen them all. But never before, not even when he had ridden back with his men from the north, when they had been roundly defeated by The Bruce, had he seen their mood so sombre.

Here the men moved about the remains of this village like lost souls. Such a small number . . . When they left London there had been hundreds. Now, perhaps one hundred remained. No more. They stumbled as they walked, exhausted. Cold and wet, they had taken every item of wood from this vill, even down to the cottage doors, in order to feed their fires, but the flames would not give them any cheer. This force was defeated before a single sword had been drawn.

CHAPTER FOUR

Second Saturday after the Feast of St Michael[1]

Near Marshfield

Paul yawned as he came out of his little cottage. He had run out of bread and had to walk down to the vill, as the Abbot was most insistent on maintaining his rights here.

It was the Abbot of Tewkesbury who owned the benefice of this vill, the manor, and the mill; all those who lived here must take their grain to his mill down near Marshfield. The miller, generally a hated individual and viewed by all with suspicion, would take his tenth of the flour after milling, and from his efforts each year, a due was given to the Abbot.

Paul had only a small sack with a few pounds of grain in it, but he hoped it would be enough for two or three loaves. With fortune, he would be able to acquire some more flour before long, but there was no doubt that this would be a very thin winter. Not so bad as when he was a youth and

[1] 11 October 1326

25

the great famine had struck at the kingdom, but still not good.

It was almost noon when he set off on the short walk to Marshfield. It was only some three miles to the mill, and he was in no hurry, but the act of walking did at least keep him warmer. He had to loosen his neckcloth after the first mile or so.

The lands here to the north of Marshfield were uniformly flat and tedious, he always felt. His little church was in the midst of them, and while there were excellent pastures, there was no protection from the wind that came from the north and east. He had already grown to hate that wind. It cared nothing for obstacles, whether flesh, clothing, or even wattle and daub. Whatever it struck, it chilled.

South from the vill, the land was more pleasing to his eyes. It was rolling farmland, leading to good woods, and hills undulating into the distance. This scene never failed to please him as he took it in.

On his way, he had to pass a cottage with a blackthorn bush tied into a bundle and bound to a pole above the front door – the universal sign of a home with ale to sell. Paul went to the door and knocked.

'Yes? Oh, Father, do you want a drop?' Anna asked.

She was a short, plump woman with a cheery face and thick, powerful hands. Paul smiled as Anna fetched him a large earthenware jug, and he drained a cupful in a moment standing by her fire.

'Come, Father, you can sit. You're an honoured guest for us here, you are. Please, take the stool.'

'Anna, I spend my life sitting and kneeling. Do you want me to grow as fat as the Abbot?'

Speaking of the Abbot in such a derogatory way was not seemly, but he knew the peasants here detested the man for his taxes. There was nothing so mean that the Abbot wouldn't take it. Whether it was the *leyrwite*, the tax for adultery, or the *heriot* when a peasant died, the local people were fleeced like sheep. It was cruel to take so much from those who had the least.

There was a sudden crash at the door, and it rasped open slowly, Anna's little husband entering with a small sack upon his back. He carried a couple of faggots of twigs in one hand, both balanced on a billhook's blade.

'Father,' he nodded, letting the sack fall to the ground. It contained three cabbages which had been badly mangled by slugs, and two little turnips. 'You staying for some pottage? Anna makes the best in Marshfield, I'll vow, and with weather like this, you'll need something hot for your belly.'

'I thank you, but the ale and the fire are all I need,' Paul said untruthfully, for the odours from the little pot by the fire had made his belly groan.

'Really?' Anna said mischievously. She lifted the lid and sniffed with appreciation. 'Marrow bones, some meat from a chicken, with all the garbage, and the last of the peas went into that. Sure you don't want any?'

It was later, when Paul was sitting replete, that the peasant looked at his wife and remarked, 'Old Puddock was in the vill this morning. He had news of Bristol.'

Paul smiled to hear that. He was still unused to the broad local pronunciation, and the word 'Brizzle' made him feel alien, but strangely comfortable too.

'Puddock is the Abbey's steward,' Anna said. 'He often comes on tour to see we're not living like lords on the money we manage to save from them.'

'Little enough,' her husband grunted. He picked up a stick and prodded at the fire.

'I really should get off to the miller,' Paul said unenthusiastically.

'Puddock,' the other man said solemnly, 'he was telling of a terrible murder in the big city. An 'ole fam'ly killed.'

'Terrible!' Anna said, while Paul crossed himself sorrowfully.

'There are many evil men in the world,' he opined.

'Because of that silly maid of theirs, the Capons have all been killed. Even the daughter's pup.'

Paul felt the blood drain from his face and throat, just before he heard a roaring in his ears, and the ground came up to strike him.

Second Sunday after the Feast of St Michael[1]

Chapel near Marshfield

The floor's little ridges and gravel were agony to his knees as Paul knelt, head bent, hands clasped tightly near his nose, but that physical pain was nothing compared with the agony of his spirit.

'Could You not have let me suffer for them? Why did You let that evil man kill them? There was no need for them to die. And my child was blameless, surely, in all this! Why should You punish him?'

He knew the answer already, of course. The child he and Petronilla had conceived was born out of an adulterous relationship. That 'petit treason' was itself an abomination. If another man had committed such an offence, it would be cause for an enraged husband to seek him out, and if he were to slay the offender, he was sure to be released. No man could be expected to endure such shame. Paul was fortunate that he was a priest. Holy Orders protected him.

[1] 12 October 1326

The child had been born in sin, and was taken to prove to all that such evil behaviour was as obnoxious to God as to all right-thinking men.

He sobbed, his head falling forward until his elbows were on the ground, his brow on the chilly, clay soil. His heart felt as though it had been twisted and torn at the loss of his lovely Petronilla, the gorgeous, winsome maid with whom he had fallen utterly in love. There was no other emotion that had filled him so entirely. Even when he had felt the hands of the Bishop on his head at his service of ordainment, the thrill had lasted but fleetingly, and by the time they had left the great church, his excitement was more or less dissipated.

That was not the case with Petronilla. He had met her one day when she and her husband arrived at his chapel near Hanham, and it had been just as though a dart from Cupid's bow had stabbed his heart. Instantly he was aware of no one else. Her face radiated perfection: it was like seeing the Blessed Virgin come down from Heaven to his little chapel, filling the place with light and warmth and love.

Of course, then he had had no idea that she might possibly feel the same for him, but there was a sparkle of something reciprocal in her eyes. He was sure of it.

She was wife to Squire William de Bar. That was the harsh truth. She was seventeen on that fateful day when Paul met her, an acknowledged beauty, but still barren. Not for want of trying, the Squire would say gruffly, ignoring, or perhaps not seeing, the pain in her eyes.

Paul could not marry anyway, since he was sworn to celibacy, but that served only to heighten his arousal at the sight of her. She was unattainable, a vision of total perfection: like Guinevere to Launcelot. An angel come to earth.

All would have been well, had Paul not seen her thrashed that day. That was the day he swore to himself that he would not let her suffer in that brutal man's company. He would rescue her.

It was that resolution which had led to her murder.

And his child's.

Second Monday after the Feast of St Michael[1]

Ten leagues from Bristol

The rain fell but they scarcely noticed it any more. On all sides men trudged on through the wet and mud, wretched in the cold. Some were wearing tattered sacking about their heads and backs; others, more fortunate, had leather jerkins, but all shivered as the dampness was flung in their faces by the capricious wind.

These were the men of southern Oxford. Summoned by a King who had lost all support among his barons, briefly arrayed with their unfamiliar weapons, they had been ordered to hurry to his defence – while all others in the land hurried to the King's enemy: his wife, the Queen.

If it had not been for Otho, most would not have struggled this far.

The Sergeant was a kindly man to those from his village. Thick-necked, with a pepper-and-salt beard and a clump of sandy hair, Otho had two boys back at his home, and Robert knew he would be as worried about them and his wife as he was about his own wife, Susan. But Otho would not allow the men under him to rest and slacken off. He inspired them by his own iron determination, forcing himself on, hour after hour.

A cart hauled by a wretched old nag rumbled past. The beast's head hung low as it plodded on, beyond despair. The rain began

---

[1] 13 October 1326

to fall again. Few among the men would spare a thought for its suffering, and when it stopped, shivering, the man at the leading rein stared uncomprehendingly as though he had forgotten he had the animal with him. A spasm passed through the pony's frame, and its head drooped so low, it almost touched the mud of the roadway. The driver and two others tried to beat it into movement, but it would not budge, whether they hauled on the reins or whipped it until its rump was red with blood.

Robert Vyke heard the low, moaning whinny, and his eyes were drawn to the pony.

'He can't pull any more,' he said.

The driver snarled, 'So, you want to carry his load on your back?'

Vyke glanced at the light cart with the boxes set over the axle. 'You can pull all you want, the beast's done.'

'Yeah, well unless we get some more like you to pull, we'll have to rely on this God-damned pony,' the man said, and tugged again. 'Come on, in Christ's name! God's body, but you'd test the patience of a saint!'

'Leave the poor brute,' Vyke muttered. He walked to the pony's head and scratched it under the chin. The creature was too tired even to whicker, but rested its head on Vyke's hand. 'He's all but done.'

'Out of the way, you prickle – we have to get on! Come on, you justler, you swiver – *move your arse*!'

Vyke would have protested, but Otho put a hand on his shoulder. 'Come on, lad. He's right, you know that. The horse has his work to do.'

Struggling on, his eyes rolling in his head, muscles tightening like bands beneath his skin, the horse began to move again, and Vyke turned away in disgust and pity as the driver swore, cajoled and yanked on the beast's reins.

Then, at the side of the road, there was a sight to drive the horse from his mind. Two young men stood, both dark-haired, their faces twisted with loss, while an older man lay between them, his hair almost white, his face grey and miserable, his lips blue.

Robert Vyke passed them with a short stab of jealousy. He was so tired, the thought of lying down amid the mud and thin grasses, to feel the rain upon his face, the coolness of water seeping into his bones, and know that he need not march further . . . that would be a sublime pleasure.

A memory snagged his mind as Robert glanced at the men. He had seen them before, in Reading, he realised. They had been with another vingtaine. The two were the old man's sons, but it looked like they'd lost their father now. There was no movement in his breast, and his eyes stared, unmoving.

But their loss was not Robert Vyke's. He had little room in his heart to feel sorrow for others when he missed his wife and child so very much.

Sometimes, while walking, he had a memory of his home. Of when he was with his Susan, her young face cracking into a smile as she joshed him, or that teasing expression of hers as she glanced at him from the side of her almond-shaped eyes. It was a look that he'd take to the grave, that was. When she did that, he had to follow. He knew what she was offering . . .

He would probably never again feel the warmth of her body against his. That was the thought that made him sigh. And all because his lord had thrown his lot in with the King. 'Only a few miles,' they kept saying. The King was only a little way ahead, over the next hill, and then they'd all see his host. There would be thousands there, they said, but no one believed it. They knew no one else supported the King any more.

A sob formed in his breast, near his heart, as he prayed that his Susan was safe and well, their little boy with her – but today, no one could tell. The country was aflame. He would perish out here somewhere, far to the west of the realm. They all would.

It felt as if the kingdom had been teetering on the brink of war for years, and now it had toppled into chaos. Old Otho had been ordered to collect twenty men for battle, and Robert had been one of the first to be chosen. That was just over a week ago now, and since then all he had done was march, first up east towards London, and now back west again. There was no sense in it. He didn't know what they were doing, only that the King himself was in danger, and Robert, Otho, and the lads from the vill must try to protect him, while others tried to stop or slay them. It made no sense. Nothing made sense any more. All he wanted was to stop, to lie down and sleep.

There was a sudden crack and a shout, then a terrible scream. The pony lay on its side, a bloody froth at its mouth, kicking listlessly with two forelegs, while the cart's body lay in pieces all about. A wheel had fallen and broken in a hole, and the poor beast had broken its heart trying to continue.

Robert Vyke walked over to the driver. 'I said the poor brute wouldn't be able to carry on,' he told him.

The driver looked at him blankly, then kicked the horse's head viciously. 'Bastard son of a sow was useless,' he burst out.

Robert's hand was on his dagger – and then the blade was out, and the driver jumped back. There was a shout, a curse, and the driver had his own dagger free in his hand, and was reaching for his whip.

'Stop that!' The bellow came from Otho, the Constable of Robert's vingtaine, and in a moment he was standing in between them. 'You want the Queen to discuss your argument, boys? You want her here so that you can put your cases to her, wait for her judgement on you? Eh? Because I can tell you what her judgement would be – that you two prickles would deserve a good, tall tree to hang from, since you're going to her enemies. Your King wouldn't be too happy to learn you'd held us all up, neither. He'd hang you as an example. Put the blades away, boys, because so help me, if you don't, I'll break your pates, both of you.'

Robert and the driver stared at each other a moment, then Robert looked at Otho. 'You think I can't cut a fool's throat like his?'

'Leave him. He's a son of a goat, and not worth getting yourself hanged over, Robert,' Otho rasped.

'I will do as you wish, Constable,' Robert said, and thrust his dagger back in its sheath.

It felt as though he had pulled the lever in a mill and turned off the water from the sluice. Suddenly he had no energy again, and he saw that his companions from the village were all near him. He walked in among them, and would have fallen but for a friendly hand at his arm. And then they began their weary trudging again.

CHAPTER FIVE

Third Tuesday after the Feast of St Michael[1]

Bristol

Cecily reached the house and pulled open the door. Trembling like a leaf, she pushed it closed behind her, then stood leaning against it for a while, her eyes shut.

'Maid?' Old Hamo the steward was at the doorway to his buttery, a cloth in his hand as he methodically wiped and polished a maple-wood mazer, a frown of perturbation on his kindly features. He was ancient, at least sixty years, and as bent and gnarled as an old blackthorn. 'Maid, what is it?'

'Nothing,' she said. How could she explain the shock that had jolted through her body out there when she saw the little boy who looked so like baby Harry? The child in his mother's arms had turned and stared at her with such an intensity, it felt as though Harry himself was there. God in Heaven, the accusation she thought she had seen in those eyes . . .

[1] 14 October 1326

'Hamo!' she said, and then began to sob, her hands over her face as she slid down the door to the floor.

'What is it, Cecily?'

She tried to turn away, but the tender concern in his eyes made her feel the guilt again. She saw Little Harry's face, and as though in a nightmare again, saw the skull shatter, the blood and brains exploding out. 'Oh, Holy Mother, save me!'

'Speak to me, Cecily,' the steward said, now seriously concerned. 'You've been getting more and more fretful these last days – what is it?'

Cecily wept, head covered in her hands. She was aware of tears pouring down both cheeks, and gave a choking sob. But it was no good. Even behind her hands, she could still see the hideous events of that bloody day: the accusing death stare of Arthur Capon, the cold, calculating expression in the murderer's eyes as he stood and slid his sword into Madame Capon's breast. The baby . . .

She must carry her guilt with her to the grave.

Emma Wrey had heard the weeping, and it was enough to make her put her needlework aside and walk to the doorway. She watched for a moment, frowning as she considered her maidservant. Curious that Cecily had broken down like this. It was the first time she had been so distraught during the day. At night she had often cried herself to sleep, and woken with a yelp of horror or pain, but Emma had assumed that the dark memories would gradually fade.

It must have been a God-awful shock. Emma didn't know how she herself would have reacted, seeing her master and mistress cut down before her, the daughter of the house dragged from her bed and stabbed to death, then the child who was her charge slammed against a wall and killed. Those were the sort of things that no one could witness with impunity. They would change a soul. Poor Cecily, she had thought.

But this recurrence of the maid's terrors was alarming. There were stories of people who were dreadfully affected by such things, who lived normally for a while and then were prey to fears that drew their lives to an untimely end. Perhaps Cecily was so badly marked by her experiences that her heart would give out.

No! It would not do!

'Hamo? *Hamo*?'

'Mistress?'

'I think a jug of strong wine would be a good idea. Cecily needs fortifying.'

'Of course, mistress,' Hamo said, walking stiffly from the room.

'Make it good wine. Not the sour stuff, mind.'

He smiled and nodded.

When Emma married Master Wrey, she had been alarmed by the sight of this paragon. He was tall, suave and elegant, and had impressed her with his cool appraisal of her before he gave a nod, as though telling himself that while she was not perfect, she was at least young enough to be moderately malleable.

And perhaps she had proved to be for the first years, until her husband died. When that happened and she found herself thrown into the management of the business, Emma had grown harder and more uncompromising, but still, every so often, she would catch that same measuring look in Hamo's eyes, and she would see him occasionally give a sign of approval, as if pleased that she had turned out so well; not in a patronising manner, but almost with pride.

Not that she needed such recognition now. She was content with her position in Bristol and her standing in the financial community. Since Arthur Capon's death, her business had become one of the leading finance houses in the city.

'Come with me, Cecily,' Emma said, walking over to the fire and patting the stool beside her. 'Maid, I've heard your tears often enough. What is it that upsets you?'

Cecily's eyes were red-rimmed, and at the question, they brimmed with tears again. 'Mistress, I'm sorry, I didn't think to upset you. I—'

'Enough, my dear. With all the angels as my witness, I declare I only want to help you. Now, ah . . . Thank you, Hamo. Put the wine there, and then you may leave us.' She waited until he had left the hall, and then herself poured two cups from the jug.

When Emma passed her a cup, Cecily took it and sipped, but sat with her eyes downcast.

'Look, the attack on the house was not your fault,' Emma said patiently. 'Squire William was a thoroughly evil man. He and his men were foul to commit such a dreadful crime.'

'I know.'

'You mustn't blame yourself. I imagine you feel a little like me – guilty, because you survived. I felt that after my husband died, but . . .'

'No! It's because I didn't protect *him*! He shouldn't have been hurt. I should have protected him, as I swore. I failed Little Harry!'

Third Wednesday after the Feast of St Michael[1]

Near Tintern Abbey

All along their route, the peasants stopped and stood staring as they heard the sounds of the marchers approaching. As the noise

[1] 15 October 1326

grew nearer, there was a rush as men and women dropped their tools, no matter how expensive, and flew away, scooping up children as they went and hurrying off to hide in the woods and shaws that stood about the vills.

No one wanted to be caught by the warriors. Everyone knew what could happen when a force arrived. Men with swords would always resort to blunt persuasion when they wanted food and drink – and women.

But the people of the village didn't realise that these men-at-arms had more pressing concerns than mere pillage. They didn't want to be caught by the host that followed so closely on their heels.

The main road was churned underfoot by the centaine of thin, anxious men in dirty jacks and leather, all stubbled, pallid-faced and sick with fear. Their legs and hosen were beslubbered with mud, and weariness made them stumble as they trudged, eyes downcast.

Sir Ralph of Evesham sat astride his rounsey feeling dejected as he surveyed the men about him. They were so exhausted, it was a miracle any of them were still on their feet. In the last twelve days they had marched all the way from London, with the perpetual fear of capture in every man's heart, but as their journey progressed, men had disappeared. The numbers were down to below a tenth of the force which had set off.

In the early days, he had managed to retain his belief that at some point they would meet with additional men who would join them to help protect the King, but now the truth was clear and stark even to his optimistic eye. The idea that the Marcher Lords would come to the King's aid was as false as the hearts of those further east who had broken their promises. King Edward II was alone but for this tiny force.

'Sir Ralph, we should ride on, sir, and make a surveillance.'

Sir Ralph nodded. Thank the Lord for his loyal men, he thought gratefully. Pagan and Alexander were both still with Squire Bernard and himself, which was little short of a miracle. So many others had seen their pages and heralds leave as the force trudged on towards Wales.

'Good idea,' he said, and lashed his palfrey's flanks with his reins' ends.

They cantered ahead together, Sir Ralph slightly ahead of his squire, and could soon see the village ahead.

'Shall I see if there's an ambush?' Squire Bernard said as they paused at the edge of the woods.

'No, we will go together,' Sir Ralph said.

They trotted down a shallow incline, both keeping a wary eye open for the threat of danger, but like so many other villages along their way, the place was deserted.

'Get back and tell the heralds that it's safe,' Sir Ralph said, and dismounted. He walked to the well at the side of the road and pulled up a pitcher of water. It was brackish, but wholesome.

He sat down to wait, and it was just then that he heard the unmistakable sound of hooves approaching at a canter.

'Sir Ralph? You are wanted, sir. The King has sent me to fetch you.'

Sir Ralph mounted and rode to the King as soon as the summons came. He swung from the saddle, throwing his palfrey's reins to a waiting boy, and dropped to his knees in front of the King. 'You ordered me to come, your Royal Highness?'

The King stood, tall and handsome with his long, curly fair hair. Nearby was Sir Hugh le Despenser and a circle of guards. This was not the camp of a man who felt secure in his own realm.

'Sir Ralph, please stand. You have excelled yourself on the

journey,' the King said. He had a quiet voice today, but whether that meant anything, Sir Ralph did not know. From what he had seen and heard, the King was prey to remarkable changes of mood; he could coo like a dove when he wanted to, only to shriek with fury a moment later. Now, if he had to guess, he would have said that the King's tone was more one of bafflement than anything else.

'Thank you, sire.'

'But the Queen is close at hand, I believe,' the King said. 'She is hunting us with the ferocity of an alaunt. How can we keep from her?'

'Your Highness, we must ride on.'

'Lancaster has gone to her, did you know?' the King went on, as though not hearing. 'After I showed him mercy and magnanimity, he ignored my friendship and now rides with *her*. *All* wish to be with her.'

'You yet have loyal knights, Your Highness.'

'Only a few, I fear.'

Sir Ralph shot a look at Sir Hugh le Despenser. The adviser was listening intently, but for all that his eyes were on the King and Sir Ralph, there was something about his demeanour that made the knight think that he was not concentrating. His expression was that of a little boy told to consider some writing on a slate, who stared, but to whom the words made no sense. He was uncomprehending in the face of so much disaster. Last year, the man had held the realm in his fist, but now all he gripped was sand, and it was running through his fingers no matter what he did.

'We have made good time, Your Royal Highness,' Sir Ralph tried. 'Soon we shall be in Wales, and perhaps there you will find loyal subjects ready to defend you.'

'I wouldn't have her hurt, you know,' the King said suddenly.

'She is the mother of my children, and I would not have her hurt.'

'I know, sire.'

'She has been misled. That is the matter at hand. She thinks that my good knight, Sir Hugh here, is her enemy. Yet he declares every day that he loves her – why should she believe he seeks to injure her? He has always put her case to me most fairly, often taking her part in disputes. Why should she feel he is not her friend?'

Sir Ralph could scarcely comprehend what he was hearing. Did the King seriously believe that the Queen would be glad to know that her petitions to her own husband had to be mediated by Sir Hugh le Despenser, the man who had wreaked such havoc in her life?

'And now *this*,' the King said, and there was a tone of such shock and dismay in his voice that Sir Ralph felt anxious.

'Your Highness?'

'They demand that I surrender, and that I yield up Sir Hugh, and his father, the Earl of Winchester. They say that Sir Hugh is profligate, and that I have taxed the realm too much to support him – when all who know the Treasury are aware that I have ever been careful with the nation's money! How *can* they say such things, Sir Ralph?'

'My lord, I . . .'

'No, it is not for you to answer this. You are right. But I fear that the Queen may come to attack us. There are other groups of men on their way here to join us, I believe. Sir Ralph, I would be glad if you could take some men and find them and bring them to us here at Tintern. We must concentrate our forces.'

'Of course.'

The King's tone became peevish. 'Sir Ralph, you will remain loyal, won't you? You wouldn't run to them?'

In answer, Sir Ralph knelt again and held up his hands, palms pressed together. 'I will renew my vow to you now, my lord, if you wish.'

The King smiled sadly. He placed his own hands around Sir Ralph's, as he had all those years ago when Sir Ralph was made a knight by him. 'Sir Ralph, good Sir Ralph, I am sorry. Your honour is not in doubt.'

He made Sir Ralph stand, and kissed him.

Sir Ralph went to his horse and mounted, but before he left, he caught sight of the huddle of men again. Earl Hugh of Winchester was next to his son, Sir Hugh le Despenser, and the King himself was alone a few yards away.

There was nothing could soothe that monarch's fretful heart, Sir Ralph thought as he cantered back to his camp.

Approaching Bristol

The exhausted men were close to collapse that morning. As they struggled onwards, desperate to find the host they were meant to join, they came across a broader roadway.

A good place to rest, Robert Vyke thought wearily. Trees ranged on both sides, and a thick hedge was to his left. There was a small building up ahead, the limewash old and fragile, falling away with old cob in places. It was the beginning of a hamlet, perhaps, or a small farm.

'Only another four or five miles, boys!' Otho was calling, entreating them onwards. 'Then we'll be in Bristol. We'll soon be with the King, then.' Spotting Robert Vyke, he nodded. 'You all right?'

'Good as I can be.'

'Aye, well, forget that tranter. He's got enough trouble on his hands moving all the gear without a horse.'

'He deserves it.'

Otho smiled as they continued. He knew the cause of Vyke's rancour.

It was almost two months since the King's purveyors had reached their village and made their demands. There were more wagons coming, and the King had need. The village was to be ravaged: food, goods, iron, all were taken and thrown into the wagons, together with all the ale they could grab. And then one of the horses had stumbled and broken a leg.

There was no pause. The purveyors had their orders, and they must fulfil them. So they took Vyke's only horse, set it in the traces, and were off. The dead brute they dragged with them, for the meat.

The horse was the only valuable possession Robert Vyke had owned. Without it, he was impoverished. His wife Susan would find life more harsh and cruel. A horse meant transport, it mean income when loaned to a friend, it meant barter: ale and eggs and cheese. But the purveyors had taken him.

Before Robert Vyke lay a puddle, and he splashed into it unthinking, unaware of anything but his own misery, but then there was a tearing pain in his ankle and leg, and he felt himself fall, the long shaft of his bill tumbling through his hands to clatter on the stones of the road, his pack of belongings thumping down beside him, while men scattered from the bill's sharp blade.

'What is it, you fool?' Otho demanded.

'My leg, my leg!'

'Get up, you hog's arse! You think we're going to wait for you?' the Sergeant demanded, and he hawked long and hard, bringing up a large gobbet of phlegm, which he spat near Robert's face. 'On your feet! By Christ's blood, you make a man want to kick you, you do. First you pick a fight with a poor bastard who's only gone and lost his pony, and now you want to doze by the wayside. Waiting for a frisky wench to snuggle up to, eh? Maybe a pair? Well, forget it!'

Otho was known for his rough humour, but Robert was not of a mind to laugh. He took a long look at his Sergeant and then, sobbing with the pain, he slowly eased himself upright. Only then did the Sergeant stare down at his leg. 'God's ballocks, man! How did you do that?'

'Mary save me!' Robert said, as he saw the blood slowly pulsing from the long gash. 'Otho, I—'

'Christ's pain! you're no good to me like that, you tarse,' the Sergeant said mildly. He was staring at the men behind them as though Robert was already passing from his mind. 'No good to us at all. You'd best stay behind and hope the bastards don't see you. They'll be after us anyway, not you. You piss off up north of this road, and you may be all right. Understand?'

'Yes, Sergeant.'

'No, better than that, lad, you make your way to Bristol after us. It's only a few miles from here. Can you do that?' Otho added doubtfully, glancing at the flap of skin hanging loose. He then leaned forward and said in a low voice, 'Look, if they do catch you, just give yourself up, eh? There's no point trying to fight. No point any of us trying to fight,' he added to himself dully. 'Right – you got a thong or some twine?'

While Robert stretched his leg out before him, Otho bent and bound the wound with a length of linen, then he wrapped a thick leather thong over it to hold it in place. 'Take care, boy.'

'You too, Otho.'

'Yeah. Well, I hope we'll meet again.' The Sergeant rested a fist on Robert's shoulder, and Vyke saw that he was thinking about something. Otho was a man who considered his actions carefully. If he wished to say something important, he would weigh his words. Now, he looked away as though saddened.

'Look, Robert, if you get home safely, see my Agnes, eh? Tell her . . . just tell her I wanted to get home,' he said.

Robert nodded. There was no need to say more. They both reckoned it was unlikely either of them would see the village or their wives again.

Then Otho hefted Robert's bill on to his shoulder and bawled at the rest of the men: 'What're you lazy gits staring at? Taking a rest while you can? It's going to be a long march before we get to see the King, me boys, so get a bleeding move on!'

Gradually, with many a curse and muttered complaint, the men began to stagger forwards again, while Robert watched from the side of the road with eyes filled with tears. He had no idea where he was, nor how far from his home, and now all his friends were walking on and leaving him. Herv Tyrel broke from the shambling mass and passed him a lump of old bread he had saved, then winked, while others either nodded and gave him a 'Godspeed', or looked away, ashamed to be deserting him.

The little party shuffled on past, and if it weren't for the pain, for the fear of capture, and the desperate loneliness that was engulfing him, Robert Vyke could have enjoyed the exquisite delight of sitting here at the wayside while the others all continued on their way.

'You'll be dead in a day.'

The vicious whisper came from his right, and he was about to turn when he felt the dagger at the side of his neck.

'Who are you?' Robert Vyke asked, scarcely moving his head.

It was the horse-driver. 'Walerand the Tranter, most call me. Won't do that again now I've lost my only pony, swyve them all.'

'Well, Walerand, I am called Robert Vyke. When you have finished serving the King, you come and find me, and I'll be glad to set my dagger against yours, anywhere, any time. Unless you're such a coward that you'll kill me here instead.'

'I'm no coward, horse-lover. I'll find you, and I'll cut your throat like a hog's.'

'Really?' Robert said, and he slowly turned his head to stare at the man. 'Next time we meet, Tranter, you'll pay for your stupidity.'

'Mine?' the Tranter said, and grinned. Then he slammed the pommel of his dagger into Robert's head, and the young man knew no more.

CHAPTER SIX

Bristol

Cecily knelt beside her palliasse and clutched the little wooden cross on her necklace, her eyes closed as she prepared herself and then began to speak.

The act of prayer had always been soothing. Mumbling her words as she drew down God's attention upon herself, on Emma, on the Capons, on all she knew, would always in the past have brought her comfort. With her eyes closed, she could sense the presence of the Almighty as she fingered her rosary beads and talked directly with Him. But not this time.

She opened her mouth to speak, but the words would not come. There was a thickness in the base of her throat that seemed to all but choke her. Even as she stared down at her rosary, she knew it could hold no spiritual solace – and that knowledge came to her with a shock that felt like an actual punch in her belly.

Her mouth closed, and the beads trembled as her hands began to shake. Moaning, she leaned forward until her brow touched the palliasse, while tears began to seep from beneath her eyelids.

'I can't, I can't do this!'

Her fingers gripped at the rosary, but there was no strength in them to move the beads along their cord. It seemed that God Himself had turned from her. Her soul was damned, because she had taken the vow to protect the child, to be like a mother to him all his days, and she had *failed* him. Now the boy was dead, and she was forsworn!

For one error, she would be cursed for all time; she was quite sure of it. Her fingers would not work the beads; her hands gripped the cross, but she felt no sensation of case from the holy symbol. With a stifled cry, she threw the cross and rosary aside and fell sobbing to the bed. She hadn't wanted those men to kill Little Harry, but it mattered not a whit; she knew her guilt. She had come to appreciate the full depth of her crime, and now there was nothing she could do about it. She was lost – perhaps forever.

'I wouldn't have done it if I could have helped it,' she whispered, and the sobs began again.

She tried to beg for forgiveness, but He made no sign that He could hear her. At last, in desperation, she grabbed at the rosary beads again, but in her snatching them up, she did not notice that there was a knot formed. As her anxious fingers pulled the beads apart, there was a sudden give, and it seemed to her that time stopped.

The beads sprang from the cord that had bound them, and flew into the air, forming graceful arcs as they rose, only to tumble back to the ground, bouncing and rolling hither and thither.

'God save me!' she screamed in horror, her eyes rising to the ceiling as though Christ was there already, staring down at her with an immensity of sadness on his face.

Approaching Bristol

'Shouldn't have been so keen to insult the bastard,' Robert Vyke muttered to himself as he opened his eyes. Some day, he told himself ruefully, he'd learn to think before opening his mouth. Not many men would accept advice on how to treat their beasts, any more than they would on their pewter, their weapons, or their wives.

The blow to his head had left him dizzy, and he hunched his shoulders in an attempt to keep warm. as he lurched painfully up the roadway.

The path ahead was muddy and badly rutted, and for all that the rain had dwindled to no more than a thin drizzle, Robert Vyke was soaked to the skin. A trickle of water ran down from his hair and followed the line of his spine to his waist.

From the light in the sky, he guessed that he had lain like a dead man for quite some time. He must get away before dark, but for now there was nothing in his mind but the need to sit and rest a little more.

Idly, he glanced at the puddle into which he had slipped. From here it looked like a shallow pool, but from his fall he knew it sank at least eighteen inches. Kneeling carefully on his good knee, he tentatively felt around the hole, testing with his fingers until he found a jagged piece of metal, which he hauled out. It was a dagger. The blade, bent almost around to the hilt, explained the injury, and he stared at it in disgust. Someone must have dropped it, and a horse probably stood on it, to make the blade form this impossible shape. It was odd that no one had seen it, for it must have been lying here on the road before being trampled by hooves and kicked into the puddle. As he wiped at the hilt, Robert saw with a sudden thrill that it was richly carved and inlaid with at least two rubies. He whistled softly. He had never touched such valuable stones before in his life! Those rubies would fetch a good few shillings, and Susan and he would be able to buy a pig – maybe a few sheep, too, as well as a new pony.

Without his bill, which Otho had taken, he had no protection, and perhaps this dagger would help him. Not that it would be much use in its present state. Better by far to rely on his old dagger . . . and then he realised that the horse-driver had stolen it. At his waist there was nothing but an empty sheath.

'Bastard son of a diseased whore,' he muttered from gritted teeth.

Well, that made his decision easier. He had to bend this dagger straight if he wanted a weapon of some kind. With that in mind, he set his good foot on it, wincing as his injured shin twisted, but the metal didn't budge; his whole weight wouldn't move it. Behind him was a hedge, and there were surely stones at the base to maintain its shape. Robert hobbled over to it, trying to find a gap between the rocks, but there were none; the vegetation was too thick. Pushing his way through further, he finally found a good gap, and here he managed to set the blade into a niche. By throwing his body's weight against it, he succeeded by degrees in setting the blade almost true.

Looking down the length of the metal, he was satisfied. Pushing it into his old sheath, he found that it fitted very loosely, but at least it should be safe there.

His next problem was the matter of a staff. To walk without one in his present state was impossible. There were no decent lengths he could take from this hedge, for the boughs were all thick, and those that weren't, were too short to be of any use. However, at the far side of the hedge was a small wood. The trees loomed overhead.

With some effort, Robert pushed himself through a thinner part of the hedge. It appeared to have been used before, for the way was already partly hacked, he noticed. Once in the wood, he was about to search for a six-foot staff, when he became aware of a strong odour in the air. To a countryman there was something familiar about that smell; like the stink of a fox, it was instantly repugnant. He realised it was rotting meat.

A gust hit him. The smell was everywhere. Keeping hold of the branch he had found, wincing with pain, he had to swallow hard to stop from throwing up. Then his eyes were drawn upwards, and he felt his breath catch.

It was like a blow in the belly, that sight. The head was that of a man with wild, dark hair, and it lay resting in the fork of a tree a scant two feet away. The eyes were heavily-lidded as though stupefied, the mouth just a little open, the lips blue and, beneath the chin was the raw meat where his throat had been hacked apart.

And Robert fell back, cursing, before his body at last convulsed, and his vomit spattered on the grass. Rising, he dare not look at that hideous spectacle, but pushed sobbing through the hedge once more, out into the clear, wholesome road.

Then something clubbed him below his ear, and he fell, senseless once more, to the muddy ground.

Bristol Castle

In the castle's hall, Sir Stephen Siward the Coroner stood warming his hands by the fire. His clerk and he had been holding an inquest into the death of a boy knocked down by a cart in the street. The matter was simple, the accidental death sad, but commonplace. But now, as the clerk carefully bound the rolls ready to be installed in the chest where they must await the arrival of the Justices, Sir Stephen found his mind returning to that other inquest.

He remembered it so well that it almost felt as if it were only yesterday afternoon that he had been called to the Capon house, to stand there watching, his heart in his throat, as those awful, mutilated bodies were dragged out and laid in a row.

The Capon inquest must have been completed legally, for his clerk, who was a stickler for the correct words and due process, did not criticise. The bodies were rolled over and over, naked, while the jury watched in grim silence, but their self-possession began to fracture at the sight of the last two. The men of the jury were roused to rage at the sight of Petronilla's slaughtered body, and that of her baby, his head crushed and bloody.

Cecily was a hopeless witness. She could hardly speak: she muttered, stared at the ground, and closed her eyes completely when asked to look at the corpses. It was all quite frustrating, for Sir Stephen needed a clear declaration of the attack. Still, she had managed, finally, to make the necessary statements, and she had been convincing enough for the Squire and his men to be arrested.

Of course, it was natural that she should be in a state of shock. The poor young woman had lived with the family since Petronilla's childhood. A long, long time.

After Petronilla's marriage to Squire William, the latter had fallen out with his father-in-law, the burgess Arthur Capon. Sir Stephen himself wouldn't have stood against the Squire in one of his rages: the man was known for his ferocity, and his impotent fury over his wife's infidelity and flight must have been all-consuming.

The jury had no need of lengthy deliberations, but simply agreed that the assassins must have been Squire William with a gang of his men. Any man would want revenge in these circumstances, especially since his woman had run away with her confessor.

Everyone knew the background to the attack, and although Cecily had agreed that she had seen Squire William, it was not necessary for her to give lengthy evidence about his part in the attack. That was quite a relief to all concerned. The Squire and his men were arrested soon after.

Afterwards, Cecily had not wanted to see Sir Stephen for a long time. Well, that was all to the good, Sir Stephen thought. He had no wish to become attached to her permanently. It was hardly appropriate for a knight to be seen too often in the company of a serving-maid.

Third Thursday after the Feast of St Michael[1]

Marshfield

The sudden darkness brought on the terror again, and he stirred and sat up, thinking that he was in danger, but there was nothing here. Only a hideous pain in his leg, and Robert groaned to himself when he recalled the horrible wound.

Opening his eyes, he saw that he was lying on a comfortable bed with a rope base over which a palliasse of straw had been laid; at the foot of it stood a large chest. It was the sort of thing in which a man would keep his spare belongings, and Robert eyed it with curiosity. Made of pale, gleaming wood, with a pair of heavy bands which appeared to pass over the lid to padlocks at the front, it was a temptation to try to open it and peer inside, but something stopped him. There was an aura of evil in the chamber: something that emanated from within the chest.

Then, despite himself, his hand moved over the chest's lid, his questing fingers stroking the blued steel of the bands, reaching down to the padlocks . . . and his heart pounded as he felt the hasp of the first lock give under his fingers. His hand went to the other lock – and suddenly the lid was flung open, throwing Robert onto his back. He screamed, and saw before him that head once more – the narrowed eyes, the blue lips – floating

[1] 16 October 1326

towards him. Robert flailed at it with his arms, but the thing drifted effortlessly past, moving ever nearer, and there was the smell of the grave about it. And then it was right in front of him, coming closer and closer until it seemed about to touch his lips . . .

'*Christ's bones!*' he screamed aloud, and this time it was enough to shake him properly awake, and he was sitting up, mouth gaping, panting, the sweat pooling on his breast. He looked around wildly, and found himself in a bright, warm chamber, lying on a good bed, and there were firm hands on his shoulders gently pressing him back.

'You are safe here, my son. Do not fear. Lie back. Be still, be easy.'

Robert stared about him. The room was sparsely furnished. One stool sat near a small, low table, and the only decoration on the walls was a stoup set at the door, and a simple cross of dark wood on a wall nearby. The floor was made of packed earth, and the fire, which burned with a steady, heartwarming hiss, lay on a hearth of clay in the middle of the room. Over it a pot bubbled, giving off a wonderful smell of rosemary and bacon.

'Where am I?'

'In my house. I am Paul, the priest for this little vill, and you have been here since your discovery beside the road.'

'My discovery . . . What does that . . .?'

'You were found there,' the priest said. He was a slim man, but wiry, with a tonsure that left the majority of his skull bald. Bright blue eyes held his own, and Robert was comforted by the sympathy in them. 'You were bleeding badly from that gash in your shin. It's a matter of good fortune that you lost no more blood, my friend, for had you done so, I doubt that you would have survived. As it is, the wound appears to have all but healed.'

'Healed? How long have I been here?'

'We can talk about that in the morning. For now, you should rest. Have some broth, settle back, and forget these horrible dreams.'

'I've had them before?'

'You have returned to the same dream many times, I think, my friend. It is most sad to see you thrashing in your fear. Do not worry, though. We shall soon have you well and free of these mares.'

Robert nodded and allowed the priest to ease him back against the wall, watching while Father Paul busy himself with wooden bowl and spoon.

But Robert did not see the priest. All he saw with his mind's eye was that decomposing head floating towards him again.

CHAPTER SEVEN

Bristol

The city of Bristol was still the second city of the kingdom, no matter what anyone might say, and Sir Laurence Ashby, the Constable of Bristol Castle, was convinced that his adopted home eclipsed London in many ways. It was better served with access to the sea, it was more pleasant on the nostrils and eye, being much cleaner than the capital, and from his point of view, as a warrior, it was infinitely more secure. Not only were there walls encircling the whole town but the river also formed a strong barrier to the south, while the fields to the north were notable for their bogs and marshes.

There was a good, strong wall about the castle, too, which was one of the most imposing in the land. Raised on a hill, its square keep reared up over the city it was intended to protect, while the curtain walls concealed a mass of smaller buildings: sheds, smiths' forges, stables, and a vast number of storage chambers. Usually the castle was manned by only a small contingent, but now the realm was on a war footing, matters had radically changed, and Sir Laurence was glad that his calls for the garrison to be enlarged had been heeded.

It was with good reason that people called this 'almost the richest city'. Merchants there plied their trade all over the world from Bristol's good, deep-water port. Many years ago, the city had begun the great work of moving the River Frome, the burgesses excavating the new line of the river in St Augustine's Marsh, so that access to the harbour was greatly improved. The sea was the source of the city's power and wealth, and as soon as that great work was completed, the townspeople set out on another ambitious project: damming the River Avon and diverting it, so that a stone bridge could be constructed over the river, giving access from the south.

'Sir Laurence, there is a messenger.'

The Constable closed his eyes for a moment, cursing all messengers. Since the beginning of this terrible dispute between the King and his Queen, the number of messages had increased to a steady flow. In the past, the Constable of a royal castle would be left to get on with his many tasks, but not now. It seemed as though the King was ever more determined to keep tight control over every aspect of life in the kingdom, especially in places like Bristol. Or was it that he was attempting to maintain the fiction that he had some control of events?

Sir Laurence supposed it was to be expected. A man who was so suddenly overtaken by fate must try to assume command by whatever means he could.

Taking the note, he read down the sheet quickly. Sir Laurence was a man of middling height in his early thirties. His head was almost as bald as a priest's, with a fringe of yellow hair curling about. His eyes were clear and blue, set in a rather pale-complexioned face with thin lips that gave him the look more of an ascetic than a man of action. The truth was, he was infinitely happier with a sword in his hand than a book, and although he had less time to spare now, he was always more content to sit in his saddle with a lance at the ready, than bent over at a desk.

Not that there was much likelihood of that, these days. Knights were no longer permitted to test themselves in jousts of honour, since King Edward disapproved of such martial displays. He had been very happy to participate in such celebrations when he was younger, but Piers Gaveston had died following a plot conceived during a jousting match, and after the loss of that most beloved adviser, the King had refused to allow any more.

'Very good,' Sir Laurence said, and folded the parchment carefully, pushing it into his shirt. The writing was atrocious again – he had scarcely been able to decipher it. The King's clerks were clearly under a great deal of stress themselves, he thought to himself.

Leaving the messenger and guard, he strolled towards his little chamber in the keep, where he pulled out the message and threw it onto his table. His clerk, David, peered at him with interest. 'More complaints about the privy?'

'Silence!' Sir Laurence snapped.

David was less a clerk, more a comrade against the world. A lean, astute man, his sarcasm was a welcome shield against the foolishness of men, especially those who tried to achieve their will by politicking. 'Oh, having a good morning, then?' he responded calmly.

'No one's grabbed me about the shit-house this morning, no,' Sir Laurence grunted.

'Something else, then?' The clerk knew all about the many troubles which dogged his master. As Constable, he was nagged about any problems with living quarters in times of peace, and now there was war, for some reason the complaints about the privy had escalated. True enough there *was* a foul stench rising, and guards and servants alike were unhappy that they might inhale some of it.

Sir Laurence himself reckoned it was less a fault with the chamber itself, or the chute into the moat, and more a reflection of the garrison's nervousness in the face of impending war. They were shitting themselves.

He kicked the door shut. 'Yes. I reckon the King has lost his mind.' It was hardly surprising: there was his wife, flaunting her adultery with the man whom King Edward had ordered to be executed, plus she had kept their son with her even when King Edward had demanded his return. Who wouldn't be made lunatic in those circumstances?

'Do you really mean that?' David set down his reed and stared at Sir Laurence, his head to one side.

'Read this,' the Constable grumbled, picking up the message and passing it to the clerk. 'He's only written from Tintern, demanding that we all hold array and provide at least one centaine of men, along with provisions and horses to equip a force of hobelars. Madness, complete madness! The King must realise that the first city Mortimer will want to take is Bristol.'

He slumped down in his chair. Bristol was the jewel of all the cities in the kingdom, and Sir Laurence loved it with a passion. Even the scars on large portions of the walls, rebuilt after the insurrection ten years ago, were like the birthmarks on a lover. He knew them all intimately.

'We don't have a hundred men to spare, and if we did have them, we'd still need them here to protect the city. We can't survive another siege.'

The last siege had been terrible. Sir Laurence had heard much about it when he first arrived here. A small group of fourteen rich men controlled the city and refused to countenance the justifiable demands of other burgesses to be allowed the same privileges and rights. The matter had come to a head eleven years ago, in the eighth and ninth years of the King's reign. First, the King was petitioned by the fourteen to have judges listen to their issues, because they were sure that they would win the matter and retain their powers. But when the judges arrived and took up their positions in the Guild Hall to open the case, a mob began to riot, convinced that the judges were biased in favour of the few instead of the majority. Harsh words were spoken, some stones thrown, and it was said that twenty or more men lay dead at the end of the fight.

Many claimed that the garrison was responsible, that the mob was innocent, but it didn't help the city. Eighty of the inhabitants were to be attached and held for judgement; they would be declared outlaw if they did not surrender themselves. However, they preferred to conceal themselves in the city, and as the situation deteriorated and the fourteen fled the city, terrified of retaliation, the city itself closed the gates and prepared for war.

The townspeople declared that the city was not rebelling against the King, but Edward II would hear none of it. His position was simple: they had rebelled against his Justices, and that meant against him. He sent the Earl of Pembroke to demand surrender, but the city refused, and the fighting began.

It was thoroughly one-sided. The river was blocked by Sir Maurice de Berkeley, while the siege was prosecuted by Sir Bartholomew Badlesmere and Sir Roger Mortimer, who had called on the *posse comitatus* to prosecute the campaign. The castle remained in the King's possession, and Mortimer's strategic mind saw how to force the capitulation of the city. It was he who decided where to position the great mangonel or catapult machine in the castle, and it soon started to destroy buildings, while the posse outside the city laid to with a vengeance.

Attacked from both sides, there was little the citizens could do, and they surrendered after a few days.

And now this same Mortimer was returned, this time with a large force of Hainaulters, and if the city were to attempt to hold out again, history would repeat itself.

Sir Laurence narrowed his eyes. Yes, but in the years since the last siege, the city had invested a lot of money in rebuilding the walls to make them more secure. So it might just be possible to keep Mortimer at bay. Not an easy task, but one surely worth attempting.

One thing was for certain: there would be no help from the King. All that could be done must be done by the city alone – if the city could do aught to defend Edward's interests.

David carefully folded the parchment and sat for a long time staring at it. 'The city will fall,' he said simply.

Sir Laurence stood, his chair grating over the boards. 'It will not!' he growled. 'While I live, I will keep this city for the King, and protect it as I may!'

'Sir Laurence, the Queen will soon be here. And she has artillery with her, you can be sure. Think what those machines will do to the city, and to the people. The King wants your men; there will not be enough to protect the city and the castle, will there?'

'I will not allow it to fall,' Sir Laurence repeated.

Then he left the room and walked up the narrow staircase to the north-eastern tower, frowning over the town from the wall at the top.

The city was sprawled beneath him, bounded by the two rivers. He was looking down over St Peter's to the Avon now, a broad, sluggish river today. He turned and stared over the long, rectangular yard enclosed by the outer walls of the castle, and then beyond, musing.

There was one thing he was certain of, and that was, while his King wanted Bristol kept, Sir Laurence would do all in his power to hold it. He wouldn't give it up willingly to a rebel like Mortimer. It was a matter of honour.

While he held the town's walls, Bristol was safe even from that scoundrel.

Third Friday after the Feast of St Michael[1]

Near Winchester

As they reached the outskirts of the city, passing by St Katherine's Hill, they had been riding like madmen for a day and a half already – a man, a youth and a large dog.

Although in his middle fifties, Sir Baldwin de Furnshill rode like a man many years younger. His beard, which trailed about the line of his jaw, was pebbled with white now, and his hair was grey but for two wings of white at his temples. He had been a warrior all his life, and his neck and arms showed that he had kept up his regular exercises. Riding every day meant that his muscles were honed, too, but his companion was only a lad, and at the end of this second day Baldwin threw him an anxious look. 'You are well, Jack?'

'Yes, sir.'

'You look as though you are about ready to fall from the horse,' Baldwin said gruffly.

If he could, Baldwin would have left the fellow behind in London, for then he would have been able to ride more swiftly, but it was impossible to find somewhere safe for the boy. With the realm sliding towards war, the city was in a turmoil, with

---

[1] 17 October 1326

bands of rifflers running over the streets, robbing passers-by, plundering houses, raping women and killing any who argued with them. Even the Tower was to fall to the London mob, Baldwin was sure of that, with the King away, and no one certain whether he would remain King. No, London was no place to leave the lad. And Sir Baldwin was also anxious to ride to his wife and ensure that she was safe in their manor in Devon.

Wolf, Baldwin's great mastiff, looked up enquiringly for a moment, before following a scent. He was an amiable-tempered brute, with white muzzle, brown eyebrows and cheeks, and a white cross on his breast, but he was as dull-witted as he was handsome, and had an annoying habit of walking in front of horses as the whim, or scent, took him. Baldwin muttered at him as he meandered across the lane again.

The sun was sinking swiftly now as they peered ahead at the city. A warm orange glow illuminated the sky, highlighting the spires, the towers of the Cathedral and the roofs of the Bishop's Palace. Looming over the city in the south-west corner, Baldwin could see the outline of the castle, a huge monstrosity in comparison with the rest of the little city. Twenty or more years ago there had been a fire in the royal apartments there, and the King and Queen had nearly died. They had been forced to hasten from their chambers as the flames took hold. There was no risk of the King and Queen of today being immolated, Baldwin told himself sadly, and turned to the city gates. They would be unlikely to spend another evening in each other's company again.

It was already too late, as he had feared. As soon as the sun began to sink, the gates of this, like all the other cities in the realm, were closed and the curfew imposed. For those inside the walls, it meant security and safety; for those outside it meant a night shivering in the cold, constantly fearing brigands, unless they could find a room for the night at a village inn.

Baldwin looked at Jack. The boy was swaying gently as the horse moved beneath him, his face looking much older than his fourteen years. With the dirt from splashes of mud on his cheeks, and the strain of the last few hours etched deep into his skin, he could have passed for a man six years older.

The boy was a responsibility Baldwin could have done without, but Jack deserved his protection. The boy had saved his life. In a short skirmish earlier in the year, Baldwin had fallen and would have died, had not Jack saved him. It left Baldwin with a sense of indebtedness that was not to be easily cast aside.

'Come, we'll find an inn for you,' he said gently.

'I can carry on,' Jack said quickly.

'We cannot,' Baldwin said. 'The roads are too dangerous. If our mounts fall into a pothole, we shall lose both. I cannot afford that. No, we shall seek a room for the night. That will be safer.'

On hearing his words the relief on Jack's face was like a warm beacon in the dark. Baldwin chuckled, for he could see it even in the gloom of twilight. It was no surprise that he should be glad: Jack was a peasant's son from Portchester who had been taken at the array and sent to help on a raid in France, but he was only a youth, with no experience of fighting and less of riding a horse. Yet in two days he had covered as much ground as a King's Messenger. His thighs must be rubbed raw, at the very least.

Baldwin spurred his horse on, calling to Wolf, and they trotted around the city's wall, following the old road. It was no great distance: the total circumference of the wall Baldwin reckoned to be less than a mile and a half. On the way they met with a carter, who warily kept out of sword's reach as he listened to their questions, and then told them that there was an inn at the southern gate of the city, which was where most would settle for the night if they missed the gate. It was to this that Baldwin led

Jack, and before long the two were standing before a great fire that crackled and glowed in the middle of the room, while Wolf slumped to the floor with relief.

Jack looked about him with eyes dulled by exhaustion.

The innkeeper was reluctant to let them in at first, but that was normal at such an hour. Most inns would prefer to err on the side of caution and bar their doors after dark. As it was, the keeper brought them ale and then returned to speak with a strongly-built man with dark hair and beard who sat on an old barrel, watching Baldwin mistrustfully.

'Do not worry,' Baldwin said soothingly, only partly to reassure Jack. 'We shall be safe in this place.'

CHAPTER EIGHT

Near Marshfield

Robert Vyke peered at his leg. The wound was not smelling foul, which was a relief, but there was plenty of pus leaking out and turning the linen bandages yellow.

'It hurts?' the priest asked.

'Very much, Father.'

'I have heard it said that this leaking fluid is the "laudable pus". It means that you should have a fully healed leg in a little while.'

'It is feeling stronger. And there is less fluid.'

'You can stay here as long as you wish, my friend. There is no hurry for you to leave.'

Robert Vyke couldn't help but glance at the door. 'Have the Queen's men been here?'

The priest was sitting on his stool, a wooden board on his lap containing some old cheese and bread. He had been about to push a lump of the bread into his mouth, but now he stopped and fixed an eye on Robert. He had a shrewd look about him, for all that he was no older than Robert himself. He would have been a good-looking man, with his fair hair and blue eyes, were it not for the sadness that seemed to lie on him. 'Have you cause to fear her?'

'I was here because of the King. I was arrayed, and marched with him.'

'I think that there will be many like you,' the priest said, shoving the bread into his mouth and chewing. Crumbs flew from his mouth as he spoke. 'There is no need for you to fear, my son. She and her army may pass here, they may not. The most important thing is that they won't be stopping here to find you. Do you think she will seek out all those who have ever shown themselves loyal to their King? No. It is not as though you are a wandering felon, is it?'

'No!' Robert protested.

'I did have to ask, my son. Your leg will heal, so far as I can tell. I have washed it with egg-white, and there is no poisoning of your flesh. Perhaps in a week or a little more, you will be able to walk again.'

'A *week* or more?'

'If you will rest it and behave sensibly, yes.'

Robert stared at his leg. He had hoped to be able to return home to his Susan. She would be so happy to see the . . . Where was the knife?

'Father,' he said tentatively, 'when I fell, there were belongings of mine in a bag, and . . .'

'Yes, of course,' the priest said. He stood, set his board on his stool, and came over to the bed. Reaching beneath Robert, he withdrew the old pack. 'The dagger is a strange device for a man of such lowly upbringing,' he noted.

All at once the memory of the face returned to Robert. 'I found it . . .' he began, but was cut off by the priest holding up his hand.

'I am sure you came by it honestly, my friend. After all, who could have wished to keep a weapon in that condition?'

'It was lying in a pothole, with the blade pointing up, and it was that blade which so injured me.'

'A great misfortune,' the priest said. 'I wonder whose it could have been?' His voice held a strange note, and when Robert looked at him, his posture was that of a priest, awaiting a man's confession.

'There was a man there,' Robert said. 'I was trying to straighten the blade, and he was in there. In the trees. His head – it was sitting on a fork of two branches, and that was when I fell. I can remember now.'

'Where was this?' the priest asked, frowning.

'In the trees.'

'Can you describe the place?'

'I . . .' He stopped. He might recognise it if he saw it again, but it was just a bit of roadway. 'There was a road, with a pothole, a hedge, and trees behind it.'

'My son, you were found in the field behind my church here. Did you walk here from the wood?'

'No, I was beside the road with my friends,' Robert said.

'Which road? Do you know which vill you were near?'

Robert shook his head slowly. 'All I know is, we were close to Bristol. We stopped there to rest, for our company was passing through on our way to the King. I hurt my leg and had to be left behind – and then a damned sumpter-man struck my head because I remonstrated with him for his cruelty to his beast. He killed it,' he added as an afterthought.

'There was no party came past here,' the priest said. 'I've heard of the King's host passing by a few miles to the north, but none down here.'

'We were only one vingtaine,' Robert said tiredly. His head

and leg were throbbing. 'And it was very early in the morning when we came past.'

'You think I'd have missed you?' the priest chuckled. 'Not here, my friend. There is no concealment for a vingtaine, I assure you. I sleep lightly, so I would have woken at the sound of a force riding past.'

'I didn't see a church,' Robert admitted. 'The road was tree-lined, and there were hedges, and a little cottage: I *saw* it.'

'Well, not here, my friend,' the priest said, and there was a kindly look in his eye. 'Don't forget, you have seen the skull rise before you several times over the last day, in your sleep. Perhaps you should lie down again?'

'I am not mad!' Robert said, but he could feel the onset of a kind of panic. Had he dreamed the whole incident – the fall, the discovery of the head? Was it all just a fiction planted in his mind by a mare?

Inn outside Winchester

Baldwin and Jack were shown into the main bedchamber. Palliasses were thrown higgledy-piggledy over the floor, and some had already been taken. Their occupants were curled up or lying on their backs, and there was little noise, apart from one man, who was snoring so furiously it was as though he was fighting for every breath. There was a boot lying by his head – perhaps someone had thrown it to silence him. The shutters were pulled tight, Baldwin noted, to prevent any thieves entering during the night, but he still looked about him cautiously.

By the little rushlight it was hard to see much. He could make out six men on the floor, of whom only one appeared to be awake still, and he was hardly a threat. He was a short fellow, scrawny as a man who'd fasted for a fortnight, and he lay watching the two of them from dark, suspicious eyes that raked over Baldwin, from his green tunic to his sword.

Baldwin undid his sword belt with slow deliberation, staring back at the fellow as he did so. Then, choosing the least noisome of the spare palliasses, he rested his back against the wall and placed his sword at his side, motioning to Jack to lie nearby. Wolf padded to his side and lay down.

There were no safe inns in the land now, he knew. The kingdom was too unstable. King Edward II was running for his life. Throughout his reign, from the earliest days, Edward appeared to have been doomed. His wars to protect his lands against the Scottish had all foundered against the resolute tactics of that devil Bruce, while the one war he had finally won, against the Marcher Lords, had been fought not for his own benefit, but for that of his adviser and friend, Sir Hugh le Despenser.

His choice of friends and advisers had been disastrous, since he had selected those who were more keen to enrich themselves than work for the good of all and govern wisely. First it had been that cretin Piers Gaveston, and more recently Despenser. There were few in the realm who did not loathe Despenser; even those who protested their affection for him were often lying. His avarice and insatiable hunger for power were despised by all who believed in chivalry and honour.

Baldwin himself detested the man. He had seen how Despenser had persecuted his friend Simon Puttock. A good, decent man, Simon had been hounded from his home and forced to give up his offices working with the Abbey at Tavistock, returning to his old home near Sandford and taking on the mantle of a simple farmer. Yet compared with others who had endured the enmity of Despenser, he was fortunate. He was at least still alive.

There were many within the King's circle in past years who

had inspired such hatred, but few could have attained such heights of influence. For Baldwin, it was a cause of conflict and frustration since, although the Despenser represented all that was hateful to him, yet Baldwin must fight to protect the man – because to refuse would be to disobey his King. And he could not do that.

The rushlight was dying, and Baldwin snuffed it between dampened finger and thumb. Instantly the room was thrown into darkness, and he listened carefully. There was no apparent difference in the sounds of quiet breathing and snoring, but he would take no chances. Reaching for his sword, he placed it on his lap, his right hand ready on the hilt.

Shutters could be closed against burglars and draw-latches, but sometimes they could seal in a victim.

Chapel near Marshfield

As the sick man began to murmur and moan in his sleep, Paul knelt beside his bed and gently mopped his forehead with a cloth.

It was expensive having this man here. He had already eaten much of Paul's store of food, and his logpile was sadly depleted, all gone to keep the room warm for the invalid. At least his leg did appear to be healing.

But it was worrying, this story he told. His descriptions were vague, but as soon as news was abroad that he had been out this way, the chances were that his story would take on a new meaning.

'God help me,' the priest muttered under his breath.

This fellow was probably the most profound danger to Paul of all the men who walked upon the earth. As soon as his story became known, everybody who had heard of the Capons and Petronilla, the faithless bride, would flock to gawp at him – her lover. It would be impossible to remain here. What would his congregation think?

Squire William had slaughtered his Petronilla and her family, even a babe who could never have hurt anyone. They had all died for nothing. Petronilla and Paul had been foolish, perhaps, but that was no reason to murder the Capons. If anyone, it was Paul who deserved that.

He closed his eyes as the tears came once more. It was hardest now, in darkness, to hold back the terrible misery; the shame that lay so heavily on his soul.

As he opened them again, the rushlight flickered and almost blew out. He glanced across. It was only a gust coming in through one of the many holes in his walls. A rat had gnawed its way through a beam at ground level, and the big hole there was one of the banes of his life. Every so often he would try to fill it with clay, but at this time of year it wouldn't hold. It would dry out on the inside from the fire's heat, then wash away outside.

Something glinted temptingly, and he turned to look around. There, in the rushlight's warm glow, lay the knife with the warped blade.

He reached down to pick it up, but something made him stop. He recognised it.

This knife had been the Squire's, he was sure. He had seen those gemstones so many times, prominently displayed at the man's belt. He suddenly realised, with a horror that almost stopped his heart, that this blade might have been the one that ended poor Petronilla's life. And here, in his bed, lay a man with his leg cruelly harmed by it – more proof of the weapon's malevolence.

To grip that hilt might take away all the last restraints which manacled him to this church. If Paul took up that knife, he could instantly plunge it into this sleeping man's heart, for bringing so much danger here to him.

Because as soon as people heard that Squire William had died, they would want to come and arrest Paul. And this fool could tell them exactly where to find him.

Inn outside Winchester

The sound was tiny. A faint, muffled crunch.

In the dark, Wolf awoke and crouched, instantly alert. His movement stirred Baldwin. He had spent much of his youth as a *Poor Fellow Soldier of Christ and the Temple of Solomon*, a Knight Templar, and the life of obedience and training had left its mark upon him. His hand closed about the hilt of the sword in his lap, and he opened his eyes slowly, casting about him for any movement.

There was no moon, and the room was as black as pitch. If a man had moved, he doubted that he could have seen it. However, listening intently, he knew that there was something wrong, and then he realised: the breathing in the chamber was not that of sleeping men, but faster – the breathing of men preparing to fight.

Baldwin put out his hand and found Jack's sleeping form at his left. Good, the boy was still there. There was a rustle from his right, just ahead, and Baldwin knew it was a foot stepping on a palliasse. He felt, rather than heard, a low, ferocious growl from Wolf.

It was that which decided him. He knew that there was about to be an attack, but the darkness meant he might as well have been unarmed. A sword in the darkness was likely to kill the wrong man, and Baldwin had no wish to accidentally stab Jack. Still, Wolf had precipitated action.

He must protect the boy. Rolling to his right, he slipped a

hand under his palliasse and threw it over Jack. Wolf was
snarling now, and a man shrieked. Springing to his feet, Baldwin
stood with his sword, still scabbarded, in both hands, then
stabbed the blunted weapon forward. There was a grunt, a muttered curse, and Baldwin knew where two men were. He
slammed his right fist forward, the pommel protruding this time,
and felt it connect with one head, as a man cried out in pain.
There was a shout and stumbling feet, a muffled protest from
Jack, and another man whimpered and screamed as Wolf bit his
thigh.

Baldwin stepped swiftly to his side, away from any retaliation, only to hear the silken whisper of steel, which ended in a
wail of terror as Wolf bit the man's hand. There was a loud clang
as a sword crashed to the ground, a shriek as the man fell with
Wolf worrying at his throat. Baldwin stamped his foot, feeling
the hand beneath his boot, and chopped down with the hilt of his
sword. It crashed into a skull, and he heard the man grunt and
collapse. Then he was thrusting at the place where another had
been.

There was a rasp, a flash, and he saw his error. In the dark he
had moved too far to his left, and now the second man was at his
shoulder. Baldwin cocked his elbow and jabbed, felt it crack into
the man's jaw, his teeth clicking together, hard.

Another flash. Someone was striking a flint. Baldwin ducked
as the flare glinted from a sword, and shoved his scabbarded
sword upwards into the man's belly. He gave a short retching
gasp and fell back as a red glow appeared. There were two more
men, and Baldwin finally drew his sword. The grey blade
gleamed wickedly, and as the tinder began to catch light, some
rushes flaring briefly and leaving a residual glow, Baldwin saw
that both had knives, one small, the other a long fighting dagger
of almost eighteen inches. The fellow with the shorter knife was

the more practised, though – it was the bearded man he had seen with the innkeeper. His skill with the knife was there in the way he held the knife low, thumb on the blade itself, his other hand gripping a cloak, which he wrapped about his wrist and forearm. He knew what he was about. The other was a mere boy, only a little older than Jack, and held his blade out as though it was a magic wand designed to hurl flames at his enemies. He almost looked scared of it.

'Stay, Wolf,' Baldwin shouted, before his mastiff could leap and be spitted on the long dagger.

Baldwin always believed in removing the worst threat first. He held his sword up in the hanging guard, the point of his sword aimed at the knife-man's belly, and waited a moment. In the gloom it was hard to see anything, but he was sure that his opponent flashed his teeth in a snarl. It looked as though he was preparing to launch himself, and Baldwin gave him no more time to think. Instead he sprang forward himself, thrusting down with his sword, and had the satisfaction of feeling his blade sink into the fellow's flank, before batting away the little knife with the scabbard. He jerked the sword back and out, punched the man on the chin twice, hard, dropped the scabbard, grasped the man's wrist, and held the knife safely away. There was a loud crunch behind him, and he turned to see the boy with the long knife collapse slowly, falling to his knees with a shocked expression on his young face, and then his eyes rolled up into his head and he toppled sideways to reveal Jack behind him with a splintered baulk of timber in his hands.

CHAPTER NINE

Third Saturday after the Feast of St Michael[1]

Inn outside Winchester

The innkeeper was wonderfully apologetic, and at least Baldwin and Jack did not have to pay for that night's lodging, although Baldwin secretly wondered how much of that was due to the fact that he had not cleaned his sword's blade; to the innkeeper's eyes, he must have looked very bloodthirsty.

After the attack, Baldwin had bound the remaining men with thongs, and they were being held in a storeroom at the back of the inn. He himself sat at the stool near the inn's fire, wiping down his sword. After the care of his horse, the most important aspect of a warrior's routine was preserving the life of his weapons. Until earlier in the year, Baldwin had owned a beautiful little riding sword with a perfect peacock-blue blade, inlaid with inscriptions and decorations, but during a fight it had fallen into the sea, and he had been forced to buy this rather inferior

[1] 18 October 1326

77

piece of work from a London armourer. There were many better swordsmiths in Exeter, and he was looking forward to purchasing another on his way home, but for now, this would have to do. True, the grey steel blade had shown itself adequate last night, but now, as he peered along its length, he could see that there was a slight bend in it already, and there were four nicks in the fine edge.

With a stone he had found in the yard, he sharpened and honed the edge of the blade until it shone again. Jack was sitting nearby on the floor, watching him avidly.

The keeper was a stolid man, broad of shoulder, but with a girth that more than matched it. His heavily bearded face was prone to smiling, but Baldwin distrusted him. There was a shrewd calculation in his eyes, and the knight sensed that he was keen to make profit, no matter what. He was reluctant now to admit to anything he might know in case Baldwin demanded compensation, he reckoned.

'I am very sorry that such footpads could find their way into my inn,' the man was saying as Baldwin eyed his blade and ran the stone along its length one more time. The slithering sound seemed to unsettle the man, Baldwin saw. He ran the stone along it again, more slowly this time.

'I am sorry too. I should report the whole matter to the local Sergeant.'

'Oh, I'm sure there's no need for that.'

'Really? And yet I am equally sure that it would be a most excellent idea to do just that. One should never attempt to conceal a crime, should one?'

'But everyone can become tainted by such news,' the innkeeper protested. 'After all, some may think that the villeins came in with others who are still here, mayn't they?'

Baldwin's sword flashed and the point came to rest near the

keeper's throat. 'You are suggesting that a man might consider *me* to be connected with draw-latches and felons? Think carefully, good fellow, before you answer.'

'I didn't mean to insult you, Sir Knight, no. Not you, I was thinking of the other man in the chamber with you,' the man said, his tone a little higher.

'And I should hate to insult you, too. It may prove to be all too painful for you.'

'I . . . I understand, sir.'

'Now, good fellow, tell me: did you know any of the men who were here?'

'No. Certainly not!'

'I saw you talking to one of them.'

'It is my job, Sir Knight. I have to be polite to my customers.'

Baldwin said nothing. In his mind was the question of how polite it was to accuse knights, however elliptically, of fraternising with criminals. He ordered the keeper to bring them eggs and some ham to break their fast and scabbarded his sword.

'So, Master,' Baldwin said when the innkeeper had hurried away to find their food, 'would you like to repeat what you said to us last night?'

The scrawny man Baldwin had seen on entering the sleeping chamber the previous night pushed himself away from the wall. He was very wary still, but at least his suspicion appeared to be concentrated on the innkeeper rather than Baldwin. However, Baldwin had great faith in the judgement of another. As the man approached, Wolf lowered his head and gave a low rumble deep in his throat until Baldwin rested his hand on the mastiff's head.

'As I said, Sir Knight, the fellows were all together. I saw the keeper talking to a lot of them at different times, and I think they guessed that I might be carrying something valuable. I wasn't, but they weren't to know that.'

'You were not?' Baldwin asked shrewdly. 'You will not mind my saying, sir, that you are not clad like a successful merchant, nor a Bishop. Why should they think you so fabulous a catch?'

He listened carefully, watching the man as he spoke. For many years Sir Baldwin de Furnshill had been Keeper of the King's Peace, and as well as chasing felons with the full might of the posse behind him, he also had been called to sit as Justice of Gaol Delivery on occasion. Listening to a man's voice and assessing where lies existed was a key part of his function.

This man showed no signs of concern, though. He spoke easily, maintaining a relaxed stance that was the opposite of a man bent on guile or deceit.

'Sir Baldwin, once I had the life of a wealthy man, and perhaps those characters saw that aspect of me and thought that I was a rich merchant in disguise, but I swear to you I have nothing. On my oath, I have only my clothes and a few other belongings.'

'What happened to you?'

'Just the usual sad tale. I am called Thomas Redcliffe, a merchant from Bristol. Until a year ago, my business was good. I have often imported wine and oils to England, and I have grown to be well-known in my city. But last year my ship was attacked by Breton pirates, and I lost all. She was on the return voyage, and all my money was invested in her cargo, so when it was taken, and my ship as well, I was ruined. I hoped to stave off the end by prayer, and took steps to protect my business while I went on pilgrimage to Canterbury, but . . .' He sighed. 'You know what the roads are nowadays. I was set upon outside London, at the place called Black Heath. All my money was taken, everything. I continued on to the shrine of Saint Thomas, but it appears to have done me little good. When I get home, I daresay my business will be no better, and I have suffered a broken head into the bargain.'

'It is a long way for a man to go for prayer,' Baldwin noted.

'A pilgrim must make an effort, surely? I thought if my misfortune was caused by some insult I had given to God, perhaps my journeying all that way might appease Him. At least I would have Saint Thomas to intercede for me.'

'I am sure Saint Thomas would be glad of the opportunity,' Baldwin replied.

He eyed the man thoughtfully. There was little about him that showed he was lying, and equally little to give the impression that he might have money on him and thus warrant an attack.

'I have no idea why they should attack me.' Redcliffe shrugged with every appearance of honesty. 'I am not clad in furs or silks, I don't have jewels draped about me. In truth, Sir Baldwin, it would be easier to understand that they had made an attempt upon *you*. You look rich, with all your expensive clothes.'

Baldwin glanced down at his new tunic, wondering if this was a subtle insult. It was only a matter of a few months old, but there were worn and faded patches at his knees and thighs, while the careful embroidery which Jeanne, his wife, had sewn at the hem was already pulled and ruined. Still, Redcliffe was right. It was more likely that felons would try to rob Baldwin, for a knight would be likely to carry something worth stealing: if not money, then pewter plate or good armour to pawn.

'Perhaps,' he agreed after a moment. 'What of enemies? Is there someone who could wish to assault you: a woman's husband, a jealous competitor in business?'

'I have no enemies,' Redcliffe said with a little smile. 'A poor man cannot afford such luxuries. And my wife is a good woman to me. Beautiful and obedient.'

The innkeeper returned, and the smell of cooked food made Baldwin's mouth water. For all the years of fighting and serving as a warrior, he was forced to accept the fact that he was no longer young, and the disruption of his night's sleep after a day's hard riding had left him feeling less than alert. The wooden trencher with the eggs and thick slices of dark ham were surely going to help him wake, and he broke off a lump of bread and dabbed at the eggs with it.

'Where are you going now?' he said after a little while, and drank from the jug of ale which the innkeeper had set at his side.

'I am heading for my home. My wife will be wondering what has happened to me already, and I would fain leave her wondering whether she is a widow.'

Baldwin nodded, considering. The men who had tried to rob Redcliffe the night before were locked away safely, but this was no time for a man to be wandering the countryside alone. There were many others who would be happy to rob a lone traveller.

There was another point at issue: he had no desire to be stuck here, a witness to the attack on Redcliffe, but if he was to arrange for the arrest of the men in the innkeeper's shed, he would be held up for at least a day. Better to avoid that. He wanted to get back to his own wife.

'Do you intend to charge the felons?'

'I would rather they were kept in a gaol until I was out of the county,' Redcliffe admitted. 'I don't want to be delayed here waiting for a Justice to listen to their tale.'

Baldwin nodded, then beckoned the inkeeper. 'Master, I wish to speak with the captives.'

Marshfield

When Robert Vyke woke next morning, for the first time his dreams had been untroubled and free of memories of that damned head. The pain from his leg had thankfully abated somewhat, and was now little more than a constant throbbing with an occasional stab of anguish if he knocked it by accident. In truth, his head hurt a great deal more than his leg, and that was when he remembered vaguely that his poor skull had suffered a second blow. Who had attacked him, after he found the body?

Slowly lifting himself from the bed, he pushed the rugs away and gently eased his feet to the ground. It was not a pleasant sensation to have his weight upon the injured leg once more, but he saw a large staff in a corner of the chamber, hopped over to it, and used it as a crutch.

Getting to the door was a lengthy process, but once there, he opened it and peered out. Immediately, his feeling of disorientation was increased.

Where he had expected to find a road, with deep potholes, mud and a hedge or shaw running nearby, instead he found himself gazing out over a flat landscape with one solitary track, and that so under-used that the grass grew thickly all over it.

'But . . .' he gasped, desperate to find anything that could even approximate to the scene he had expected. Hobbling out into the thin sunshine, he stared about him wildly. Behind him was a little church, and there were some trees in the small graveyard, but not enough. He was sure that as he and the vingtaine approached that latest vill, there had been trees lining at least one side of the road. As he had fallen, looking up he had seen their branches against the sky. He couldn't have *dreamed* that. There had been branches framing Otho's head when the Sergeant bent to him. And when he found that head, it was in a little wood. He couldn't have dreamed it all!

'You are awake, then? Good. How is your leg? It must be a little improved for you to be out here,' the priest said. He was walking towards Robert from the open church door. Seeing Robert's look, Father Paul gestured back to the building and said, 'There are so many strangers travelling the country, peasants who were arrayed and deserted, felons who will take advantage at any opportunity, as well as warriors who are seeking whatever plunder they may discover, that I have to keep a wary eye on my altar in case one of them steals it to sell. Thieves are no respecters of the House of God, you know.'

But Robert paid little heed. 'This isn't where I was,' he lamented.

The priest looked at him oddly. 'It isn't?'

'No. When I fell and hurt myself, I was in a little wood, on a busy roadway.'

'I found you about thirty yards down there,' the priest said, calmly but firmly. 'Would you like to see?'

'Yes,' Robert said eagerly, and carefully followed him. It was hard going, even with the tall staff to cling on to, and Father Paul had to point out holes and puddles as they went so that the injured man didn't fall again.

'It was just here. You can see,' the priest added helpfully, 'where you have flattened the grass here.'

Robert looked around at the flat lands, the treeless pastures and low hedges. He felt confused, weak and sickly. Like a small child who has lost a toy.

'No, this wasn't it,' he said. 'I wasn't here!'

Inn outside Winchester

Baldwin walked into the little shed and eyed the men held inside with disfavour. The innkeeper had argued against it, but Baldwin and Redcliffe had insisted that the prisoners should be bound. It would be too easy for them to escape if they had their hands free, which was one reason why Baldwin suspected the innkeeper was in league with these fellows. At least there was no fight left in them. They were all sitting sullenly, their wrists tied securely, and probably painfully.

'Who among you wants to hang?' Baldwin said.

They tensed visibly, and the boy who'd had the long dagger, whom Jack had knocked down with a timber, looked fretfully at the bearded man who appeared to Baldwin to be their leader.

In the grey daylight, Baldwin saw that this man had brown hair, and his beard was brown and ginger, as though he had carelessly painted a wall and splashed ochre over his chin. He had the narrow, deep-set eyes that to Baldwin indicated that he was untrustworthy. The knight was not keen to make snap decisions about any man, but felt that when someone had attempted to test his blade in Baldwin's breast, he was entitled to take a dim view. At least the fellow was in less of a position to hurt anyone now, from the look of the blood seeping through the linen wrapping his flank.

'You,' he said, pointing. 'Are you the leader of this band?'

'We don't have leaders.'

'You don't have a lot, do you?' Baldwin said. He leaned against the doorframe and folded his arms. Wolf came and stood at his side, head lowered aggressively.

The men were all unrested, he could see. Even without the bruises and injuries it was clear that they were strained. There was a smell of sweat and fear. 'You realise that I can have all of you hanged? Men who rob by night are the lowest criminals. And in your excitement, you chose to attack a Keeper of the King's Peace. A word from me, and you will all die.'

Silence greeted his words. The boy looked down and rested his brow on his arm, sobbing without a sound, while another man stared at Baldwin in confusion. He was one whom Baldwin had punched with the pommel of his sword. There was the imprint of the steel on his forehead, and the eyebrow beneath was torn and bloody.

The bearded man said nothing, but his eyes were fixed on Baldwin as though unsure how to respond.

'You have nothing to say in your own defence?' Baldwin enquired. 'In that case, I shall have to ask for the Bailiff to come and take you, then.'

'What would you have us say, master? You want us to pretend it was an accident?' the man sneered.

'Since you ask, I would know this: why did you choose to attack us last night?'

'We're going to hang, so why should we answer you?' the man with the injured brow demanded.

'Fair enough.' Baldwin looked at them all, one by one. 'If there is no mitigating circumstance, as Keeper of the King's Peace, I have no choice but to hand you to the law.'

'What does that mean?'

'Simply this: as draw-latches and robbers, you are felons, and you will hang. Of course, if you were motivated by some other . . .' He let the sentence hang, watching the bearded man again.

The boy lifted his head and began to speak. 'Sir, I didn't know we were—'

'Shut up!' the bearded man growled. 'Don't go speaking when it's not your turn.'

Baldwin looked at the boy. 'It is your turn, fellow. If you want to live, you should speak your mind.'

'I don't want to hang! We were paid, sir, and I—'

The bearded man turned and hissed viciously at the boy, who paled and withdrew, shuffling his arse towards the wall.

Baldwin sucked his teeth. 'You, boy, will be taken outside in a moment,' he said, and then his tone hardened as he eyed the bearded man. 'I am inclined to hang one of you today as a deterrent to all those who think that they can waylay a knight. So you will die. And then I can learn all I need about you from the boy there.'

'You can hear what you want from anyone when I'm dead.'

'If you reconsider, you could all live. Which would you prefer?'

'You will release us if we tell you the truth?' the bearded man scoffed. 'Is that what you're trying to tell us?'

'I have no desire to see bloodshed. I only want to know why you chose to attack us last night. You must have seen I had little enough with me. Did you mean to steal my horse?'

'Not you, sir. We didn't want to attack you,' the boy protested.

'Who, then? The man with us had no money, that much was obvious when you looked at him.'

'We didn't mean to rob him,' the boy said. 'We were paid to *kill* him.'

Bristol

That day began much like any other for Cecily. She rose before dawn, and left the house to seek bread for the breakfast, and then began her chores while Emma Wrey set about her board.

Cecily had not expected her new mistress to be quite so accommodating and generous. Bristol was a good city, with many kindly folk, but not many would want the bad fortune of someone like Cecily in their houses. There were too many superstitions about servants from unlucky households bringing bad luck with them for her to expect such a pleasant home again.

Emma was different. Perhaps it was the fact that she was responsible for herself. Her husband had been a good man, like some kind of angel. But even angels can die, and eventually he fell dead in the street after an evening's drinking with friends at an inn.

It was some little while after the murders that Cecily had found herself in this house. Before that, she had been forced to find what she could on the streets again, hawking eggs and flints for whatever she could charge. It wasn't easy, but at least she gathered in some store of coin.

There had been nothing for her when the murders had been investigated and the men caught. Certainly nothing in Arthur's will. That was little surprise, but she had hoped that she would be protected by a gift of some silver or a spoon from Petronilla. She had two shillings saved, but that was all she had in the world. The Coroner had offered her money, but she wouldn't touch it. Instead, she found herself what work she could.

It was the purest good fortune, so she thought, that Emma had heard of her plight and called Cecily to her house. She had been looking for a companion and maidservant for some weeks, she said, and when she hired Cecily soon afterwards, it was a huge relief. Life on the streets was growing alarming. Cold weather meant that selling goods from her basket left her fingers like icicles each evening. Often the only way a woman could survive was by joining the ranks of the prostitutes, and at the age of thirty, Cecily would find that a hard profession.

This morning being a Thursday, she wandered along to the fleshmarket to buy meat for their meal, and spent some time musing over the different cuts before making her selection; she dawdled a little, buying eggs, and some larks from a poulterer. She would cook them with honey later, she decided, and serve them before the main meats. Larks were such tender, sweet little birds.

It was while she was there, packing her purchases into her basket, that she saw the men.

Neither paid her any notice. Not even when she dropped her basket, smashing the eggs, her mouth gaping. Fortunately, she was too far away.

But she knew them. Their faces were all too familiar. They were two of the men she had seen and pointed out at the inquest.

The men who had been gaoled for going to her mistress Petronilla and holding her while Squire William stabbed her with his
gold-handled dagger. They were the men sentenced to death for
snatching the child from Cecily's arms and dashing his brains
out against the wall in the front courtyard of the Capon house.

It felt as though her heart would stop with the horror.

CHAPTER TEN

Inn outside Winchester

Baldwin walked back inside the inn and glanced about him. Seeing Redcliffe sitting at the table still, he closed the door behind him, and then walked over to the innkeeper's door and closed that too.

'Master Redcliffe,' he said, crossing the floor.

Redcliffe saw something in his face as Baldwin strode to him, and stood hurriedly. 'What? What have I done?'

'You have lied to me,' Baldwin said. He pushed Redcliffe back, both hands on the man's shirt. 'Those men weren't here to rob you, were they?' he continued as he thrust Redcliffe against the wall. He lifted the man and shoved him a little harder against the rough limewashed surface, smiling thinly. 'You lied, because you said that no one had a reason to hate you, that you had no enemies, didn't you? Yet someone has paid those men out there to kill you.'

'I didn't think—'

'No, I don't suppose you did.' Baldwin was furious to have been lied to, and the thought that he had given his sympathy to this man made him still more angry. 'I think you should remain here with them, and we should let you explain the position to the local Bailiff.'

'It would be a mistake,' Redcliffe said.

'What – you threaten me? You seek to threaten *me*?'

'No, Sir Baldwin. Hear me out, but in God's name, let me down first.'

Baldwin opened both hands and let him fall. 'If it were up to me, I would leave you in the gaol here to tell the Bailiff what the reason for this was, and the local Justice of Gaol Delivery might decide whether you or the felons were more guilty.'

'I am not guilty, Sir Baldwin. Are you a loyal subject of the King?'

At that, Baldwin shoved Redcliffe against the wall again, while his other hand grasped his sword hilt.

'No, Sir Baldwin, please, I must ask this: are you loyal to the King or not?'

'I am his loyal subject,' Baldwin rasped. 'Why, do you mean to insult me?'

'No, but those men wanted to kill me because I am the holder of secret messages for the King. I am a King's Messenger.'

Bristol

Sir Stephen Siward wore his accustomed affable smile as he walked from the market, but in his heart he knew that there was trouble brewing – trouble that could affect him personally if it was not nipped in the bud as quickly as possible.

Cecily had plainly been shocked to her core. He had seen her while he stood buying a pie. She appeared moonstruck, as though she might faint away at any moment. Women were prone to such odd humours – it was the womb, he had heard. It was a curious organ, and could move about the body through the month, causing much of their temperamental behaviour . . .

And then, even as she turned and fled, he saw the men, and with a shock of recognition equal to her own, knew where he had seen them before. They were the fellows Cecily had accused at the inquest.

The King, in his desperation to find any man who might support him, had proclaimed that all those in prison for theft or homicide, or those who had abjured the realm, if they would go to the King they would receive *litteras de pace*[1], and could return to their homes as free men after serving in his host.

Sir Stephen had heard that Squire William was to be freed some weeks ago, but he hadn't expected the men to come back here, not to the place where they had been accused and held, ready for hanging.

As Cecily fled, Sir Stephen eyed the men. If the city grew aware that the killers of the Capons had been released, there could be widespread unrest, he thought. And that maid may just stir it up. Where she had seemed unstable before, now she looked wild, and a woman in her frame of mind could be irrational.

If the men noticed her, they could well decide to take revenge for her evidence against them. They could capture her, torture her, kill her . . .

She might turn to *him* for protection. She might assume that he would defend her. True, she had thrown his money in his face when he tried to offer her support – but then, she probably thought he was buying her off and was proud enough to be offended. Truth was, she had also admitted to him that she held an affection for him. But her feelings were not reciprocated, and

[1] pardons

he could hardly waste time with her now. Not with the kingdom on the brink of war.

Sir Stephen sighed heavily. If those men learned where she lived . . .

Near Whitchurch

Simon Puttock looked about him warily as they rode on westwards.

It was two days since they had passed over thc great bridge at London, and he had kept a suspicious eye on any who so much as glanced at him or his wife as they trotted down into the Surrey side of the river, away from the great city. That first day of travel had been one of intense anxiety at all times. After witnessing the mobs wandering London's streets on the rampage, seeing so many deaths, no one could be unaffected.

The lanes of Southwark stank, filled as they were with the Bishop of Winchester's brothels, tanneries, and other more noisome businesses which were not wanted in London itself. It had been a relief to escape to the orchards and fields just outside. By the time they had reached a little village called *Wandelesorde*[1], Simon had already felt a little safer.

Yesterday they had made better time, travelling from dawn to dusk, and getting as far as a small village outside Farnham, where they had been able to sleep in a friendly peasant's barn; today they had already made good progress, and with every mile that they put between themselves and the city, Simon grew more content.

'I never want to see that place again,' his wife breathed.

Simon was not surprised to hear her say so. They had both been shocked by the sudden explosion of violence as the King fled his capital and the Queen approached.

[1] Wandsworth

'Nor me, neither,' he said. 'Nor Westminster.'

In the last months he had been forced to travel here too often, mostly supporting his friend Sir Baldwin, but also on the King's own business. This last time, he and Baldwin had witnessed the hideous slaying of so many people, including their good friends . . . but he wouldn't dwell on it. He would have gone to their rescue, but luckily Baldwin had stopped him. There was no courage or cowardice involved. It was simple mathematics: there were so many men in the crowd that anyone attempting to divert them from their prey would himself become the target of their uncontrollable rage and immediatcly be killed.

'We shall soon be home,' he said. 'A week, no more, and we'll be away from all this.'

'I hope so,' his wife said.

He had fallen in love with his Meg the first time they had met. She was tall, slender, and blonde as a ripe cornseed, while he was heavier, squarer of feature. He hadn't expected to be able to win her heart, but she had succumbed to his charm, and they had soon been married.

'Don't suppose it's time for lunch yet?'

This was Rob, a whining, malcontented lad whom Simon had acquired when he was Keeper of the Port at Dartmouth under Abbot Champeaux at Tavistock. Such a short while ago, that seemed, and yet so much had changed. The Abbot had died, the post at the port was taken from Simon while the Brothers at Tavistock bickered over who should take the reins of power, Simon's own home had been stolen from him by the Despenser, and now he had only his farm for his livelihood. Yes, much had changed.

'Shut up, boy!' Hugh, Simon's servant, snapped.

'Are you sure it will take a week to get home?' Margaret asked.

'I am afraid so,' Simon said.

'A whole week of that fellow complaining,' Margaret said wonderingly. She knew her man too well, and his concerns were apparent to her now. He was worried about their son, Peterkin. She hugged her son to her belly. Peterkin was already yawning, and while he was safe enough here, she didn't want to drop him. The boy was not yet four years old, and very precious to them both. He was their second son – their first-born son died when only a baby, of some foul wasting disease that took him gradually over several days – and both were ever wary of danger to this, their second. Meg had suffered miscarriages and had fallen pregnant only after many attempts, which made Peterkin still more important to them both.

'He may improve,' Simon said, glancing at Rob without enthusiasm.

Margaret nodded. 'A week . . . I had not realised it was so far.'

'When we came from Porchester, that was a shorter distance,' Simon agreed. They had been forced to stay at the coastal town for some time, helping search for spies, whose messages were rumoured to be sent by ships. The King had ordered that all men with experience in such matters should monitor all shipping and capture the letters. As Simon had said, it was about as effective as searching for a needle in a field of corn. An utter waste, in fact, of his time.

'I believe that as the crow flies it is some seventy leagues[1],' he said, peering ahead. 'We should be home again in a little over five days, with fortune.'

They had asked directions as they left Farnham, where they halted to buy provisions, and were told to find their way to Winchester, and thence to continue west.

---

[1] There were three miles to a league, so two hundred and ten miles.

'Are we likely to be waylaid?' his wife asked in a lower voice.

'I don't think so,' he said, and grinned at her. 'And the Queen's riding north of us.'

'We hope.'

'The King's been gone for two weeks,' Simon said. 'He's probably in Wales by now.'

'Why would he go there?'

Simon shrugged. 'From his point of view, he needs friends. He hasn't many, but at least Despenser is still with him, and Despenser owns the whole of South Wales. It's his power base, so I suppose the King thought it would be the best place to install himself. From one of the great castles he can begin to form a host so he can stand up to his wife and son.'

'What a terrible position,' Margaret murmured, pulling her cloak about her shoulders and tightening her grip on her son. 'To know he has the enmity of his wife and child.'

'He should have kept closer to them,' Simon said without sympathy. 'It was his choice to ignore them and turn to Despenser in their place.'

Margaret nodded, but her thoughts were far from the King and his wife.

Simon cast an eye at her. 'You are thinking of Edith, aren't you?'

Their daughter Edith had married only the last year, and had given birth to her first child, but before the birth, her father-in-law became estranged from Simon. The Despenser had decided to make use of Edith and her new husband in an attempt to force Simon to his will, and as a result the newly-weds had been separated and forced to suffer greatly. Edith's father-in-law swore after that that his son would have nothing to do with Simon and his family, and that if Edith wanted to maintain her marriage, she must renounce her father and mother, and agree never to see them again. It was a terrible act, and one that made Margaret and Simon desperately sad, for they had not been able to see their grandson. The only contact they had was through Baldwin's wife, who managed to keep in touch with the girl.

'She'll be fine,' Simon said.

'Yes,' Margaret said, but without conviction. There was no telling how their daughter might be. Not while they could not speak to her.

Third Sunday after the Feast of St Michael[1]

Bristol Castle

Sir Laurence left the pile of requisitions and other papers with his clerk David, and walked out to the battlements, as was his wont, checking that the men on the ramparts were awake and alert, seeing for himself what the mood of the city below was, and glancing about the castle's inner ward as he walked. Only out here in the open air, did he feel a man again. He was not suited to dealing with clerks and papers.

It was one of the regrets of his life that he must now subject himself to this office incarceration each day. Staring out over the city, he felt the resentment of a prisoner. This castle might be a glorious fortress, and the city might be his favourite in the kingdom, but when a man was effectively tied to them, it took the savour from both. He gazed longingly out to the east, over the woods and fields. The trees of the ancient woodlands and coppices rose high, while the cattle in the pastures moved sluggishly

[1] 19 October 1326

in the cold morning air, and he felt envious of those men out there now, peasants with their billhooks ready to attack the trees in the coppices, preparing to go hedgelaying, or merely running or riding for the pleasure of it.

If he closed his eyes, he could imagine himself on horseback again, the wind in his face freezing his shaven cheeks, his hair flying behind him, the smell of sweating horse in his nostrils as he bent down to hurtle all the faster along the roads . . .

He opened his eyes as he heard footsteps, and saw his porter hurrying along the walkway towards him.

'Yes?' he said testily.

'Woman to see you, Sir Laurence.'

CHAPTER ELEVEN

Near Amesbury

They had started off in good spirits, but by noon it seemed the day was to end in disaster for Simon and his wife.

Their beasts were well-rested, and Margaret had slept better than for many weeks past in that little inn. It was not too busy this morning, for most people were sensibly keeping close to home at this time of trouble for all. The alehouses in the villages, by contrast, would be making plenty of money as the locals gathered to swap stories about the progress of the Queen in pursuit of her husband, for men enjoyed gossip as much as women, but the amusement ended as the men left the ale behind and went home. None of them was certain what the future would hold.

This part of the country appeared to have little enough reason to fear battle, Margaret thought. The crops and apples in the orchards had been harvested, and the peasants were out in their fields preparing for winter, trimming hedges and collecting faggots for their fires, and dealing with the numberless little jobs which had been put off during the harvest. None had suffered from the ravages of violence in the same way as the people about London, or the folks of the Welsh Marches in the last four years. The Despenser had enraged other barons to the limit of endurance, and they had risen against him, rampaging over the Despenser territories, killing, looting, pillaging wherever they went, and finally marching on London itself, where they held the King hostage until he agreed to exile his favourite.

But King Edward had had no intention of honouring his promise. While Despenser agreed to take to his boat and leave the kingdom, in reality he based himself on the coast, while the King prepared to bring him back. The resulting war devastated swathes of peasant lands, and Despenser returned, only to bring ferocious revenge upon those who had dared to try to curb his ambition.

Here, thank God, there was little evidence of such violence. Margaret cuddled her son closer to her and began to relax, but in the middle hours of the morning, trouble arose once again.

They had ridden into a large village not far from a place called Basingstoches, when they were accosted by a man riding fast from the south.

'Beware! Stop! There are men up there who've clubbed others for what they can steal! Don't head that way, friends, as you value your lives.'

Margaret could see that her husband was on his guard immediately. Hugh was the same; he trotted on his little pony up to Simon, his large staff in his hand, to listen carefully, while motioning to Rob to join them. Rob appeared not to notice, and despite the situation, Meg had to stifle a giggle to see Hugh's scowl as he prodded the boy sharply with his staff.

Unaware of their antics, Simon was asking, 'Where have these men come from, fellow?'

'They've just appeared in the last day or two. Bastard thieves, the lot of them. There's a tale told that a poor widow backalong was found in her house when they passed by, and they made play with her. Sorry, mistress, but the truth can be shameful.'

'I don't know,' Simon said. 'We are on our way homewards, and that means Exeter.'

'You'd be best served to take a wide circuit of Basingstoches, friend. I'd not see a family attacked if they can be saved.'

Simon nodded, his eyes staring back the way the fellow had come from. 'What's that?' he asked.

The scene was pleasant, the sun breaking through the clouds and sending shafts of golden light stabbing at the ground to the south. A natural curve of the land gave them a view past two gently undulating hills, and through the pass between them. There were woods on top of the hills, but the lower-lying ground was all pasture and field. In among the trees there was a fire, seemingly, and the smoke rose in a thin stream. It appeared to climb a little above the trees, only to be whipped away by the little gusts of wind that licked at his face moments later.

'Oh, God's bones, it's them!' the man said with a gasp of horror. 'They've come nearer than I realised. Master, you must ride from here.'

'How many are they?' Simon said.

'Thirty, perhaps? Too many for you to protect your family against them.'

Simon shot a look at the rest of his party, and reached out to his wife. 'Meg, give me Perkin. I can carry him more easily than you. Hugh, you stay with her, and Rob – *keep up*. This is no time for whining about bloody horses, boy! Now, ride!'

Margaret gave him Perkin, and then leaned forward

impulsively to kiss him. She cast a swift glance towards the smoke, and then he saw her mouth fall open. Two men were approaching at the gallop, and then behind them he saw another – and then another. 'Meg: *ride!*' he shouted, and slapped her horse's rump to get it moving.

Looking over her shoulder, Margaret saw him turn to face them, assessing the threat, his horse springing up on its hind legs, sensing the excitement.

If it were only the two, and he hadn't already taken Perkin, she knew he would have chanced his luck. One rider could hold two at need; but there were more and more appearing, tumbling out of the trees on horses that appeared fresh – six . . . no, eight. Margaret could see that Simon's own mount was not exhausted yet, but they had covered some miles and hadn't yet taken a rest, for they had been planning to stop and take some food shortly. She saw him curse their bad fortune as he wheeled his horse round to follow the others, and clapped spurs to the flanks, one arm about their wailing son's waist, the other gripping the reins tightly.

Margaret could not watch, for her mare was always likely to stray too close under a tree, forgetful of her rider. It was all she could do to cling to the beast, head low over her neck, trying to avoid the mane as it whirled about in front of her, and shoving her face into the horse's coat every so often as a branch flashed past. Only when they had ridden into a patch of more open road-way did she look back once more, and see that her husband was falling behind.

'*Simon!*'

Bristol

Emma had been waiting in the gatehouse for an age, or so it felt, when the damned man deigned to come down and see her, and her mood was not of the best. Christ's bones, but she was a woman of some position in this city! The fact that she was clad in her richest clothes, the bright crimson cloak with the squirrel fur trimming, the green velvet tunic, sewn to taper in at her waist and show off her bosom – all was designed to prove that she was wealthy enough to be taken seriously. Yet she was left waiting here like some common petitioner at a lord's doorway. It was outrageous!

When the figure appeared, she remained on the bench where she had been sitting, so that their roles were subtly reversed. She eyed him contemptuously from his boots to his head. 'You are Constable here?'

'I am Sir Laurence Ashby, Constable of Bristol under the King,' he acknowledged, and gave her a bow.

He at least appeared to have some manners, she conceded. Still, his voice showed that he was a foreigner, and as such, not to be trusted. She could tell he was not from Bristol.

'I am here because of an error,' she said stiffly.

His eyebrows lifted. 'Yes?'

'Some weeks ago, a man and his wife, the Capons, and their daughter, Petronilla, along with her child, were all killed, with their bottler; they were murdered by their son-in-law, Squire William de Bar of Hanham.'

Sir Laurence nodded, a slight frown at his forehead. 'I have heard of the case. It was most distressing.'

'But the curious matter is, my maid saw his men in the city, and after asking at the gaol, I learn that he has been released with them. Is this so?'

'I fear it is.'

Her voice hardened. 'Then I respectfully ask that you have him taken into custody once more, sir. He is an enormously dangerous man, and should be held in the gaol until the Justices can listen to the case and see him executed.'

'With respect, madame, I cannot. He has been granted a royal pardon.'

Emma opened her mouth to speak, but for a moment no words would come. Then, 'I think I must have misheard you, sir. A fellow who has killed two women, a babe and an innocent bottler and his master, *cannot* be granted his freedom. He is a convicted felon, and should pay the price for his crime.'

'The King has himself granted the pardon. There is nothing I can do, madame.'

'It is not possible that a man with such a heinous record could be released!'

'The King has need of any man who can wield a sword or bill, madame. I am very sorry, but that is all there is to the matter. The Squire is free and his past crimes are forgiven, in exchange for which he will be required to serve his King once more.'

Emma stood. 'I consider this an insult to the whole city of Bristol!'

'I do not expect you to comprehend the necessity, madame,' Sir Laurence said. 'All I can do is apologise for the distress you clearly feel. Has this fellow offended you personally?'

'No! That is not the point. My maid was in the house when he rampaged through it and killed all those people. Now she sees him strutting around in the street with his men – the very man who stood with gore on his sword and threatened to murder her in her turn! How can she possibly feel safe here again? She is a weak woman, sir, perhaps only of low birth, but a decent, obedient maid for all that. Her ease of mind is taken from her, and so is mine. Can you not have him held?'

'No. I am afraid I cannot.'

Emma stood and stared at him. 'So any felon may be released from the gaol, so far as you are concerned?'

'Madame, as I have explained, I have no authority to deny the King's decisions,' Sir Laurence said patiently. 'I assure you, if I could, I would have held him here longer. I have no love of homicides.'

'Your assurances mean little to me while that man and his friends walk the streets.'

Near Amesbury

Simon bent low, his world encircled by noise: the snap of his cloak in the wind, the squeals of terror from his son, the snorting of his rounsey's breath, the clatter and crash of his horse's hooves on the stones of the road . . . but now he could sense the beast's energy draining away. The poor beast had already covered half the day's ride without a break, yet despite that, the creature was doing all he might, exerting himself as never before. Simon knew, however, that the chase would be lost.

Simon Puttock had been an officer of the law, a Bailiff, and had fought often enough. On Dartmoor he had chased murderers, even large gangs of outlaws, and killed when he needed. There had been moments of fear, it was true, but in the main he reckoned he'd been courageous enough.

This was different. He had his wife and son to protect. He was aware of a curious tightening of his scalp, as though it was readying itself for a crushing blow from a mace or axe, and he knew only the terror that here, today, he would see his last surviving son die at another man's hand.

The fear lent new urgency to his frantic spurring of his mount, and the rounsey seemed to gather himself and pound onwards, as if the beast too realised the enormous danger of their position. Simon ducked to avoid a low branch, and risked a glance over his shoulder. The nearest man was a scant two yards away, a heavy-set fellow with black hair and a roughly-stubbled chin. He wore a green tunic, much patched, but it was not his clothing that held Simon's attention: it was the long sword in his hand.

And then Simon's mount stumbled. A momentary lapse, that was all, and suddenly the sword was within striking distance. Simon knew he was done for: he couldn't get away fast enough, not with his poor rounsey flagging. Then the man was almost level, and Simon saw the sword flash, the blade slashing at his cloak, but by a miracle missing his torso.

It was at that moment, when he was about to lose all hope, clinging to Perkin, who was sobbing now in his panic, that Simon saw salvation lurch into view: Hugh.

His servant rode with an expression of grim truculence, heading straight at the outlaw, and at the last instant, the fellow saw his danger. He jerked his reins, and his horse rode almost into Simon, missing by a mere half foot, while he stabbed with his sword at Hugh. But Hugh wasn't close enough to be hurt. His horse hurtled past, more than two yards distant, with him wielding his staff like a lance. He held it firmly under his armpit, and the inch-thick timber struck the outlaw under the chin like a rock from a mangonel. Simon heard the man's jaw shatter, an eruption of blood flying into the air. The fellow arced backwards over his horse's rump, to hit the ground with a hideous thud that Simon could hear over his hoofbeats.

Hugh now turned his mount and came after Simon, but the others were almost on him. Simon bit his lip, wanting to turn and help his servant, but knowing if he were to do so, he would risk his son's life. There were six men in close proximity, and Simon dared not turn back.

As he watched, he saw Hugh suddenly canter off to his right. One man in the pursuit seemed to waver in seeking this new quarry, but then he thundered off after Hugh. His beast was large, heavy, and not built for great speed, but he was a better rider than Hugh, Simon could tell, and he felt the fear assail him again, even as he saw Hugh suddenly stop his mount dead, swinging his staff in a circle. The man chasing him was slashed across the face, slamming his head back. Then more trees blocked Simon's view, and he peered to where he could see Meg, with Rob riding a few yards behind. The boy looked like a sack of grain, both legs out-thrust, his entire body bouncing up and down with each of the pony's movements. It was a miracle he hadn't fallen off.

And then he saw his Meg stop and look back. Sweet Mary, Mother of God, she had stopped – she was calling to him!

Simon felt the breath catch in his throat, for to pause here was to die. The men were so close, they would surely catch them all, and Meg, his lovely Meg, would be raped and killed, her body plundered like Simon's purse. At that instant, he was flooded by and uncontrollable rage. He would *not* submit and die without taking as many of these murderous lurdans with him as he could. Perkin would not be slain without Simon losing every drop of his own blood to defend him. Three, four, or more of their attackers would die first.

He forced his beast to slow, and then stop, pulling its head around to face back the way they had come. And now Simon took his son and kissed him quickly, about to set him gently down upon the ground, saying, 'Perkin, my lovely boy, go to a tree and hide behind it.'

That was when the cries reached him. There was a swirling of dust from the road, a thunderous sound, and seven men-at-arms galloped past him, whooping and shrieking, two with lances couched, while the others bore heavy swords. They crashed into the outlaws, and Simon saw a fountain of blood rise through the dust that enfolded them, saw men tumbled from their horses, heard the whinnying of petrified beasts, the echo of axes against armour, the crunch of steel crushing bone.

The bloodlust suddenly left him, leaving him overwhelmed by a terrible exhaustion, and he had to force his fingers to keep hold of his son. It felt as though to drop him would be to lose him forever, and Simon knew he must not do that.

CHAPTER TWELVE

Near Hanham

He was still in pain as he left the priest's little home, but Robert Vyke couldn't remain there any longer. He hobbled along the roadway with a large stick to serve as a staff, looking about him carefully.

'Master Vyke, where are you going?' The priest appeared, carrying wood he had gathered.

'Father, I am sorry, but I have to see if I can find where it was that I was struck down.'

'I can understand your confusion, my son. But I do not think you should be using that leg yet. Will you not stay here a little longer and rest it?'

'I thank you, but no. I cannot sit idly, while a man's body lies rotting.'

The priest nodded slowly. 'Do you have any idea where you should go?'

'No, but it cannot be too far from here, as the man who knocked me down must have carried or carted me here.'

Paul looked dubious. 'Perhaps so. Well, if you head east from here, and a little south, you will come to Bristol. That may be a good place to aim for, my son. Perhaps you will strike the place on the way. Otherwise, you will have to search in all directions trying to find it, and I do not know that you would be content to hunt all over the shire.'

'No, I am sure you are right there, Father. Will you give me a blessing?'

Paul gave him a hug, and muttered a prayer, making the sign of the cross over his brow and wishing him Godspeed, and soon Robert was on his way, following the road as Paul had suggested.

But as he set off, his teeth gritted against the pain, he knew that the reason he wished to seek that body was less because of the dead man, and more because he was determined to learn what had happened to himself.

He remembered finding the head, remembered crouching to vomit – and then nothing. Perhaps it was the effect of the knock on his head the previous day, but surely the blow wouldn't still have had such an awful impact on him after such a long time.

Stopping in the road, he ran his fingers questingly over his skull, quickly finding the area of intense soreness where the tranter had hit him. And then his finger found another place, right above his left ear. Touching it was enough to make him wince. So that was it, he thought. Someone had knocked him down again.

But why would his attacker take him somewhere else, unless it was to confuse him and hide the location of the dead man? If that was all the fellow intended, surely he would simply have killed Robert too, as a witness to his crime? It made no sense.

Robert suddenly set his face to the north. There were trees in the distance, and he was sure that there was smoke, too. It was painful to walk on his bad leg, but it would heal sooner if he kept it moving. Resting it too much was the surest way of losing his mobility for good and all.

The way soon became overgrown with brambles and black-thorns. Robert struggled on for a while, until he found himself on the edge of a small wood. He turned off through the trees, hoping that the way would become easier, and at first it was, but only if he followed a shallow incline to a little valley below. Here there was another trail, this time heading more southwards and getting marshy. He went carefully on the soft ground, test-ing the ground with his staff before putting his foot anywhere dangerous.

It was a slow, painstaking progress along this track, and he could have wept when he saw that the track was bending around to head south-east of here. He was going in the wrong direction entirely. Soon, if he wasn't careful, he would be back at the priest's house where he had started.

And then he saw the trees. There was something about them . . . He stopped, and stared hard, before setting off again in his jerky manner, moving carefully to protect his bad shin and skull, all the time aware of his emotions being pulled this way and that.

At the forefront of his mind was the necessity of finding the dead man, if there was one. If a fellow had been killed, and his body dismembered, Robert wanted to find it so that it could be reported. There were many people who would hurry away from a corpse on the basis that they would not want to be attached as first finder. Robert himself didn't want to have to pay any man to be bound over to return to this place when the Coroner came to hold his inquest, and later, when the Justices came to listen to the evidence in court. No, of course he didn't want to get caught up in all that, but still less did he want the murderer to escape.

Also, it was only by finding the body that he could assure

himself he wasn't mad. His dreams had been growing more and more grotesque, the dead man's head following him as though begging him to return. Maybe if he did so, peace would be granted to him.

The path led in among a stand of trees, and he saw with a thrill of excitement and trepidation that there was a hedge on one side, with a puddle nearby. With a grunt of resolution, he forced himself to look at the hedge. Sure enough, there was a gap in it large enough for his body to have crawled through. If he was right, the head was just over there . . . He bent and peered in.

And saw the head still sitting on the branches where it had lain before.

Near Amesbury

Simon and Margaret sat gratefully on the stools provided, and sipped the wine passed to them.

'So, Master Puttock, I think you must be glad we appeared when we did, eh?'

Simon looked up at the man who had appeared. He was a big fellow, but a man encased in a coat-of-arms and mail tended to have a commanding presence. This one still had his face concealed by his helmet, and Simon stood, a little unsteadily, and bowed. 'Sir, I am very glad to see you and to be able to offer my profound thanks. I don't . . .' Then he paused. 'How did you know my name, sir?'

'How would I not know the name of a friend?' The man laughed, and lifted off his helmet. 'Remember me?'

Simon gasped with pleasure to see Sir Charles of Lancaster. 'Sir, never was a knight more welcome!'

The knight nodded with a grin. He was a tall, confident man, with clear, blue eyes that told the world he knew it existed, in large part, in order to entertain and amuse him. Sir Charles was not a man to suffer from a sense of inadequacy or jealousy. He believed that he had a right, by birth and position, to enjoy his life in any way he wanted to.

There had been some significant changes since the last time Simon had spent any time with Sir Charles. That had been in France, and there, Sir Charles had suffered the loss of his most devoted man-at-arms when he was murdered, and Simon and Baldwin had helped him.

It was apparent that Sir Charles recalled the same incident. 'So, it seems I am able to return your favour to me,' he said. 'You helped me in Paris, and I am able to help you here.'

'What are you doing here?' Simon asked.

'The country would seem to be growing a little fractious,' Sir Charles said loftily. 'I have been asked to come and try to keep this area quiet, and I've been doing my best, but I confess, it appears that my best is inadequate. There is,' he added thought-fully, taking a large mazer of wine from his servant, 'quite a vast amount of unrest among the peasants.'

Sir Charles and his men had killed all the members of the gang which had attacked Simon and Margaret. There had been one survivor, whose horse had died in the attack, and who had tried to bolt for some trees to escape, but two of Sir Charles's men cantered easily after him, and in a few moments, the man was hacked into pieces. There was no sympathy for such scoundrels. Outlaws could expect instant justice.

'This is the first we have seen of it since leaving London,' Simon said. 'I had thought we had left the madness behind.'

'When a kingdom collapses, I fear that some men will always rise up and take what they want,' the knight said, airily waving his mazer while his servant struggled to unbuckle his greaves. 'You have these peasants who toil in their fields musing about life, and when they see law and order dissipating, they think,

"Aha, I could steal a shilling or two, and live like a lord for the day." They really are that simple: they only look for the next ale, the next pie. Further than that, they are blind, poor fools.'

Simon was irked by the knight's facile explanation, but there was little point arguing, he knew. Sir Charles had the ability to see what he wished, and took the view that other opinions were supremely irrelevant. Simon glanced across at the others. The man they had met on the roadway was over beyond Meg, who was playing five stones with Peterkin, while Hugh and Rob stood guard behind her. 'We all owe you a great debt of gratitude,' Simon said solemnly. 'And now, I suppose we'll have to make our plans for escaping any other mishaps on our way home.'

'You think to travel to your home in Devon?' Sir Charles chuckled. 'I would not advise it.'

'We have to return,' Margaret said firmly. 'Our daughter is in Exeter, and—'

'Will be considerably safer than you,' Sir Charles finished for her. 'If you travel the roads, you will be at risk from every felon, outlaw and disgruntled peasant. The roads, Madame Margaret, simply are not safe. You cannot possibly ride that way. The King has ridden westwards, and no one knows when he will return. The Queen and Mortimer are after him, and he has yet to gather his host.'

'He has issued instructions for his knights to gather, surely?' Margaret said.

Sir Charles nodded, but grimly now. His cheery manner was put to one side for the present. 'Oh, yes. He demanded his first men before he left London. I was given a writ myself – but no one would obey the summons. I am told there were sheriffs and knights who arrayed their men, formed their hosts – and then took them straight to the Queen. It appears her forces have been swollen a great deal since her landing, while the King's have declined. The force you see with me here is the best I could gather together. We are on our way to join the King now.'

'If you are right, and the Queen's strength is growing,' Simon said, shocked, 'you surely don't think that the King could lose, do you?'

Sir Charles eyed him. 'I would not say so. But until the final reckoning, all may change in an instant. And for now, the fact is that the roads are far too dangerous for any small group to hope to travel so far alone. In any case, as I said, your daughter is sitting in Exeter, behind sturdy city walls. If she is in danger there, she is in danger anywhere in the realm. For now, the King and Queen are not near her.'

'What will you do, then?' Simon asked.

'I am inclined to head towards the King and join him in Bristol,' the knight replied. 'I think that there I should be able to see how matters are developing.'

'And then?'

Sir Charles smiled, but didn't respond to the question. 'I would recommend that you join me in my journey. Bristol is said to be a fair city. I am sure you would find it delightful.'

Simon glanced at Margaret, who nodded, gazing up at the knight sadly. 'Yes, thank you, Sir Knight. But I am so worried about Edith, Simon.'

For once the knight appeared to show some sympathy. He bowed low. 'Madame Puttock, I am afraid that many will fear for their loved ones in the coming weeks. But there is no need for you to rush into danger to be with her. Better that you travel safely and arrive in one piece, than travel unwisely and never see her again.'

*

David was still working at his table when Sir Laurence threw the door wide and marched back into his chamber.

She was *insufferable*, that woman! As if a castellan had time to worry about her maid, just because she was upset at the sight of some men who scared her. He had a mind to go to the wench and give her a short instruction about the responsibilities of a man at time of approaching war.

'You have been a long while,' David observed.

'Oh dear, have you been bored?' the Constable snapped. 'Don't you have enough to do without me commanding you?'

David lifted his eyebrows. 'This was nothing to do with the garderobe, then?'

'The privy has been safe from me today,' Sir Laurence grunted as he slumped into his chair. 'Let's not talk about it.'

David eyed him uncertainly a moment before beginning to discuss the business of the day: a small fire that had damaged one of the storerooms, fodder for the horses and how many ought to be stabled within the court, a report on the total sacks of grain for bread and ale-making, as well as the honey, charcoal and brimstone stored for making the new blackpowder. The King had ordered two barrels of honey to be held at his castles for this purpose four years ago, along with all the other items necessary for repelling a siege, and Bristol was well served in all.

Sir Laurence tried to concentrate, but his mind kept returning to his interview with Emma Wrey. Cecily was an object of some fascination in the town, because of her narrow escape, and she had been pointed out to him a few times, usually by men using that hushed undertone that denotes some sort of notoriety.

It was said that only one man could have wanted to kill Arthur Capon and his family, but most people in the city knew that was ballocks.

Many, like Sir Laurence, had had cause to visit the man in his great house, less a merchant's humble dwelling and more of a palace, with the great paved and grassed court at the front, and high walls to keep it all private from wanderers in the street outside. Yes, every so often even a castellan needed money, and Arthur Capon was always prepared to help a man, with his sly little smile and oleaginous manner, and huge funds of ready coin. It was only later that his clients learned how they had been fleeced by the ruinous charges Capon levied upon them.

All too many of these disgruntled citizens would have been happy to enter his house and slit his greedy throat for him. There were fewer who would have killed his wife and daughter too, but in these days of violence, when even the throne itself was rocking with dissent, was it so surprising that a murderer should seek to eradicate the whole family? No. To leave a son would be to leave a future avenger.

And that, Sir Laurence thought, would have been simply foolish. A man ruthless enough to kill the father had to be prepared to kill all in the house.

CHAPTER THIRTEEN

Near Salisbury

Baldwin and Thomas Redcliffe were riding abreast, while further back was Jack, today looking remarkably relaxed as he trotted along. Wolf was jogging along happily at the side of the road, sniffing occasionally at the grasses and brambles.

'Another day and we should be in Bristol,' Baldwin said.

They had set off almost as soon as Baldwin had spoken to Redcliffe at the inn yesterday, telling the innkeeper to release the felons. The bearded leader's flank was giving him some grief, and it was plain enough that they would not be able to follow in a hurry. In the event, Baldwin and his companions had made good time after Winchester. The way to Salisbury and thence to the plains had been surprisingly clear of all other travellers, and Baldwin was glad of the views in all directions from up here on the clear grassland. Any man attempting to waylay them would find his task made infinitely more difficult by the absence of trees and other means of concealment.

'I am enormously grateful to you, sir,' Redcliffe said once more.

It was a refrain which Baldwin had heard too many times in the last days. He made no reply now, staring at the horizon ahead, but inside he raged with himself for agreeing to come all this way. Travelling to Bristol would add at least two days to his journey home, and he was desperate to get to Jeanne and make sure that she was safe. But as soon as he had admitted to the men in the shed that he was a Keeper of the King's Peace, he had found himself bound. The men who had attacked Redcliffe had received his promise to release them, and no matter what he wished, he could not retain them without breaking that promise. That Baldwin would not do. Meantime, he had a duty to protect the King's Messenger. Not that the fellow looked much like a messenger, in his opinion; he looked much more like a spy, and Baldwin had a healthy dislike of such men. Usually they were motivated by money, and he detested all forms of mercenary. Men who conspired and plotted were all untrustworthy, to his mind.

'You are good to help me in this way,' the man said.

'I had placed you in a position of danger; it was the least I could do,' Baldwin said.

'But still very kind. Many would not have helped me.'

'I wish I had realised the danger those men posed.'

'I wish I had known myself!' Redcliffe said. 'I still wonder who it was who paid them.'

The fellows had all denied any knowledge of the man who told them to hunt Redcliffe. It made Baldwin wonder who could have had such a violent hatred of the man that he was prepared to pay a gang to murder him. It was possible that Redcliffe knew who this man could be, but he vehemently denied it when Baldwin asked him, and from his apparent shock when he heard what the men had said, Baldwin reluctantly had to believe him. He was the subject of someone's irrational hatred, apparently.

Well, such things did happen. Or perhaps it was merely that the Queen had heard Redcliffe was coming this way, and had set men to catch him. It would depend on the importance of the message he carried.

Redcliffe himself had suggested that it could be a past competitor in his businesses. Not only had he been successful as a merchant, he had been known as a good judge of horseflesh, and had three times travelled to Lombardy and Spain to buy destriers and other mounts for the King and his nobles. Were others perhaps jealous of his trading? he wondered.

'I confess, I find it astonishing that you do not know who this murderous enemy could be,' Baldwin said now. 'Surely it was a man who saw you on your travels and set those fellows on you at the inn.'

'There was no one I noticed.'

'You are certain you have not offended any other fellows on your journey? I recall one man who felt himself offended.' Baldwin recounted the tale of a murder some years before: in that case the murderer had been a parson, from Quantoxhead in Somerset. He had taken umbrage at a man who accidentally jostled him in the street. In a sudden rage, he declared that he would see the man in hell within a day, and was in fact better than his word. The fellow was found dead the same afternoon, his servant also murdered at his side.

'The idea that a man should seek to have me killed is appalling,' Redcliffe said with a shudder. 'I have never been in such a situation before. It is most extraordinary to think that I could be the target of a killer.'

'You have much to remember this year. Losing a ship, then being attacked while on pilgrimage, then this latest incident . . . It was Black Heath where you said you were robbed, was it not?'

'Yes.'

'Those men: did they appear to want to kill you, or were they interested only in robbing you?'

'Oh, they seemed solely interested in my purse. If they had wanted to, they could easily have slain me. They had me at their mercy.'

'Did they get anything else?' Baldwin asked. 'Something that told them you were a King's Messenger? You could have become the target of someone who seeks to support Queen Isabella against the King.'

'No, only money,' the man repeated.

Baldwin glanced at the purse at his belt: it was a very old, worn-looking leather one. 'I am surprised your purse was returned to you,' he remarked.

'Yes. I was fortunate,' Redcliffe said. 'I found it later in the roadway.' He put a hand on it as though protectively, although there was not much money in it, from what Baldwin could see.

'And it survived the robbery, too. That was lucky,' Baldwin said.

'It is valuable to me, this purse,' Redcliffe said shortly. 'A sentimental object.'

Baldwin nodded. It was true that a man could become attached to a number of items. He had himself been most attached to his blue sword, now sadly lost in France; but he did find Redcliffe's attraction to what was a simple leather purse to be a little surprising in a man who said that he had once been very rich. He would have expected such a merchant to be more attached to a richly embroidered purse, perhaps with gold threads, and a decoration of precious stones.

'Are there many merchants in Bristol?' he asked. 'It is one of those cities which I have never before visited, only passed nearby.'

'It is a great city,' Redcliffe said enthusiastically. 'Beautiful, clean, with excellent lands all about, and access to the sea from the Severn. There could be no better place in all the realm.'

'You are proud of it, then?'

'Very. I love Bristol. Even though I have suffered in recent years, I cannot blame the city. It is not, perhaps, so well-governed as some others, but it—'

'In what way?'

'Oh, we have the usual problems. There is a small number of men who will regulate all business to suit themselves, and they are not accommodating to others.'

'We have a similar situation in Exeter,' Baldwin said. 'The Freedom is a jealously guarded liberty.'

'So it is in Bristol. There are a mere fifteen men who control the working of the city. Nobody may do what he wishes without the approval of them all.'

'You sound bitter.'

'I was promised by one, a man I trusted, that he would help me by paying some of my debts and support my return to business, but when I actually needed his help, he turned upon me and demanded all his money back. It was he who ruined me after all my problems.'

'Was he a friend?'

'I should not speak too ill of him. It is not kind, for he is dead, but yes, I had thought him a friend. It only serves to prove that in business no man may be counted your friend. All may smile and allow you to join their mess, but when it comes to a matter of business, you must assume that each and every one will stab you in the back. Capon did not appear to care about my feelings. It was only a business transaction to him. He did not feel my pain when he forced me to sell my property and leave the city. He had won, I had lost, and that was all.'

'You say he is dead?'

Redcliffe nodded, and related the story of the Capons and Squire William.

'I have heard many similar stories,' Baldwin said. 'Yet it is difficult to comprehend how someone could take his revenge on an entire family . . . that beggars belief. But I suppose if he had been cuckolded, knew that his father-in-law was denigrating him . . . There are many men who would find that difficult to swallow. He must have felt entirely betrayed.'

'Oh, I can imagine a man killing when he realised his wife had betrayed him like that,' Redcliffe said, 'but not the other deaths. The wife, maybe, while in hot blood, but that case was not a hot-blooded affair. It had been carefully planned. He slew the family with a gang of his henchmen. They were so subtle and careful that they all escaped the city before the hue and cry. It was only when the poor dry-nurse recovered herself enough to raise the alarm that people realised anything had happened.'

He shook his head, frowning slightly. 'You know, Sir Baldwin, it helped me a little. I had not yet paid off the last of the money I owed him, and God's body, but I had no reason to feel sympathy for him. Yet I do feel sorry that he died in that way. It was a hideous death. And the Squire was found in his manor near Hanham, denying that he had any part in the murders, the deceitful fellow.'

'Men will deny their crimes,' Baldwin said heavily. 'Even when their lies are tested and proved false.'

'As happened here,' Redcliffe said. He glanced at Baldwin, who was turned in his saddle and now gazed over his shoulder at the way behind them. 'You are worried, Sir Baldwin?'

'There is one thing that concerns me,' the knight admitted, turning forward once more.

'You are worried that those fellows might follow us? I don't think so. The way that you bested them in the bedchamber was surely enough to persuade them all to relinquish any ambitions against me. Hah! The bearded man would scarcely be able to walk with the prick you gave his side.'

'No,' Baldwin said slowly. 'My thought was that, while you have been enormously lucky so far, and have travelled by curious routes, yet twice you have been discovered and attacked.'

'I am surely the most unlucky of men.'

'Or there is a man following you who has pointed you out,' Baldwin said. 'Someone so committed to his task that he is prepared to follow you for many leagues to rob you – or to kill you.'

Third Monday after the Feast of St Michael[1]

Near Hanham

Robert Vyke was woken by a kick to his belly, and he curled into a ball, retching on his empty stomach.

'Get your arse up, you bladder of piss!'

Forcing himself onto all fours, Vyke managed to lever himself upright, taking tight hold of a metal staple in the wall. The pain in his leg was a fire that seared his soul, and the bruises from last night were sore and throbbing.

'Let me speak to your Bailiff,' he managed to croak.

'Shut your mouth, or I'll shut it for good,' the man snarled. He was a big, bull-bodied fellow, short but incredibly strong, with a face that was red from cider, wearing a four-day beard of coarse black stubble. In his hand he held a short length of thick rope, that hurt like a cudgel when he swung it, as he had last night.

Once more Robert Vyke had good cause to curse his miserable fortune.

[1] 20 October 1326

He had come here, to the nearest house, as soon as he had found the head. It was his duty and his responsibility to call up the posse to discover the perpetrator of this foul murder as soon as he could. The rule was that first finder must go to all the nearest houses, at least three of them, and announce that a body had been found. Then it was up to the local officers to demand that a Coroner be called, and that the jury gather so that the whole matter could be investigated and all pertinent details noted. All too often men who found bodies would run quickly in the opposite direction to avoid being attached, which meant you had to pay a fine to guarantee that you would come back when the Justices convened their court.

'All I did was—'

'You came to the wrong place if you thought you could kill a man like that and get away with it,' the man spat.

'I didn't kill anyone!' Robert said. His belly was a mass of anguish now, both from the beatings he had endured and from the hunger.

'No one else here could have done it,' the man said unsympathetically and swung his rope-end.

It caught Robert on the side of his jaw, and he felt blood begin to course down his face as the flesh was slashed open. Wordlessly, he stumbled forward, and almost fell into the hands of the men waiting outside.

Blinking in the sudden sunshine, he tried to grab at something to hold himself upright, but his hand missed the door's lintel and instead he found himself snatching at thin air. With a cry of despair, he tumbled to the ground again, stifling a scream of agony as his bad leg slammed into a stone.

'Get up!' his gaoler said again, poised to kick, but this time a sudden command made him pause.

'Stop! I know you are as dull-witted as the sheep in the

pasture, Halt, but you will not kick that fellow again. It looks as though you've been using him for a game of camp-ball as it is, man. Dear God, have you killed him?'

'I just held him here, sir, until you could come to view him.'

'You have misused him appallingly. Someone get a bucket of water and wash the poor devil's face. If you seriously think that this man is a danger, when he has been so badly abused already, you are a bigger fool than I thought.'

'Coroner, I—'

'Haven't fetched the water yet. Get to it, man, or I'll have you gaoled instead of him. Understood?'

Robert Vyke heard all this, but it was too much of an effort to open his eyes. He remained lying on the ground, his whole soul encompassed by the flames that rose from his wound. He wondered if the pain would cease when the leg finally burned away entirely, or whether the flames of agony would continue up his frame to engulf him.

'Open your mouth, man. Drink this.'

He did as he was commanded, and a blessed gulp of ale soothed his throat. A second gulp, and his eyes could open again, and take in his surroundings.

There was a circle of faces about him. All scruffy fellows generally, with worn linen shirts and threadbare hosen, apart from the short, tubby clerk with black hair, who stood nearby, an anxious expression in his pale brown eyes. He held a reed in his hands, and was prepared to scribble notes on behalf of Vyke's rescuer. The latter was a tall, dark-haired man clad in a crimson tunic and heavy brown cloak. He had blue eyes and a perpetual smile on his round, amiable face. He was standing with his legs spaced widely, thumbs stuffed in his war belt, and staring down at Robert.

'Master, you have suffered a considerable amount in recent days. Did that cretin Halt cut your leg like that?' he said.

'No, sir, that was in a pothole.'

'A hole in the road did that to you?'

'There was a bent and damaged dagger in the hole, and it caused this cut.'

'I see,' the man said, and smiled kindly.

'It is in my pack. The man Halt took it last night. It's a good knife, with jewels in the hilt.'

'Is this true, Halt?'

Reluctantly, the squat man grimaced and went into his hovel to fetch Robert's belongings. The dagger was separate, and he did not meet Robert's accusing stare, merely passing it to the Coroner, who turned it over and over with a surprised look about him. 'This is a valuable knife, masters. The man who lost this would have been seriously discomforted. And you say this was in the hole?'

'Yes,' Robert said, and told the story about his falling into the hole and then trying to bend the blade back into a straighter line and finding the body.

'Where was this head, then, fellow?'

'In the little shaw over there,' Robert said. 'I came here as first finder to report it.'

'I found him in there, Sir Stephen, and knocked him on the pate to hold him until you could get here,' Halt said proudly.

'Yes,' Robert Vyke said, 'this fool held me and beat me. He said I must have killed the man myself. I don't even know who it is!'

'Halt is a fool of the first order,' the Coroner said. He turned to Halt and suddenly swung his gloved fist backhanded across the man's face, hard. 'That is a lesson to you. If a man comes and reports a crime, it is *hardly* likely that he is the criminal. The felon will be long gone. And a man who has such a wound as that leg deserves care, *not* a beating.' He glared. 'Besides, if you had a brain, you would have realised that the dead man has been here for days, if this fellow speaks the truth. You beat him before you bothered to go and view the body, didn't you? That makes *you* the felon here.'

'It was growing dark,' Halt said. His lip was bleeding where it had been smashed into his teeth. 'I couldn't go out and—'

'Shut up. You have nothing to say which can help us in any way. The only saving grace you possess is that you would not have sent for me if you had killed the fellow yourself. Has anyone else seen the body yet?'

No one had, from the way that the people all about suddenly began to shuffle their feet and murmur about their fields, and how busy they all had been.

'Good, so the vill shall be amerced for that. You do know that you are supposed to send a man to guard the body from the moment of its discovery to the moment your Coroner arrives?' the man asked the assembled men rhetorically. There was another shuffling of feet.

Robert Vyke eyed the Coroner closely. He wore his dark hair very closely cropped, and with his bright blue eyes, at first glance he looked as though he was smiling all the time, as if genuinely happy and contented. He had crows' feet at the corners of both, and his mouth seemed formed specifically to grin. But Robert knew enough knights to be aware that any initial impression could easily be false – he didn't need to look at Halt's broken nose and bloody lips to remind him that knights obeyed only those laws which appealed to them.

Back at home in his own vill, the lord of the manor was a knight who looked rather like this one: a man called Sir Hector who seemed equally amiable. But when you looked carefully into his face, you could see the cruelty in his eyes, a disdain that encompassed all who were not of his rank. It was no surprise to

Robert to learn that a knight could be guided by the power that his status gave him. They were trained to kill and maim from an early age, so it was scarcely to be wondered at that they would turn to violence as a first resort rather than a last.

The jury appeared to know the man, from the way that they all avoided his gaze. And yet there was no proof of this knight's viciousness. Thinking about it, Robert Vyke was unwilling to hold the blow at his gaoler's mouth against the knight. That, he felt as another twinge of pain shot up from his shin, was entirely justified.

As all were herded off along the lane to the place where he had been struck down again, Robert Vyke had the support of a young peasant who, although he smelled strongly of sheep, was possessed of a strong arm. And then they arrived at the place where the head still lay upon the branch. The knight stood here and stared around him as though dazed. There was no cruelty in his eyes here, only sadness. 'This,' he said slowly, 'is terrible.'

The head was much deteriorated now, with the flesh falling away, the eyes . . . well, he couldn't look at them again. They had haunted his dreams for too long. Instead Robert gazed about him at anything else, rather than the face – and that was when he saw a fresh horror.

On the ground, a few yards away, lay a torso, presumably belonging with the head. One arm was almost removed, while the other, the left, was hideously marked. The palm of the hand was scored with great cuts and slashes, and insects and small animals had nibbled and worried at the loose flesh. The belly had been opened, and animals had gorged on the corpse's entrails. For all that, the victim had been wealthy, from the look of his clothing. A rich scarlet material covered his upper body, and his cloak was of good quality – a thick, emerald-coloured item that had fur at the edge of the collar.

129

'You did not notice this, Halt?' the knight demanded, his face twisted into a rictus of disgust at the smell.

'I haven't been this way in a week or more,' Halt said whiningly. 'Been working out the fields and hedging with everyone else, these last few days.'

'Oh, really?' the Coroner said unsympathetically.

The inquest was brief enough. Standing in the midst of the shaw, the Coroner gazed about him, announced fines for the people there, declared that the body had been slashed and stabbed twenty or more times, and the head removed. Then he asked who the dead man was.

There was a renewed bout of nervous coughing and shuffling before someone admitted that they had no idea. It was not a local, they said. He must have come from some distance, because a man clad in such rich clothing would no doubt be famous to people for many miles about his hall.

The Coroner nodded to himself pensively as they said all this. 'Yes, very interesting. But I happen to know him. It is Squire William of Hanham, who lived little more than three leagues away, I think. So the vill is fortunate. You will not be fined the *murdrum*, since you can present Englishry, but will only be fined for the death – and for not reporting it properly. However, because you are not a rich vill, I doubt you will manage to pay it. Which means I shall have to return, no doubt, and seize what I may in order to pay the King's fee. I am very sorry for all this, but it is the law.'

'Squire William, you said?' the clerk confirmed.

'Yes. And I think his death may be fortunate,' the Coroner said musingly. 'He was responsible for the murder of the Capons, and there could have been trouble in the city, were he found there again. We don't want the folks of Bristol falling into chaos and disorder.'

'But who would do this to him?'

'To dismember and behead a man . . . it implies a punishment for treachery. Perhaps because he killed his own father-in-law? I wonder if the family left any heirs.'

'Shall I note all that?' the clerk asked.

'If you wish, John. Perhaps you would like to see me prosecuted for my behaviour, eh? I do not think it will happen. There are more pressing matters for the King to be troubled by without his concerning himself over my affairs. Right, you, Halt: is there a spare horse or pony here?'

'No one has any animals to spare, Sir Stephen.'

'Then I shall require one that you cannot spare. This first finder is coming with me. I will not have him left here to expire from lack of care by you and the others in the vill. Find him a pony or ass, or I will increase the fine on you for contumacy.'

CHAPTER FOURTEEN

Fourth Tuesday after the Feast of St Michael[1]

Chepstow

It was another miserable day, Sir Ralph of Evesham thought as he listened to the rain splashing outside. The clouds were all low and rimmed with black, and the views were of greyness in every direction. It was hard to remember a time when the sun had shone, he sighed as he mopped at the back of his neck with a square kerchief. He had been out to squat, his bowels playing merry blazes after too many days and nights with poor food and lodgings, and got a soaking in return.

They had been here in Chepstow for a couple of nights now, and in that time they had heard several reports about the progress of the Queen. It was enough to make a man weep. All were going to her, none coming to support the King.

'More wine?' enquired Bernard, his squire, holding up the wineskin.

[1] 21 October 1326

'Why not?' Sir Ralph said, lifting up his cup.

They were seated about a fire in this little chamber. They had not stolen anything, but the owners were not around. As so often happened, the moment a force of men arrived, many house-holders fled. It was natural enough. No man wanted to wait in order that his daughter could be raped. Troops were always an untrustworthy mob at the best of times, and these were not the best of times.

'You heard about the Queen's proclamation at Gloucester?' his squire asked, poking their fire with a stick.

'No.'

'It's all over the camp. She has said that the King isn't at fault, she's not here to harm him; her argument is with Despenser, and she's come to remove him from her husband's side for the good of the realm.'

'That'll wash well with the people,' Sir Ralph said.

'Aye. But it won't work.'

'What do you mean?'

'If she is serious about getting rid of Despenser, she'd have to kill him. The King exiled him before, didn't he – and how long did that last?'

Sir Ralph nodded. Sir Hugh le Despenser had been forced from the realm, but he didn't go far. Instead, he based himself on the South Coast of England and preyed on the shipping in the English Channel, acting the pirate. To this day the French King had a price on Despenser's head for the French ships he had robbed, so if he were to appear in France, he would be executed on sight. Then, as soon as the King felt strong enough, he had invited his most favoured adviser back to his court, and launched a war on those who had thwarted him. No, he would never will-ingly give up Hugh le Despenser, and it was equally unlikely that his Queen would believe him if he promised to do so.

'There's a story going round about London, too,' Bernard added.

'Oh yes? London has rebelled has it?' Sir Ralph said dully, staring into the flames and playing with the cloth in his hands.

'They've killed Bishop Stapledon,' Bernard said quietly. 'I heard they cut off his head, threw his body in a ditch, and sent the head to the Queen. She received it in Gloucester.'

'God's blood!' Sir Ralph looked up at that. '*Stapledon*? He was a good man. Christ's pain, but the country's falling apart. It'll be a wonder if we any of us survive,' he breathed, shaking his head.

There was a shout, then a rattle of armour – the sound of many men hurrying.

'Alarm!' Sir Ralph hissed, and grabbed his sword. Bernard darted to the back of the chamber, calling for Pagan and Alexander, snatching up his own sword-belt and buckling it as he went. In short order all four were outside, running towards the tumult, and then, as they drew nearer, they all began to slow.

'What is it, Sir Ralph?' Pagan asked, frowning. His eyesight was never very good.

'I think it's the King,' Sir Ralph said, listening intently.

It was. Edward's speech was short. The entire household was to be disbanded, he said. Sir Hugh, Roger Baldock the Treasurer, and a few of the King's closest retainers and servants would remain with him, but all others were released from their service.

Sir Ralph had heard the King speak many times, but never with such poignancy and calm honour. Sir Hugh le Despenser stood at his side, head bowed, sometimes pushing a fingernail into his mouth and worrying at it, but for the most part avoiding the looks of all the others ringing them.

The King looked about him as he spoke, smiling and giving occasional nods of encouragement to specific men. 'My friends, for I can call you all friends, you who have remained so loyal to your King, enduring all the hardships of our journey here, all the trials of the long march from London in so short a time. My friends, I am betrayed. Doubly so. My General, Sir Roger Mortimer, is now my greatest enemy; my Queen, the mother of my children, has turned from me and openly cavorts with Mortimer, of damnèd memory; and as we have marched, none of those from whom I demanded aid has helped us. Even today, I have learned that Leicester has turned from me, and now gives his support to the Queen along with all his retainers. My friends, I fear that my time here is to be ended. I must travel away to gather a new army, and when I do, I shall return to this unhappy kingdom and crush this rebellion. With your help we shall punish all those who seek to thwart my rule and who defy God by rejecting me; and I shall reward handsomely those who have sought to aid me. For *I* am God's anointed King! I *alone* can rule this realm. *Me!*'

There was a low growl of support from the gathered men, and then, slowly at first, but gathering pace, men slammed their weapons against their shields, or rattled dagger-hilts against their pairs of plates, or simply clapped, until there was so much noise all about that the King could not be heard. He held up a hand, nodding and smiling, and then both hands, high over his head.

'Friends! Friends, wait! I must board ship now, and I sail for Ireland with my good friend Sir Hugh le Despenser, where I hope to gather up such men as will follow me. I will come back, do not fear. Protect yourselves as you may. Go to your castles, your manors, your peasants, and hold them safely. For when I return, my friends, there will be many rich lands for all of you to share. Those who defy me will find their lands broken up and given away, all their animals slain or passed to you, all their costly silver and plate, all their buildings, all their honours – gone. They will lose all!'

Now the noises reached a peak, and there came a hoarse roar from hundreds of throats as the men began to cheer, weapons waving in the air, enthusiastic in the promise of largesse to come.

'Sir Hugh's father, the renowned Earl of Winchester, left this morning, because I have given him a new responsibility: command of all the men of the West Country. He is in charge of the men all about here, including Bristol. So those of you who live far away, go to Bristol to join with him, and protect that city for me. The rest of you, go to your homes and guard them against my return.'

'All you have to do is prove yourselves loyal and hold on to what you own now,' Sir Ralph muttered drily. 'While the Queen and her men wander the land punishing all of you!'

'Sir Ralph,' Bernard said, touching his arm.

Sir Ralph followed his gaze. In front of them, the King was walking away down towards the sea, but Sir Hugh le Despenser was still in the same position, and now looking directly at them. As Sir Ralph met his gaze, Despenser raised a hand and beckoned him.

'Damn. Bernard, take Alexander and Pagan and break our camp. I'll be back as soon as I may.'

Bristol

Simon had entered many cities in his life, and although this was not the most imposing one, there was something about it that attracted his attention. It seemed neater and better regulated than London, and as he headed with Sir Charles towards the castle, he liked the feeling of airiness about the place. The limewash on the buildings was cleaner, the thatch newer, the streets less smothered with ordure generally. Which could have been the work of the rain over the last weeks, he reminded himself.

'I like this, I reckon,' he said to Margaret as they entered the bridge.

This was a smaller version of the great bridge over the Thames at London, with massive stone arches raising the road over the water, while houses and shops thronged the roadside, leaning out over the river on jetties.

They made Simon whistle. 'Look at them, Meg – wouldn't you like that? You could sit at your parlour and stare out over the river, watching the shipping. It'd be a little like Dartmouth, but without the fog and the sea pounding at you in winter, or the sailors cursing and swearing all day long. And your privy would be right over it, too. No need to have a box of ashes and empty it over the field every so often.'

She shuddered. 'No! I'd be constantly worried that the house would topple over and fall into the river, and as for the sailors, the ones who go to the quayside up here would be just as rude and unmannerly as any in Dartmouth, I reckon.'

Simon chuckled. She was a farmer's daughter, and he would never convince her that life in a city was remotely better than a quiet life in a rural haven. It had been hard enough to persuade her to join him at Lydford when he had been given his job there by the Abbot of Tavistock, Robert Champeaux. Until his death, Abbot Robert had been Simon's patron in all matters. The kindly gentleman had seen to it that Simon had been promoted to Bailiff of the Stannaries, and then, as an especial reward, he had given Simon the post of Keeper of the Port of Dartmouth – a generous gift which had unfortunately missed its mark, since Simon had no desire to move to the coast and, more to the point, neither did his wife. In the event, the post was only to be short-lived, for the Abbot of blessed memory died quite suddenly and Simon found himself removed, but the sadness at Abbot Robert's death was tempered by the fact that it helped refresh his marriage, which had been tormented by the inevitable separation while he was based in the south and his wife remained in Lydford.

It was strange to think how much they had both travelled since then. Simon had been to London, to Paris, and many strange places between. Margaret herself had joined him on his last journey, which had proved to be the most dangerous yet, because of the mobs. At least now, they should be safer.

'Simon, please, join me at the castle for ale,' Sir Charles said with a laugh. He cantered past them as they walked slowly on their horses up the slight incline towards the castle itself.

'It is a lovely city,' Margaret admitted. She smiled at two urchins who ran beside her, begging for coins, found a farthing and threw it to them. One caught it and bowed gravely, while the other danced and skipped.

'You shouldn't spoil them,' Simon grumbled.

'They will hardly be spoiled for the cost of one farthing,' Margaret said tartly.

'If they learn that they can get all they want by begging, they'll never see the need to work,' Simon said.

'Perhaps they will see the advantage of money, and thus learn to love work, husband,' she replied.

'And perhaps they will learn to love reward without effort, woman.'

Margaret leaned forward and laid her hand upon his wrist. 'Are you angry, Simon?'

'No,' he smiled.

'Good, because you are speaking like a horse's arse, dear,' she said sweetly.

'I don't think—' he began, but stopped as they turned a corner and saw the castle before them.

The curtain walls were enormous, at least as large as the Tower's in London, and as befitted the second city in the realm, the castle within was as imposing as the White Tower. However, it was not the sight of the buildings or the enormous walls that stilled them both.

It was the carts, wagons, and men who lined the roadway, waiting to enter the castle with provisions. Simon felt ice invade his bones. He and Meg had seen that selfsame picture only a matter of weeks ago, in London.

'They think they will soon be under siege!' Margaret breathed. And the sob in her throat was enough to make Simon's heart lurch.

CHAPTER FIFTEEN

Near Chepstow

The ship was an old cog, a round-bellied sow in the best of weather, Sir Ralph of Evesham thought to himself. He hated sailing.

Sir Hugh le Despenser led the way to the gang-plank, and from thence out to the rear of the vessel. There was an ill-fitting door here, that squeaked loudly as it opened, giving access to a small cabin. Sir Hugh walked in, leaving the door wide for Sir Ralph, and went to stand at the window. It was an opening covered with a sheet of waxed parchment that allowed a yellowish-grey light into the chamber, leaving it brighter than it would have been, while keeping the worst of the wind at bay.

'Sir Ralph,' he said, 'we must sail as soon as practicable. We shall take some few men with us. You, I would prefer to remain behind.'

He studied a forefinger, then thrust it into his mouth and worried at the stub of a nail. His nails were already bitten back to the quick, leaving half the bed exposed, and when Sir Ralph glanced at his hand, he saw that there were little red crescents about each nail where he had chewed down too far and made them bleed.

The sight was repugnant. No man should so lose control of himself that he made such a display of weakness. 'What do you want of me?' he asked.

'Today the King will send two friars to meet with the Queen and try to negotiate for the lives of all aboard this ship.'

Both men knew what that meant. The Queen would not have any desire, surely, to murder her husband, nor would she have much against the inoffensive Baldock. She had only ever harboured a detestation for two of the King's friends: Bishop Walter Stapledon, and Sir Hugh le Despenser. Those two she hated with all the ardour of a lioness who has witnessed the death of her cub. Stapledon had aided others to curb her authority and power, while Despenser had taken away her husband. She would want to see Despenser suffer for all the insults he had offered her in the last six years or more.

'The friars will return here. We are to try to make our way to Ireland, if we may, and the friars will join us there, with fortune. We would ask that you serve the friars and ensure their safety.'

'I shall do so, if it be the King's desire.'

'It is.'

'Where shall I bring them afterwards?'

Despenser took his finger from his mouth with an expression of pain. He stared at it a moment, then looked up at Sir Ralph, and for a second or two, Sir Ralph could swear the man had forgotten he was there.

'I didn't mean for this, you know,' he said. 'I never intended to hurt the king. I love him.' He put the finger back in his mouth, and turned to face the window.

Speaking with a low, thoughtful tone, he went on: 'It all began as a simple way to support him. They put me into his household to watch him, you know. Thomas of Lancaster, Walter Stapledon and the others all wanted the King observed so that he could be controlled. But Bishop Walter and I disagreed with the whole idea when it became clear that Earl Thomas wanted to control him. What right did we have to keep an eye on him all the time? None. So soon after I was made Chamberlain, I began to learn how to help him. He is a kind man, you know?'

He turned as though seeking support. Sir Ralph had little idea what to do, so he nodded his head. It seemed sufficient, and the King's closest adviser turned back to the window.

'I gradually began to win his trust. And we discovered a closer friendship, too. A mutual affection. It was little more than that, I swear. But we have similar interests; fascinations. Why should we not? And I have enriched myself, but that is no crime. All before me in the same position have taken what they can, just as I have, and just as any will do after I am dead. Any man who doesn't enrich himself when he may, is a fool.'

'I think I need to join my men.'

'I'm finished, aren't I?' Despenser said suddenly. He turned from the window and seated himself in a little chair. 'There's nothing we can do. If we raise a host of men from Ireland, will we be able to bring them back here? I doubt me that. And if we do, there will be a bloodbath, and the people of England would never forgive me, nor the King, for the waste of English blood. That *bitch* has managed all without killing a single man. She landed without dispute, runs about the country without hindrance, and soon she will be here and will have taken the whole kingdom.'

'If the King were to hold his banner against her, perhaps her allies would refuse to fight him,' Sir Ralph said. 'Just as during the Marcher Wars. The Lords Marcher would not lift their standards against his. All submitted.'

'That was then. This is now. She has already put money on

my head, did you know that? The impudence of the bitch! She dared to offer money for my capture, yet she is the invader. But her men are all from Hainault, and they will obey her, the daughter of the King of France, rather than bow to King Edward of England on his own land.'

'Perhaps so.'

'So I will be exiled. I'll have to go to the Holy Roman Empire or beyond, to avoid her clutches, and those of her brother. I shall become a wanderer without home or property. And Mortimer, her lover, will win all he wants. His family has beaten mine at the end.'

'You want me to bring the friars where, when they have had their negotiation with the Queen?'

Despenser stared at him, and now Sir Ralph was sure that there was genuine desperation in his eyes. Sir Hugh had wanted him to understand him, to understand his position.

'Take them to Cardiff. My people hold that town, and it should remain safe a little longer.'

And with that Sir Hugh le Despenser stood and went to the window again, saying nothing more.

Sir Ralph waited for a dismissal, but when it was clear there would be none, he walked from the room without speaking further. Sir Hugh was obviously convinced that he would be caught and slain, just as others had been before him.

Fourth Wednesday after the Feast of St Michael[1]

Outskirts of Bristol

After riding steadily, it was a relief for Baldwin to see the city ahead of them as they came out of the trees. For all his vigilance,

[1] 22 October 1326

there had been no sign of a man following them, and he began to wonder if his alarm and suspicion had been justified, but then the memory of the bearded assailant at the inn came to his mind, and he urged his horse and his companions on to greater efforts.

It was a great problem that horses could not cover more than a man on foot in a day. The King's Messengers were aware of that: a man on foot was expected to cover thirty to thirty-five miles, which was the same as a man on a horse. It was only at times of extreme urgency that a messenger would be given free passes and the right to demand a change of horse at every twenty miles or so. Other men had to accept the fact that if they wanted their mounts to survive a long journey, they must allow the beasts to rest at regular intervals.

Their journey had not been easy for the last day or so. From Salisbury, as they pressed on, they had come upon a number of men who were being arrayed and counted for the King. More and more were filling the streets and lanes, no matter which road they took, and it was growing dangerous. Baldwin could understand the quizzical looks he received from some of them, but it was unpleasant nonetheless. Many of them clearly wondered where he was going, and why. Some believed he could be a messenger for the Queen and Mortimer, and would have had him arrested and held, and it was only his belligerence as he demanded to speak to their commanders that ensured his release at the various stopping points.

'We will be there by noon,' Baldwin said, gazing at the city.

'It will be an immense relief to be home again,' Redcliffe said. He had not survived their journey unscathed. His face was more lined and fretful, his complexion more sallow and unhealthful, and now he sat on his horse with his fingers tapping at the reins as though keeping time with music only he could hear.

The sight of his distress was enough to convince Baldwin.

'We shall wait here and rest our mounts. We are near enough, there is no need to force the beasts on without account for their health. They have brought us far enough already today.'

'There are more, look!' Jack called out as the three swung sore legs over their saddles, pointing down into the valley before them.

Baldwin stared, shaking his head. 'The sight of so many men marching to their doom is a terrifying one,' he said.

There must have been more than a hundred of them. All clad in fustian and other cheap cloths, a mass of brown, green and faded red clothes, walking with their heads hanging, weapons of all types over their shoulders, dangling from slack hands or sheathed. Baldwin could see them as though they were walking only a yard from him: brown faces anxious and alarmed, boys of fourteen, men of fifty, all drawn along by that same responsibility to their lord. All knowing that they must stand in a line and defend each other against the force arrayed against them. Many must die, because with cheap helmets and little steel protection, they were mere targets to the arrows and lances of the professional killers who stood opposing them.

'It is a terrible sight,' he breathed.

'Nay, Sir Baldwin,' Redcliffe said, and now he had a gleam of excitement in his eye. 'These are courageous men, all of them prepared to fight and die for their King! What could be more glorious than that?'

Baldwin turned to face him. 'When they have chewed on a battle, and have survived, then you can tell me that they will enjoy their glory. Most will not. War is a hideous grinding of men and bodies, not a cause for celebration. These men will soon face Mortimer's knights and squires, and when they do, they will learn what it is to endure pain.'

'You have fought, Sir Baldwin. War is sad, I make no doubt,

but the fact is, these fellows will have the honour of serving their King and their lord. There is nothing better for a man than that.'

Baldwin shook his head. He *had* served, and those were battles which served a purpose, for they were to defend the Holy Land from the depredations of the Saracens. When he had been at Acre, fighting alongside the Knights Templar, he had fought for the protection of God's holy land, and to serve the pilgrims who wished to visit it. He had seen warfare at close hand, and had killed his foes. Yes, and seen his friends hacked to pieces, pierced by arrows, slammed against the walls by enormous ballista bolts or splashed across masonry by a mangonel's rocks. There was nothing pleasant, honourable or good about such a death.

Afterwards, of course, all that sacrifice had been made irrelevant by the self-serving greed of the French King and Pope, who had agreed a pact between them to have all the Templars arrested and all their valuables and treasure confiscated. The Templars had been branded heretics and, worse, accused of devil-worship and other atrocities, and many were tortured and killed.

'Those fellows know they are fighting in a good cause,' Redcliffe said.

'Perhaps. But many more will not know why they fight, nor for whom,' Baldwin said firmly. 'This war, if it comes, will pit brother against brother or father. It will be a woeful battle that seeks to put another's interest between members of the same family.'

'The answer to that is easy, Sir Baldwin. The foul enemies of the King must surrender, as they did before during the Marcher Wars.'

'I have taken my oath for the King. I do not need reminding of the duty of his knights and men to protect him,' Baldwin said.

'Jack, do you bring the food bags. We shall have a little bread and cheese.'

He was tempted to say more to explain the horror of war, but when he looked at Redcliffe, he thought he saw a cynical twist to the man's mouth. Baldwin suddenly had the feeling that Redcliffe was jesting, and that thought made him wary. Who would dare to joke about fidelity to the King at a time like this? But no, he told himseslf, he was merely being over-sensitive. To him, warfare was no joking matter.

He held out his hand and took the satchel from Jack, but his eyes were drawn back to the lines of men marching in the dust.

'You feel sorry for them?' Jack asked quietly.

Baldwin looked at him, and rested a hand on his shoulder. The boy had also seen battle, and had shown himself valorous. 'Do you?'

'I feel sorry for all of us,' Jack said.

'That is good,' Baldwin said heavily. 'They serve, and it is good that they answered the summons – but I hope and pray that Mortimer and Isabella will come to their senses and stop before we have more bloodshed!'

Bank of the River Severn

Bernard was not happy. It was clear in the way that he scowled ahead, eyes always studying the ground as he searched out any possible dangers.

They had waited the previous evening with all the other members of the royal household, watching as the King and his closest guards boarded the ship and moved away from the shore into the middle of the River Severn, where the sails began to fill, and the ship rolled slightly as the wind caught at them.

There they had remained on the banks of the river, Bernard keeping watch, Pagan and Alexander moodily hunkered down beside a fire, casting glances at the two religious until a large boat arrived. Despenser had arranged for it to take them across the river, which was very broad here, and before too long they had managed to get horses, packhorses and friars on board, and were crossing to the other side, where they camped for the evening.

It was very curious. Over on the Welsh shore, almost as soon as the King had gone, his men began to disappear. When Edward boarded, there had been 200 men there, but when Ralph left to supervise the loading of his goods on the ship, that number had already halved, and when he looked back at the banks from the river as they coasted along, he saw only a few men, all standing about the fire Pagan had abandoned. The others seemed to have faded away into the trees to escape the Queen when she arrived.

They slept the night on the eastern bank, one standing guard through the watches in case a man from the Queen's host should happen by, since they had no idea where her forces were yet. All were glad when the sun finally appeared.

Not that it was visible for very long. The day was dry, which was a blessed relief after the last days of rain and misery, but the sky was overcast before they had broken their fasts, and all wrapped themselves tightly in cottes and jacks before they mounted their horses, Sir Ralph tying his kerchief about his neck to keep the worst of the cold from his throat.

'Where shall we find her, do you think?' Bernard asked as they set off.

'Last you heard, she was at Gloucester, wasn't she? I'd wager she was somewhere between there and Bristol,' Sir Ralph said. 'The speed she has followed us, she cannot be far.'

Bernard absorbed this with an expression that matched the skies. 'So we should walk into her before long.'

'I fear so.'

'Where are we heading?'

'First to Bristol, then we shall see what we can hear of her.'

Bernard nodded and dropped back a little. They were all riding at a moderate pace now, and Sir Ralph checked to see how the friars were coping with the speed.

The pair were of a similar age, between eight-and-twenty and thirty, and both had the reputation of being well-versed in the practice of negotiation. One, Brother Mark, was very short and had a goitre that clearly gave him trouble, but his blue eyes were bright with intelligence. His tonsure was very wide, and the hair fringing it was pale brown. The other, Brother Daniel, was a little taller, but his features were marred by a thick scar that cut across his cheek and left his nose broken. His brown eyes were full of merriment, Sir Ralph thought.

Seeing his glance, Brother Daniel grinned broadly. 'Don't worry about Brother Mark here. He'll fall off soon enough, and unless you tie him up, he'll keep on denting the roadway every few yards, but he won't feel it.'

'The danger, Sir Ralph, is that this fool should fall on his arse,' Brother Mark said. 'It would irreparably damage his brains if he were to do that.'

For all their banter, the pair appeared perfectly comfortable on horseback, and Sir Ralph guessed that both were quite well-born. 'Let me know, Brothers, if you need to take a little rest,' he said. 'I would prefer to hurry our pace for we have some distance to cover.'

'The faster, the better,' Brother Mark said. He had the look of a man who was keen to undertake his task. 'We should meet Queen Isabella before there is any bloodshed.'

'God willing,' Brother Daniel intoned.

'God willing,' Sir Ralph repeated.

He understood Bernard's discontent; he felt much the same

himself. The idea of riding into their enemies' camp was not one which appealed to his own sense of self-preservation, and yet the Queen herself was very keen to honour the rules of chivalry. Men who were arrived in order to negotiate should be welcomed with offers of safe conduct. That, at least, was what he hoped.

They reached a hill overlooking the city of Bristol some time before noon, and Sir Ralph gazed ahead in search of signs that the Queen was near. Certainly the vills outside the city looked dead, and he suspected that the peasants had fled before the Queen's mercenaries could arrive and begin to lay the area waste. The city itself looked secure for now.

'I think we should go to the city and learn where she is supposed to be,' he said.

Bernard nodded. 'Why not? That'll put off the moment when we actually have to greet her and hope she doesn't lop off our heads before she hears us out.'

'Thank you, Bernard. I needed that reminder,' Sir Ralph said.

CHAPTER SIXTEEN

Outskirts of Bristol

Thomas Redcliffe watched as Baldwin and Jack prepared a loaf of bread, breaking it roughly into three large pieces, then cutting wedges from a cheese they had bought earlier.

It was fascinating to see how the knight worked. He was calm, thoughtful, more intelligent than the usual knights whom Thomas had met, and yet there was that firm edge to his character, a honed quality that could cut a man when he least expected it. Thomas had never met a man quite like this knight before. His presence was invaluable, though. Redcliffe would not have managed to get this close to Bristol without his help, that much was quite clear from the way that the wandering men-at-arms had suspiciously pushed swords and lances in their direction as soon as they had been discovered.

The last ones had been the worst. There was a particularly unpleasant churl with one eye and a perpetual leer who had slowly drawn a long dagger and walked menacingly to Thomas as though to cut out his heart. It was only Sir Baldwin's rapid intervention that had stopped the man, and then his Sergeant had heard the noise and come to see what was wrong. Again, the knight's position had saved them all.

To think that a warrior so devoted to the King could have saved him . . . Thomas sighed to himself at the thought. There was a time when he would have done all in his power to protect his King without considering his own position. He had been entirely loyal, a true devoted servant.

Not any more. Such commitment was worth little today. Thomas would have served until death. He had sold horses to the King for less profit than he could have won, and his delicate work taking messages to the Christian Kings of Aragon and Portugal had been singularly unprofitable too. He'd done it to help his King. And now that he was ruined, had Edward helped *him*? No. Worse still, he had not even deigned to see him. Thomas had been turned away from the gate at the Tower like some beggar demanding alms! The shame had been appalling. He had told dear Roisea that soon they would be saved, without explaining how exactly, and the shock of realising that his King would leave him to starve, and her too, had shaken the wind right out of his sails. His future stretched before him, an endless barren life without possibility of recovery.

And then he had seen what he might do. A letter, a short ride north, and he had his response. It was all he needed.

Yes, it was fortunate that Thomas had managed to persuade Sir Baldwin to join him in this journey. Without him, Thomas would have been stopped and searched, and the thought of what could have happened then was enough to chill him to the marrow. No one with messages like the one concealed at his belt would be permitted to live. And if Sir Baldwin had learned of it, he would himself have denounced Thomas. Or run him through.

Which was why Thomas was so glad the scrap remained concealed. He wouldn't want to have to kill the knight.

Bristol

It was still afternoon as Baldwin and Thomas Redcliffe rode down towards the city and clattered over the stone-flagged way to the bridge.

Baldwin himself was glad of the sight of the city. 'Good porter, I am Sir Baldwin de Furnshill, lately come from London.'

'Aye, good, Sir Baldwin. We'll have need of all the men we can find, I dare say, before long,' the man said, standing aside for the three to ride in.

'What did he mean by that?' Jack asked.

'I expect everyone is on tenterhooks about the Queen and her host,' Baldwin explained. 'The whole of her force must be riding to us now.'

'At least the castle and this city look strong enough,' Redcliffe said.

'Yes. But the strength of a city like this lies less in its walls, and more in the people who are there to protect it,' Baldwin said. 'Will they wish to support the King and Despenser, or will they feel, like the London mob, that they should join to overthrow the Despenser?'

'They will remember their loyalty, I am sure,' Redcliffe said sanctimoniously.

'Are you?' Baldwin said.

They took an eastern road which Baldwin was told was named Wine Street, and a short way along here, Redcliffe took them to a little tavern, where he declared the wine to be the best in the city. He wished to reward his saviours, he said, and when they had drunk their fill, he would take them to his own home outside the city walls.

Baldwin was nothing loth. They left their mounts in a stable-yard, where hostlers hurried to groom and feed them, while the three went for a welcome drink.

'Thomas, how are you?' was bellowed from the bar at the far end of the room as they entered, and a large bear of a man, with a thick, bushy beard and arms muscled like a string of small ale barrels, came out and strode towards them, wiping his hands on an apron of linen.

'I am well, God shield you, Matt. And you?'

'I'm as fine as a summer's day, Master Thomas. Wine?'

'Aye, a flagon for me and my friends.'

'You know this tavern well, then,' Baldwin said.

'I come here most days, yes. But there are not as many men here as usual,' Redcliffe commented, glancing about him. 'Where are they all?'

Matthew was returning with a stack of four large mazers in one beefy hand, and a quart flagon in the other. 'They've all gone to talk about things, master. You heard who is coming here today?'

'No, we've only just arrived.'

'The Earl of Winchester. He's come to take charge of the castle, but they say he's got control of all the King's men from Hampshire to Cornwall. Every able man who is held true to his oath to the King is to muster.'

'So,' Baldwin breathed, 'Hugh le Despenser, Earl of Winchester, has come, has he? He was said to be a wily old warrior, but I don't know that he would best Roger Mortimer. After all, Mortimer was the King's most successful General until Despenser's son alienated him and persuaded the King to sign his death warrant.'

The Despenser family had been long-standing rivals of the Mortimers. The Earl of Winchester's son was the same Hugh who was now the King's favourite and chief companion, and it was his grandsire, the Earl's father, who had been slain on the battlefield at Evesham by Roger Mortimer's grandfather. Since inveigling his way into the King's affections, Sir Hugh had managed to see his father elevated to the earldom which he himself coveted so greatly.

Baldwin mused on this. 'I have met the Earl. I believe him to be honourable.' He was at least, as he reminded himself, far less avaricious and self-serving than his deplorable son.

Matthew the landlord leaned down and beckoned Baldwin and Redcliffe closer. Speaking quietly, he said, 'He'll need all his skills and authority to hold the city. It matters bugger all what he's named. It's said that the Earl of Lancaster has declared for the Queen, and marches to her aid with all his retainers.'

Thomas Redcliffe shrugged. 'Even a man so powerful as he would not on his own swing the affair. If the King stands firm on a battlefield, he can win. Remember the battles on the Marches. All the rebels declared that they would fight Despenser, but not the King. Not many would dare to stand against the man whom God Himself has anointed. When the King showed his own banner, the rebels were forced to submit. They wouldn't willingly break their vows to him. He might manage the same again.'

'The King won't be here,' Matthew said. 'Word is that he'll leave the land. He won't wait here to be caught, you mark my words.'

'What?' Redcliffe scoffed. 'You think the King would desert his own kingdom? And where would he go? Would he sail to France, where the King hates him for refusing to pay homage for the French territories he holds, and hates him even more for the way he has treated his sister, Queen Isabella? No, he couldn't dare sail there. Where else would he be welcomed?'

Baldwin sucked his teeth. 'Ireland, I would guess. He has allies there, and the land is pacified. Where better for him?'

Redcliffe frowned a moment. 'But if he were to do that, surely he would lose the kingdom.'

'Perhaps he thinks to lose a kingdom is one thing – to lose his head . . .' Matthew murmured.

'That could be considered seditious,' Baldwin said sharply. 'Be careful to whom you speak.'

'Oh, I am, sir, I am. There is more, too. They say that the Queen is only a short way away from here now. Bristol will soon be under siege, and when it is, the King's commands will carry little weight. This city is independent.'

'It is a city in the King's realm,' Baldwin declared hotly.

'Sir, it's only ten years ago we had the King's host outside our doors hurling rocks at us. They took the city, banished eighty of our people, and taxed us so heavily we could hardly afford food or drink. We don't forget.'

'Perhaps,' Baldwin said, 'you also remember who was the King's officer at the time? The man positioning the artillery of war was the Queen's associate, Roger Mortimer. So you could fight the man who ordered the attack on your city, or the man who actually attacked. The choice is not so easy, my friend.'

North of Bristol

The rain started again a little before noon, and Sir Ralph hunched down so his neck was protected from the drips. They were riding through a small wood, and he could hear the pattering of the heavy drops on his felt cap. The water dripped from the tip of his brim onto his groin, which he knew would become increasingly uncomfortable as he rode on. There was already a cool, damp sensation all down his legs, and he tried to pull a fold of his cloak over himself again, but it wasn't large enough.

It was dark in among the trees, and he was anxious for a while that they might be waylaid. Everywhere moisture gleamed, from leaves, from bark, from the very mud of the path. And now the rain seemed to ease a little, and suddenly they were in the open.

There was a man on a horse, a man-at-arms, who turned to face them as they trotted out. 'Who are you?' he shouted out.

'Sir Ralph of Evesham,' the knight growled. Bernard was quickly at his side, and the two of them kept their hands near their swords.

'Where do you ride?'

Sir Ralph looked at Bernard, and the two began to move towards the man, increasing the distance between themselves to provide better fighting space.

'Who are *you*, and where do *you* ride?' Sir Ralph asked with an edge to his voice, reining in his horse.

He was suddenly taken by the sight before him. There was a large encampment, with men and horses resting. He saw the Earl of Winchester's arms on a banner, and felt relief. 'It's all right,' he said to the picket. 'We're with the King.'

Bristol

Simon and Margaret had been installed in a small inn a short way from the castle's western gate, and Sir Charles had visited them the previous evening to ensure that they were as comfortable as they might be. He had done so by the simple expedient of explaining to the innkeeper that these were friends of Sir Hugh de Courtenay, the Baron of Devon, who would have the innkeeper stripped and held by the thumbs for the sport of the entire city if he didn't see to it that Simon and his lady were fed only the best foods and drinks during their stay.

The quality of their food was certainly good. Simon and Margaret were also taken with the bed, which was the first comfortable one they had enjoyed for many long miles. Even now, unusually for Simon and although it was only close to noon, he felt the need to return to his bed and rest a little, and for once Peterkin expressed a desire to sleep too. Rob was already snoring, curled by the fire in the hall.

'Simon, when do you think we can go home?' his wife asked, entering the chamber with him.

Sitting on the bed and pulling off his boots, Simon twisted his face into a grimace. 'I don't know, Meg. The roads will still likely be filled with men looking to fight for one cause or another.'

'I am still keen to return to Exeter, to see Edith.'

'So am I, my love, but I don't know when we may be able to leave. It's a hundred miles from here, I think, and with the kingdom in an uproar, it wouldn't be safe.'

'But we cannot blithely sit here in comfort and hope Edith's all right, Simon!'

'Meg, she is married. Her safety is the responsibility of her husband.'

'But she is your daughter!'

'She's my daughter, yes. But that doesn't mean I have the right to take her from her husband, does it? And what could I do – what could *we* do – if we reached Exeter and learned that she was in danger because of the King's forces besieging the city? Or Isabella's men? We could do nothing, except get caught in the same trap, which would endanger Peterkin's life as well as our own. I love Edith as much as you, wife, but there is nothing we can do just now to help her or anyone else.' He closed his eyes.

'It's not good enough. I have to see her. I *will* see her!' She stamped her foot, which made Simon open his eyes in surprise. Margaret had never been prone to displays of anger.

'Meg, you can't leave the city, not just now – be reasonable! It's too dangerous. Now, please, just leave me a little while in peace? My old bones need rest.'

'Yes, and I would hate to deprive you of your rest, while my own peace of mind is flown forever,' she snapped.

'Meg, please—' he cried, but the door was already slammed behind her. Simon grunted, then rose to his feet and went after her. 'Meg! Please take Hugh with you if you are going outside. We don't know this city well.'

His wife looked back at him and nodded, just once, before continuing on her way.

Simon returned to the bedchamber, where his son was sitting on the bed, staring at him with wide eyes and an expression of innocence. 'I'm very tired, Father.'

'Yes, so am I,' Simon said heavily, and sat on the edge of the bed again. He lay back, an arm going about his son, and closed his eyes, but sleep would not come for a good while.

He was stirred by the shouts.

North of Bristol

'I'm taking these friars to meet the Queen to try to negotiate protection for the King's friends, my lord.'

The Earl of Winchester was sitting on a chair chewing some choice tidbits when Sir Ralph was taken in to see him. He pulled the leg from a honeyed lark and bit into it, before wiping his fingers on a cloth presented by his laver.

Earl Hugh was a bright man, who had earned respect from knights and barons on all sides over many years of loyal service to this King and to his father. He was about sixty-six, a strongly-built man with almost uniformly white hair. His eyes were keen and penetrating, and he displayed little of the anxiety his son was feeling. Where the younger Hugh was nail-biting and fretful, the elder Hugh was still calculating the odds, a gambler with the strength of character his son seemed to lack.

His was a career characterised by loyalty, commonsense and

ambition. Sir Ralph personally reckoned that ambition was the main ingredient of his make-up which had been passed on to his son, but where Earl Hugh was keen to improve his standing, there were limits to his avarice – perhaps because he had been born into troubled times. The son of a rebel, his father had died fighting his King at Evesham, and from the age of four, Hugh was tainted with an associated guilt for which he spent the rest of his life trying to atone.

By dint of hard effort and martial skill, he worked his way into the King's affections. King Edward I was a warrior who knew little about peace, so to find a man like Hugh, who was not only a thoroughly competent fighter, able to prove his loyalty to the King at every battle, but was also a highly skilled administrator and negotiator, was very useful. Sir Hugh le Despenser gradually climbed the ladder of appointments with a stealth that would have impressed a fox.

By the time of Edward I's death, Sir Hugh had become an honoured member of the King's household, and practically a father-figure to the young Prince Edward. As King, Edward II grew to trust the older Despenser's judgement, and as Sir Hugh the Younger rose in the King's affection, his father also was rewarded. Sir Hugh the Younger became the supreme manager of access to the King, and Sir Hugh the Elder became an Earl.

Now the Earl glanced at the friars behind Sir Ralph. 'If you vouch for them, Sir Ralph, I am content.'

'I do. Have you seen sign of the Queen?'

Earl Hugh shook his head. 'But her forces are closing in quickly. The bulk of them lie north of Bristol, working their way here. I understand that Berkeley Castle has turned to her. She may be anywhere near. Certainly some of her men have crossed the river and are pillaging and riding out south of the city too. Soon it will be encircled.'

'Can Bristol hold?'

'Yes, if the leaders of the city are resolute and loyal,' Earl Hugh said, and Ralph saw the conviction in his face. 'It will require a firm hand, however. I shall strengthen the resolve of them all. First of all, the gates must be closed as soon as I have reached the city. There can be no more pretending that the country is at peace. The Queen has been able to ride about as though on a perambulation of the realm. Ridiculous! She is a rebel, leading a force of mercenaries and traitors, and she is no more a friend to the people of this country than a wolf is a friend to a sheep. She can feign amity when she wishes, but she will soon bare her teeth, and I think it best to force her so to do. If she can show her true spirit, her cruelty and spitefulness, the people may rise up again to defend their King.'

'I see.' So that was the plan, Sir Ralph thought: to try to force the Queen to raze Bristol, and thus show the entire realm that they should protect King Edward and themselves from her.

'You may assist us,' the Earl added. 'If you tell the Queen that our resolve is to hold it against her for as long as our supplies last, she may be persuaded to turn her full attention upon us. She cannot dare to leave Bristol behind her when she enters Wales. The risk of her supplies being attacked will be an immediate threat to her ambitions. Mortimer will see that. He is many things, but not a fool. You tell them we intend to fight, and we'll see what she does.'

'I shall rest the horses, then, and ride on,' Sir Ralph declared.

'Godspeed,' said Earl Hugh, and after a short interval, Sir Ralph and his little party were riding north and east.

It was less than an hour later that they met the advance guard.

CHAPTER SEVENTEEN

Robert Vyke found himself one of the very last to enter Bristol before the gates were locked, and he rode under the gateway with great relief.

The last few miles had been a hideous race. They were still some miles from the city when they had come across riders who were clearly up to no good. The men shouted at them loudly, with curious, foreign accents, but fortunately their old nags weren't up to the chase, or they were too drunk to bother, and the Coroner's party rode on unmolested. That was worrying enough, but soon things grew rapidly worse, because as they came past a small wood, they realised that the fellows they had seen were only part of a much larger force.

The Coroner was idling along on his rounsey, snapping questions at the clerk on his old donkey, and paying little heed to the road ahead, when Robert spotted the first of the great wagons. 'Sir!'

'Oh, in Christ's name!' the Coroner grumbled, muttering some other choice curses which Robert missed, and snapped his reins. The beast whinnied, and then leaped away to the north, so as to navigate a route past all the men and their provisions, but it was too late. The rearmost carters were already bawling and pointing, and men were pelting towards them. Coroner Stephen bowed low in his seat, galloping at full tilt, with Robert clinging on for dear life on his own chestnut mare, but falling behind, while the clerk was squeaking ineffectually and bumping along, lashing his donkey to little effect. He was soon overwhelmed, and Robert looked back to see him encircled by rough men. Then there was a narrow gateway, into a field divided into long, narrow strips for the peasants, and he was thundering along the line, praying that he might make it to the other side without falling and being taken by these murderous-looking fellows, when he was suddenly out the other side, and staring at a wide river.

The Coroner was a little way ahead of him. He and Robert set off again, along the side of the river, both horses flagging a little. There were men at the banks, watering their own beasts, there were dogs, yelping and snapping at their hooves, and other men, standing with polearms or swords drawn, who scattered as the two men lowered their heads and galloped onwards, and there were the flocks of sheep, no doubt stolen from every homestead and farm along the way for food on the hoof, which bleated and bolted as though the hounds of hell were after them.

And then . . . then they were through, and their mad career could slow, while they gasped for breath and stared about them wildly.

After that, their journey was less eventful, fortunately. Until now, reaching the gate. 'What will happen to your clerk?' Robert asked.

'Him? He'd smell of roses if he fell in the city midden,' Sir Stephen said dismissively.'A luckier man never was born. He'll be fine.' But now they were in the city, he bellowed for the gate-keeper. 'Keep an eye open to south and east, man. If you see anyone approach, lock the gates immediately. There is a host of men out there, and they'll be here very soon, God save our souls!'

Margaret was angry with herself more than with Simon. She knew as well as he that it was dangerous even to think of leaving for their home, but the sense that they were betraying their daughter was so strong, she felt a powerful guilt, as if their inaction was itself about to put Edith into danger.

The inn's yard was almost empty at this time of day. Usually it would be full of merchants, traders, hawkers and others jostling for space. There would be carts and wagons arriving every few moments with foodstuffs for the inn, and straw and hay for the stables. The inn was one of the largest in the city and, with its proximity to the castle, often took all the excess visitors from there as well – but right now it was all but silent. There were no travellers to the city.

It was mute proof of the fairness of her husband's words, but it only served to increase Meg's bitterness. The realm was falling apart, and the thought that they might soon be snared inside a besieged city was like a needle in her brain. It was a miracle that they had managed to escape the city of London, and doubly frustrating that their freedom had been of such short duration.

Hugh and Rob walked behind her as she made her way out and along the wall of the castle to the river, where she stepped silently, staring at the waters. There was a slight breeze, and clouds were covering the sky, so she had to wrap her arms about her breast to keep herself warm. There was something soothing about the river lapping against the bank, the trickling sounds, the sudden gurgles, that cooled her hot temper.

It was unlike her to be angry, and to respond so fiercely to Simon. It was not his fault, after all.

She had been married to Simon so long ago now, it was hard to remember a time when she had been free. He had come to their farm, and she had been taken by his looks and manner immediately. The son of the steward to the de Courtenay family, Simon was a man of some importance in their county, and Margaret was proud when he asked for her hand. And she had never had cause to regret her choice. He was kind, he was faithful, he was witty, and he had given her and the children a good life. What more could a woman ask from her man than all that?

Yet in the last months their lives had been entirely disrupted, and this last obstacle had been the final straw on the camel's back. All along, she had coped with the strain of her daughter's marriage, then the enmity of Sir Hugh Despenser, who had so cruelly broken them by seeing them thrown from their home of ten years or so at Lydford, and then the horrid periods when Simon had been sent off to London or Paris to do the King's bidding. But like a thread wound too tightly, the tension of the last year or more had finally made her snap.

They had walked on and were near the main bridge to the city from the southern side of the Avon. She stood a moment, gazing out over the waters to the lands in front, wondering how long it would actually take to ride to Exeter, to go to her daughter's house and make sure that she and her little child were safe. Five days? Perhaps three if she made haste. One hundred miles was not so terribly far, after all.

There was a bellow, and she looked up to see a small group of men riding fast towards the city gates. The man at the head of the group was an older fellow, and he had a herald with him who bore a fluttering standard, while behind him were thirty men-at-arms, all well mounted, and with armour that glittered and shone.

As they approached, a Bailiff of the city stepped forward with his polearm at the ready. 'Who are you?'

'Stand aside for the Earl of Winchester, Constable of the Castle of Bristol!' the herald roared, and the men rode in at the canter, their hooves clattering on the cobbles as they made for the castle.

'Hugh!' Margaret said urgently. 'Take me back to the inn. We have to tell Simon!'

Bristol Castle

He heard the shouting in the yard and hurried to the door of his chamber, pulling it wide open. There was a small corridor before the walkway on the castle's wall, and Sir Laurence reached it almost before the first riders had swung down from the saddle.

'Oh, Mary, Mother of God,' he muttered, and went to the stairs in the tower nearby.

This was not what he had expected. The Earl of Winchester was one of the most powerful men in the country, probably somewhere after the King and his son, Sir Hugh le Despenser. Sir Laurence knew that in the realm there were few who could equal the Earl's authority. Even Bishops and Archbishops did not have the same access to the King, because Sir Hugh was Edward's most favoured adviser, and if the King's adviser recommended an action or sought a specific end, it was highly unlikely to be refused.

He came to the bottom of the stairs and emerged into the courtyard. 'Earl Hugh, my lord, you are very welcome.'

'Don't give me that ballocks, Sir Laurence! You're wondering what in God's name I'm doing here, aren't you?' the Earl said as he carefully climbed from his horse. 'Time was, I'd have jumped from my mount. Beware old age, Sir Laurence. It creeps up on you like a draw-latch, and takes away all your abilities.

I've been riding too quickly in the last few days, and my muscles are all complaining. I didn't realise I had so many in my backside, in God's name!'

He stood a moment with a hand rubbing his lower back, and then nodded towards the hall. 'Let's go and talk.'

The castle's hall was a good-sized room, with a fireplace set into the northern wall that was already filled with flames from some small logs. A pair of larger logs lay before it, warming before they too could be set on the hearth. There was little decoration here, apart from some paintings on the wall behind the dais, which showed scenes of hunting: men on horseback winding their horns as they galloped towards a glorious hart, raches and alaunts leading the way. It was a scene which Sir Laurence had always loved, being a keen huntsman himself. Away on the right of the picture was a final scene, in which the alaunts had encircled the hart and were preparing for their final attacks, teeth bared, while the poor creature remained at bay.

For the first time, seeing the picture, Sir Laurence was suddenly struck by this scene. It was as though the artist was depicting the final days of Bristol, the noble hart encircled by ravening foes preparing to rip it to pieces. The thought made him feel chill.

The Earl stomped into the room, glanced about him with a glower, and made his way to the fire. He barked an order to his page, who ran to the dais, snatched up a chair, and brought it to the fireside.

'Well!' the Earl said as he allowed himself to fall into the seat with a grimace. 'We are in a pretty pickle. What's the status of the castle?'

'The outer walls are all strong. No weaknesses in the towers. It seems the foundations are all well-laid, and the undercrofts are provisioned. We have enough, with the full garrison, to last three months or more. The men are in good heart, and all are loyal to the King.'

'I'm glad to hear it,' the Earl said, and wiped a hand over his face. Suddenly he looked more grey, as though he had become enfeebled. His eyes were watery as he looked into the fire, and he gave the impression of immense sadness.

Sir Laurence told his steward to fetch wine, and waited while the Earl sat thinking.

He took the wine when it arrived and lifted his mazer to Sir Laurence in a mute toast of appreciation, then drained it. 'Well, you will know already that the Queen is outside your city. She has a force of thousands. The King has a few tens remaining. His reign is in trouble. If we can just hold the city for a little, we may yet prevail. She cannot sweep past us and hope to be safe. I would immediately order an attack on her supply-lines, and try to raise enough men to attack her flanks, if I may. We could destroy her, with only a little luck. Mortimer's a shrewd devil, so he'll know that. They'll do their best to reduce us to rubble. That's my feeling. Do you disagree?'

'No, my lord.'

'So, we must hold the place. The King has placed me in charge of all the west of the country: Somerset, Devon, Cornwall, Dorset, Hampshire, Wiltshire – it's all mine. While he attempts to raise his own forces, it is our duty to hold the Queen and her rabble here for as long as we can.'

'Very well.'

'What is the mood of the city?'

'Generally good, I think. The people here are a contrary lot. They tend to hate Mortimer more than the King, though.'

He went on to discuss the stores within the city, the different city walls and the options for defence. It was not overall a bad situation. 'With a strong garrison, we can maintain the castle without problem even if they break into the city.'

'I see.' The Earl looked at him. 'I know, Sir Laurence. It's not a bad position for us. We must only pray for God to look over us – and over our families,' he added quietly, staring into the fire again.

That was when Sir Laurence realised the truth: that the Earl did not expect to be able to hold the city. He only hoped to keep it long enough to allow his son and the King to escape.

Sir Laurence's eyes flew back to the picture of the hart, but now, in his mind's eye, he saw the city encircled, while blood-thirsty demons laughed and gibbered about it, ready to crush the city for ever.

Simon was relieved when Margaret arrived back. She sent Peterkin out of the room with Hugh to find Rob.

'The Earl, eh?' Simon said. There was a note of hope in his voice. 'That's better news. He's a fair man, I reckon. His son is a prickle of the first rank, but the father isn't so bad – and he's had some experience of warfare. Perhaps he can hold things together here.'

'What will we do, Simon?' Margaret could feel the onset of tears in her eyes, and there was a panicky feeling in the pit of her stomach. 'I can't stay here and suffer another siege, not after all that we went through in London.'

'Meg,' he said, rising and putting his arms round her. 'Where can we go? The way home is bound to be dangerous, with armed men wandering about at will. The only safe place for us is here in the city. Would you really be prepared to leave Bristol if it meant you were putting Peterkin's life at risk?'

'Simon, if the city is besieged, the first thing the locals will do is throw all the useless, foreign mouths from the gates. That

would mean me and Peterkin.' She pulled away from his encircling arms. 'If we stay here, are you prepared to watch as
Peterkin and I are forced out of the city and left as a barrier
between the wall and the army? That's what you said happened
in sieges before now, Simon – that the women and children were
evicted and left to starve so that the besieged and besiegers
didn't have to feed them. They'd keep you here because you can
handle a sword, but us? No. We'd be thrown from the gates.'

'I don't think it'll come to that,' Simon said.

She tore from his grasp. 'Don't *say* that! Don't try to calm me,
when you have no idea what may happen! You don't *know* that
we'll be safer here in the city than on the road, do you? You
don't *know* that Bristol won't be fired and pillaged, with many
people inside slain, which means all of us! How can you stand
there and try to be so *rational* when it's our lives you're gambling with?'

He was infuriating her! Did he mean to insult her? She was
intelligent enough to manage his household when he was away,
and yet now he was treating her like a *child*!

It was only then, when she had spat the last words into his
face, that she saw his own despair. He was not arguing because
he seriously believed that one choice was better than another:
both had strengths and pitfalls – and he was confused and desperate. He needed help to choose the better option. In his face
she saw her own anguish reflected. He was disheartened by this
latest proof of his inability to serve his family.

'Oh, Simon,' she said, and felt the tears beginning to flow as
she put her arms around his neck again and held him close. She
was relieved to feel his arms about her waist, his head resting on
her shoulder.

'I'm sorry, Meg,' he said, his voice curiously quiet. 'I had
thought we would be safe here, and I had thought all our

problems were over, but no decision I take ever seems to work in the manner I intend. I didn't *want* Edith to marry when she did; I didn't *want* to work in Dartmouth; nor did I *want* to become stuck in the King's arguments with the barons or upset Despenser – but it's all happened. I've lost our treasure, our daughter, and now we're in danger too. I no longer know what to do for the best!'

She shushed him, stroking his head as she would a weeping child's. 'You are a good man, Simon Puttock. Be strong for me. Don't let my complaining offend your good sense. You make the decisions based on your reason.'

'My "reason",' he repeated bitterly, and pushed himself from her, walking to the window. 'My "reason" told me we would be safe here because no one in their right mind would want to harm the second city in the realm. And now the Earl of Winchester is here to defend it with all his might. Well, every choice I have made so far has turned to disaster. So no, Meg, I won't choose this time. This time, I will follow *your* judgement. It is always better than mine. So we shall pack and leave the city, and make our way as swiftly as possible to Exeter.'

CHAPTER EIGHTEEN

Fourth Thursday after the Feast of St Michael[1]

Bristol

Next morning was dry, but the clouds were hanging low in the sky, and Margaret thought they looked like dirty muslin dangling from a line. But there was nothing could spoil her mood today. They were leaving. They were going home at last!

It had been a horrible evening, with Simon quiet and introspective, and she tormented with the thought that she had brought him to this pass. It was her task, as his wife, to support him in all he did, and make him content with his lot. She knew that. It was how she had been brought up, how her mother had taught her, how people expected a woman to behave – not to carp and argue and force her husband to change his mind, no matter what the provocation. And this time, surely he might well be correct.

She made her way to the church of St Peter, a short way from

[1] 23 October 1326

the castle's bastion, and there prayed with absolute dedication for their journey to be safe. Like many travellers, she would often beg for God's aid when going on a long journey, but this was more serious and the dangers more clear than at any other time she had set off. And there was the feeling that she needed to beg forgiveness for insisting that they should depart. It wasn't fair that she should have forced Simon into changing his mind about staying here in Bristol.

When she rose, making the sign of the cross, she felt a conviction that her prayers had been heard, and it gave her a warm glow. With fortune, He would watch over them as they made their way homewards.

It was with this comfort in her heart that she walked from the church and returned to the inn. Here, she found Simon already loading the last of the packs on their horses, while Hugh was testing the saddle-straps and harnesses, glowering suspiciously as usual.

'Our room is cleared,' Simon said, seeing her. He did not try to embrace her. His face showed that he was still greatly troubled. 'Everything is ready.'

She smiled, and gave him a quick kiss on the check, before taking the reins and walking her mare to a series of steps to mount. Once upon her horse, she felt again as though things must now begin to improve. Peterkin loudly demanded to be allowed to walk as far as the bridge, and Margaret indulged him today. The last thing she wanted was a row before setting off. That would be a dreadful augur. She desired calmness, for herself, but also for her husband.

As Simon and Hugh helped Rob to his pony, and then the two clambered aboard their own beasts, she was reminding herself that the further they descended into Devon, the safer they would be. Men who wished for battle and war would all be up here, or in Wales, not in the quiet lanes of Devonshire. With luck, they would be home within five days. That was all that mattered.

The small group walked their horses out of the inn's gates, past the barbican to the castle, and thence along St Peter Street towards the High Street and the bridge. The sun was fighting hard to escape the clutches of the clouds, but didn't quite succeed.

As they approached St Mary-le-Port Church, it became clear that there was some kind of blockage ahead, for carts, horses and shouting men thronged the way as far as the High Street itself. Hugh dropped down and, ruffling young Peterkin's head, lifted him on to his mother's sadddle, out of harm's way.

'What's the matter up there?' Simon demanded of a man nearby, who merely shrugged.

'Probably a cart's broken a wheel. You know what this place is like.'

Simon muttered a curse under his breath, and began to cast about for a different way to the bridge. However, if there was one, he thought the other inhabitants of the city would surely have availed themselves of it rather than queue up like this.

There was a man shoving his way through now, heading back the way they had come, and Simon hailed him. 'Friend, can you tell us what is holding us all up?'

'The gates are closed. The Queen's host is approaching, and all the city's gates are barred against her.'

Near Gloucester

Sir Ralph was glad that they had given him a place to lie down inside a tent. The weather worsened during the night, and the misery of trying to sleep on wet ground was not an experience he intended to repeat. He had been forced to do that often enough in his youth.

The Queen's men were a curious mixture. There were voices from all over the world, with the guttural tones of those from Hainault and Frisia, clear, refined French, rougher Breton, and plenty of English from different parts of the country. She had truly gathered together one of the most cosmopolitan forces ever seen on English territory.

He recognised her as soon as he saw her.

The Queen was a slim lady, perhaps nine-and-twenty years old, and her reputation as the most beautiful woman in the whole of Christendom was not to be disputed. Her dress was black, a widow's weeds, because she had declared that her marriage was being broken by Sir Hugh le Despenser, 'this Pharisee', and until she was avenged on him, she would dress like a widow; however, the black clothing only served to highlight her blonde beauty, as she must surely have known. Sir Ralph bowed low as he entered her presence, remaining bent until commanded to approach.

'Sir Ralph of Evesham. It is a long time since I have seen you. Please, don't bow again. You will give me a crick in my neck!'

'Your Highness is most kind to remember me,' Sir Ralph said.

She still had that little lilt of a French accent that had proved endearing to so many when she first arrived in England fifteen years ago. Then the child bride had been lonely, installed in this strange country without friends, apart from the few who were allowed to remain in her household. But soon it became clear that the King was more interested in certain among his advisers than a young girl, and her misery was complete. It was only after the barons revolted and forced the King to agree to limits on his powers that Isabella began to come into her own, and at last her husband started to treat her as a woman and wife, not an irritating little child.

That happy time was all too short. Then Sir Hugh le Despenser flexed his own ambition and the Queen started to be sidelined. The King preferred the companionship of his friend to that of his wife. Gradually the snide remarks grew into open hostility, and Queen Isabella lost all. Her lands, her dower, even the income from her possessions, such as Bristol, were taken from her. Then, after years of wrangling, the French King grew furious at the English prevarications about the French territories, and invaded King Edward's possessions in France.

Malicious courtiers were happy to drip poison in the King's ear. They pointed out that the Queen was herself French. She would support a French invasion, naturally. And her lands in Devon and Cornwall would provide the perfect location for an invasion force. To prevent this, her lands were sequestered, her income confiscated, her children, all of them, taken from her and placed in the protective custody of Lady Eleanor, Sir Hugh le Despenser's wife; the Queen's own worst enemy.

As soon as a chance presented itself, she fled to France, and began to raise her own force to wrest the kingdom from Despenser's control.

Queen Isabella stood and clapped her hands. A steward arrived with jug and goblets, and soon Sir Ralph was sniffing a good, strong wine that made his mouth water.

She looked to the steward and nodded. Immediately, all the servants left the tent, and there was only the Queen and Sir Ralph. Instantly he felt more endangered than before.

'So, Sir Ralph. I am glad to know that you are here.'

'Where are the friars?'

She waved a hand in an impatient gesture. 'They are safe and comfortable. Doing what they were sent here to do – to haggle. They are like a farmer who seeks the best price for his bushel of wheat, dickering for a day, while other men agree a price in the morning and enjoy the use of the money in the afternoon. Your friars are quibbling over details. Nothing more.'

'They were to negotiate with you, Your Highness.'

'They have seen me, and now they see my negotiators. Later, I shall speak with them again, perhaps. For now, they serve me better by meeting with others while I speak with you.'

'What would you say to me?'

'These friars, they came from my husband?'

'Yes, my lady.'

'How is he?'

Sir Ralph considered. 'Hale and hearty. He has the heart of a lion.'

She smiled. 'So, he is very anxious? Worried?'

'I . . .'

'Do not answer and forswear yourself, good sir knight. It does not suit you. You will not tell me that my husband is weak and worried, I can understand. Instead, tell me, how is the good Sir Hugh? Is he still as full of bile?'

Sir Ralph knew as well as any that Sir Hugh le Despenser was the primary cause of her leaving the country. He grinned. 'I think you would be pleased to see him,' he said.

'Ah,' she said, and chuckled. 'If only that fool were here. So! You know that my husband is attempting to demand that all those with him should be spared. He wishes for safe custody for Sir Hugh and others. Yes, of course you know. Well, I think you also know the answer as well as any.'

'You will not permit Sir Hugh to live.'

It was not a question. Her feelings towards Sir Hugh were clear in her eyes. When she mentioned his name, it appeared to burn her lips like acid, and her face momentarily lost its beauty.

'Allow him to live?' she said quietly. 'I will give no such undertaking. Good men have died in the last days. You know

177

Bishop Stapledon? Even though I had reason to deprecate his behaviour in recent years, I admired him. Yet the London mob hacked off his head and sent it to me. I received it at Gloucester. Poor man! Many others have been dispossessed, robbed or killed, and all because of the arch-felon Despenser. No, I will not permit him to live. He is a danger to the entire realm. His greed is without bounds.'

'I am sad to hear that,' Sir Ralph said. 'You know that the King will not submit without his friend's protection.'

'It is sad. I am desolate at it myself. Because my husband *will* submit. He cannot survive – there is nowhere for him to go. The kingdom will not support him, for all know that I only came to remove Despenser and return to my husband's side.'

'Your Majesty,' Sir Ralph said. 'You are here to remove the King from his throne.'

'Would you blame me?' she said. 'He has taken my children from me and installed my daughters in the protective care of Despenser's wife. Poor John is in London, I think, but all the while I was here, my children were alienated from me. So – I ask you again: would you blame me?'

'He is the King, Your Majesty. Blame matters nothing. It is clear that you wish to end his reign.'

'And if I do?' she asked coquettishly. She turned from him and walked towards the middle of the tent. As she spoke, her voice was quieter, and he was forced to approach her again. 'If I do, and place a Regent in charge of the kingdom until my son should be old enough to take the crown for himself, what would be so wrong about that? I love my son, Sir Ralph. I love him dearly, and would do all I may to protect his inheritance.'

'The King has been anointed by God,' Sir Ralph said with a shrug. 'When he is dead, I will serve his son as I have him: loyally.'

'Ah, but you will not hasten that moment?'

Sir Ralph felt the blood wash from his face. There was a tingling sensation in his belly at what he thought he had heard. 'You suggest I should kill my King?' he said with a hushed horror.

She spun round to face him, alarm in her eyes. 'Kill him? *Kill* my husband? No, no, never!' she said emphatically. 'I wish only to see him surrender so that we can protect the nation and prevent any more bloodshed. Did you think I could ask such a thing as murder?'

'My lady, I am truly sorry,' he said, kneeling again. 'I misunderstood. It was my error, and I am deeply sorry for it.'

'Do not abase yourself,' she said, and there was a tinge of exhaustion in her voice now. 'I am not so surprised that any would think that I could plot such a happening. But what? Would it help me to have my husband killed? No! My son would hate me, and I would hate myself. I gave myself to my husband. I would not commit petit treason against him. Not for anything. But what should I do? Despenser is a devil who has bewitched my husband, and now I must force him to leave the King's side. Is this reasonable? Why should I have to do this?'

'My lady, perhaps if you were to permit him to escape to Ireland, insist that his exile be permanent, then Sir Hugh might flee.'

'You do not know the man, do you?' she said sadly. 'Come, you shall have to leave soon to take your charges back to the King. Finish your wine and be gone. And Godspeed, Sir Ralph. I hope we may meet again in calmer times.'

'I too, my lady. Your Highness,' he said, backing from the room, bowing as he left.

Outside, he took a deep breath, and wondered what the woman would do. Well, it was none of his concern. He had other

179

matters to deal with. He could see Bernard sitting on a portable trough, and bent his steps towards him, but all the way he was considering the Queen and her words. It was troubling to see her in such clear distress. And all knew who had driven her to this final act of despair.

He could almost pity Sir Hugh le Despenser, for when the Queen captured him, his end would not be good.

CHAPTER NINETEEN

Bristol

Baldwin woke with a curse on his lips. During the night a flea or similar malevolent creature had found its way to him, and now he had a series of lumps on his back that itched like the devil.

The house was a large one in a part of the city that had once been the Temple lands, and he had been struck with a strong sense of nostalgia as he rode this way with Redcliffe last evening. They had left the tavern while it was still just light, before the gates were closed against all intruders, and made their way southwards into the warren of little streets and lanes that made up the Temple area.

They had passed through this suburb on the way to the bridge, but seeing it in the morning light, Baldwin could understand why the merchant had decided to take him for drinks in the city itself. Last afternoon they had all been too tired to pay attention to the buildings about them. Now, as he stood in the stables over the road, Baldwin looked about him without favour.

'I don't suppose that Master Redcliffe is a very successful

merchant,' was Jack's opinion when he saw Baldwin. He was grooming their mounts as he did each morning.

'I think you could be right,' Baldwin said. He noticed that Wolf was looking well-groomed as well, and he glanced at Jack, but the boy was concentrating on the horses.

Later, when their host brought them bread and some cold cuts of meat, he offered them his apology. 'I did tell you I had lost everything when my ship sank. My creditors demanded all that I owed immediately afterwards, and I was forced to sell my house and gardens within the city. I am no longer a burgess, but at least I am fortunate to have my health and this little home.'

'It is a good size,' Baldwin commented.

'Much smaller than the last, I fear. That was large, and with an excellent stables. I used to help the King to import horses from a Galician stud. Excellent, they were, too. I lost four magnificent destriers on my last ship. They were worth a lot of money.' Thomas sighed at the memory.

The house had a goodly-sized hall, and behind it was a yard with some outbuildings, in which he hoped to store goods when he could buy space on a ship and try to return to his past career. For now, he relied on his wife to maintain the house while he worked on recovering his fortune.

'If war comes,' Baldwin said, 'what then?'

'There is always money to be made for a man with determination,' Redcliffe said, but his voice was tired, and Baldwin thought he looked as though he had been knocked down so often that the prospect of another fight was too daunting for him.

Redcliffe was sitting on a small chair, and he looked up as his wife, Roisea, went to his side. He put his arm about her waist as he spoke, and smiled up at her now. It eased the lines of concern at his brow. They were much in love, from the look of them, Baldwin thought, and at that moment, Roisea was tugged, protesting, on to her husband's lap. She leaned forward to kiss him enthusiastically, as if the two were alone in that chamber.

'I am sorry, Sir Baldwin,' Thomas said after a few moments. He grinned at his wife as she sprang from him and stood at his side once more.

She squeaked as he tried to encircle her waist again, moving out of his reach. 'Husband,' she chided, 'your guest hardly knows where to look!'

'You're right, my love,' Thomas said. 'So, Sir Baldwin, if real war comes here, I shall sell and trade whatever I may once more. As I say, there is always money for a man who is bold enough.'

Baldwin nodded, unconvinced. 'There are often more men with determination who possess weapons and help themselves to all that they can,' he pointed out. He did not want to say so, but there were enormous risks for young women like Madame Redcliffe. She was a short, but slender woman in perhaps her middle twenties, with a round face that was particularly attractive. She had a pale, peach-coloured complexion, lovely clear blue eyes, a broad, intelligent forehead, and full, soft lips that seemed made for smiling.

In many ways, she was the picture of desirability, and yet Baldwin could think only of his own wife, so many miles away, surely worrying about him and what he might be doing. He missed her, his lovely Jeanne. He had loved her since the first moment he had set eyes upon her in Tavistock all those years ago.

He looked again at Roisea and this time saw the fear in her eyes, while her mouth smiled.

'Madame Redcliffe,' he said gently, 'I am most grateful for the use of your room.'

'I am at your service, Sir Baldwin. It is very kind of you to

183

honour us with your company, when you could have rested in any of the inns in the city itself.'

'But such inns would not have so charming a hostess,' Baldwin said with a slight bow.

'You will stay with us a little?'

Baldwin glanced at her husband. 'I fear I must return to my own home. My wife will be missing me, and I would prefer to be there in case of unrest.'

'It is difficult when you have responsibilities,' she said, and threw a look at her husband that Baldwin could not comprehend.

Women were so difficult to understand – he had spent too much of his youth in the convent without female companionship.

'You will stay one day, at least?' Redcliffe said. 'I wouldn't want to think you had to set off so soon, without any rest.'

Baldwin could feel Jack's eyes on him as he said politely, 'I am most grateful to you, Master Thomas, but no. I must return. At this time, I have a responsibility to my wife, but also to the King.'

'You are a supporter of the King, then?' Roisea asked. Her lips were parted, as though she awaited his answer with an especial keenness.

It was not a question he had expected, and Baldwin felt his brow crease in a fleeting frown. 'I have given my oath to him, and I owe him my service as my Lord. Just as any knight must who holds lands from the King.'

'You are a man of honour,' Redcliffe said, pushing his wife away so that he could reach the food. 'Come, Sir Baldwin, please eat.'

Bristol Castle

In the castle, Robert Vyke was happy to find that he was not to be held in one of the cells. All too often, as he knew, a city's castle would contain the very best facilities for holding men – cold, damp chambers near the moat, plenty of smiths keen to show their skills at producing fetters of different types, and quite a lot of men who were equally enthusiastic about methods of enquiry involving the use of hot metal and pliers.

For Robert, the idea of the torture chamber was one that returned to his mind that morning when he was told that he was needed. He was called by a Sergeant with foul breath and a peculiar-looking beard which had a large gap in the left side of his jaw. When Vyke looked more closely, he saw that the man had suffered a ferocious wound there; the skin was all scarred, as though some weapon had torn away an inch-wide section of flesh.

'Horse kicked me,' the man said, seeing the direction of his attention.

'In a battle?'

'No,' the Sergeant said, scowling. 'I was grooming the bastard.'

Vyke was unsure what to say, so he followed the Sergeant out from the garrison's sleeping chamber, where he had been installed for the night, along a short passageway, up two flights of stairs, and into a long, warm, rectangular room.

It was heated by an immense fire in the left-hand wall, and the glorious light illuminated rich hanging tapestries of hunting scenes, and a number of stools, chairs and two large tables. At one, a smiling older man was sitting, while opposite was a thin, grey-faced old fellow with wiry frame and grizzled hair. At the fireplace stood Sir Stephen, the Coroner.

'Get in here,' the Coroner said. His face was blank, just as it had been at the inquest. He was a strange serious man, who was either amused and jolly, or completely serious, concentrating on matters of importance. Now, clearly, he was considering something that gave him little cause for amusement.

185

The man with the smile was the Earl of Winchester, Vyke knew. He had heard about him from some of the garrison last night. Not a bad man, this one – unlike his son, by all accounts.

'Come in, fellow. Come in. Now, the good Sir Stephen has said to us that you are bright, and capable of thinking for yourself. Is that right?'

'I suppose so, sir.'

'Good. You come from where?'

'I'm from East Henret, sir. Oxfordshire.'

'Oh. You're a long way from your home, then.'

'Sir. The men in the vill were arrayed and mustered and marched off. That was a while ago. We went east towards London, then we were turned about and came here instead.'

'And your companions?'

'They went on, sir. I was left behind because of my leg,' he added, pointing.

'You are loyal to your master?'

The impatient, grey-faced man interrupted him before he could reply. 'You *are* loyal to your King, aren't you?'

'Yes, sir,' Vyke said. He didn't like the direction of the conversation.

'You may be able to help the King in his trials now,' the man said briskly. 'We need to send him a message. Can you do that for us? Can you take him a message?'

'I suppose so, sir.'

'Good. Do this, and you'll have the gratitude of the King, the Earl here, and of me, Sir Laurence Ashby.'

'I'd gladly help, but I'd need directions. I don't know this country.'

'It should be easy enough to follow the King's trail,' the Earl said.

Sir Stephen folded his arms. 'This is very important, Vyke.

We have to make sure that the message gets through to him. You understand me?'

'Yes. I understand, sir.'

'Good. Then you can go now.'

'One minute,' the Earl said. 'How bad is your leg? Can you use it for a long walk, do you think?'

'If I need to. The cut was deep, but it's not gone foul, my lord.'

'You're sure of that, are you? Has anyone looked at it?'

'A priest did, my lord. He seemed very competent and—'

'My friend Sir Stephen Siward here says you were hurt by a bent dagger: it sounds a curious accident. It is usually enough for a man to fall into a pothole without the additional encumbrance of a dagger inside. Do you have the dagger here?'

'It is in my pack, my lord,' Vyke said.

'Good. Can you fetch it for our friend?' the Earl said to the Sergeant, who still stood behind him. The Sergeant nodded and hurried from the room.

Sir Stephen pushed himself away from the wall and walked to the table where the Earl was sitting. He poured himself a goblet of wine from a pewter jug, but made no effort to offer it to the Earl or the other man, to Vyke's surprise. It was almost as though the Coroner thought himself superior to the others in the chamber. Either that or he was so distraught at the idea of the coming days that he forgot himself.

There was the sound of steps approaching, and then the Sergeant walked in again. He had Vyke's pack with him, and opened it on the floor near the Earl.

Earl Hugh took the dagger when it was offered to him, and Vyke saw him shake his head. 'A valuable piece. I would think any man would rue its loss. You have done well to discover it, Vyke.'

187

'I was going to see if I could straighten it,' Vyke said.

'You mean to keep it?' Sir Stephen asked.

'Well, I don't know whose it is, so . . .' Vyke said, flustered. It seemed to him that Sir Stephen was planning to take it from him, and he was alarmed at the thought after all he had endured because of this damned blade with its pretty hilt.

'I would think you would be better served to sell it,' Sir Stephen said. 'It is a valuable piece of metalwork, and if you were found with it, it may go evilly with you. Give it to me, and I will pay you a fair price for it. Six shillings?'

Vyke was about to take it gratefully when he spotted something out of the corner of his eye. It was the look on Sir Laurence's face, an expression of sadness.

'You know whose dagger that was, don't you?' Sir Laurence said. 'It belonged to Squire William de Bar, who murdered Arthur Capon.'

'You knew Capon?' Sir Stephen said.

'Many knew him. He was a useful money-lender to many nobles. I had reason to use him a few times – but I never expected to hear that he could have died at the hands of a man like that. Squire William deserved his end, for killing him and his family.'

Bristol

That afternoon, there was a bad feeling in the air as Cecily walked about. It was not only her and the weight of the guilt that bore down upon her shoulders, it was the atmosphere of the whole city.

There was no sign of the besieging force as yet, but the traders were already closing up as though they had sold all their wares. In reality, all knew that they would have to be more careful with their food and money.

Cecily had endured the siege here ten years before, and knew how people would change. Those who seemed happy-go-lucky could suddenly become depressed; others, who were rude, quarrelsome and argumentative could suddenly discover their Christian kindness and start to help their neighbours. Most, though, just tried to keep their heads down and survive.

Women, of course, were the most fearful of all, for when men were convinced that they were soon to die, they often lost all shame and fear of justice. During the last siege, Cecily had known women who had been raped by those who sought a momentary escape from the fears of death. She herself had been pulled into an alley by a neighbour, but had drawn her little knife and he had immediately slunk away, to stand sobbing at the alley's entranceway.

It had shocked her more than anything, because he had always seemed a pleasant old man: thoughtful and amiable. To see someone like that suddenly turn into a monster who sought to rape her had been more terrifying than the thought of strangers attacking her, somehow. Perhaps, she wondered, it had been her fault? Maybe he had seen her so often, he had assumed she would welcome an advance from him? Or had he thought that she lusted after his body, just as he lusted for hers? Was it possible that she had, in her friendship with him, given him the impression that she would welcome his natural desires? Perhaps. But he had used the siege as the excuse. Yes, that was it: he was glad to have a reason which he could use for blame, rather than his own lustfulness.

Later, she had heard he had killed himself, taking a razor to his throat, and she felt sorry for him, although she couldn't forgive him.

So now, as the mood of the city turned to fear and uncertainty, she walked in the wider roads, her head downcast beneath a hood, avoiding the eyes of passers-by.

It was when she passed along Peter Street that she felt the terror strike her again, and had to stop and breathe carefully so that her heart did not leap from her breast.

The two were lounging at the side of the street, chatting as though it was the most natural thing in the world. Anyone looking at them would think that they were normal men doing normal things. Only she, of all the people walking past, knew the truth about them both. *They were murderers.*

'Come on, maid, you want to come and play?' one called, seeing her and making an obscene gesture.

She could not look them in the eyes. Her loathing would be too clear, if she did that. She was no pretty young maid, but these men were drunk, and would go with any woman. She must walk on past them . . . if she could.

'Maid, didn't you hear us? Come here, let's play the afternoon away.'

There was an edge to his voice; a hint of threat. If she could only walk on, simply placing one foot before the other, she would survive. Her knife was no match for these two.

'Are you deaf? Or is it that you don't *want* to lie with us, maid? Come on, you can say that. No? Ah, then you *do* want to?'

A loud laugh, a high giggling from the other, and she was aware of them both approaching her. She had to run, get away from here, as swiftly as she could, escape to the house where she lived now with Mistress Emma. But Cecily was frozen with panic.

'Leave her, you men!'

There was a hand on her arm, and she squealed, wrenching it free, as Sir Stephen Siward smiled and said, 'Come, Cecily. Do you not know me, then, that you look so fearful?'

CHAPTER TWENTY

Near Gloucester

It was already growing dark as the group was shepherded to their horses, and Sir Ralph mounted his beast with a feeling of enormous sadness.

'Your Highness, I hope to meet you again in happier circumstances,' he called.

She was standing some distance from him, but her pale face was fixed on him, and he saw her hold up a hand in farewell.

'They're ready, Sir Ralph,' Bernard said, nodding towards the friars, and they set off, weaving their way past the unnumbered men.

The camp was enormous. From here, Sir Ralph could see tents stretching off into the distance, while many slept in the open, wrapped in cloaks and blankets, huddled close to the fires that burned fitfully. There were some houses with men inside, the peasants fleeing, and doors and furniture had already been thieved for firewood. The places all about here had lost everything. Only shells remained.

Any optimism on the faces of the two friars was gone now. They rode silently looking downcast.

When Bernard asked how they had fared, the younger friar shook his head sadly. 'There are no guarantees. The only thing they would say was that the body of the King would be respected. He is inviolate, naturally; not so the others with him. Those who have committed the most manifest crimes must pay for them. There is no humility there, you see.'

'Who was negotiating with you?' Sir Ralph asked.

'It was Sir Roger Mortimer,' the friar answered. 'He is a most resolute man.'

'And his soul will burn in hell,' the other friar added. 'The devil himself could not have been more inflexible.'

Sir Ralph rode on without listening as Bernard asked what Mortimer looked like, what sort of character he had, how he held himself – those things didn't matter to him. All he could see in his mind's eye was the King's few friends and retainers, struggling on, while the great mass of the Queen and Mortimer's force swallowed them up.

'We shall take a rest soon,' he said, interrupting Bernard. 'There is no hurry to bring news of this sort. I weep to think how the King will react to it.'

Bristol

The hammering on the inn's door in the middle watches of the night was enough to make Simon curse loudly.

Their evening had not been restful. Margaret had been weepy and miserable, and Simon was convinced that his indecision was the cause of their current situation. If only he had made up his mind to do as she suggested sooner! If only he had agreed to leave that very night, rather than wait until the morning, they would be past the great line of hills to the south by now. If only he had been able to make a decision, his wife would be out of this damned city, and perhaps on her way to safety.

'What do you want?' he demanded.

Hugh was already awake and had taken hold of his staff as he rose, yawning and blinking, from his palliasse near the door. Margaret was awake beside Simon in the bed, while Peterkin and Rob slept on, huddled together on their own palliasse, wrapped in coverlets, Peterkin snoring gently.

'Master Simon Puttock, if he is awake,' came the drawling response, and Simon cursed as he pulled on a shirt, walking to the door and pulling it wide. 'Sir Charles, what sort of hour do you call this?'

'One of the more unpleasant ones, Master Bailiff. Madame Puttock, I am sorry to disturb your rest. I trust I may bring your husband back very soon.'

'You want to talk?' Simon asked, rubbing his bearded face and yawning.

'I would like to take you to see something, master. But not, perhaps, until you have had a chance to clothe yourself. You may find the night air a little inclement. And it's raining.'

Simon grunted and reluctantly went to his pile of clothes. Drawing on his hosen and binding the cords about his waist, he cast a bitter eye at the knight. 'So what is it? Some debate about military matters? How to defend the city? I'm not experienced in matters such as those, you know.'

'No, Bailiff,' the man replied, and now his manner was deadly serious. 'No, this is a case of murder, I think. And I am sure that I need help in the matter.'

Bristol

Sir Charles had said that the body was a fair distance away, but since the whole city bounded by the wall was tiny, Simon doubted that it could be far.

'Christ's cods!' he spat as he stumbled into a rut. 'Why do you want my help?'

'You have experience of dead bodies, Bailiff, and investigating them. I remember that much from our meetings in the past. There has been a woman killed, and I would appreciate your experience.'

'You'll be disappointed,' Simon grumbled. 'If you really want help, it's Baldwin you should speak to. He is the one who understands death and dead bodies. I am the one who tries to avoid them. My help was only needed when he had less knowledge of a local village, and I knew more of the people. Anyway, isn't there a Keeper of the King's Peace or someone else here to investigate such matters?'

'Yes, there are plenty of people here in the city, Master Bailiff, but in case you had not noticed, they are all rather busy with arranging for the defence of the city just now.'

Simon grunted. 'I see. But what is the reason for calling on me at this time of night? I ought to be with my wife. We have not had a good day today. We'd hoped to leave and make our way home, but were turned back at the gates.'

'I think there are a lot of people who will soon wish that they had escaped Bristol,' Sir Charles said with sudden sombreness. 'Myself included. I didn't intend to come here and be imprisoned in the city.'

Simon nodded as he followed Sir Charles up a lane, along a broader street, and then into an alley that narrowed until it took a turn at the end.

It was clear that this was where the unfortunate body lay, because there was a large group about it. With the curfew operating, these people must be neighbours, called like Simon from their beds to witness the body. A pair of horn lanterns flickered and cast a baleful light on the area, making faces look devilish or unwholesomely pale by turn. Sir Charles called out to a pair of watchmen, both older men with grim faces and figures that would compel a man to be polite. They held thick staffs, one as short as a cudgel, the other as long as a bow, and both looked entirely competent to handle them. Hearing Sir Charles's shout, they stood back, and commanded the rest of the people to give way, pushing with their staves to clear a wider circle.

Simon shoved his way through and found himself confronted by the body of a woman in her middle years. She lay on her back, her eyes wide open. One arm was at her side, while her right had the elbow bent, and her hand was up near her shoulder.

Simon knelt beside her and closed his eyes for a moment or two. Not so very long ago, he would have reached for a bucket – but he was grown more accustomed to the horrors of murder, and as he opened them again, his eyes began to take in the details even as his mind rebelled at the sight. He had often heard Baldwin say that a dead body was a person with a story to tell, but who had been struck dumb. The killer had left his reasons for the killing all about the corpse, and a man who had eyes to see and a brain to think, would be able to read the tale.

In the dark he had to peer closely, but first he surveyed her body, how she lay, the ground about her, searching for any little hints as to what might have happened here.

The first thing that sprang to mind was rape, naturally. A man who felt he had been rejected might, after some ales, decide to repay the woman who had spurned his advances. Rape followed by homicide was all too common.

Her skirts were lifted, but here in the dark he was reluctant to investigate her intimate parts further. In the morning when the inquest was held they could see whether she had been savagely assaulted; perhaps the story here was that simple? Certainly, when Simon peered at her face, he was sure that there was bruising about her mouth. He motioned to a boy and took a lantern from him, studying her more closely. Yes, her mouth had been roughly gripped, which could mean she had been held down to stop her calling for help. It brought to his mind a picture of this woman squirming, trying to break away, her eyes wide with terror and horror . . . It was a thought to make his stomach turn.

He felt her body gently, seeking a wound, but at first could find none. Her flesh was still quite warm, although there was no breath in her. She was plainly dead, but she must have died quite recently. Then he felt the little patch of stickiness, and beckoned the moon-curser[1] to him.

The boy lowered his lamp and Simon lifted a fold of material. There, just under her breast, was a stab wound. At least an inch in breadth, he reckoned.

She had been stabbed only once that he could tell; was there another wound? In his experience, men and women often had defensive cuts on their hands when they tried to shield themselves. He studied her palms but there was no mark there.

He squatted on his heels, thinking. Perhaps she had been hit on the head. If she had been knocked down, she wouldn't have been able to defend herself. He reached behind her head, lifting it and feeling the scalp all over. The ground here was rough, and taking his hand away, he saw blood on his fingers. It was not proof of anything, of course, but the way she was lying here, the bruising about her mouth, seemed to imply that she had been held down, a hand over her mouth, her head pressed into the ground.

Simon stood, and spoke to Sir Charles, explaining his findings.

---

[1] the boys who lit the way of walkers in the dark were often called 'moon-cursers' because when the moon was bright they would swear at the loss of their trade.

'I see. There is nothing more to learn, you think?'

'In this light it is not easy, Sir Charles,' Simon said sharply. 'I wouldn't think she was killed a very long time ago, because the rats haven't been at her yet, and she is still warm.'

'So she was thrust on the ground, a hand over her mouth – what, while she was raped?'

'Yes, possibly,' Simon said. 'At the moment, I cannot tell whether she was raped.' He beckoned the moon-curser and went back to the body, picking up her hands and studying her finger-nails. 'No, there is no blood under her nails. I had hoped . . .'

'So her killer has not even gained scratches to show he was here,' Sir Charles said.

'Do you know who she was?'

In answer, Sir Charles beckoned the watchman with the shorter cudgel. 'Tell the good Bailiff here all you know.'

'What is your name?' Simon asked.

'Reg Bothel, Bailiff.'

He was a sturdy-looking man, this Bothel. As he spoke his eyes remained on Simon's face, which impressed him: he liked the fellow's honesty.

'She was called Cecily, I think. Lived at Emma Wrey's house which is over at the top road from here.'

'This Emma, was she a relative?'

'No, she was just Cecily's mistress.'

'Has anyone told her that her maid is dead?'

'We haven't had time yet,' Bothel said.

'And now it is late,' Sir Charles said, and soon they were returning to Simon's inn, leaving the poor woman's body to the care of the watchmen.

Simon waited until they were out of sight of the huddle of men and women by the body before saying, 'All right, Sir Charles. What was that really about?'

The other man gave him a quick look, but then shrugged, saying, 'I was asked to look into that woman's death, even though I have no experience of investigating murder. Still, since the fellow asking me to look at her was the Coroner, I thought I should do the best job I could.'

'Why didn't the Coroner come himself?'

'Busy. He's helping with the city's defences.'

'And you wanted my help just to view her?' It did not sound to Simon as though the knight was being entirely straightforward

'I do not like to think of that poor woman lying dead without taking action to get the culprit brought to justice.'

'I doubt you'll have much luck with this one, my friend,' Simon sighed. 'The fellow is here in the city, for as I know to my cost, there is no way out of here. But trying to find him? Well, that is another matter.'

'And that is why I would be grateful for your help,' the knight replied. 'I told you true, Bailiff Puttock. I do not like to see a woman killed and her murderer go unpunished.'

CHAPTER TWENTY-ONE

Fourth Friday after the Feast of St Michael[1]

Bristol

Margaret was still distressed as she sat with her husband the next morning. The reappearance of Sir Charles was not welcome.

The knight entered the inn with a mildly distracted air, but smiled at the sight of Simon and his wife. 'Old friend, I am glad to see you are not still trying to flee the city, like so many. They are queuing all about the gates, demanding the right to leave. They won't be allowed to do so, though. We cannot afford to let them.'

'Why not?' Margaret asked quietly. 'Surely it would be better to have the city emptied of all the unnecessary mouths? Couldn't some, like us, be allowed to leave?'

Sir Charles turned his smile upon her. 'My dear Madame Puttock, it would be too dangerous. How many of those leaving

---

[1] 24 October 1326

could tell the enemy how to break into the city? How many know where a weak point in the wall lies, or where a postern to access the castle may be found? They may not wish to betray us, but if they are captured and put to the torture . . . No, better to keep everyone caged here, and ensure that none go to the Queen to tell her the secrets of the city.'

'We are strangers here – we know nothing of such things,' Margaret protested.

'The rule is to be enforced nonetheless, Madame.'

'I am not happy that we are to be kept here as prisoners,' Simon said.

'I know – and if I could find a way for you to escape safely, I would do so immediately. But the way things are just now, you'd not get far before being captured. If the stories are true, the Queen's men are almost in sight now. They encircle the whole city.'

Margaret turned away, hiding her tears. They were trapped here in this damned city for as long as the Queen maintained her siege. She wondered whether she would ever see her daughter again, whether she would at last see her grandson. But no. It was likely that she and her son would perish here.

Despair made her bitter. 'Simon, I should like to find food,' she said curtly.

'My love, I think that all the food is likely to be locked away now.'

'I want dried meat and some bread here, for Peterkin and me,' Margaret snapped. 'As soon as this siege begins to bite, the city will likely allow all strangers and foreigners to starve. You will be all right, Simon, because you can help guard the city, so they will feed you. What about Peterkin and me? Simon, I don't want to watch our son die!'

This last was a wail of despair, and Simon felt it like a punch to his belly. He stared at Sir Charles, wretched in his inability to help his own wife, to protect his family.

Sir Charles was not the fastest-thinking knight Simon had ever met, but now he held up both hands. 'Madame Margaret, you and your husband will stay in the chamber allocated to me in the castle, and I shall find somewhere else. Then you will be able to eat the food stored for the siege. Nothing could be easier. I will not permit you to go hungry, my lady.'

Simon had gone to his wife and held her in his arms. 'You are sure?' he asked.

'Of course. My lady, do not worry yourself – it is all solved. There is no need for you to be alarmed. Now, Simon, let us discuss this unfortunate peasant – Cecilia? Cecily?'

And Simon went to sit and talk with the knight about the woman found the night before, while Margaret watched unhappily. Because it was one thing to say that they would be fed within the castle, but another for Simon and she to be safe, when all the Queen's forces were now to be aimed at that self-same castle, with bolts and stones hurled from the siege machines of her artillery.

She glanced up at the ceiling as though expecting the sky to begin to rain rocks upon her head. It was terrifying. And there was no escape.

South of Bristol

Exhaustion kept Baldwin in a deep slumber, and it was only when a hungry Wolf thrust his nose in his armpit that he was jerked fully awake.

Although the knight was keen to be away on the road to Furnshill, he found himself content in the hall with Thomas Redcliffe and his wife. The couple chattered happily, and it was pleasant to see their ease with each other this morning. They clearly enjoyed their domestic existence, even with the disaster of his business failure.

Their companionship was not the only reason for Baldwin's reluctance to make a start. From the moment he had woken he had heard the steady thrumming of rain on the roof, and as soon as he pulled open the shutters, he knew that the day would be miserable. It reminded him of the time a decade earlier, when the rain had been so unrelenting that crops failed and famine struck the whole of Europe. People died in such vast numbers that English Coroners could not view all the bodies, and a special dispensation was given to all vills to hold their own inquests — unless there was good reason to suspect foul play.

Sir Baldwin offered a prayer that there would be no such repetition. None who had lived through the famine had survived unmarked by tragedy.

At the table, while he and Jack ate a large breakfast of thick pottage in which cubes of ham floated, Redcliffe spoke of the trials of the King.

'It is a terrible thing for the Queen to have deserted her husband,' he said.

'I am sure that it was not a decision she took lightly,' Baldwin said.

'You do not mean to support her in her treason?' Redcliffe asked.

'I myself intend to ride to the King's support,' the knight pointed out. 'A man can do no more. But I do not condemn.'

'There are few who would be so moderate as you, Sir Baldwin.'

'Perhaps we should talk of happier matters,' Roisea suggested, seeing their guest's discomfort. 'How far is your home, Sir Baldwin?'

'If we ride well, I suppose three days from here,' Baldwin

said, and tried to block out the noise of falling rain. Wolf sat at his side, shoving his head under Baldwin's hand. 'Yes. We should be on our way,' he muttered.

They completed their meal, and after a short period of leave-taking, Baldwin and Jack were on their way. Redcliffe had advised on their best road. They should follow the great river westwards, and then take the coastal route towards the moors. From there Baldwin would be able to find his own way, he was sure.

It was a relief to be setting off on the last part of their journey, and Baldwin tugged his heavy riding cloak about him as he and Jack trotted slowly up the road which led away from the city, Wolf behind them. Soon they could see the hills rising in front of them, and in the miserable weather it was good, Baldwin reflected, to have such clear, distinct targets to aim for.

The weather had worsened, and the rain had penetrated even Baldwin's sturdy clothes. Usually his cloak would serve against the worst that even Dartmoor could hurl, but not today. The rain was so heavy it made Baldwin blind. It was simply impossible to keep on peering ahead in such foul weather. Jack, who had no decent clothing, was already soaked through to the skin, his jack and shirt hanging shapelessly from his body, while his hat with its broad brim drooped so badly he was forced to lift it in order to gaze ahead.

It was enough to persuade Baldwin that they should turn back. The roads were grown too slippery and dangerous. The horses were picking their way with care, but it would only take one pot-hole to break a leg.

'Jack, we'll have to make our way back,' he called through the biting wind. The rain was clattering all about them, and much too loud for he had to bellow just to make himself heard, but when Jack turned to him, his expression was one of sheer horror.

Baldwin followed the direction of his eyes and felt his mouth drop. There, before them, was an army.

'Back to Bristol, my boy, and quickly!' Baldwin bawled, pulling his horse's head around to the north, and clapping spurs to the beast's flanks.

Bristol

'Shite. If this was but a little warmer, it would be as miserable as hell,' a man joked as Simon wandered towards the group.

He could not argue with his sentiment. The rain pattered about the roads, and Simon's boots splashed in puddles all the way.

He had left Margaret at the inn with Hugh to guard her and Peterkin. Seeing her mood, Sir Charles had set a watchman at the door of the inn to protect them too. Now he and Simon were standing at the edge of a small crowd while the formal inquest began.

'I had assumed that you would hold this inquest,' Simon whispered.

'Me?' Sir Charles murmured. 'No. I am no Coroner, only a humble seeker after truth. *He* is the Coroner: Sir Stephen Siward.'

'Then why did you call me last night? And why drag me out here now?' Simon asked with a frown, but Sir Charles merely indicated the tall fellow approaching.

The Coroner was of a similar build to Sir Charles, but had dark hair and blue eyes – a combination that Simon instinctively mistrusted. The man looked too much like a murderous Cornishman. His smile was oddly out of place at such a meeting, too, as he chatted quietly to a clerk sitting with a board over his knees and parchment, reeds and ink set out ready.

He did at least seem to know his business. The jurors were called forward, the men ranging in age from one lad of perhaps thirteen, to the oldest who was at least sixty. When they had given their names and the clerk had enrolled them on his parchment, the Coroner asked who was missing. These names were noted too, so that they could be amerced for their non-attendance later, and then the jury had to swear on the Gospels held to them by the clerk that they would tell the truth on all the points the Coroner put to them. Then the body was studied.

The Coroner had the duty of viewing and feeling the bodies which were found, so that his clerk could record every injury. So as usual, Cecily's body was unceremoniously stripped and then displayed naked to the Coroner and the jury. Her limbs were moved, her flesh pressed and prodded; the stab wound was measured and her throat studied for signs of throttling. There was remarkably little damage, only a faint path of bruising about her mouth and the stab to the heart, and when they investigated, no sign of rape.

Still, Simon looked away. It felt like a second violation of the woman, for her to be displayed in such a lewd manner before so many men – all of them seeing the parts of her body which only a husband should have known. It was degrading to all of them, he thought.

When he glanced about, he saw that all the jury bar one man were gawping at the body. The last, though, was a rough-looking man, slim, ferrety-faced, with dark, slightly squinting eyes. He was not looking at the body, but instead stared at the Coroner with an expression of fear.

Then his attention was taken by the Coroner again.

'I, Sir Stephen Siward, find that this maid was killed by a dagger with a blade of about one-inch width at the hilt, and perhaps six inches long,' the Coroner said. He studied the wound again. 'The blade was double-edged, I'd say. The wound is diamond-shaped, not triangular. It's a good-sized blade – a dagger.'

He turned to the jurors after the body had been rolled over and over twice, an ungainly mess of arms and legs without dignity. 'Well? Jury, do you find that this woman has been slain feloniously, died by misadventure, or that she died of natural causes?'

His tone was ironic, but it was the normal form of the questions, as Simon knew. The jury must answer all to the best of their ability or risk a large fine.

'Feloniously killed.'

'Very well. I agree that this woman was unlawfully killed by a person or persons armed with at least a small dagger. Do you all know the woman?'

'She is Cecily,' two men called out, and the clerk noted that too.

'Good,' the Coroner said, and began to rattle through the other questions: where did she live, had anyone witnessed the killing, had there been any noises in the area before the body was discovered, and had anyone seen somebody in the area.

It was a perfunctory affair, Simon thought, perhaps because the jury and the Coroner himself were distracted. Why concern themselves with one death when at any time an onslaught could be launched that would slaughter hundreds? However, Simon was sure that there was something else in the Coroner's eyes when he looked at Cecily's body. Something akin to sadness, as though he had some feeling for this particular woman. It was rare, in Simon's experience, for most Coroners were immune to sympathy. They saw too many dead men and women for that.

The summary was given, the bill of amercements called out that all in the area should know how much they must pay, and then the Coroner ordered that the body be taken at once to the nearest cemetery for burial in accordance with the law. Soon, poor Cecily was placed upon a cart, and two men began to wheel her away, her clothing bundled separately in order that it should be sold later.

'So why *did* you bring me here?' Simon asked Sir Charles once more. 'If you have no authority in this case, I cannot understand why you asked me to join you last night and today.'

'I did not wish to see that woman's homicide go unreported. If her death was felonious, then I wanted to make sure that the Coroner recorded the fact and that she had a proper enquiry into her murder. You see, Bailiff, I don't think that he would have done so, had I not forced him.'

'Why? He seemed perfectly competent and obedient to his duty,' Simon argued.

'Come with me. I will show you.'

CHAPTER TWENTY-TWO

North of Bristol

When the news had spread of the Queen's forces approaching the city, there had been an immediate panic, and it was felt not least by Robert Vyke as he had hurried to gather up his belongings and shove them into his little pack, before going to the northernmost gate of the city, where he was told by Sir Laurence that he could best make his escape.

He had not bothered to walk far in the gathering gloom, but took his rest in the meagre shelter of an old shepherd's hut, where the roof had fallen in. This morning it was the rain that had woken him, landing on his face.

Eating a little bread with cheese, he stared back at the city through the rain. His thick cloak and hood were enormously heavy, now that they were soaked in water. There was no point in trying to keep dry in this weather, he decided, and hefted his pack again. At least the rattle of the coins in his purse was comforting. He couldn't remember ever possessing such wealth in his life before, and the thought of the look on his Susan's face when she saw the money was wonderful. It would make her so happy, she would be unable to speak for a long time, he thought with a smile. Six shillings was untold wealth for a peasant.

The way was fairly steep here, for he had left the road to continue on his own path. The main road was bound to be filled with the Queen's men, and he had no intention of being caught. No, he would continue on his way here, towards the King. He was supposed to be in Chepstow or somewhere near. Robert would just keep on going until he found him. It couldn't be too difficult to find a King, after all, he told himself. You just had to look for the big standard flying. If you could in this weather, he added miserably.

He clambered his way to the top of a hill among some trees and peered out. There was no sign of anyone. Here, so he had heard, the land began to drop down towards the great river, and he must cross it to reach the town. There were many boatmen at that point, even though there was no bridge, so he was moderately confident that he could reach the other side without difficulty. Once there, he must find the King and pass him the little sealed document in its leather tube, stoppered with thick wax, and await his answer.

It was not a task he had thought himself capable of in the past, but he hoped he would be rewarded. Surely a messenger who braved the weather and his monarch's enemies to bring him news of the garrison of Bristol would be given at least some shillings, or even a golden ring.

With thoughts of still more astonishing wealth shortly to come his way, he emerged from the trees and found himself in a little lane. Looking up and down, he turned right, as being the direction to take him further away from Bristol, and continued on into the thick greyness.

Bristol

The man in the jury had turned to leave when Simon and Sir Charles reached him.

Simon did not like his face. There was something about the squint that implied a shifty nature, and his habit of shuffling his feet did not inspire confidence either.

'Tell this man what you saw,' Sir Charles said encouragingly.

'I don't know, sir, mayhap I was wrong. It was dark and—'

Sir Charles's smile broadened, and then he snatched out with his hand and gripped the man about the throat. 'I hope you don't soil my glove, fellow, because I don't want to have to take your money to buy new ones. They are expensive.'

The man's eyes popped wide, and he gulped. 'I'll talk, I'll talk!'

'I know,' Sir Charles said pleasantly.

'That woman Cecily – I saw her yesterday. With a man,' the fellow said desperately, his voice weakened by the pressure on his neck.

Simon felt coldness wash over his body. 'You lied? After you swore on the Gospels? You *lied* to the Coroner?'

'I couldn't tell!'

Sir Charles turned to Simon with that smile still on his face, but in his eyes there was no humour. 'No, he couldn't tell the truth, Simon.'

'God's teeth! Why not?'

'Because the man he saw, the one with whom she left, was another knight – a man called Sir Laurence Ashby. And a mere churl like this would never dare accuse a noble knight.'

South of Bristol

Baldwin and Jack had ridden hard to the outskirts of the city, all the way fearing capture, but their luck had held so far. Now they paused, and Baldwin peered behind them. His face was streaming, and he put a hand to his brow, wiping it away and flinging it to the side. It was hard to see anything yet, and he prayed that he and Jack had out-ridden the encircling men.

The force was that of the Queen; he had little doubt of that, because he knew that the King was already passed through and into Wales; his host would come to Bristol from the north and west. The men Baldwin had seen were approaching from the south and east.

He knew the Queen and Mortimer, having met them a few times in England and in France. While he rather admired the Queen, for not only was she beautiful, she was resolute, intelligent, and fiercely determined; yet Baldwin was less certain of Mortimer.

Roger Mortimer had been the King's General – it was largely due to him that Edward had been able to pacify Ireland – but Despenser and Mortimer hated each other with a loathing that went back two generations. It was Despenser who had managed to see Mortimer, already a prisoner in the Tower of London, served with a death warrant. For that reason, Mortimer broke out of the prison and made his way to France, where he became the focus for all those who had cause to detest the reign of Despenser in London. Every malcontent, including the King's own brothers, went to him and swelled his forces.

When Mortimer and the Queen landed in the east, they had only a few hundred men with them, but wherever they went, it seemed as though the people of the country flocked to them. The Queen had made a strategically successful statement when she stated that she was not in the country to oppose her husband, but to depose the tyrannical reign of Despenser. That struck a chord with almost every Englishman, for Hugh Despenser was universally hated. And then, the Queen also had the banner of her son, Edward Duke of Aquitaine, raised before her forces, so

Baldwin had heard, so that even those who might have been inclined to support the King felt unable to raise a sword against her, because that would mean obstructing the next King.

That, Baldwin was sure, was the Queen's own idea. She was shrewd and crafty, and would see that her son's banner would help her. However, when she had enlisted the support of Mortimer, she was running a great risk. He might one day decide to throw her and her son aside.

Those were questions for another time. For now, Baldwin had other problems to consider. First was how to reach the far side of the river. The bridge, he knew, was blocked, for the city was already under a siege footing. They would not open the gates to any men from this side of the river now.

'Come!' he cried, and led Jack along the narrow streets and lanes all the way back to Redcliffe's house. Here Baldwin threw himself off his horse and pounded on the door.

'Dear Heaven, Sir Baldwin!' Redcliffe said, starting in amazement when Baldwin and Jack were brought dripping into his hall. 'What is all—'

'The Queen is here already,' Sir Baldwin said tersely. 'You must tell me, how may I cross the river, for there is no escape on this side of the Avon.'

'The Queen? With her host? Dear God!' the man gaped.

Baldwin knew that Redcliffe was now faced with the prospect of being overwhelmed in fire and warfare, with all his remaining possessions being ransacked and stolen.

'I am deeply saddened to bring such news to you,' he said, 'but my need is urgent. How can I escape?'

'There is a ferry which crosses the river to the west of the bridge, Sir Baldwin. But if you take it, there will be little possibility of your coming back. No man will wish to cross the river again until the siege here is over.'

'I don't intend to cross it again,' Baldwin said grimly. 'I ride to the King – I have my oath to fulfil. I swore to support him and his realm, and I will not fail in my duty.'

Redcliffe swallowed, then said, 'Sir Baldwin, I have urgent news for the King. May I travel with you? I will take you to the crossing myself.'

Bristol

'It makes little or no sense,' Simon frowned.

They were back at the inn, and he and Sir Charles sat side-by-side before the fire, sipping warmed wine as they considered their morning's work.

'Why would he ask you to investigate the killing, Sir Charles, when *he* is Coroner?'

'When the murder was reported he was busy discussing the defences with Sir Laurence.'

'And this Sir Laurence is castellan, you say.'

'He gave me the impression that he thought the city was more important than one death,' Sir Charles said. 'But then I spoke with that man from the jury, and realised that Sir Laurence could be the murderer, but I don't want to accuse him without evidence. That is the last thing we need at the moment – to have the castellan under suspicion. If a king's official was thought to be guilty of murder, the city would rebel and there could be a riot.'

'And you think Sir Stephen did not expect you to learn anything?'

'No. And I shall not learn anything.'

'Eh?'

'Simon, my friend, there is no point in my trying to seek for the woman's killer. If I do, Sir Laurence may learn about it and use his influence to stop me accusing him. It would distract him from the matter of our defence, which could be disastrous. Also,

I have duties here to help in the protection of the city. Whereas a man without responsibility . . .'

'I see,' Simon said heavily.

'It need not take you long. But if you could learn whether Sir Laurence has any connection to the dead woman, and whether he had any reason to wish to see her dead, that would be a great help.'

He smiled at Simon. 'That isn't too much to ask, is it?'

Sir Stephen finished his cup of wine and stepped out into the rain. There were four men at the end of the street, all drunk and shouting incoherently at each other.

It was a sign of things to come. Sir Stephen had not endured a lengthy siege before, but he knew men who had, and was aware that the first thing to fall apart was law and order.

He walked towards them, and felt the usual tingle of excitement in his belly as he saw two of the men stare at him, one unfocused, the other with a look of malevolence. It was he who picked up a stone from the roadway.

His voice was slurred, but his meaning was clear: 'Look, a lazy, thieving knight, just like the others who got us into this mess. Sod the lot of them! Gits who argue, and when things go wrong, who do they use to try to get them out of the shit? Us, that's who! Let's get him!'

Sir Stephen did not slow his footsteps. Soon he was within striking range, and then, as a stone was flung, only to miss him by a foot, he sprang forward. His gauntlet caught the bold man about the mouth, and the steel plates cut him badly. Then Sir Stephen shoved hard, and the drunk fell back onto his rump, while the knight stood contemplating the rest. 'Any more?' he said pleasantly.

The three picked up their bleeding companion and were off in a hurry. It was pathetic, but the mob could not be permitted to gather about a ringleader like him, Sir Stephen thought as he walked on.

He found the place a few moments later. The church had a small gate, and he walked inside, bowing at the altar.

The priest was already holding a small service, and Sir Stephen stood at the rear of the great empty space, listening to the monotonous droning of the man's voice, wondering how long the fellow could last. But finally all was done, and the body was carried outside into the rain. Sir Stephen walked along after it, and as it was lowered into the freshly dug hole, he saw that the water had already pooled in the bottom, and mud was soaking into the winding sheet. It was a sad end to an unhappy life, he thought.

At his side the priest muttered the ritual words quickly, in a hurry to get back inside his church and hide from the rain. A man should take a little time over a burial, Sir Stephen thought, giving him a frown, especially when the corpse had no family to mourn her, no husband or child. No one but himself.

The priest slowed, scowling, before reluctantly bending over, grabbing a handful of sodden soil, and babbling on in his uneducated Latin, hurling the mud at the body. Soon he was finished, muttering the last lines, and then he made the sign of the cross, before turning and almost running inside.

'Cover her,' Sir Stephen said to the fosser, who nodded, took up his spade, and began to shovel the earth into the hole. The first throw slapped wet soil onto her face, and the damp linen took on the lines of her mouth, nose, eyes. It was almost as though she was watching Sir Stephen through the gauzy material. A fresh shovelful landed on her belly, making the points of her breasts stand out, and the next smacked into her shoulder.

It was enough. He looked away, and then he reached inside

his jack and pulled out the little bundle. He hefted it in his hand a moment, looking at it sadly, before glancing into the grave, and throwing the pack in.

Turning, he left the cemetery and went out into the road.

The fosser had buried more than a hundred people here in this graveyard, and he had often seen people throw in little trinkets of no value as he covered the bodies. And more than once he had seen those people return, peering in to make sure that he had actually left their gift to the dead and had not stolen it.

This time, he was not going to take any chances. He carried on piling in the soil at the foot and at the head of the woman's body, until it was not possible to continue without burying the gift. Only then did he crouch quickly, slip the edge of the shovel under the packet, and slide it up the side of the mound of soil at Cecily's feet. Taking it from the grave, he whistled in surprise as he slipped the wrapping from it to reveal a golden hilt and two rubies.

He quickly covered it in the waxed linen again, shoved it under his shirt, and finished his work.

CHAPTER TWENTY-THREE

It had taken Simon little time to decide to visit Emma, the mistress of the maid killed the previous night. The idea of leaving poor Cecily's body unavenged did not sit well with him. He was not a sentimental man, he told himself, but the notion of a man taking a woman and then slaying her as though she was nothing more than a toy to be discarded was repellent. He loved his own wife and daughter too much to be prepared to let it go.

However, it was unthinkable that he should leave Margaret alone in the city when she was already so scared.

Her concern was entirely rational, of course. He knew that. They had been in the Tower at London when the city began to fall apart in early October, but although there had been the threat of danger there, there had not been engines of war, such as there would be here. The idea of those monsters lurking out beyond the walls was enough to make any man or woman fear for their lives. It was natural. Once those things began to fling rocks at a city, that city must fall. Nothing could withstand the onslaught.

Simon was certainly not happy to be here as the threat of battle loomed ever nearer, yet curiously, he was not afraid.

During a siege, terror affected all differently. Some would find the nearest alehouse and consume as much drink as they could, which was why there were so many scared men wandering the streets, bellies filled with wine and ale, and muttering bellicose threats to all and sundry.

No, Simon most definitely did not dare to leave his wife alone. Instead, all four of them set off from the inn in the middle of the rainy morning. Their way took them under lots of buildings whose jettied upper storeys loomed over the streets, so their progress was a series of quick sprints from one area of moderate dryness to another.

Margaret was unhappy to be taken from her chamber, especially in this weather. They should never have come here in the first place, she thought resentfully. They could easily have ignored Sir Charles and ridden on along the coast. Soon they would have been out of the reach of the Queen's men, and could have taken it more easy as they wandered down to Exeter and beyond. There was no need to be stuck here, in this ridiculous little city. Or the castle, the focus of the coming battle.

However, after a short way Meg found that her mood was lightening. There was something gay and carefree about this journey. None of them could maintain the fear of men on the streets full of ale, because no one else appeared silly enough to brave the elements. The roads were all empty. Instead, Margaret was struck with the urge to giggle helplessly as she saw an enormous wash of water sweep down from a gutter overhead, to soak her husband. Simon stood scowling furiously up at the offending gutter, and turned to his wife with an expression of utter rage, only to be struck again. This made her howl with laughter, and after a moment or two, Simon began to chuckle as well.

After all, they were all still alive, and with God's help, perhaps the siege would not prove too lengthy or irksome.

Their way took them from a wealthy area, through a part that was clearly very poor, and thence to a section of the city that was not so rich as the merchants' houses down by the castle, but still clearly well-to-do. Here, Margaret found herself peering in at the windows, where candles were lighted, trying to see what sort of hangings there were, and guessing at what type of person lived inside.

'It is not like London, is it?' she said, gesturing at a house with a large sign showing that here lived a glover. 'In London there is much more ostentation; everyone wants to flaunt their riches. Here the people seem more sober.'

'It's the way folk are over here,' Simon agreed. 'In London a man doesn't think he's alive unless he's rubbing another man's nose in his wealth. This is a smaller city, so people have to muck in together. Just like home. We don't have time to have grudges and feuds, do we? It's more a case of trying to help everyone to survive when the winter's bad and the sheep won't lamb and there isn't enough food to last. In London they can buy what they need always, I reckon, so they don't care so much about getting on with their neighbours.'

'Well, Master Philosopher, I don't disagree, but I think it's more that the people here are less rushed. They take time to enjoy their lives. Look at that magnificent bridge! London has one too, but theirs is so . . . I don't know. These people seem to have more pride in their city, while in London all the displays seem intended to show you how mean your life is in comparison. Here, men wish to allow others to enjoy it with them. They want to share it.'

'Perhaps that's why the folk of Bristol always need controlling,' Simon said wrily. 'Too much freedom of spirit is worrying to a King.'

They were at a neat house now, with limewashed walls and

door, and the smell of a good stew emanating from the unglazed, barred window. Simon knocked at the door.

When the door opened, Meg saw a woman a little older than herself, dressed in a tunic of fine green wool, with a red woollen cloth over her shoulders; her hair was decorously covered by a sober white linen cap instead of a wimple. 'Yes?'

'I am looking for the lady of the house,' Simon said. 'Emma Wrey?'

'I am she. What do you want?'

'Did you have a maid working with you? A woman called Cecily, of perhaps thirty, with fairish hair and—'

'Sir, who are you to question me?'

'Madame Wrey, I am sorry to bring sad news,' Simon said, 'but she was found last night. She's been killed. I am called Simon Puttock, and was asked to look into the matter by Sir Charles Lancaster.'

Emma Wrey's face paled. 'Dead? I . . .' She shivered and clutched at the door. Margaret stepped forward, but before she could help the woman, Emma Wrey pushed herself upright again.

'Oh, the poor maid! The silly thing! I did tell her to be careful when she went out. She obviously didn't take my advice.'

'When did you last see her?'

'Last afternoon – almost evening. She was here to eat with me, and when she had finished, she went out.'

'Would she have visited an alehouse or tavern?'

The woman looked at him. 'Sir, this city is under siege. All are anxious. Of course she might have visited a tavern. Who wouldn't?' She finally gave an ungracious jerk of her head to invite them all inside. 'I suppose if you are trying to help poor Cecily, the least I can do is ask you in out of the rain.'

'I thank you,' Simon smiled and followed Margaret inside.

Hers was a large hall, with a high ceiling and magnificent carvings on beams and panels. As they walked in from the screens, Simon was forced to stop and purse his lips as if to whistle. It was like entering a church, he thought, apart from the great fire that burned in the middle of the floor. The walls were painted and decorated with religious scenes, while there was a great halling over at the far wall depicting a garden with ladies and their gentlemen enjoying their leisure.

'Please be seated.'

Simon motioned to Hugh and Rob to remain at the door, but Hugh had already decided that it was not his place to walk into a room like this. He stood scowling ferociously in the door to the screens passage, clutching his staff like a man preparing to defend himself against a ravening horde.

It was astonishing to see so many chairs, Simon thought. There were five of them, all comfortable chairs with highly decorated backs to them, and thick, soft cushions. He sank into one with a feeling that he could easily become used to living like this.

The lady had a large handbell, which she rang now, and an elderly man appeared. Sent away, he soon returned with wine in large sycamore mazers with silver bands.

'Well?' she said when they were all comfortable. 'I suppose you have more to ask? I knew something must have happened when she didn't appear this morning – but I did not expect to learn she was dead.'

'What can you tell me of your maid?' Simon asked.

'Cecily was a good, quiet, somewhat reserved woman. I was her second mistress. Her earlier home was torn apart. A very sad event.'

Seeing Simon's keen interest, the lady sat back in her seat and eyed him indulgently. 'Cecily used to live with the family of

Arthur Capon. He and his wife were . . . good fellows, very popular in the town, and known for their generosity to charities. But not, perhaps, for their generosity towards their servants. When Cecily was sent back to them from Petronilla's side, she was sure that come the next Michaelmas fair, she would lose her position. You see, Arthur Capon did not want any hangers-on in his household. But his daughter left her husband before he could throw Cecily from his door.'

'Their daughter?'

'I am ahead of myself, I am sorry. Petronilla was their daughter. She married Squire William de Bar. You see, the Capons were wealthy, but only burgesses, and they sought a connexion with nobility. That was their big mistake.'

'What do you mean?' Margaret asked.

The widow tried to explain. 'Poor Petronilla was only fourteen when they married her to Squire William, and for a while, all seemed well. The parents were grateful for access to the nobles of Bristol, Bath and Wells, and Squire William was glad of the money they supplied as dowry. He had a small manor which was sadly dilapidated. His father had made an enemy of King Edward I, the King's father, and this enmity meant he lost all patronage. The hall itself was in a terrible state, and it wanted but their money to be rebuilt. But you cannot change a man's spirit by paying him. They had not been married long when the bullying started.'

She drained her wine and beckoned her steward, who refilled all their cups as she spoke. 'Cecily was there with Petronilla, for she had been the child's nurse and remained her maid from then on. But she saw terrible behaviour. The Squire was an obnoxious fellow: he would beat his young wife often, and without need. After some time, her parents came to stay, but they were discontented with the household and the way their daughter was treated. I think they had believed that Squire William was moderately wealthy, and when they saw the squalor of his home, it shook them. The reality was a shock. The Squire even threatened his father-in-law with a beating, when Arthur Capon remonstrated with him, would you believe? Cecily was the only friend Petronilla had. Apart from her confessor, anyway.

'Matters grew worse after her parents had gone, since it was then that Squire William learned that Petronilla was not their natural child. She had been an orphan, and they fostered her when she was a child.'

Simon winced. 'That must have irked him.'

'He was furious. If he had been unreasonable and cruel before, now he was ungovernable.'

Margaret shook her head. 'I don't quite understand.'

'Since the child was not their own, her parentage was . . . questionable. Some said she was daughter to a dead prostitute. The Squire threatened a legal action for their misrepresenting her position to him, and the Capons in return threatened to prosecute the squire for misrepresenting his own financial position. I think Capon even started proceedings to have the dowry returned. Squire William refused to discuss it, declaring it was his for the marriage. However, then he began his own case against them for marrying their daughter to him, when they knew she was not of their own blood. It was an awful situation. And he sent Cecily away in an act of spite against Petronilla. The maid was packed off back to Bristol, where Capon wanted to dismiss her, saying she was no longer needed; he told her she was a reminder of his daughter.'

Madame Wrey sighed at the cruelty.

'All this took some years, and Petronilla was eighteen by this time. She had endured enormous shame, hardship, and beatings. The only friend she had left in the world, once Cecily had been sent from her side, was her confessor. At her husband's manor, she was hated, not only by Squire William but also by all his family, for she had brought shame to them, and now there was the threat of financial disaster if they must return the dowry. She decided she could not remain there suffering abuse, so, determined to become free, she ran away.

'As luck would have it, her young confessor was convinced that she had every good reason to escape her husband and commit the act of treason. So he helped her, but not very successfully. She was captured only a matter of miles from her house, and the priest himself escaped by the skin of his teeth. But they had already been alone for a month or more.'

'I see,' Simon said.

'And nine months later . . . you understand.'

'Of course,' Simon said. 'So what happened?'

'There was a great noise at the time. In the end, the priest was taken away and put in a convent, I believe. He was certainly punished. The girl was also taken and held in a nunnery, although not as punishment. I think there was some fear that her mind was being harmed. She was so young, and had married so young, that I think the Judge wanted her to have a time to herself. So she was placed in the nunnery until she was considered sufficiently recovered, and then she was returned to her family. However, one terrible day her husband and some friends broke into the house and slaughtered the entire family. They killed her parents, they took her and stabbed her more than thirty times, and then they took her child too, and dashed the little babe's head against a wall. Poor Cecily saw it all. She was there.'

Margaret gave a small gasp. 'The baby too? Dear God in Heaven. This Squire, he was captured?'

'Oh, yes. He was captured,' Emma said. 'And now he has

been released. Like so many, he has been pardoned so that he might fight for the King.'

'That is disgusting,' Margaret said. 'Was there no outcry?'

'There was some, but what would anyone do against a friend of the King?'

Simon sucked at his teeth. 'Did she know Sir Laurence at the castle? I've heard she knew him.'

'I doubt it,' she said. 'A knight? However, Sir Laurence could, so we hoped, have the Squire taken to gaol again and overthrow his release. But although I went and asked him, the man refused our petition. I will not speak with him now.'

'She too could have tried to talk to him about that,' Simon considered. It was possible. 'And Cecily came to you after all that sad tale with her past employers?'

'Yes. The poor woman was still very shocked. She had been without work for a while when she came here. I wanted to give her a home where she could feel safe, and . . . and I suppose I failed her.'

To Simon's surprise, the woman suddenly collapsed, sobbing, covering her face with her hands.

Margaret rose and went to her side while Simon exchanged a look of embarrassment with the steward. Neither was comfortable in the presence of a woman in tears. They resorted to conventional male behaviour. Simon looked all about the room except at Emma or his wife, while the steward stared at his jug as though willing it to fill itself.

CHAPTER TWENTY-FOUR

Bristol Castle

It was a foul morning, Sir Laurence Ashby thought as he gazed over the surrounding lands through the heavy rain.

He had been brought up near here, and the weather was no surprise, but it did add a mournful aspect to the day. Bad enough, surely, that the city was about to be attacked, without these stormy skies. Ach, God's ballocks! There was never a good day to fight; never a good day to die. He slammed his fist on the wall and went back inside.

The last few weeks had been dreadful. Sir Laurence was old-fashioned enough to believe in the oath he had given the King so many years ago. Then he had been a young man, one of the first whom the new King had knighted after his accession, and Sir Laurence had remained staunchly loyal, although his loyalty had been sorely tested in recent years.

When he marched into his chamber at midday, he stopped just inside the doorway. Sir Stephen Siward was sitting on his desk's edge, teeth bared in a grimace as he fumbled with a splinter of wood. 'Damned piece of meat stuck in my tooth,' he said.

Sir Laurence nodded and walked to his seat. 'Can I help you?'

'Planning. We have to try to get our plans ready for when the bastards arrive. Won't be long now.'

'I think that the plans are well enough advanced already,' the castellan said.

'What of the citizens? I don't trust them beyond an inch. They'll give up the city soon as fart. None will support us and the King. They recall the King's siege ten years ago.'

Sir Laurence smiled thinly. 'I do not fault your summary. They will doubtless enjoy giving up their houses to the Queen's men. There are too many stories already about how she is stretched to keep most of her forces under control.'

'We have to be able to spoil the confidence of the town somehow. Can't we point out that most of her men are mercenaries? No one likes a damned mercenary – whether it's a soldier or a banker. Bastards are too keen to make money all the time instead of sticking to their oaths.'

Sir Stephen coughed and went on, changing the subject: 'You knew the man whom William of Bar killed, didn't you? Capon. Arthur Capon. Did you know that his maid has been killed?'

Sir Laurence shot him a look. Sir Stephen was eyeing him strangely. 'I knew him a little. Did you learn who could have killed the maid?'

Sir Stephen shook his head slowly. 'No. I suppose it was one of Squire William's men.'

'Yes,' Sir Laurence said. 'Perhaps it was.'

He saw her face again – the sharp, bright eyes, the thin mouth – and remembered how she would keep whining on about Squire William and his men now that they were freed. She had been a pain in his backside, especially when she had her mistress set on him as well. It was inexcusable!

Sir Stephen was watching him. 'You knew her?'

'She came to speak with me – complaining about feeling scared since the Squire and his men were released from gaol. God knows what she expected me to be able to do about it!'

'And we all have enough to worry us just now,' Sir Stephen said quietly.

'Yes. At least we know our duties. It is our place to remain here and protect this castle. While the castle survives, we are safe and the approaches to Wales and the King are guarded. They couldn't bypass us and hope to make it to the King. They would always fear a sally from us.'

Sir Stephen nodded, and he studied his splinter. 'How long do you think we could survive?'

'We have food for at least twelve weeks if we are cautious. I suppose it's possible we could acquire some more, if the siege is not effectively maintained. The city, though, is a different matter. I assume that it will be running short within the week.' Sir Laurence walked over to the small table in the corner, where a jug of wine stood. He took up his gilded goblet, which he filled and drank deeply.

'So we have a week before the city itself decides to surrender. That is when our own predicament becomes more acute,' Sir Stephen said.

'No,' Sir Laurence said firmly. 'Our predicament is acute from the moment the Queen appears. Have you heard nothing of her progress? She has been stopped by no one. All the men whom the King has sent against her have surrendered to her and her son; not a one has tried to oppose her.' He strode to the middle of the floor, where he paced up and down, as was his wont when anxious. 'The Navy refused to leave port to defeat her at sea, even though they could have done so with ease; the men of the coast who were told to prevent her landing preferred to bow to her and go to her side; towns and cities from London to Oxford have rebelled and murdered the King's own advisers, even the priests. Bishop Walter of Exeter had his head hacked off, and his body thrown to the dogs, did you know that? A *Bishop*, in Christ's name! What of the others – the men who are his servants? They go in fear of their lives. Some have been pilloried in London and elsewhere. There is nobody to stand up for them, my friend. No one.'

He slammed his fist against his sword hilt.

'And the worst of it is, it is our own Queen and the King's heir who stand against us. What is a man to say – that his own Queen is to be rejected? That her son is? The kingdom is at risk of disaster, yet the disaster doesn't come from a foreign power or even a traitor amidst our own barons. It comes from within the Royal Family.'

'Aye, well, we can hope that we merely do our duties and that the Queen honours us for that,' Sir Stephen said.

'I would trust Queen Isabella with my life, and I would trust the Duke of Aquitaine too. But not Mortimer,' Sir Laurence said, but his anger was flown, and now he wandered to his seat once more and sat. 'There are few men I would trust less than Sir Roger Mortimer. He is burned up with jealousy and bile. God forbid that we should fall into his clutches.'

'It is said he only ever seeks more money,' Sir Stephen remarked, looking at the gilded cup.

Sir Laurence eyed him coolly. 'That could be said of many.'

'Yes,' Sir Stephen agreed. He shrugged. 'Perhaps that poor maid Cecily was lucky to die when she did. Who can tell what will happen to this sorry city in the coming days?'

Bristol

It was some little while before Emma was recovered enough to be able to continue. 'I feel so ashamed to have let her down.'

'Madame, you have let no one down,' Simon said kindly. 'This Squire William – is he still in the city?'

'I do not believe so. I certainly have not seen him for a long time now. I think he left Bristol when he was released – else many could have attacked him. I hope the shame drove him away, but then I doubt he knows what shame is. The man was a monster. It is one thing to slay those who threaten you – but a mere child of a few days old? How could he be so brutal? He is probably with the King's host, fulfilling his parole.'

'What of the boy's father? This priest – you think he was the father?'

'I would imagine so. I am sure that Squire William had nothing to do with fathering the child.'

'Clearly. But if this Squire is gone, who else could have killed Cecily?'

'There are others who were with Squire William when he committed his murders. Perhaps it was one of them?'

Simon considered. 'This all happened when?'

'Some months ago.'

'Why, then, would the men seek to hurt her now? They were pardoned, why punish her and risk imprisonment again? Surely even murderers would be more rational than that?'

'I do not pretend to understand such men,' she said, 'but I do understand how they might like to take revenge on someone who had caused them trouble. It's a matter of honour to some of them.'

'Yes, I suppose so. But what about the Squire? Is there aught else you can tell me about him? What did he look like?'

'Middle height . . . very dark hair, the sort that looks thin always. Green eyes, I remember. Very pale and calculating. And his face wore a look of cruelty.'

Simon nodded as though noting her words, but for the most part he thought them useless. A man who had a 'look of cruelty' to a woman who considered him a foul murderer might well look like an amiable old charmer to another. Still, if the story was true, this man had deserved a far harsher punishment than a short period in gaol and then release. Which led him to the next logical question. 'What happened to the priest?'

'Father Paul? He was sent away. You'd have to ask someone else where he went.'

'I shall do so. And you do not think that she knew Sir Laurence, apart from going to him to plead that these felons be re-arrested?'

'No. He is the last person she would speak with.'

'Very well. I am sorry indeed to have to tell you of your maid, madame. If there is one good piece of news, though, it is that she did die very quickly. There was one thrust, straight to her heart, so far as I could tell. She wasn't raped, either. The inquest did make sure of that.'

'I see. I am glad of that at least,' Emma said. She dried her eyes and sniffed a little, then sat back. 'So, master, will you search for her murderer?'

Simon gave a sad smile. 'If ever a man picked a good time to commit a crime, it was this fellow. If you are right and the Squire has long since left the city, it will be difficult to accuse him. Also, he could not return with the gates locked. And if Squire William did not kill her – who did? Cecily was only a maid-servant, so I do not imagine that she had anything of great value to attract a thief. Did she carry a purse?'

'Only a small one.'

'So the motive was unlikely to be robbery.'

'Perhaps the Squire *is* here? He could have got back yester-day before the gates were locked,' Emma said.

'Perhaps so,' Simon said, unconvinced.

'So you will seek the murderer? Please?'

'I will do what I may,' Simon said. *While the city holds*, he wanted to add, but he could not be so unkind. Meanwhile, he would need to speak with the castellan.

River Avon near Bristol

Baldwin and Jack fretted as they waited, although Redcliffe was quick enough, throwing clothes into a leather satchel while his servants were packing the few belongings of any value and concealing them about the house. A hostler prepared his mare, and soon he was with them again. 'I am ready, Sir Baldwin.'

'Then let us go!' Baldwin said, keen to be off.

'One moment.'

There was a clatter of hooves, and Baldwin turned to see Roisea trotting around the corner on a great bay mare.

Baldwin turned to stare at Redcliffe. 'You think to bring your wife?'

'Would you expect me to leave her here, so that she can be raped and perhaps slain?' Redcliffe said anxiously. 'Come, follow me!'

They were soon out of the suburb and hurrying along towards the west. It was dark and grim, the rain still falling heavily. Baldwin's rounsey twitched his ears irritably as the rain began to soak his coat, but beside him, Baldwin saw, Wolf wandered contentedly. There was no weather that could upset him. Still, it was a relief when the rain began to ease a little, just as they were making their way down towards the river.

It swept about here in a great arc, bulging northwards into the belly of the city but, following Redcliffe, Baldwin rode westwards towards the lower level of the river. They cantered along a track by the banks and soon came across a little shed with a thatched roof over cob walls. Down at the water's edge, a large boat lay rocking gently.

'Ferryman? Is there a ferryman here?' Baldwin called, and dropped from his horse.

The door opened a little, and a bearded face peered out at him suspiciously. 'What do you want?'

'What should I want with a ferryman?' Baldwin asked reasonably. 'I want to cross to the other side of the river. How much for us and our horses?'

'Just the four of you?' the man asked.

Redcliffe sprang from his horse. 'You know me, don't you, old man? Remember Thomas who used to pay you in wine when my ships came in?'

'Oh, Master Redcliffe. Course I remember you.'

'Have you space for we four? The Queen's men are behind us.'

'Suppose so. There aren't any others, then?'

'What, do you expect me to bring the King's host with me?'

'Wouldn't be surprised to find some o' them trying to escape,' the man grunted. 'It'll be getting exciting enough for anyone soon.'

'I hope it will,' Jack said.

The ferryman shot a look at Baldwin. 'Aye, well, those who've not fought are always keenest for a fight,' he muttered, and set about preparing his boat.

'What did he mean?' Jack asked.

'Just what he said,' Baldwin said. 'Jack, war is not easy or pleasant. It's not something to hope for.'

'But I want to help the King!'

'Perhaps so. And I do as well. But if there is a war, it means many good men will die on either side.'

'If they are fighting against our King, they can't be good,' Jack said, and Redcliffe nodded.

'The boy's right,' he said 'The King's enemies are the enemies of all.'

'Men are men. On both sides there are good and bad. It is not the side on which they fight, it is the way that they live their lives and honour their responsibilities and duties. Remember that, if you can.'

'I don't understand,' Jack frowned.

'Yes, well, I doubt fewer than half the men who go to war will either,' Baldwin said with a sigh.

It was Roisea who comprehended best. She dropped lightly from her mare and looked up at him sympathetically, but without speaking.

'You lot ready?' the ferryman called out sourly. 'I don't want to be waiting here all day.'

Baldwin helped his horse down the bank and into the boat, then stood soothing the worried beast while the others brought their own down, and then, as the ferry edged into the water, he watched the bank behind them gradually fade away. It seemed to him then that his old life was being left behind in some way, and there was no possibility of his ever finding it again. It was a deeply sad feeling.

Bristol Castle

It was the beginning of the end, Sir Laurence Ashby told himself. From here on the tower's battlements, he could see the mass of men appear. They arrived like dark ink flowing over a page – men on horses in the centre, while at the edges were bowmen and men-at-arms. All wandered closer in their centaignes while their Captains rode about, agreeing the dispositions of the host.

There was one figure whom Sir Laurence noted in particular: a big man on his destrier, with armour that shone even in this grey light. He sat on his horse staring fixedly at the castle and city, and Sir Laurence saw him pointing at specific locations. They were the places he himself would have chosen for placement of artillery. That must surely be Sir Roger Mortimer.

'So they've arrived at last,' Earl Hugh said, coming to join him. 'They have taken their time.'

Sir Stephen then emerged through the little door, peering about the landscape with interest. 'They have chosen their places with skill.'

'Don't forget Mortimer was here only ten years ago. He knows all the weaker points of the castle and city,' Sir Laurence said glooomily.

'Ah, of course. So he will try to attack from the same positions as before.'

'The city can withstand the assault better now,' Sir Laurence said. 'He destroyed much of the walls, and they have been rebuilt since.'

'What quality is the rebuilding?' Sir Stephen asked.

'Not first quality, perhaps, but good,' Sir Laurence said defensively. The Coroner's words sounded like a criticism, and that wounded his pride. 'The city is strong enough to withstand a serious enemy for some weeks; the castle is stronger still.'

He ran though the items in his stores. Food was good, while water was better, for with all this rain, the cisterns would be full. He had store of brimstone, charcoal and saltpetre, and barrels of pitch to be heated. When the enemy tried to storm the place, they would find themselves meeting with stronger resistance than they could have expected.

'The garrison is ready?' Sir Stephen asked languidly.

'They'll serve,' Sir Laurence responded.

'I hope so,' Earl Hugh said.

Sir Laurence could see in his face that same determination mingled with despair. It made him sorry for the old man, but he had no time to worry about him. The Earl would have to resolve his concerns some other way.

'Do not worry, my lord Earl,' Sir Stephen said. 'They look terrible in such an order, but they will have the devil's own task if they want to break in here. You will be safe for a while.'

'A while, yes,' the Earl said.

'And then,' Sir Stephen continued, 'we shall have to hope that they will be happy to accept our terms for surrender.'

Sir Laurence gaped at him. '*Surrender*? You are thinking of surrender? They have not yet fired a single arrow!'

'Sir Laurence, we need to be realistic. Look at all those men out there. Do you think the Queen wants them all to be here, tied up in front of our city? No. So what we must do is decide when we can give up the castle on the most advantageous terms. Because if we do not, if we say that we shall fight to the last man, we will be crushed and every man within the castle executed. So, no. We shall have to surrender. It's simply a matter of how long it will take.'

Earl Hugh leaned back and eyed Sir Stephen. 'We will *not* surrender the castle,' he said. 'The King demanded that we hold it, and hold it I shall. With or without your help.'

'I shall not fail in my duty, my lord Earl,' Sir Stephen said with a deep bow.

'Good. I would not wish to have so noble a knight held in the dungeon for sedition,' Earl Hugh responded, his teeth gritted.

Sir Stephen's smile was wiped from his face. 'Do you seek to threaten me, my lord? I would not allow any man to call me coward or traitor.'

'I said nothing about your courage, Sir Stephen,' the Earl noted.

Sir Laurence saw how Sir Stephen squared up to the Earl, who was himself standing more firmly, his legs fixed as though they had been planted in the stone slabs of the floor. His eyes were unblinking beneath his heavy brows.

'They have artillery, my lord, Sir Stephen – look!' he said quickly.

The tension dissipated as the two walked, one either side of Sir Laurence, to gaze out over the fields.

There were several slow-moving ox wagons, the great beasts lowing and plodding on under the constant urging of their drivers. On the back were the immense timbers that would be raised to make the siege engines.

'That is that, then,' said the Earl. 'They will begin to fire tomorrow, I expect.'

CHAPTER TWENTY-FIVE

Banks of the River Severn

As the rain lessened and they could see ahead more clearly, Sir Ralph tried to urge his party into a slightly faster gait. It was not easy. The two friars were unused to riding, and their inability to maintain their balance on slippery leather made the going all the more laboured.

Sir Ralph was reluctant to take an exposed route, because of the ever-present risk of being apprehended by a Hainaulter. While Sir Ralph had a letter given him by the Queen which gave him safe-conduct, he did not wish to put it to the test with an armed group of men, who might decide to try their blades on human flesh and search the contents of his purse rather than listen to him explain what the words meant.

But if for preference he would have taken them along a riverbed, the fact was that the streams were all filled with water, and it was too dangerous.

'Bernard, you ride on a little before us,' he said. Alexander and Pagan could ride to the rear of the cavalcade, and with

Bernard spying out the way ahead, all should be well. 'Keep your eyes open for any dangers.'

He didn't know this part of the country very well. There were bridges up to the north, if he followed the line of the River Severn, but they were leagues away. It was for that reason that he had decided to come here, back to the ferry which had brought them from Chepstow. That was at least a direct route, and it should take them further away from the Queen and her men. With luck, they would not meet any of her mercenaries.

Then Bernard lifted a hand urgently, and Sir Ralph threw a look all about them.

They were riding around a small wood, thick with brambles and thorns. It would be difficult to ride in there, for the horses would balk. To their right was a large pasture, with nowhere to conceal themselves. If they were attacked there was only one option – to retreat.

He hurried forward, gazing at Bernard questioningly.

'Men. Look!'

There was a fire. Smoke rose and trailed into the sky from a hollow up ahead, and as he stared, Sir Ralph saw a head appear over the edge. A lean man, dark-haired, climbed up and stared at them without flinching or hiding.

Sir Ralph studied him a moment. Then, 'Wait here with the others, Bernard. I will be back shortly.'

Baldwin had made them ride fairly hard as soon as they were over the river, but he still had reservations about Jack's riding ability. The boy was sat on his horse like a man with a spear's shaft stuck in his spine. He didn't slouch, but instead his manner was one of utter terror as he jolted and lurched. He had fallen twice this morning, and now had a large bruise over his temple that was blueing already. Thomas Redcliffe had muttered to himself at the sight, but the boy's plight was enough to stir the active sympathy of his wife. She insisted they take a halt to allow Jack to recover himself when he fell the second time, and Baldwin agreed. They had made a temporary camp in this hollow, and set a fire to warm their aching bones.

The sight of the men approaching was initially alarming. The two in front appeared to be wearing armour, which must mean that the Queen's forces were close, Baldwin thought. These two in particular were professional soldiers, by the way they stopped and looked carefully around them before continuing.

'Good day,' he called when the one rider trotted forward.

'And to you. Friend, you are travelling far?'

'We ride away from Bristol. We do not wish to be held in a siege.'

'Neither do we. The Queen's men are close to encircling the city.'

Baldwin nodded, and now he could see that there were two friars in the other man's entourage, he felt more comfortable. Friars were rarely involved in fighting. 'You are welcome to join us, friend.'

'I have to ride to the ferry,' Sir Ralph answered.

'We go there too.'

The knights exchanged a look. 'I would be grateful for company,' Baldwin said at last.

Before long, the friars and Sir Ralph were seated with Baldwin near the fire, while Pagan and Alexander saw to their mounts under Bernard's watchful eye.

Baldwin too kept a careful eye, on the woods themselves, and on the lanes at either side.

But most of all, he kept his eyes on these strangers.

Fourth Saturday after the Feast of St Michael[1]

Bristol

Margaret lay wide awake in their chamber that long, weary night, wishing to Heaven that she was already in the safety of the castle, and not out here in the city, feeling vulnerable.

The sounds of preparation for the siege were all around. Men were hammering on doors, rousing householders and shouting orders, while smiths beat at metal on their anvils. Other men were building obstacles in the streets, taking doors and furniture to block thoroughfares and create killing areas where the invaders could be trapped and slaughtered. There was one shrill scream of agony early in the morning that made Simon stir for a moment and roll over, but apart from that, he slept through it all.

She wished she could do the same. Lying here in the bed, with her husband snoring gently, Perkin whiffling in his little truckle bed, and Hugh grunting and mumbling over by the doorway, she felt restless and exhausted.

In the background was the steady rumbling of heavy machines, the slow, inexorable journey of the enemy's massive engines of destruction being levered and hauled into position so that they might pound the city into dust. For that was what they wanted, surely: to demolish this city without counting the cost to the people inside.

Yes, she could discern all the sounds of two forces preparing to kill or be killed. The furious effort of one to make defences strong in the few hours that remained; and the ferocious desire in the others outside the walls to get into the city and rob, rape and pillage.

[1] 25 October 1326

241

Margaret had no illusions. She knew that if the enemy got inside the city walls, she was certain to be raped. It was not to be borne.

Rising, she fetched her dagger and slipped the thong over her head so that the sheath with the wicked little blade sat between her breasts.

She was not angry or desperate. Instead she felt cold emptiness. All emotions were pointless. No, she knew her position all too well. If any man tried to take her, she would kill him if she could, and in the last instance, she would kill herself.

CHAPTER TWENTY-SIX

Banks of the River Severn

They had reached the river late in the afternoon, and there was no sign of the ferry. It could well have been on the opposite shore, but in the darkness, there was no way to tell; even a large fire could have gone unnoticed.

When he returned to Redcliffe and his wife, he found that Sir Ralph and the others had begun to make camp as best they could. There was no shelter to be had, other than that of a few trees. Jack had been given the task of carefully feeding the fire and making sure it didn't go out. He had succeeded in keeping it smoking gently until Pagan pushed him out of the way and began to tease a full, hot flame from the glowing embers.

Baldwin made himself a bed of branches laid cross-ways over each other. They would be soggy, but better than nothing in this weather. He eyed Sir Ralph's simple tent with a jealous eye, but resignedly told himself that in his youth he had been happy enough with a simple mattress of branches and the sky as his ceiling. Not that it convinced him. He had been younger then.

It was not only Sir Ralph who had a tent. Roisea and Thomas

Redcliffe had a heavy strip of canvas which they spread out over a bent limb, and used some pegs of sharpened sticks to stab the corners into the ground. It made a simple tunnel, in which the two could sleep. Baldwin eyed his own bed without enthusiasm, and decided that he would see what protection he could achieve from hooking his riding cloak to a bush and draping it over his upper body. At least that way his face would remain drier.

It was a relief when dawn broke and he could rise, rubbing his hips. There was no doubt that he was not the fit and healthy, nor the young man he once had been. The branches felt as though they had moulded his very bones to fit them, and the ridges in his flesh felt permanent. His blanket was a soaked mass of wool, and he experimentally twisted it in his hands. Water ran from it in a stream, to his disgust. That explained why he felt so wet and miserable.

He went to the fire, and set about adding some tinder to the warmer part of the grey ashes, and to his surprise, it caught. Working swiftly with small twigs and some more tinder, he soon had a little fire burning, and he prodded Jack until the boy was awake, ordering him to fetch more sticks while he kept the fire going. Before full light they had a good fire blazing, and a pot of water already boiling, with wine warming beside it.

Sir Ralph appeared soon after Jack had supplied a second load of logs, and the man looked as refreshed and contented as a cat after a bowl of cream.

'The ferry should be over here before long,' he said.

'Where will you go then?' Baldwin asked.

'The King should be at Cardiff by now. I will ride to him.'

'I too,' Baldwin said. He sighed.

'You are upset?'

'I do not wish to see the kingdom at war, but I would not break my oath.'

Sir Ralph stared at the fire morosely. 'We have the duty of service.'

Baldwin would have said something in reply, but before he could speak, he peered over Sir Ralph's shoulder. 'Troops!'

The enemy had not seen the fire or the encampment yet. There were only four men, all on horseback, with cheap helms on their heads and for the most part wearing only boiled leather armour without insignia – and no banner, which made them surely mercenaries or felons, Baldwin thought. 'We must stop them before they can ride back,' he whispered.

'I have safe-conducts from the Queen,' Sir Ralph murmured.

'You think they'll care?' Baldwin said. 'The Queen isn't here, and they'll probably be happy to kill us and steal our swords and horses.'

Sir Ralph nodded. 'We cannot wait to saddle the horses,' he said. 'They'll have ridden off before we could catch them.'

'No. We'll have to trap them here,' Baldwin agreed.

But any hope of surprise was already lost. Even as they spoke, Baldwin saw one of the men stop and point at them. Immediately, the four began to trot towards them, their mounts spreading out as though understanding that this could end in a fight. 'They have seen us,' he said.

'Pagan! Bernard! To arms!' Sir Ralph hissed.

Baldwin appreciated the tightness of the training in Sir Ralph's team. As soon as he spoke, there was a swift rustling, but no shouts, no questions, just organised preparations. For his own part, he took his sword in its scabbard and set it close by, leaning against a little tree.

The men approaching were within thirty yards already, and the leading man had a lance which he pointed at Baldwin as he trotted forward.

'Godspeed,' he called, and poured some hot wine from the pot over his fire into a cup. Sipping it, he rose, comfortable that his weapon was easily accessible.

The first man was within ten yards now, and he stopped, looking about the little hollow where Baldwin and the others had slept. He was a rangy man, unkempt, with a thin beard and eyes that moved all over the place quickly, but seemingly absorbing all. 'Who're you?'

'We are travellers. And who are you?'

'I'm Ivor from Hereford, and we're with Queen Isabella. What are you doing here? Answer or I'll have you taken to her to be questioned.'

Baldwin smiled. 'We are merely travellers, my friend. Now, Ivor, if you would like a little wine, we have some warmed.' He took up the jug again, welcomingly.

'You'll come with us, then,' the man said, and he trotted forwards. 'Yield,' he commanded, his spear's point close to Baldwin's breast.

Baldwin eyed the forge-blackened tip with the silver edges where the armourer's wheel had ground. It was nearly a yard from his breast, and he waited until Ivor was closer, the point a scant foot from him, before bending to set the jug in the flames.

'No,' he said, and grabbed the timber, pulling.

The man was seated firmly in his saddle, but his lance was a weight that unbalanced him. By pulling it, Baldwin had removed it from beneath Ivor's armpit, and now Baldwin grabbed his sword and flicked it free of the scabbard. At the same moment, Wolf came charging over. He had seen the way Baldwin grabbed at his sword, and now set up a baying that alarmed Ivor's horse, which bucked and reared, and Ivor was forced to drop the lance and snatch at his reins to control the beast.

Baldwin waited until the horse was all but calmed, before slamming the heavy butt of the lance into the side of Ivor's head.

His eyes rolled into his head, and he fell from the back of his saddle, landing with a thud on the soft ground.

Instantly Baldwin was at the horse, grabbing the reins and speaking to it gently. There was a short scream from over to the left, and he saw that the Squire called Bernard was standing and thrusting downwards with his sword, three, four, five times, to make sure of his man. Sir Ralph was further on, standing with his sword ready, while another man slowly moved about in front of him, a long sword in his right hand, his left empty, but already wrapped in a cloak so that he could bat away Sir Ralph's lunges.

The last of the men, Baldwin could not see. And then he spotted a man pelting away on horseback, and peering hard, he saw another horse in front. That must be Pagan, and without further thought, he mounted the captured horse and set off after Pagan and his intended victim.

Pagan's man was riding fast. Very fast indeed, Baldwin realised. Pagan's old palfrey couldn't possibly keep up, and Baldwin's beast was finding it hard to make headway, but then their quarry slipped left into a small wood, and had to slow down.

Baldwin spurred his beast on, and he lengthened his stride, neck straining, a snorting coming from his nostrils, as Baldwin gave him his head. The brute was a keen racer, and needed little by way of encouragement.

They pounded on the soft grass and mud, occasionally throwing up great gouts of muddy water as they hit puddles, and then the light was eradicated as they entered the woods.

Pagan was up ahead, and Baldwin bent low over his horse's neck to avoid the branches and twigs that snatched at his hair and shoulders. There was one, a splinter from a snapped bough, that caught his left shoulder and raked along it, ripping the material and making him grit his teeth at the swift rush of pain, but then he concentrated again, and saw the figure of Pagan lift as though by magic, legs flopping, arms reaching ahead of him as though trying one last time to grab his quarry, before slamming down on the ground and lying still.

Baldwin was riding at such a speed, he was already on the body; his horse sprang over it and carried on. The sight of Pagan was only fleeting, but Baldwin saw the stubby crossbow bolt protruding from his breastbone. It made him realise that he could be riding into a trap, but the thought was irrelevant. If there were more men here to ensnare him, he would be no safer if he turned and fled back to his camp.

And then, blessed relief, he was in an open space in the midst of the woods, and the man he sought was attempting to span his crossbow. Seeing Baldwin, he gave a howl of despair and aimed his horse at him, his crossbow raised in his hand like a club. Baldwin charged, and his first sword's stroke took off the man's arm at the elbow. The fountain of blood sprayed over Baldwin's face, arm, torso, and in his hair, where he felt it congealing. Then he was back, and the man was screaming shrilly, staring at his stump, waving it, oblivious to Baldwin and all else.

With one stroke Baldwin took off his head and the body rode on a short distance, the arm still waving wildly, a gush of blood erupting from the neck, until the body could topple slowly to the ground.

Not that Baldwin was watching it. His attention was fixed on the bearded head staring up at him from the grass, jaw slowly opening and closing like a fish's.

'You again,' Baldwin breathed.

Bristol

He knew his wife was unhappy. Leaving Emma Wrey's house yesterday, Margaret had sunk into a deep gloom, and their journey did nothing to lift her spirits. Returning by a different route, they came to a large barricade thrown up by the city, and that seemed to heighten her anxiety even more.

His Meg, his lovely Meg. He had loved her from the first moment he had seen her, when she was little more than a child, but tall, slender, fair . . . She was utter beauty. They married young, and their lives had been joyous until their first son had died. That had been hard. And it was then that he had last seen her looking like this. All the trials and difficulties of the last years, even when Despenser forced them from their home, had not caused this collapse in her appearance.

She was exhausted. Her eyes looked sunken, and there were shadows beneath them.

'Come, my love,' he said. 'You need to eat something.'

'No. I want nothing.'

'Wouldn't you like an egg, or warmed milk?'

'I am fine,' she snapped. 'I don't want food.'

It was not the time to try to force her. For now, he would have to hope that he might be able to tempt her later.

A groom arrived and told them that Sir Charles had arranged for them to have a room, so they left the inn and walked the short distance to the castle's gate, but when Simon asked where they could lodge their horses, he was told there was no fodder for the beasts; they would have to remain in their stable at the inn.

Simon felt that blow keenly. Even as Sir Charles came and confirmed that there was nothing more he could do, since the only beasts allowed inside the castle were those which were needed by the garrison, and those which were to be slaughtered, Simon fretted.

'I am worried, if they are taken . . .' he said.

'I know,' Sir Charles answered. 'But there is no point arguing with this command, Simon. In truth, you are better not to comment at all. The castellan is concerned about conserving food, and if you were to make a fuss, and people realised you were here solely to gain food that may not be forthcoming in the city . . .'

He needed make no further comment. Simon knew that if it came to a decision, any castellan in the land would order him and his family out of the castle. There was no room for sympathy in time of siege.

The chamber to which he led them was large, with a good fire already crackling in the fireplace. There were tapestries about the walls to keep the warmth in, and rugs thrown over the floor. Yet there was only one bed, no truckle, and one bench for Hugh to sleep on.

Sir Charles saw Simon's look. 'I shall order a palliasse for your servant and your son,' he said.

'You are very kind, Sir Charles,' Simon said. 'I don't know what I'd have done without your assistance.'

'There is no need to thank me yet, my friend. Wait and see what happens before you do that,' Sir Charles said. On hearing a bell, he spun about, startled. 'That's the alarm bell. I must go. Simon, would you come too?'

Simon threw an anguished look at Margaret, who was sitting on the edge of the bed with Peterkin on her lap. She nodded, almost without meeting his eyes. Peterkin did, though, and as Simon ran along the corridor and out onto the upper battlements with Sir Charles, all he could see was his son's petrified expression.

It set a new thought racing through his mind. He had lost one son. He *couldn't* lose this boy too.

Banks of the River Severn

Baldwin left the body in the clearing, but brought the man's horse back, leading it through the woods and out the far side, then over the grassy plain towards the camp. There was no sign of Pagan's horse. Baldwin assumed it must have bolted, and he struggled to lift Pagan's body on to the captured mount. It was enormously hard work, for the body would keep slipping and sliding off, but at last he had Pagan thrown over the saddle and lashed in place.

The others had finished off the men from the reconnaissance. The one who had been knocked from his horse by Baldwin was dead. Stabbed once in the heart and once in the eye, he would never rise again. Sir Ralph had taken his own man, too, and the fellow lay with a great slashing cut in his neck, while the last was pierced many times by Alexander's sword. Bernard too was injured, with a terrible cut along the line of his shoulder and down his right arm, but he swore it was only a scratch and hardly worth looking at. Baldwin did try to clean it, and bound it in an old cloth he found among Bernard's clothes. With luck it would heal.

But when he spoke to Sir Ralph, he learned that the intruders had done more than kill Pagan and wound Bernard. They had succeeded in finding Thomas Redcliffe too. One of the men had slipped into his makeshift tent and run him through several times with a dagger. The man who did it had been chased away by Pagan, a sobbing Roisea said, so Baldwin was at least happy that he had avenged her husband.

Sir Ralph was pleased with his own victory. 'The fellow was a good swordsman,' he said appreciatively. 'He had a fair amount of training, I'll be bound, to be able to hold his own so effectually against me.'

Baldwin shook his head as he saw the body. 'The men who came here were determined, I'll give them that,' he said.

'What do you mean?'

'The leader who killed Thomas was in charge of a group

which tried to kill him in Winchester some days ago. I was there, and that was why I decided to come up here to Bristol in the first place. I'd intended going straight home, but seeing that Thomas had been attacked, and because he admitted to me that he was a King's Messenger, I thought that joining him was my duty.'

While they had been talking, Roisea had joined them. Her face was streaked with tears and dirt, and she wiped at her eyes with hands that were stained with blood.

'What do you say about my Thomas?' she asked. Her voice was broken with despair.

'Madame, he was a messenger for the King, so he told me,' Baldwin said.

'No – he cannot have been. He has never travelled much.'

'Perhaps he was given a message to bring to the King when he was on pilgrimage.'

'Pilgrimage! I find it hard to believe that story,' she said. 'He told you that, didn't he? When he left home, he said he would walk to St Thomas's shrine, but I was ever doubtful. I never saw him try another pilgrimage in his life. Why should he suddenly begin now?'

'What did you think he was doing, then, madame?' Baldwin said.

'I thought he travelled to London to speak with other merchants, men who did not know him and were not aware of is failure, to seek his fortune with them somehow.'

'Why should he mislead you?'

'I don't know,' she admitted sadly. 'I think because he did not want me to grow hopeful. He felt as though he had failed me when his business folded, but it was not his fault all his lenders demanded their money back. Especially old man Capon. He was the most insistent.'

'But Thomas would not have found it easy to get money from

the merchants of London,' Baldwin said. 'He must have known that. They are the most hard-nosed, unpliant businessmen in the world. Prising money from their coffers is harder than getting it from the purse of a tax-collector!'

'My Thomas did, though. He persuaded them.'

Baldwin eyed her pensively. 'You say he succeeded in winning money from them?'

'He told me that he would soon have his reputation and his resources renewed.'

'He meant he would have money again?'

'He was quite sure of it,' Roisea said sadly.

Baldwin looked over at the body of her husband. 'And he made no mention of being a King's Messenger?'

There was no need for her to answer, and in any case, Baldwin was as keen as Sir Ralph to pack everything and leave. He left her there, ordering Jack to help her, while he gathered up his own belongings, before going to the body and searching it quickly for a message. There was nothing. Any message he held for the King must have been in his head, not committed to parchment.

They were on their way as soon as Baldwin had finished and Thomas's body had been set slumped over his own horse. Thomas and Pagan would be given a Christian burial when it was safe so to do. It was the least Baldwin thought they could do for the two men.

Riding to the ferry, they were pleased to see that the boat was clearly visible, and bellowing and waving, they succeeded in gaining the ferryman's attention. It felt like an age, but at last the vessel landed on the shore and the men could begin to board her. Sir Ralph insisted that the friars and Roisea should take the first sailing, and Baldwin was equally insistent that Jack should be safe.

Jack kept looking at Baldwin with a strangely earnest expression, rather like a lady's lapdog begging for a treat or to be allowed outside. He was obviously shocked by the suddenness of the fight, the swift deaths of so many men. But Baldwin had no time for the lad's fears, especially since he was nervous that the party's disappearance must surely lead to an investigation before too long. He did not want to be caught between the River Severn and the whole of Queen Isabella's host.

It was a glorious relief to see the boat sail away, and then a blessed age before it completed its cruise to the opposite bank. Baldwin paced fretfully up and down the shoreline all the while, chewing at his inner lip, casting an equal number of glances towards the ship and back towards the woods where the men lay dead.

'The boat is coming back,' Bernard stated laconically. Alexander was whittling at a stick with his short dagger, while Sir Ralph sat on his horse saying nothing. The three appeared perfectly easy in their minds, even with their friend and companion tied on the horse a short distance away.

The ship made its slow progress over the water towards them, and after what felt like half a day, ground its way up the shore. Sir Ralph and his men were first aboard, while Baldwin waited, and then he took the reins of the horses with the dead men on their back. As he did so, there was a cry from the ship.

'Get on board quickly! They're coming!'

Baldwin snapped his head around and saw a small contingent of horse, perhaps a vingtaine, milling about at their camp. Then the enemy saw the ship's sails, and there was a flurry of orders and activity as they remounted, ready to pursue Sir Baldwin's group.

There was little time. Baldwin took his own horse on first, and waited until the beast was aboard and held firmly before returning to the horses carrying the dead men. He had the reins in his hand, but some of his anxiety must have been communicated to Wolf, as the brute gave a bark, and set up such a row, that the two horses became nervous, and one began plunging wildly. There was a crack, and the lines holding Thomas snapped, the body tumbling to the ground, and then the horse was off, leaving Baldwin with a rope burn on the palm of his hand. Alarmed by the plunging of the other, Pagan's horse too began to rear. There was no time to calm it. Cursing, Baldwin released the beast, and it galloped off after the first.

He was about to run to the ship, when he remembered Redcliffe's purse. The man had been so proud of it and in any case, it was possible that there was money in it which his widow could use. Whipping out his dagger, he sliced through the laces holding the man's purse to his belt, and then ran for the ship. It had already pushed away a little from the shore, and Baldwin tumbled into the freezing water, holding the purse aloft, but then he almost fell under from the weight of his mail on his back. He recovered, and Wolf was at his side. On a whim, he thrust the purse into Wolf's mouth, and the solemn-faced dog took it gently, continuing paddling through the water to the ship.

Baldwin floundered on, and would have failed, had not Sir Ralph thrown him a coil of rope. Clutching it, Baldwin pulled himself up aboard, falling on his back to gasp for breath.

It was Alexander who reached down, grabbed Wolf by the scruff of the neck and tail, and hauled him bodily from the water.

CHAPTER TWENTY-SEVEN

Bristol Castle

Simon had never seen the host gathered before. He had heard of the massive forces which King Edward II and his father had gathered for their wars in Wales and Scotland, but had never thought he would see such huge numbers of men arrayed outside an English city. It was terrifying – and humbling.

From the battlements he could see north over a broad swathe of land, and everywhere there were men. Tents and canvas shelters covered the farther flat lands, and all about there rose smoke from a hundred fires. No, more than a hundred, he guessed. The sheer scale of it all was incomprehensible. It was like looking at a reflection in a pair of mirrors and seeing the images reflected on and on into infinity. Simon had never been particularly concerned about heights, but today, looking out at all those men, he was suddenly assailed by dizziness, as though he could topple from the walls.

'They're serious about taking the castle,' Sir Charles remarked.

Simon was grateful for his relaxed attitude. When Simon

looked at him, Sir Charles was peering at the men scurrying about below them with an air of calm amusement. This was what the knight had been bred and trained for. Not so Simon. As he watched the great siege machines being prepared, their arms being slowly winched down, their cradles loaded with massive rocks, he felt a sinking in his belly. Those rocks would slam into the side of the walls here with devastating effect. Surely nothing could withstand them.

A few minutes later, Sir Stephen and Earl Hugh arrived on the walkways, and the Earl stared out with as much shock as Simon himself had felt. 'So many! So many!' he said. 'What have we done to deserve all this?'

Simon had not been so close to the Earl before. He had grown to detest the man's son, Sir Hugh le Despenser, because the knight had selected Simon as an enemy, and Simon had been badly tested, but seeing Earl Hugh's horror, he felt sympathy for him. The scene was enough to rock any man to the core of his soul.

He gazed around at the other side of the river to the south. There too, large numbers of men scurried about, building wooden shields to protect fixed positions. Trees were being felled from a little wood, and hauled to the city by oxen, then cut up and attached to frames to protect archers and artillery from the arrows of the castle and the city.

But when he glanced east over the city itself, he was struck by the lack of preparation. True, there were some barricades in the streets which would serve to slow men attacking along them, but surely they would not stop a force like this, were they to gain entry.

Sir Charles saw the direction of his gaze, and commented, 'I do not think we can count on the city to halt their attack.'

'I can see no one trying to save it,' Simon said.

'These fellows are merchants and peasants, not warriors,' Sir Charles said with a chuckle. 'They saw their city captured only ten years ago, and they felt the indignity of failure, as well as seeing the result of their disobedience. Exile to many, the loss of property to more. It was a disaster. And their city was sorely hurt by the King's siege train. Why should they wish to see the same happen again?'

His attention was already moving on. Now he eyed the streets below, and Simon followed the direction of his gaze. There was a group of men walking from a large building, and all standing before it, involved in animated conversation.

'Sir Charles, what are they doing?' Simon asked, pointing.

The knight shook his head. 'I wonder.'

While they stood, Sir Laurence had arrived and stood grimly surveying the people down in the street. 'This is not good.'

Simon looked at him from the corner of his eye, wondering how to broach the subject of Cecily's murder. But it did not seem the moment, somehow. Not while the city was at risk of being overrun. Instead, he glanced down into the streets again.

Where Simon had seen the little huddle, now there was quite a group, all standing together and talking. Simon could see one man expostulating with another, then three or four who appeared to hurry up to them, listening. After a short altercation, the bulk of the men ran towards the castle, and there Simon could see nothing of them because of the line of the western wall, but the others set off at a run to the northern gate, and Simon watched with a frown as they disappeared behind a building. 'What are they up to?' he wondered.

Sir Laurence paled. 'They are going to open the gates! Sir Stephen, Earl Hugh, the city is about to capitulate, I think.'

Earl Hugh spun round and stared. There was a greyness in his features. 'No! No, they wouldn't. They must know that they only have to hold faith to the King and he will rescue us. They'd be mad to open the gates now! Don't they realise the King will exact terrible revenge for a betrayal like that?"

Sir Stephen said nothing. He had darted to the corner of the battlement, and was staring down at the roads. 'Leave it to me, my lord,' he said, and was off into the tower. Soon he was below in the court, bellowing for his squire and servants. In a short space of time, there was a hoarse shout, and Sir Stephen ran from the gates with six men behind him, all armed with axes, knives and swords. A moment or two later, Simon saw them pelting up the roadway in pursuit of the men he had seen before, chasing north towards the city gate.

'Odd,' Simon said musingly.

'What?' Sir Charles said.

'I'd thought that the second party were going to guard us here, so that no one could get to the city gate and prevent their opening it.'

Sir Laurence stared at him, and then cupped his hands and shouted to the guard on the gatehouse: 'Is there a band of men before the castle's gate?'

The answer came back that there was, but Sir Stephen had passed through them without trouble, and now they stood apparently ready to repulse any force from the castle.

Sir Charles leaned against the wall and closed his eyes, while Sir Laurence set his jaw and glared down at the city. 'I could get some men,' he muttered. Bellowing down into the ward, he ordered a party of men-at-arms to gather weapons, and strode to the tower's door.

Earl Hugh looked from Sir Charles to the city with perplexity. 'What is happening?'

'It would seem that Sir Stephen is also about to capitulate, my lord. I think that he is helping the city to open the gates.'

It was as he spoke that they all heard the roaring noise: the sound of a thousand men cheering as they entered the city.

Earl Hugh slumped as Sir Laurence returned. The knight gripped the nearest battlement and stared, but Earl Hugh could not look. He turned and slowly made his way to the staircase, his face waxen, like a man who had already died.

St Peter's Church, Bristol

The job of fosser at St Peter's Church in Bristol was not generally an arduous one, Saul thought; mind, it was possible that his duties would soon become more onerous.

As Saul the Fosser hobbled along St Peter Street, he reckoned that it was all to the good. Men tended to die quite often, and if their deaths were hastened for reasons outside his own control, he was content to take the pennies each body represented as his due.

'Ach, God's pains,' he muttered as he came to another of the irregular barricades flung over the roadway to stop horses. 'Oi! How do I get past here?'

A face appeared at the top, that of a boy aged ten or eleven. 'You'll have to go round, Grandad. There's no path here.'

Cursing all little boys under his breath, the fosser went along an alley as the lad had indicated, and soon found his way to the church.

There was no burial today. He left his spade in the lean-to shed at the side of the church, and instead walked over the long grass of the cemetery. There were three mounds of soil. Two had sunk quite well now, both being a few days old, and only Cecily's was yet rounded and proud of the grass.

He went to the nearer of the low graves and cast a wary look about him before thrusting his hand into the loose soil. It took no time to find the packet, and he took it out, shaking the

muddy soil from it and shoving it into his shirt. Then he rose
and strode from the cemetery as quickly as his gammy leg
would allow.

It was an ancient wound, that. When younger, he had been
apprenticed to a bowyer, but then he had had an accident: borrowing his master's horse without permission he took part in a
race against a friend. His horse put a hoof into a rabbit-hole at
full gallop, and crashed to the ground, throwing Saul over and
over. His prize was a badly broken leg that left him crippled, and
the loss of his apprenticeship. He was lucky that he wasn't
forced to replace the beast, which had to be put out of its misery.
That was the end of his aspirations. Now he lived from one day
to the next, surviving on the pennies he was given for each burial
and a small sum for keeping the cemetery neat.

Which was why the discovery of the little dagger inset with
rubies had been so thrilling. It represented a sudden change in
his fortunes. Every so often Saul had been able to 'rescue' some
item from a corpse – a pilgrim badge, a cross, or perhaps a silver
pin – but each was trivial and hardly worth the bother. Were his
theft to be recognised, of course, the consequences would be
catastrophic. The rector of St Peter's was ever-vigilant for mis-
demeanours, and Saul would lose his post for ever.

But this dagger made all the other items pale into insignifi-
cance beside its gleaming gilt and precious stones. And Saul
knew just the man who would be prepared to pay for such a trin-
ket, too.

Guy le Dubber was a short, thickset man in his early forties.
He had a flowing grey beard that entirely concealed his throat,
and covered the whole of his face from the cheeks down. A perpetual scowl almost hid his eyes, and what was visible glittered
with a shrewd speculation. Any man meeting him for the first
time had the impression that his value was assessed in the first

moments, and generally the result was unfavourable, if le Dubber's expression was anything to go by.

Saul had known le Dubber for many years now, and he entered the little chamber with a swagger. 'You'll like this,' he said confidently.

Le Dubber was sitting at his fireside, and stared at the little fosser with his habitual frown. He had a spoon in his hand, which he placed down, then wiped his moustache with the back of a hand. He rose from his stool, pushing aside a pair of hams hanging from a rafter, and said, 'I'm eating.'

'I've something you'll want,' Saul said without moving.

The broker hawked and spat onto his floor, then scratched his buttock and jerked his head to beckon his visitor closer. He walked around the hearth to the board under the window and waited.

Saul passed him the parcel, and the broker pulled at the twine holding it. He undid the wrappings, then Saul saw his brows rise with surprise at the sight within.

'Nice, eh? It'd made anyone happy, that would,' Saul said.

'Shut up.'

Saul subsided, watching. He had seen the gleam of interest in le Dubber's eyes as soon as the first ruby appeared from its wrappings, and knew that the broker would be able to make a lot of money out of it. He would start bargaining at five shillings, Saul told himself, and allow Guy to gradually knock him back to three. Three shillings! It was more money than he had ever possessed in one time. Thirty-six pennies!

'No. Not interested.'

Saul stared at le Dubber as the broker pushed the knife back towards him.

'What do you mean, no?'

'It's too dangerous. I don't want it.'

He's playing hard to knock me down, Saul thought to himself. 'If you don't want it, there're plenty who will.'

'Yes. I expect there are,' le Dubber said, and walked back to his stool.

Now Saul was feeling desperate. 'But, master, you can sell it for a lot of money! It's worth at least eight shillings, isn't it? I'll sell to you for five. Five shillings, that's all.'

'No.'

'Four, then – I can't say fairer than that, can I? It's worth double, and you'll make all the money.'

'You aren't listening. I don't want it. It's worthless to me. It's too valuable for me to have in my pantry, and I don't know where you got it from. Looks to me like someone's been murdered with it. You think I want people believing I killed someone for his knife?'

'No, but you can make a good profit out of it.'

'The kind of profit that gets you hauled off in front of the Justice of Gaol Delivery isn't good. *No*.'

'Three shillings.'

Saul watched as Guy picked up his bowl again and began to noisily suck at the pottage on his spoon.

'Two shillings?'

There was no response. Saul stared at his broker, then back at the dagger still sitting on the board.

It broke his heart. He breathed quietly, 'One shilling.'

'Not one penny. You don't listen very well, Fosser, do you? I said no. I wasn't dickering with you. I don't want it.'

'What shall I do with it, then?'

'Try a smith. He may be able to get the rubies out and melt down the dagger. It's the only way you'll get rid of it.'

'Melt it?' Saul said, appalled.

Le Dubber looked up at him. 'You want something back for

it? Right. That's what you do, then. Now, take it away from here. I don't want anything to do with it.'

Welsh bank of the River Severn

The ship reached its little dock with a soft scraping as the rope fenders rubbed on the wood, and the shipmaster ran to the ropes, flinging them to the waiting boy, who slipped them over upright posts so the seamen could haul the ship tight and steady.

It took a little while to get some of the horses from the ferry, and then the crew helped Sir Ralph and his friends to the shore.

Baldwin's horse was one of the first off, and he joined the rounsey on the decking, leading him away, off the hollow-sounding wooden planking and up to the grassy banks. From here, he could see all along the south and he felt a pang as he gazed down towards Devon and his home. If only he had gone straight to his wife instead of stopping and then agreeing to help Redcliffe . . . But then it was foolish to think that way. He had made a decision which had seemed logical and right at the time.

'Sir Baldwin,' Jack said quietly.

Baldwin glanced at the boy. He was standing with his hands tightly gripping his own mount's reins, and wore an anxious expression.

Seeing the knight nod, Jack blurted out, 'I think I must be a coward, Sir Baldwin!'

'Why is that, lad?' Baldwin asked kindly.

'When those men rode at us, I wanted to hide! I didn't want to be killed, and I ran.'

'Jack, that is natural. You are a brave boy, I know – you saved my life in France, didn't you?'

'Yes, but that was different. There wasn't time to think. Here, I didn't even want to protect the lady, but hid out with the baggage instead.'

'Well, you aren't a trained fighter, boy. It's not surprising.'

'But all of the rest of you went to protect the place.'

'We are older, and we have been taught our arms.'

'I had wanted to fight for the King. I wanted to take a sword and help defend him, but now . . .' There were tears of shame in his eyes.

'It is no bad thing to want to help defend your King,' Baldwin said, 'but it is a better thing by far to hate war. And I have seen enough men die to know that there is nothing good about it.' In his mind's eye he saw the fellow from Winchester, his stump of an arm waving as he screamed his horror at the realisation that he would never be able to use the arm again; his shock blinding him to the fact that Baldwin's sword was about to remove his head.

The boy gulped. 'Do you think I could learn to be brave?'

'Of course. Later, perhaps you will learn your weapons, and then you can decide whether to fight or not.' Baldwin gave him a kindly pat on the back, and the lad was comforted.

The knight's thoughts went to Thomas Redcliffe. The merchant did not have the training or skill to fight against men who had both. He must have been an easy target for the bearded man's dagger.

Baldwin wondered fleetingly if there had been more to Redcliffe than he had realised. Perhaps he had been carrying a message, and the bearded man had found it. Baldwin should have searched his body too.

It was curious to think that Redcliffe was dead. The men with him were all experienced, from Sir Ralph to Alexander and Pagan: they should have protected the man and his wife without difficulty. The idea of Jack throwing himself into the fray was ridiculous. He was much better suited to the delivery of messages – like Redcliffe, Baldwin thought to himself, remembering the purse.

When he had reached the ship, he had given the purse to Redcliffe's wife, Roisea, as the money inside was surely hers. However, he had not checked inside beforehand, and he wondered now whether he should have done. There could have been a message inside that would have explained why one of the men with Sir Ralph could have killed him, rather than one of their attackers. It had happened when Sir Baldwin had ridden off to help Pagan, so he had no proof that one of the bearded man's gang was responsible. He had not been overly concerned at that moment, though. Uppermost in his mind had been the idea of warm, dry clothing.

When he had an opportunity, he would ask Roisea, he decided. She might be able to cast some light on the matter. In the meantime, he would be forced to keep a close eye on the men.

Sir Ralph was walking up the bank from the ship. When they were all mounted, he gave Baldwin the signal, and they set off at a sharp pace heading westwards, to Cardiff and, they hoped, the King.

CHAPTER TWENTY-EIGHT

Bristol Castle

The castle was filled with urgent activity. The men inside began to rush about, making for the armoury as the alarm rang out, then hurrying back to the walls with polearms and helmets. One lad was tall and lanky, and his over-large helmet rattled and moved as he walked; normally, his mates would have poked fun at him, but not today.

Simon fiddled with his sword in its scabbard, pulling it loose and checking how easily it came free. It was a nervous reaction to the knowledge that there would soon, surely, be a fight. But the tension came from not knowing when, or what form it would take. Whether there would be a sudden assault or a gradual build-up of violence, he didn't know and couldn't guess, but he felt afraid.

It was less fear for himself and how he might acquit himself in battle, more that he was fearful for his wife and child. There was a terrible irony in his decision to bring them here inside the castle, since it was now the cause of their danger.

'They have given up the keys of the city,' Sir Charles said.

The men-at-arms from the Queen's forces were striding arrogantly about the city from all the gates already. Some Captains were already standing little more than a bowshot from the castle's walls, pointing out likely places of attack, while others brought up huge shields of timber covered with leather, and crossbowmen scurried nearer. Soon, from these safer vantage-points, quarrels would be fired at all the guards on the battlements, and there was little the garrison could do to defend themselves, other than keep their heads down.

Sir Charles turned to Simon as he was drawing his sword again. 'I am sorry, Bailiff. I had not expected the city to give up and throw open the gates with such indecent haste.'

'It's not your fault,' Simon said.

'It is, though. I should have considered how the city was likely to behave. Why should they risk themselves for the King, when Edward has already fled? Why would anyone try to hold true to him?'

Simon shot a look at him. It was the first time he had heard the knight talking in such a cowed manner; it was most unlike him. 'We should try to ensure that as few people as possible are hurt,' he responded.

'You are not a friend to Despenser, are you?'

'Not to Sir Hugh, no. But his father, the Earl, is not the same kind of man. I hold no grudge against him,' Simon said truthfully.

'Well, one thing is certain sure,' the knight sighed, peering down over the battlements. 'If we hold this castle against the men out there, it will not endear us to the Queen or Mortimer.'

'No. What will happen to us, when they break in?' Simon said.

'I don't want to think about that,' Sir Charles said.

Bristol

Saul the Fosser felt as though he was carrying a dangerous secret with him as he made his way down the street back towards his own home. He didn't know any smiths, and the thought of enlisting the help of a man he did not know was alarming. The fellow might just take the rubies and keep them. After all, Saul could hardly run to a law officer and complain. There was no one who could mediate for him if the things were stolen.

The fosser hobbled along with a face like a slapped arse as he considered the position he was in. His dreams of wealth were gone, his hopes for a sudden financial windfall evaporated. 'Might just as well have left the damn thing in the soil,' he muttered spitefully. But returning it to the grave was the last thing on his mind.

The broker had suggested one smith who was more reliable than most – a man called David, who lived nearer St Mary le Port, and Saul found that his feet were bending their way in that direction almost of their own volition. The road broadened out here, and the smithy was soon located: a man only had to follow the sound of ringing steel.

David Smith was slim and wiry, with hands callused and grey from the coals he worked with. His face was dark, but his eyes were as bright as a shrew's. 'I don't do horses,' he declared as soon as Saul appeared.

'I don't have a horse.'

'Didn't think so,' was the response, and Saul stood a moment, frowning, trying to work out whether he had been insulted or not.

'I have something . . .' he began hesitantly.

David was gripping a length of steel in a coal forge, working a great bellows with one hand to heat the steel to red heat. Leaving hold of the bellows, he used both hands to pull the bar from the fire and dropped it on his anvil. Grabbing a hammer, he began to beat the metal around into a curve. 'Best get it out, then,' he said loudly over the din.

The fosser looked all around, and then pulled the dagger from his shirt. He tugged the wrapping away, and held up the hilt for the smith to see.

David whistled. Reaching out for it, he motioned to the steel which he still gripped. 'Take this.'

Saul reached for it, passing the dagger at the same time. His hand closed around the end of steel, and he watched as the smith held the item up to the light. Suddenly realising that his hand was burning, he dropped the bar with a little yelp. Seeing the smith's disgusted face, he hastily picked it up again in a fold of his jack, and held it back on the anvil with his good hand, while he surreptitiously blew on the injured one.

The smith held the dagger up to the light, eyeing the two bright stones in a cursory manner, and then peered at the blade shaking his head and muttering. Then he rubbed at the top of the blade with his rough old thumb, and peered closer. He walked to his anvil and took a fine-graded stone, dampened it, and began to rub at the metal.

Saul, forgetting to blow on his scorched hand, craned his neck. 'What're you doing?'

'Seeing if there's a mark here. Polish away the old metal at the side, and you'll see the print more clear.'

The smith stopped, held the blade almost to his nose, and gazed at it. Then, with a nod to himself, he wrapped the dagger in the waxed material once more, and strode from the forge.

'Hi! Oi! What's your game?'

His attention split between the disappearance of the valuable blade and the danger of dropping the steel, Saul put down the metal bar and hobbled painfully outside.

He could see the smith up at the top of the alley, and hurried to join him.

'This is the one,' the smith was saying to a short, stolid-looking man.

'Fosser, eh?' the man said. 'How would one of them get his hands on a lord's dagger like this, eh?'

'Why? Who cares?' the fosser said spiritedly. 'That's mine, that is. Give me back my knife!'

'*Your* knife?' the smith said. His hand whipped out, and he took Saul by the shoulder. Saul squeaked and tried to dart away, but the grip of a smith is not so easily broken.

'It's not your knife, Fosser. I know, because I made it for Squire William de Bar. But I don't see him around here, so how did you get your thieving hands on it, eh?'

Bristol Castle

Sir Charles invited Simon to join him after he and Margaret had eaten some dinner. Simon was to be allowed to join the rest of the men in the hall while they discussed the various options open to them. The meeting had grown into a heated discussion within moments of them walking in.

'We know what the situation is. The Queen is outside, and gives no guarantees to any,' Sir Laurence said. 'We have to choose: surrender or continue to hold the castle and pray that the King may return to rescue us.'

'You dare to say that he wouldn't?' Earl Hugh growled.

'No, I say nothing. I speak only as logic dictates, my lord. I am sorry if it is offensive to your ears, but we must try to be realistic. While the city held, there was the possibility of holding the assault off, because at least they had a broad target to try to breach. If they were to pick a specific point, we could see that and run to the defence. But now? We have the castle curtain wall itself, that is all. They can bring all their machines to bear at any point they wish, and there is nothing we may do to prevent them.'

'This castle can hold. It *will* hold!'

'For how long?' Sir Laurence rasped. 'I am a loyal subject to the King, and to the Queen, too, but first to the anointed King of our land. I would prefer not to be in this position, but this is the situation we have been placed in by God, and by His faith, I will hold this to the last man breathing if that is the feeling of the men here. But it is not a course we can take without risk.'

There was a shuffling of feet at that.

'Are you all against me?' the Earl roared as the men began to look away or down. 'Listen, men, listen! The King, God bless his soul, has ordered us to hold this castle. He gave me the command of all his men, he gave me the stewardship of the city and castle. I will have any man hanged who tries to negotiate with the enemy!'

'I am sure you do not mean that,' Sir Laurence said sharply. 'If this was a question of discussing with enemies, my lord, I would agree wholeheartedly. But here, sir, we are talking about meeting with our Queen and her son. That means the next King of our country! You have no authority to prevent us from talking to them. This is not treason or sedition, it is commonsense.'

'I will *not* have you gainsay me, Sir Laurence! I am Commander here, damn your eyes, and I will see my orders complied with.'

'You have overall command of the King's forces,' Sir Laurence countered. 'However, *I* have a duty to the castle and the people of the city as well. And although it is a terrible responsibility for me, I have to execute my duty as I see fit. I will not permit the city or the castle to be laid waste just because of our interpretation of how the King would most like to see us behave.'

The Earl rose and slammed his fist on the table, making the cups and horns leap. 'I will not listen to this bullock-turd! You say you agree I am Commander, and that is enough. I am in charge here – *not you* – and we shall hold this castle, no matter what.'

'My lord Earl,' Sir Charles said smoothly. 'It cannot harm anybody to ask for an audience with the Queen. If we enter discussions, it does not mean we actually have to accept any terms given. All it does mean is that we know exactly where we stand. If we are informed that none of us will be allowed to leave the castle with honour, it makes all other discussions pointless. However, while we talk, we are delaying the enemy's plans, even if by only a little. We have supplies here, so the time will not hurt us. And when the talks break down, as they almost certainly will, they will have to start from scratch with their siege machines. It is a delaying tactic, my lord.'

Earl Hugh looked at him, and in that moment Simon realised that the old man was at the end of his tether. He plainly knew that if all went foul with the King, his son must die. Sir Hugh le Despenser was the most detested man in the realm, and for him there would be no hiding-place.

What was more, if the mob tracked down Sir Hugh, they might decide to enforce the most brutal punishment. Others had suffered that final torment, of being hanged, drawn and quartered. It was the most appalling revenge society could inflict, and Earl Hugh knew that if the mob caught his son, he could expect no sympathy.

Simon looked away. It was a hideous prospect for any father. He himself was fearful that his own son might die here in the castle, but how much worse must it be for a man if his son were forced to endure ritual public slaughter? It was at that moment that he began to feel sympathy for the Earl.

The meeting ended shortly thereafter, and the Earl walked

from the room like an old man; Simon noticed that none of the others in the chamber could meet his eye. It was like watching someone go to their execution, he thought. It only required the priest intoning prayers as Earl Hugh shuffled out.

But Sir Laurence was still at the table, toying with a reed while others muttered and mingled. Simon thought that this was as good a time as any to question him.

'Sir Laurence, may I speak with you?' he said.

'Are you going to call me a coward or fool, too? No? Then yes, you may speak with me.'

'I was asked to view a body the other day,' Simon began. 'It was that of a maidservant called Cecily. Did you know her?'

'Everyone in the city knew of Cecily. She was notorious as the maid whose family was butchered,' Sir Laurence said, leaning back in his chair. He aimed the reed like a dart, and threw it at Simon. 'Well?'

'You were seen with her on the night she died, and I wondered . . .'

'You want to talk to me about that? She had come to me to ask about the men who'd been released – Squire William and others – and I was able to tell her that he was dead. That was all.'

'You said just that and left her?'

Sir Laurence's eyes narrowed. 'You are asking whether I killed her, Bailiff? I did not. I was walking around the streets assessing the barricades I had ordered to be built. I didn't have time for her petty concerns – especially since the man she most feared was dead.'

'The Squire – where was he killed?'

'East of here, some miles away. Sir Stephen viewed the body.'

'At least she would have been comforted by that knowledge,' Simon said.

'Yes, so you would have thought – but, if anything, she was

more distraught. She only demanded that his men should be arrested in his place. Nonsense!' Sir Laurence blew out an irritated breath.

'So, what then did—'

But the Constable cut him off, standing abruptly. 'Enough. I spoke with her, she left. That is all that happened, and now, master, if you will excuse me, I have a castle to protect.'

Simon sighed. Sir Laurence was short-tempered, but that was not necessarily a sign of guilt. He had a lot on his mind at the moment.

Sir Charles led Simon to the buttery where the pair drank off a quart of strong wine each, but the drink had no effect on either of them. Outside the castle, they could hear cheering and singing, and the steady beat of a drum somewhere as people in the city celebrated their release and safety.

'What will happen?' Simon asked him, staring at a very drunk guard who was staggering along the wall of the hall.

Sir Charles shrugged. 'We will either fight, in which case we shall very probably die together, or we shall arrange a peace and walk out of here with our heads held high.'

'Which do you think it'll be?'

Sir Charles looked at him. 'Come, Bailiff. Let us try another jug of that wine. I'm not sure it wasn't off, eh?'

Fourth Sunday after the Feast of St Michael[1]

Bristol Gaol

The morning was, for once, blessedly dry, and even inside the repellent little chamber in which Saul the Fosser had been

[1] 26 October 1326

thrown together with three drunks, one of whom threw up for the early part of the night until he had emptied his belly, and then retched until he passed out, lying snoring in a pool of his own vomit, the difference in temperature was noticeable. Not warm, but not as icy cold as it had been.

'Fosser? Someone wants to talk to you.'

The door was pushed open, the rusty hinges screeching. In that enclosed stone space, the sound was like a dagger being thrust between the ears. Saul climbed to his feet, then made his way out through the door, past the gaoler, with his reek of old garlic and armpits, and found himself in a small chamber. There was a man there, who stood playing with the little dagger with its two rubies.

He was a very calm, quiet man, with a peculiar slow blink of his brown eyes. His hair was very dark, while his flesh was quite pale, a curious combination. He was wearing a long, dark-green tunic of very soft-looking woven material. It made Saul feel even chillier than usual to see such a rich, warm-looking fabric.

'You are the man who was trying to sell this?' the stranger asked.

'It wasn't my fault!' Saul said immediately. 'I was trying to make a little money, my lord, not—'

The man wasn't impressed by his assumption of his rank, nor by his protestations of innocence. 'Know that the man who carried this weapon was a felon who deserved the full penalty of law. If you killed him, it will not be weighed against you. But, if you know where his body lies, you must tell me now. I want to see him dead with my own eyes.'

Saul considered. There was the risk that this man was lying, of course, but he had the impression that the fellow was telling the truth. There was certainly no indication of any sorrow on his part for the late departed owner of the dagger. On the other hand,

Saul had no idea who the owner was, unless it was the tall knight at the graveside.

'I don't know who he was,' he said, and told all he knew. About the knight watching the burial of the woman, how he threw the packet into the grave while Saul replaced the earth, and then disappeared. 'I think he was in the castle. Perhaps he is in there now?'

'Perhaps he is. Describe him.'

'He was tall, with a long crimson robe, and . . .' It took only a little time to describe the man standing in the cemetery.

The knight considered him without speaking for a while. Then he nodded to himself. 'Very well. I believe you. You will remain here for a little longer, Fosser, but it's not a punishment.'

'Please, my lord, no! Let me go home. It's not as if I'll be able to run away,' he said, gesturing at his leg, hoping for sympathy.

'It is not in order to punish you, Fosser. It is for your protection,' the man said.

CHAPTER TWENTY-NINE

Bristol

He had not expected to be treated quite so well as this, but Sir Stephen knew that the Queen must be grateful for the gift he had brought her. There were not very many men who would bring her an entire city. In the great Guild Hall, he felt honoured to he allowed some time with her, her lovely little maid and one guard.

Isabella was a delightful woman. Quite the prettiest he had ever seen. Her fair hair and pale features were set off exquisitely by the black material of her widow's weeds, and everything about her appeared designed to drive a man's fancies to thoughts of bed.

'I am very keen to learn what is happening inside the castle, Sir Stephen. Do you know upon whom the Earl of Winchester depends most of all? He is a strong-willed man, I know, but all must have one or two whom they can trust above all others.'

He was tempted to make a flippant comment about her husband and the way that the King had always selected unsuitable advisers, but saw that such a view would be safer kept to himself.

'My lady, Your Highness, I think that the Earl is less strong now than when you last saw him. When would that have been?'

'It was last year, more than a year ago.'

'And his health has not improved. He fights because he can see no alternative if he wishes to protect his son.'

'His son will die for the crimes he has committed,' Queen Isabella said flatly. 'You know how he has insulted even me, his Queen? He took my city, this Bristol. All the revenues which were mine by law, he acquired to his own benefit. The city was a part of my dower, and yet he seized it all. It was ever an especial favourite of mine, Bristol. So pretty, is it not?'

'I find it so.'

'So, the good Earl is not content? And yet he must know that he cannot stand in our path.'

There was a knock at the doors, and in walked a youth. It was only when the guard snapped to attention, and the maid curtseyed deeply that Sir Stephen felt his heart lurch, and he bowed low.

'My son, this is Sir Stephen Siward, who yesterday brought us the city of Bristol.'

'You turned from your friends in the castle?'

Sir Stephen heard the pointed challenge. 'Your Royal Highness, I thought, and still feel, that it is more important to remain loyal to the Royal Family than to others.'

'Which others?'

Sir Stephen looked up. 'Men who would use the law to terrorise and steal. I have had experience of the murders committed by the Despensers. I would not be able to support a Despenser.'

'That is good.' The Duke of Aquitaine, Edward, son of King Edward II, walked to his mother's side, bowing and kissing her hand, before turning and studying Sir Stephen. Fair-haired like his parents, he had a glorious mane of hair, and his build was already that of a warrior, even though he was only just fourteen years of age. He also had some strength of character, from the way that he studied Sir Stephen with those serious blue eyes of his. 'But I wouldn't see all Despensers punished by association, either. The fact that one is dishonourable, dishonoured and must be punished for his manifest crimes does not mean his father is a felon. I respect the Earl.'

'So do I,' Isabella said. 'He has been good to us in the past. Perhaps he would listen to reason and surrender the castle, do you think? There can be no benefit in his keeping the fortress only to see it destroyed about him. The rubble of a ruin is hardly worth a single life.'

'I think he would plan to keep it in order to hold it for your husband, Your Highness.'

'I have no husband,' she said, and there was just a hint of heat in her response, although she recovered her sangfroid quickly enough. 'But were Edward to come here, it could not be for a very long time. Did you not know?'

'I am not sure what you mean.'

'The King has left the country. That is why we are gathering today. He has left his kingdom, and that means the realm is without a monarch. It has been deserted.'

Cardiff

It was a relief to see the castle appear in the distance at last. Huge, and beautifully proportioned, it was a sight to make Baldwin smile: so regular and symmetrical, it appealed to his sense of balance.

He was at the rear of their party as they rode down the final plain towards the castle with the great town at its foot. There were men at the entrances to the town itself, and Baldwin and Jack rode slowly to the gates as the rest of their party rode on ahead.

Here at least there were signs of normality. Flags and banners flew from the turrets and there was an air of calmness and peace about the place that made Baldwin's soul feel refreshed.

Their journey today had been uneventful, merely a fast walk through the woods and valleys of South Wales.

It was a countryside he particularly liked: verdant and hilly, it was much like his own Devonshire, although the peasants were perhaps rather poorer. They had come down a little green valley from the Severn, and Baldwin had been taken by that. At the bottom of the valley was a little house, the smoke rising from the end of the thatched roof. There was a cattle shed, badly dilapidated, and some other cottages as they rode past, but only the main farmhouse appeared to have anyone living in it, and even there the people looked poverty-struck. In fact, they looked to be no better off than Baldwin's villeins had during the famine of ten years before.

For all the beauty of that little valley, Baldwin had been glad to ride away from it, and point his rounsey's head westwards again. At least from there it was only some five-and-twenty miles to the castle.

The friars were happy to be away from Bristol, that much was clear. But they were also clearly of the opinion that they were leaping from the chafing dish into the coals: the King's anger on hearing that his timid requests for letters of safe-conduct for all those in the household with him was to be entirely ignored did not bear contemplation. Since Baldwin had endured the King's displeasure before, he did not envy the two their task.

Still, for the most part of the journey, all were taken with the constant threat that the Queen might have other men in the area here to attack them. She was as able to throw some forces ahead of her into Wales as any other warrior. And since she had Mortimer with her, who was the most experienced fighter of any in the realm when it came to border wars, a screen of horsemen around here was very likely.

They made good time, hurrying without over-tiring their mounts, for the most part without talking as all kept their eyes skinned on the trees and other likely ambush positions. However all had been well so far.

Poor Roisea rode with her face concealed beneath a veil, her head hanging, the picture of misery. The death of her husband had been most untimely. If what she had said was true – that he was about to make his fortune again – it was particularly hard for her because the money had not yet arrived. Now, she would remain as poor as before. She had lost everything.

He remembered their little house to the south of Bristol. At the time he had been in so much of a hurry to be gone, that the couple had not occupied his thoughts much, although Roisea's and Thomas's behaviour had seemed vaguely improper in front of him. It was hardly polite to be display such affection in front of a guest, especially a guest they hardly knew, and yet now, in retrospect, it seemed fortunate that the man should have died in the knowledge that his wife loved him.

Baldwin had already stabbed the bearded man who had led the attackers in Winchester. He had followed them all that way. Baldwin thought about it. It was very curious. He had never known of footpads showing such determination before. What's more, the fellow was with different companions, too, which implied that he was a leader of men, who was prepared to hire others to help him as he planned his attacks. Why attack Thomas Redcliffe? There would have to be a significant reason, to persuade a fellow to hunt a man all the way from Winchester, let alone from London.

The alternative, that he was trying to catch a King's Messenger, was more likely. Perhaps Redcliffe was thought to carry some dangerous message that must be stopped? Or perhaps it was more simple: he was killed because he had taken some business from a London merchant who resented his interference. The merchant could have paid someone to hunt him down and execute him.

But there was little point speculating. Better to leave such hypotheses to others.

Their way took them down a grassy bank to the road itself, a stony track that pointed like an arrow to the castle. Baldwin almost unhorsed himself riding down a particularly steep part, and he glanced back with a grin on his face, only to see Alexander a short distance away, gazing about him with caution.

It reminded him that even this close to the King, they would not be safe until they were inside the castle's wall – and with that thought, he spurred his rounsey on again.

Bristol

The hall was filled.

Sir Stephen Siward was one of the most powerful knights in the country, one of only two thousand men who could call themselves members of the Order of Chivalry of England – and yet he had never seen a gathering like this. The Bishops of Ely, Hereford, Lincoln, Norwich and Winchester, the Earls of Kent, Lancaster and Norfolk, as well as barons, bannerets, knights and squires, thronged the large chamber, all presenting themselves before the Queen and her son as the new rulers of the country – and that itself was shocking.

It was the sort of gathering that a man would see once in his lifetime. The prominent nobility of the realm and the Church were never usually to be found all in one place like this. It was a proof of the importance of the matter, and yet it was profoundly *wrong*. Sir Stephen knew it, and despite his part in helping bring it about, this gathering was enough to make his flesh creep, for all these people were here in order to change God's decision. His anointed King was being forced from his throne. In King Edward's place sat the Queen and her son.

A steward bellowed, and his staff struck the ground. The people in the chamber fell silent and the meeting began.

Sir Stephen knew that he would never again witness such an event, but it passed like a dream, and afterwards, also as in a dream, there was little he could recall. The main part was the declaration being read out: the King had deserted the realm. He was *extra regnum*. That phrase somehow remained fixed in Sir Stephen's head when so much else was gone. *Extra regnum*, outside the kingdom, and leaving the kingdom without a Regent.

That was not going to continue. Before the assembled nobles, Edward, Earl of Chester, Duke of Aquitaine, was declared Regent during the King's absence.

Watching him closely, Sir Stephen felt the Duke's mood was less joyous than he would have expected. A man who was presented with a kingdom should be glad, and the Duke would know that the people wanted him. There was near-rapture in the city when he entered, and Sir Stephen felt certain that his reception would have been no less enthusiastic wherever he had gone.

But as Sir Stephen watched him cast an eye over the men before him, he realised that the boy could see only rats gorging themselves. Edward had been held in France by his mother and her lover for the last year; since returning, he knew that his was the authority that allowed Queen Isabella and Mortimer to take over the kingdom. It was he who was being used to topple his own father, a distressing position in itself, but with the added irony that it would set a precedent for a future King – for Edward himself.

By destroying his father, he could well be planting the seeds of his own destruction.

Bristol Castle

When Simon left Margaret in their chamber with Peterkin, he was scarcely able to think straight. His wife was distraught with terror about the siege, and nothing would comfort her.

'Come, Bailiff,' Sir Charles said, seeing him in the corridor, and taking him to the Constable's chamber. 'You and I should witness this.'

Sir Laurence was at his table, which was piled with documents and scrolls, but his attention was not on them or his clerk, but on the man who sat before him.

Simon could scarcely recognise this ravaged figure as the man who had only yesterday been so sure of himself. There could hardly be a greater contrast between Earl Hugh then, and now. It was astonishing to see how he had fallen apart since the defection of Sir Stephen Siward.

'So, two are least have not deserted their King,' he said with a certain doleful satisfaction. He reminded Simon of a whipped hound that had expected another thrashing only to be given a tasty morsel instead. 'Not all have run away.'

'We have just learned that three more men of the garrison have climbed over the walls and run,' Sir Laurence said.

Simon nodded. 'How many are left?'

'What does it matter?' the Earl snapped bitterly. 'If the cowards will run, who gives a farthing for them? Their courage and valour has flown. Sir Stephen *ballocks* Siward took it with him when he ran, the bastard!'

'Surely we still have enough men?' Simon said calmly, although inside he could feel his belly grinding with trepidation. It was awful to think that the place could be left undermanned in the face of so strong an enemy. For the attacking forces it would surely be easy to scale the walls if there was no one to watch for them. And then, were some of the garrison to be tempted, a rebellion inside the castle could see all the loyal men at risk of death. Meg, too. And Peterkin. He wanted to be sick.

Sir Laurence said nothing. He sat with apparent composure as the Earl expostulated about the quality of the garrison and their leadership: 'Look at them! What sort of men are there here? The coward Siward has taken his men, and we don't know whom we may trust. I know my men will remain loyal to me, but what of the others?'

'My lord, we are all loyal to the King,' Sir Charles said. 'You know you can trust us.'

'I know no one!' the Earl spat. 'We are lost! You will not aid me!'

'This castle can hold with only a few men-at-arms, so long as we all stick to our purpose,' Sir Laurence said quietly. 'I am content that we can uphold our honour here. I made a vow to the King when I was made castellan here and I would not break it. But now it is different. The situation is changed.'

Simon was impressed with him. He was firm and calm under what must be immense pressure. Not so Earl Hugh.

'You think I *wish* to surrender?' the Earl cried out. 'In Christ's name, the King placed me in charge of all the south and west of the kingdom, and he ordered me to protect his realm so far as I may – and now, already, I must think of submitting, according to *you*.'

'To avoid unnecessary bloodshed,' Sir Charles murmured. 'If it were only we men, it would be easy to bear. But think of all the others – the women and children – who must also die. That is harder to support.'

'Yes, yes,' the Earl agreed, but his mind was already moving on. 'So, are we agreed?'

Simon looked from one to another, wondering what he could say. 'I don't know what . . .'

'We cannot continue to fight,' Sir Charles said smoothly. 'Not now.'

'I don't understand,' Simon said helplessly.

'The Duke of Aquitaine has raised his banner along with the Queen's,' Sir Laurence said. 'If we resist, we will be resisting the Queen and the King's heir. We will be committing treason. If we surrender, we shall be failing in our oaths to the King. But if we do not, we shall condemn ourselves. I would not willingly lift steel against the King's son.'

'There is nothing more to be said, gentlemen,' the Earl declared, and rose. He gripped the table as he wobbled. 'We must surrender and pray for terms. I cannot ask the men to fight their next King.'

CHAPTER THIRTY

The actual transfer of authority was an anti-climax, Simon thought. He had returned to the chamber to fetch Margaret and Peterkin as soon as the decision was made, and with them and Hugh, he made his way to the gatehouse as quickly as possible.

Down at the gates, Sir Charles was bawling for a man to whom he might speak, while the castle's castellan stood beside him, a finger pulling at his bottom lip thoughtfully. While Simon watched, he heard a sniffling and weeping, and when he turned, he saw two of Earl Hugh's men unashamedly sobbing. All knew that their master would be arrested. The Queen and Mortimer had good reason to think that a man like the Earl should be kept in a dungeon for the rest of his life. With fortune, he could be held in a decent chamber in the Tower, perhaps, or at Corfe or one of the other great royal castles. It was certain that he would not be permitted to go into exile. As the Queen now understood only too well, sometimes exile could mean an opportunity to recruit supporters.

There was a shout, then Sir Charles began to issue orders. In a short space, the gates were thrown open, and a small number of men walked inside, crossing the area to run up the ladders and stairs to the battlements. The guards already there were marshalled and marched down to the courtyard to wait. Simon was grabbed unceremoniously and brought to join them, as was Hugh. He threw a look at Margaret, and felt his heart wrench to see the tears streaming down her face.

They must wait for a short while, and then there was another order and a new man walked in.

Simon had seen Sir Roger Mortimer before, but then he had been in France, and Mortimer had worn the look of a man who was sure he was about to die. He was in exile, declared traitor by his King, and under sentence of death.

Not now. This was a man returned to pride and position. Confident, arrogant, certain of his authority. As soon as he entered the courtyard, he was looking about him, and then he began to point to specific points at the walls and inner buildings, ordering men to those vantages, others to hunt through the entire castle for people concealing themselves. Only when he was happy that the castle was secure, did he deign to look at Earl Hugh.

'So, my lord. It appears your scheming to execute me has come to naught.'

On hearing that voice, Simon felt his heart turn to ice. Mortimer was devoted to honour and chivalry – but was also known to have no scruples about punishing those who stood in his way. And Simon was one of those who had held the castle against him.

Earl Hugh made a brave effort, but his voice was querulous. 'I did not plot your death, Sir Roger.'

'Truly?' Mortimer said. He was clad in mail under his tunic, looking quite old-fashioned for such a modern warrior. But at nearly forty years old, he was already quite an age for a man

who had dedicated his life to serving the King by leading
Edward's men in battles from Scotland to Ireland. His hair was
grizzled now, Simon saw, but his build was still that of a fighter,
trim at the waist, powerful in the shoulder.

Earl Hugh stood with slow deliberation, as though his knees
and hips were giving him pain. As he stood, Sir Roger Mortimer
said nothing, but turned and beckoned, and then Simon heard the
sound of hooves walking slowly. Soon two beasts appeared
under the gateway. The first to appear was Queen Isabella, riding
on a bay mare that ambled in to stand at Roger Mortimer's side;
the second was the young Duke of Aquitaine, Earl Edward of
Chester, the King's son.

Earl Hugh bowed to both, and he smiled. It was clearly in his
mind, as it was in Simon's, that this lady would not order the
death of a man she had known for so long. 'Your Royal
Highness, I surrender the castle of Bristol to you. In the name of
the King, I beg that you treat all the men within with honour, and
that you respect the King's property.'

As he spoke, Sir Roger stood with arms akimbo as he looked
down at the older man, and his low, controlled voice carried over
the whole courtyard. 'Earl Hugh, you will be held until we can
convene a special court to consider your crimes. You should
compose your soul for death, my lord. I will take no pleasure in
it, but you have stolen and robbed for so long, you can receive
no other punishment. The realm demands it.'

'We agreed when I surrendered . . .'

'Nothing.'

The Queen called out, 'Sir Roger, there is no need to punish
the good Earl. He is not the man who caused us so much grief –
that was his son.'

'My lady, I am afraid that this man is guilty of numerous
offences. We can discuss them during his trial.'

The Earl shook his head, expostulating, 'We agreed that the innocent would be released! You promised that.'

'We agreed that you would surrender the garrison and the castle in the interests of protecting the innocent. There was no need to kill all the people in the castle, certainly. I am no blood-thirsty warrior. I only carry out those acts which are necessary for the good of the realm. Take him away!'

And Simon watched as the old man was grasped by both arms. His sword belt was unbuckled, and the sword and dagger allowed to fall to the ground, while he was firmly marched away to the little gaol set into the wall.

Fourth Monday after the Feast of St Michael[1]

Bristol Castle

There was a stillness in the cool air that morning, and Simon was stiff and uncomfortable as he rose.

They had been given some few blankets, but for the most part the garrison had been forced to sleep on the stone paving of a hall near the entrance to the castle. The chill felt as though it had entered his very marrow, and Simon prayed that his wife and son were safe. One thought nagged constantly at his mind. He could imagine Peterkin huddled in a corner while men took Margaret for their own pleasure – the little boy forced to watch, Margaret biting her lips to stop her cries so that he shouldn't be too alarmed.

Hugh's voice was low and sulky. 'Reckon we'll be released?'

'What do you think?' Simon snapped. 'They've taken our weapons, and we're stuck here like felons. I doubt they intend to give us gold for a journey home.'

[1] 27 October 1326

Hugh said nothing, but shifted so that he was sitting upright. The man on his right was snoring, with a great bloody mark on his nose. He had been slow to respond when given an instruction to move towards this chamber, and the guard with him had slapped him across the face with a steel gauntlet, breaking his nose and almost knocking the fellow unconscious.

Seeing his servant shivering badly as he huddled himself into a small shape, Simon was instantly stabbed with pangs of contrition. 'Hugh, forgive me. I was thinking of Meg when you spoke.'

''Tis all right. I just don't like being stuck in here.'

It was more than that. Simon knew that Hugh had never liked towns. He was a son of the moors. Raised near Drewsteignton, he had watched flocks as a boy, learning how to fight, how to cook and eat on his own out on the rich pastures bounding the moors. For him to be locked in here, in a small room with a lot of other men, was like taking a lion and caging it. He needed to be able to breathe the clean air.

Rob lay in the corner of the wall; his mouth was open, and he was the picture of ease and comfort. His childhood had been spent in the port of Dartmouth, and to him a bed of stone floor and a scrap of rug was plenty. Having had threats of a thrashing from the sailors who were his mother's lovers all through his life, the risks of his execution did not seem to affect him. It was just one more hazard. He had survived so many already in his short life.

Simon's further contemplation of his servant was stopped as the door's bolts slid back noisily. There were two, and as the last shot open, the door was pushed inwards. Three men with cudgels in their hands blocked the way, and the man in front, an ill-favoured watchman with a week's growth of beard and the eyes of a ferret, slapped his against his open palm as he gazed about the room. 'Where's the one called Bailiff Puttock?'

Simon stood. 'I'm here.'

'Come out here.'

Simon glanced at Hugh. 'What of my servant?'

'I didn't call him, I called you. Get out here!'

There was little choice. Simon walked out, trying to catch Hugh's eye, but the servant hardly looked his way.

Bristol Castle

The walk from the cell to the hall was brief, and yet to Simon it was as though he had walked from a scene of Hell into Heaven, and the fact filled him with a strange euphoria.

Inside the castle's hall, he felt his belly lurch as he saw Margaret and Peterkin sitting on a bench engaged in animated conversation with a man in a bright green tunic. It was only when he turned that Simon recognised Mortimer.

'Sir Roger,' he said, bowing.

'So, Bailiff. We meet again, and this time in our own lands! Please, come, sit with us. We have much to discuss. You would like some food?'

'I would be very grateful,' Simon said, and threw a quick look at his wife.

'I am fine,' Meg said, and in her face he could see no untruth. Her smile told him that she had slept safely, which was more than he could have hoped.

'She has been kept safe from the men of the castle, Master Puttock,' Mortimer said, seeing Simon's expression. 'Don't fear for her.'

'What do you want from me?' Simon asked. 'You have pulled me out of the prison, but you've left my men in there.'

'Perhaps I can release them too before long,' Mortimer said, and gave a sharp whistle. Soon a steward entered the room carrying a large cauldron of pottage, which he set beside the fire.

Another man brought two loaves of bread, which he broke open and left on a trencher, while a bottler supplied a pair of large wine jugs. 'First, though, eat and listen. I have much to tell you.'

Simon sat on a stool and took a mazer of wine, which he drained. He hadn't realised how hungry he was, but the lack of a meal the previous night, followed by no breakfast, had left him with a belly that felt like a pig's bladder with the air let out. There was a rush of warmth as the wine hit his empty stomach, and then a sensation of near-dizziness. It was so intense, so delicious, he held out his mazer to the bottler to be refilled.

'You were investigating a murder, I believe, when I arrived here?'

The question so surprised Simon that he almost choked. He shot a look at Margaret, but her frank incomprehension was a picture. 'Yes.'

'The dead woman was called Cecily, I believe. And she was slain by a man who may still be here in the city?'

'He's bound to be, since he killed her after the city's gates were locked.'

'That simplifies matters. Very well – the woman was killed by a man called Squire William de B—'

'I think that is unlikely.'

'Perhaps you should tell me what you know first.' Sir Roger smiled thinly.

'She was found dead,' Simon said, and went on to tell about the murders of the Capons and their daughter and grandchild by the Squire and his men. 'I have not managed to get far with the discovery of the killer. I had supposed it could be the Squire himself, but now Sir Laurence has told me that Sir Stephen held an inquest over Squire William's body before she died, perhaps Cecily was murdered by one of his confederates:? But if so, why wait so long to kill her? They could have got rid of her much sooner.'

'True enough,' Mortimer acquiesced.

'It is the case that finding anyone in the city in the last days has not been very easy,' Simon added heavily.

'Perhaps so. But I would have the murderer pursued. He is guilty of a reprehensible crime, and I would see him punished for it.'

'Oh. Aye.'

'You sound doubtful?'

'I see little profit in chasing about the countryside trying to find a man who could be almost anywhere.'

'That is not the point,' Sir Roger said sternly. 'If it is felt, or believed, that a man can escape punishment here, the whole city could begin to behave in the same manner and I shall not permit that to happen. All those guilty of crimes will be held up to exemplary punishment so as to deter others. And it is important that this particular man is discovered. After all, Squire William was a friend and ally of the Despenser. That, so I have heard, is the true reason why he was released after the killings of Cecily's master and family. I will *not* let it be said that those who kill my enemies can rely upon a more gentle judgement than others. Those murders were a disgraceful act, and we have to show now, more than ever, that all felons will be sought, found, and brought to justice. That is what the law is for. Under any King, the law must be supreme.'

'Yes,' Simon said. He wanted to ask about his servants again, but there was something in Sir Roger Mortimer's face that put him off for the moment.

'No one can be above the law, don't you agree?' Mortimer repeated.

'Yes, I do,' Simon said. 'I have served the law all my life.'

'Then I would like you to find this murderer and bring him to me for justice,' Mortimer said.

Simon nodded, but he was doubtful as he eyed the tall knight. 'Sir Roger, there is clearly more to this than is apparent. If it is not disrespectful, may I know the reason for your interest in the woman's murder?'

'All you need know is that this dagger,' Mortimer said, pulling the bent knife from under his tunic, 'was thrown into the grave by a man who came to witness the woman's burial. The fosser himself retrieved it. Speak to him. He may be able to help you.'

CHAPTER THIRTY-ONE

Cardiff

The excitement in the town was palpable as the ship was seen approaching early that morning.

Like the day before, the weather was sunny, and warm when the sun touched a man's face or hand, but the breeze was chilly, and Baldwin saw Jack pulling his cloak tighter about his body as the wind from the sea picked up.

They had slept the previous night in a stable. Hunt as they might, there seemed to be no beds available for any money. Cardiff was packed with men who had depended upon the King for their livelihoods. With the turmoil in the country, they were hoping for some form of rescue before Mortimer arrived, which they were all convinced would not be long.

It was a smooth sea that the King's cog sailed on. It came about the harbour, and then put in at the quay a little before noon, the timbers scraping and echoing hollowly. Sailors idled on the ropes about the sails, hauling on the canvas and tugging it up before lashing it in place, while others lounged about the deck in attitudes of boredom. Theirs had been a short journey, but with the weather they must have endured, Baldwin was sure that they would have had enough excitement.

After docking, although some of the crew strolled ashore, and a tall sailor with a large axe waited at the gangplank as though preparing to guard it against any who would dare to attack, the ship remained quiet for some while, and Baldwin began to wonder whether this was the right one after all. Sir Ralph was nearby, the friars behind him, and all were waiting with tension in the air. Nobody knew how the King would react to the news the friars brought.

At last the ship's little cabin door opened, and two men stepped out. They walked to the gangplank, and then Despenser himself strode into the air, staring about him with a furious eye. It was that which made Baldwin think that he was beginning to lose his mind.

It wouldn't be a surprise after the last weeks. Everything which Sir Hugh le Despenser had built up – his money, his properties, his lands – all were at risk now, because he had thrown his hand in with the King. In the last month, he had seen the whole of his empire topple and fall. It would be enough to make any man despair.

However, Despenser's present pallor was not caused by the losses he was incurring; they sprang from a more mundane cause. As Baldwin watched, he saw how the man's attention kept wandering to the ship's rail, and then realised that he was suffering from sea-sickness.

The King came to the deck a short while afterwards, and sprang up onto the gangplank with the enthusiasm of a much younger man. Once he was on land, the other men joined him.

'Sir Ralph, I am glad to see you!' the King said, striding up to them.

Baldwin, bowing as low as Sir Ralph, was slightly surprised

by the effusiveness of the greeting. It was as though Edward had decided to become the most popular monarch the realm had known.

'Sir Baldwin too, I am most pleased to see you. I trust you are both well?'

'Very well,' both men said, shooting a glance at each other.

'Good. And the two estimable Brothers. My friends, I hope I find you unharmed after your travels? Excellent!'

'Your Royal Highn—' Sir Ralph began, but the King cut him off.

'No, Sir Ralph. Surely we need a little wine and food first. Poor Sir Hugh has been terribly upset by the voyage. It was particularly rough until yesterday, and I am very afraid that he has lost his sea legs. You know, we were almost hurled against the rocks at Lundy; a ferocious wind, it was.'

The King's men had already prepared him a chamber in the castle, and it was to this that they went, the King marching briskly along as though finding it hard to suppress his enthusiasm. Despenser was a pale, anxious wraith in comparison, his whole demeanour that of a man who knows he is cursed.

When they reached the chambers, the King strode to his seat near the fire and sat, stretching luxuriously. His handsome face was a little burned by sun and wind, and his blue eyes appeared to gleam with more intelligence than before. The journey by water had done him good, Baldwin thought. To escape the immediate risks and dangers had apparently worked like a tonic on his frayed nerves.

'You know, Sir Baldwin, I was intending to break our journey on Lundy Island, just to be away and rest. We could not stop, though, for the wind and high seas threatened to dash the vessel on the rocks, and so it came into my head that we should aim direct for Ireland, but that too did not work. The winds were

299

quite contrary for us, and we beat up and down, but made no headway – is that not so, Sir Hugh?'

Sir Hugh mumbled something, and when Baldwin glanced his way, he saw that the adviser had a finger in his mouth and was worrying at the remains of a nail. The repetition of his tale of the rocks surprised Baldwin, and then he realised: the King was not refreshed at all. He was merely acting the part, demonstrating his confidence so that those about him would not guess at his inner desperation.

The King was talking again.

'And then it came to me, Sir Baldwin. You see, I am the King. I cannot leave my realm, can I? That would be to deny my duty, which is to protect my kingdom. And if the kingdom ever needed protection, it is now. With my poor wife so woefully misguided, and my son led unthinking into the clutches of Sir Roger Mortimer, that evil traitor, clearly the worst thing I can do is sail off to Ireland. After all, by the time I return, Mortimer might have done untold harm to my people. So it is better, I think, that I return. And it is God's will, that is clear, for his wind blew me straight back here.'

'I see.' Baldwin did not look at Sir Ralph, but was keenly aware of the knight at his side.

'Now, I trust that the Queen had a message for me?'

The friars tensed, and then both bowed their heads.

'Your Highness,' Mark began. 'She did *not* promise to protect those who are with you. She swore that those who were guilty of crimes against the realm, against her or your son, would be punished. There would be no safe-conduct for any of them.'

'None?' the King asked, the smile still on his face. Behind him, Sir Hugh le Despenser began to worry at another nail.

'None at all,' the friar said quietly. He had his eyes closed,

Baldwin saw, as though expecting to receive a sword-blow at any moment that would end his life.

'Then we shall have to ensure that none are captured by that harpy!' the King suddenly exploded. He rose, stalking about the room, a hand on his sword hilt, while he gesticulated wildly with his right. 'The bitch chooses to threaten us – *all* of us? When did she accumulate such authority in my realm? Does she seriously believe that the mere possession of my son will force me to accept the threats of rebels, traitors and foreign mercenaries? The bitch will soon learn: she will learn that my will is the will of the *King*! If she seeks to pit herself against me in battle, she shall do so! I will stand with my banner, if there is only one herald who will hold it with me! I will never submit to such foul threats and dishonour, damn her soul forever! Sweet Jesu, as You sit at the right hand of God, hear my prayer! Protect my son, save him from her wiles, and aid me to strike down the foul traitor Mortimer. God help me in this. I will not rest until he is dead.'

'My lord, there is more,' Sir Ralph said. 'As we left, the city of Bristol was being surrounded. I fear that . . .'

'It is besieged, I know,' the King interrupted. He took a deep breath. 'I need more men to go and lift the siege.'

'Sire, I am afraid it is too late for that. The siege has ended. The city capitulated.'

King Edward slowly turned to stare at him. 'What? No, Bristol would not surrender. The walls are strong, the city is powerful . . .'

'It is true, my lord,' Sir Ralph said, and brought forward the messengers.

Robert Vyke felt overawed as he cast a look at all the great men in this chamber. He was one among three messengers here, and had been told to wait until he was called inside. Seeing the

King, he fell to his knees. 'Your Majesty, I am sorry to bring such news. I have to tell you that the good Earl Hugh of Winchester arrived, but he could not hold the city for long.'

'Had the city fallen when you left?' Despenser demanded.

'No.'

Despenser gave a satisfied nod. 'Then what of the castle?'

It was another messenger who answered now. 'Sire, the city had fallen when I left it two days ago. There was a traitor in the castle who ran to open the city gates to the Queen and Sir Roger Mortimer. They rode into the city without opposition. It was shortly after that, that Sir Laurence Ashby asked that I ride to you to warn you. He said that the castle would likely not be able to fight on.'

'I too fear that the castle itself cannot survive long with the city in Mortimer's hands,' Sir Ralph said.

'Why?' Despenser shot out. 'There are sufficient men there to protect it, and they should have been provisioned well. Why wouldn't they be able to defend the castle? It was held before, when the city rebelled against the King ten years ago.'

'Sir Hugh, when the castle was last attacked, it survived a long while. But then there was a strong garrison inside, and they knew that the *posse comitatus* was outside the city. They had a clear view of their rescuers. This time, they know that the Queen is all-powerful. How can even your father maintain the fighting spirit of the men there, when they know that the King has no force with him. How can they hope to be relieved? Without that hope, there can be no commitment to holding on to the castle. Why would men risk their lives for a vain hope?'

'*No*. They can't have given up.' Despenser had gone even paler of hue. 'My father's there, he'll put some spirit into them. The garrison won't submit so easily with *him* in charge. He's a good motivator. Knows his men.'

'Sir Hugh, I believe that the city must fall before any form of relief could be gathered,' Sir Ralph said. 'For that reason, I recommend that you, Sire, should seek to return to your ship and make your way to Ireland. At least there the population may have remained loyal to you.'

'My people *are* loyal! It is only the damned barons who seek more control over me – they're the ones who want to have me as a puppet, pulling my strings for me, telling me what I can and can't do. Well, I won't let them! I will gather a new host from here, from the Welsh.'

'Your Royal Highness,' Sir Ralph began.

'Shut up!' Despenser snapped. 'The King has spoken, Sir Ralph, and you would do well to consider how to help him, not hinder him with pointless objections – if you wish to keep your head on your shoulders!'

Bristol Castle

The hall was filled with smoke from the fire, and the steward had already sent for more wood that was better aged and would smoke less.

When he was led in, at first Earl Hugh of Winchester was hopeful that this might prove to be a swift meeting designed to fine him and perhaps strip him of some of his honours, but the first glance about the chamber was enough to drive a dagger of ice into his spine.

If it were not for the strong arm of his servant, he would have toppled and fallen right there before the men, but he managed to make his way to the chair which had been set before the tribunal.

He could feel his legs tremble on his way there. It was the longest walk he had ever undertaken. His worst enemies were seated staring at him as he crossed the floor.

Sir Roger Mortimer, the Earls of Kent and Norfolk, brothers to King Edward himself, then two retainers of the Earl of Lancaster, who had himself been killed by the King, and Henry of Lancaster too. All detested the Earl and his son, and all would take delight in destroying him. He knew that.

His life was to end.

'My lords, where is the Queen?' he asked, and was surprised by how firm and steady his voice sounded.

'Silence, Earl Winchester. You have no right to speak in this court,' Mortimer said flatly. 'If you speak, you will be gagged.'

'May I not speak in my defence?'

'No. We accord you the same rights you accorded to the Earl of Lancaster when he was captured. Your crimes are so manifest and obnoxious to all thinking men that you deserve no defence.'

'Of what am I accused?'

'Silence!' Sir Roger snapped. He nodded to a clerk at a table nearby, who stood and nervously began reading from a list.

Earl Hugh listened with his face kept carefully blank. There was a slight pain in his breast over his heart, and his bowels felt as though they had turned to water, but over all that he was aware of a slow, building anger. That these men should think they could dare to bring him to trial! He was an Earl, the same rank as the highest in this chamber, and they thought they could serve punishment to him like some churl from the street? They would learn differently. Surely the Queen wouldn't allow them to continue, once she heard. He had never hurt her. And the fact that he had agreed to give up the castle must count for something. He only prayed that his son would get to Ireland, that his own predicament would delay matters sufficiently for his son to make good his escape.

Not that they would dare to carry out any punishment. Not of a truly condign nature. He was a friend to the King, and

Edward's fury would know no bounds, were he to learn that someone had hurt one of his chief advisers.

So, his crimes were legion. He was to pay for supporting his son and his son's government, for making laws that stopped men from defending themselves in court, for enriching himself at the expense of others, of stealing from the Church, and for participating in the execution of Earl Thomas of Lancaster, the Earl who had himself tried to accroach all power in the realm to himself, and control the King. A number of crimes. All perhaps repellent to the men here, while all were also designed to service the King. It was he who had demanded the removal of Thomas of Lancaster; he who had wished for strong government. Earl Hugh's crime was to have supported his son. He was a father! Who would not do the same in those circumstances?

He opened his mouth to reject these ridiculous allegations, but Mortimer glanced at him, and in that look, Earl Hugh saw pure malevolent glee. This was not a show trial to scare a man before throwing him into confinement. This was a trial for his life, but a trial at which no argument might be submitted in his defence. His judges put on a fine show of deliberating over possible penalties, but the crimes themselves were accepted as proven. And there was only one punishment to suit the crimes, he realised: he was to die.

It was curious, to sit here and listen to the men talking about him in this abstract manner, as though he was not there. Only Mortimer and Lancaster would occasionally look at him, as though to remind themselves how repellent he truly was. The others tended to avert their eyes, as though they too felt a little of the guilt of sentencing a man without giving him even the semblance of fairness in his trial. It was a formality, this court, not a court of law in which the truth was weighed and assessed among other evidence.

He had treated men in similar ways in the past. Sometimes it was necessary to make a show of a man before his comrades so that they might see the all-powerful nature of the law. But today, here, Earl Hugh was less convinced of the merits of that argument than when he had himself sat on the seat of judgement.

The Queen – she would save him. They must give him time to speak with her, he decided. Even Mortimer wouldn't want to execute him out of hand. The King would assuredly avenge the death of a man so senior in his household.

'You are sentenced to be drawn from this place to the place of common execution in the city,' Mortimer said. 'There you will be hanged by the neck until nearly dead, and then beheaded.'

The Earl nodded stiffly.

'The sentence of this court will be carried out at once,' Mortimer finished.

Earl Hugh felt his throat close up. His muscles, when he tried to stand, had lost their vigour, and he must remain seated for a few moments before he could rise. It was as if he had been given a blow on the skull. For those few moments, he found it impossible to concentrate.

A glance at Mortimer did the trick. The sneer on the man's face was sufficient for Earl Hugh to wave away the hand offered by his old servant, and to be able to rise to his feet. Haughtily he turned from the tribunal and set off to the door.

He would have to speak with a priest and consign his soul to God. There was to be no period of grace. He was to die today. Now.

He had only one hope: that his son would at least have made it to Ireland. That was where he and the King were heading for, and perhaps they were already there. If so, at least the his death might serve some useful function, because it would ensure that Mortimer and his army remained here in Bristol.

If there was one thing he wished, it was that he might have a little time to see his son. To talk to him, and to advise him how to strive to capture the men here in the room. To catch them and see them punished for their presumption.

But mostly he just wished he could see his son one more time.

CHAPTER THIRTY-TWO

Cardiff Castle

The outburst from Despenser had stilled everyone in the room. Sir Ralph said nothing, but there was a gobbet of spittle on his cheek. He reached up and wiped it away without comment, before bowing low to the King and slowly walking backwards from the room.

'Where do you go?' Despenser demanded.

'To prepare the remaining members of the King's household to ride wither His Majesty commands,' Sir Ralph said with cool politeness, and was gone.

Edward gave a loud expostulation, lifting his hands and letting them drop again. '*Oh*! Why do I have to suffer in this way? If only I had one General in whose efforts I could trust. A man with the tactical genius of . . .'

He was quiet before he could say the name, but Baldwin was sure that he was about to say, *Sir Roger Mortimer*. The man had been his best Captain. All knew it. Mortimer had been the King's very finest Commander, not only tactically and strategically, but politically too. And now he had turned against him.

Shortly afterwards, the King and Despenser left the chamber for a smaller, more private one, and as soon as the door had slammed behind them, the men in the hall were able to stand upright again, rising from their knees. Baldwin saw that one of the messengers needed assistance to rise, and he walked over to him. 'Can I help you?' he asked. 'Are you fatigued after your journey?'

'No – well, yes, but it's not that,' Robert Vyke said, wincing as he put the weight on his leg again. His shin was on fire, and he wondered whether he should pay to have it looked at.

'What happened to you?'

'A foolish accident. I fell into a pothole, and inside was a dagger. It sliced my leg open.'

Baldwin pulled a face. 'It is one thing to be stabbed by an opponent in a fight, but to get slashed in a muddy pool, that is the height of bad luck. The fool who left it there deserves to be punished severely.'

'I think he was,' Robert said, and told Baldwin of the head and dismembered body.

'Really? That is an intriguing story,' Baldwin said. 'I suppose there are small factions fighting all over the country. Lots of grievances being settled, feuds brought to a conclusion.'

'There are plenty who say that they have a score to settle,' Robert agreed, sighing heavily.

'And I dare say that most will never be resolved,' Baldwin replied. 'It is sad to think of so many dying without a grave, without a mourner or prayer said over their bodies.'

'I think I do know who he was,' Robert said. 'I was told that his name was Squire William. At least, that was the name that Sir Laurence mentioned when he saw the dagger.'

'Squire William who, I wonder? We shall perhaps never know. Where was the man's body?'

'It was left near a vill some little way from Bristol. There was a priest nearby, who found me and tended to my wounds until I could walk again. Then I made my way to Bristol, where they asked me to come here. I suppose I wouldn't have managed to help much in the fight there in the castle.'

'I suppose not,' Baldwin said. He watched the injured man limp over to a bench. 'It is healing?'

'Think so. You know how these wounds can be. Sometimes they heal quickly, others you have a barber take your leg off, and sometimes a man will die from the lockjaw or gangrene. I think this will be all right, but it is still very sore. I've walked long and hard in the last few days.'

'You must take your rest,' Baldwin said. He turned, only to see Bernard nearby. 'A question, from interest,' he said to him. 'Are you aware of a Squire named William who lived near to Bristol?'

'Only the one,' Bernard said with a chuckle. 'He wouldn't be popular there, though. Married the daughter of a merchant in the city, and then treated her like a cur. Poor chit was only fourteen or so when they got wed. She ran away when she was eighteen.'

'And?'

'She ran off with a parson, and nine months later she had proof of his catechism! He must have been a right holy fellow, for he was always on his knees. The fool must have had his brain in his tarse. Anyway, when the crime was uncovered, the girl went home to her parents, and as soon as her husband heard of her baby, he went to her home with a group of ruffians and killed them all. His wife, her parents, and her son.'

'I see,' Baldwin said slowly. The sheer ferocity of such an act sickened him. He himself could imagine killing any number of men who had hurt his wife or children, but to go to a house from jealousy or from the position of cuckold, with a group of others, and slay all within, especially the babe, was the act of a madman.

'They even killed some of the servants,' Bernard went on. 'The porter at his door was stabbed, and a maid.'

Baldwin nodded. 'It is terrible how the lust for blood can blind some men.'

'Well, they didn't kill all the servants, I suppose, so that's a mercy. The maid looking after the baby didn't die. They left her where she was.'

'But they took the child from her,' Baldwin said. 'That is truly foul. It must have sent the woman lunatic to see the babe killed.'

'She was made of hardier stuff than that, I reckon.' Bernard rubbed his chin. 'She's still in the city, I heard.'

Baldwin nodded, but he had no idea how his future was about to be so closely entwined with the woman he was discussing. Nor with her death.

Bristol

Simon had been allowed to finish his food, and then to see his servants released and fed, before he was led away to discuss the murder.

It was strange to be taken out to the main city. After such a short time, it had begun to feel as though the castle was a gaol from which he would never be released. Now, he was able to walk the streets with Hugh again like a free man. Margaret and Peterkin, he had been told, would be safer staying in the castle. With so many foreign mercenaries about the city, Simon could only agree with that. He left Rob with them.

He and Hugh were taken along the main street near St Peter's, and then his guard stopped and suggested that they wait.

'Why?'

'Sir Roger Mortimer wanted you to be here,' the guard said

imperturbably. He set his polearm on the ground and leaned on it like man with a staff, yawning.

'What's your name?' Simon asked.

'Herv Tyrel.'

'Have you come with the Mortimer from Hainault?'

'Me? No.' The man was surprised, Simon saw.

Herv Tyrel was a thickset fellow with the brawny arms of a farmer. His brown eyes were gentle, set in a broad, amiable face, and he looked as though he would be more at home in a field with oxen than here in a city.

'Where are you from, Herv?'

'A little vill in Oxfordshire, a place called Henret,' he sighed, gazing about him without relish. 'Wish I was back there now. I've already lost one mate, and now God knows when we'll get back.'

'I think we all wish we were at home,' Simon said. 'I would that I was at home in Devon. This city has been too exciting already for my tastes.'

That made the man grin. 'I know that feeling. I left home in the pay of the King, and halfway here, our Captain decided to become a servant of the Queen. I mean, the Queen's son will be the next King, so I suppose joining their men is a good idea, but I don't really understand . . .'

Simon shrugged. 'It's all beyond me. I just want there to be no fighting while I'm in the middle wondering what to do. Do you know what we're supposed to be waiting for here?'

Herv shook his head. 'I was told to wait here with you, then take you on.'

'I see,' Simon said. He did not care overmuch and was simply relishing his freedom. The memory of that chamber with the others was still close to the front of his mind. The light here, the scents – all were glorious reminders of life going on.

Hugh was less cheerful. He stood leaning on the wall, staring dourly at everyone in the street. He mistrusted all city dwellers as a matter of principle, and after being held captive overnight, was even less inclined to change his mind.

'How long are we to wait?' Simon asked. 'I have business on behalf of Sir Roger.'

'Not long, I hope,' the guard answered, staring back the way they had come.

There was a shout, the sound of horses whinnying, and an outbreak of laughter. Then two horses were led from the castle's gates, two large beasts, with a pair of ropes extending back behind them.

And then he saw the hurdle, and the small, sad figure that lay strapped to it.

Earl Hugh was clad in his armour, with a surcoat over it, but on this surcoat his arms had been reversed, the final proof of his guilt. For this signified the end of his arms – the end of his earldom. No man would inherit his estates entire as a matter of course. His son could not.

Simon watched the sad figure pass him by. Later he heard that the Earl was given no opportunity to speak on the gallows. He was taken to the place of execution of common criminals in Bristol, a demeaning enough position for a man who had risen so high in the King's household. There he was strung up on the oak beams, and throttled until nearly dead, before being cut down, gasping and retching, to be beheaded. There, in front of the crowds, his old body was stripped and rolled off into the kennel, the gutter in the road's centre. Later, his body fed the dogs of the city. His head, meanwhile, was taken away to be put on display at Winchester.

For all the last long years, Simon had detested the Despenser regime with a passion. He had been attacked, had lost his home, had been nearly killed, and all because of this man's son. Now the Earl had fallen from his high pedestal and would suffer the death of a traitor.

'What now?' Simon said, watching the old man being dragged past on the jerking, jolting hurdle.

'Now you can go and continue your investigation,' Roger Mortimer said. He was walking along with three men-at-arms a few yards behind the hurdle.

As the hurdle rattled past, people threw rubbish at the occupant, while some laughed and jeered. A pair of dogs scuttled along, barking, and all the while Earl Hugh stared up at the sky as though it was his fervent wish to imprint that on his mind as his last memory.

'Come, Hugh,' Simon said thickly.

'What did he want us to see *that* for?' Hugh grumbled as they set off with Herv.

'To make sure that we behaved,' Simon said. 'Another man's death is a prime example, isn't it?'

But although he didn't say so, in his heart he was thinking that Sir Roger Mortimer was no better than the Earl and his son Sir Hugh le Despenser.

The room into which Sir Charles was brought was a large chamber, and he was glad to see that the man sitting on the table was unharmed.

'Simon, my friend, I am glad to see you well,' he said effusively. 'When I saw you were not in the room with all the guards, I immediately thought the worst.'

'Are you well?' Simon asked.

'Oh, yes. I made sure that when the surrender went ahead, I was there to give a warm welcome to the Duke of Aquitaine. He and I know each other from my time in France, and he was very happy to vouch for me, I am glad to say. So I was not held like you.'

'I have been freed, but I must learn who the killer of that woman was. And I have been advised by Sir Roger to speak with a fosser.'

They crossed the city together, Simon's servant Hugh still gazing about him with that air of barely controlled disgust, and came to the gaol where the fosser was held. Here it took one penny for the gaoler to realise he would like to introduce them to his prisoner, and they soon reached the chamber where Saul sat on a stool.

'I don't know why I'm here,' he declared mournfully as Sir Charles and Simon walked in. Hugh stood at the door with his staff in his hands.

'Perhaps it began when you bethought yourself that taking a dagger from a grave might be a good idea?' Sir Charles said consideringly. 'What do you think?'

Simon smiled to himseelf, then asked the man to tell him all about the dagger and the man at Cecily's grave.

'I told the other one already,' the fosser complained. 'Why do you have to keep me here to tell you about it all over again?'

'Which other one?' Simon asked sharply.

'The tall one with the dark hair. He was in here yesterday morning.'

'What was his name?'

Saul the Fosser screwed up his face in the act of memory. 'Roger Mortimer, I think – a knight.'

Simon listened carefully to what the gravedigger said. How Mortimer had arrived and questioned him, then left with the strange dagger.

Outside a little later, Simon was baffled. 'Why would Sir Roger send me here to hear something he already knows?'

Sir Charles smiled widely. 'Simon, you are a simple soul like me. The reasons why the great fellows of the land do things is far beyond us. What we need to do is look at the murder itself and see what we can learn. Maybe the great Sir Roger felt he didn't have time to follow this up.'

'I wonder,' Simon mused. 'I wonder . . .'

Cardiff Castle

Baldwin was about to walk from the hall when a page called out to him. 'Sir Baldwin, sir, the King would like to speak with you. Would you come with me, sir?'

Cursing under his breath, Baldwin strode after the man. The last thing he wanted now was another opportunity to listen to the King or his adviser ranting about the state of the kingdom. It was their own fault that the realm had sunk into this disastrous state, and it would be difficult for Baldwin to maintain a calm demeanour, were they to begin to pass the blame on to others.

The chamber into which he was brought was a pleasant, airy room with a large fire roaring in one wall, while all about were pictures of religious scenes. The king sat in front of the fire with a fur-trimmed cloak pulled over his shoulders. 'Come in, Sir Baldwin. Please, come here.'

Looking around the room, Baldwin was surprised to see that Despenser was absent. He was alone with the King and three servants, who all stood at one side like statues. They were Edward's most trusted men, the ones who would never repeat a word that he said.

'Sir Baldwin, you are loyal to me, I deem. As my crown gradually slips from my head, I learn that the very men I once considered dangerous or unfaithful are those who have grown most dear to me, who have become most close by reason of their loyalty. Those in whom I should have been able to place most trust: my brothers, old companions, my General – all these have become my enemies. But you are still here.'

'I gave you my oath, my lord. You are my King. I can do no more.'

'You are a man of integrity and honour, Sir Baldwin. I am most glad.'

The King appeared distracted. He stood up and wandered over to sit at a bench beneath the large window, away from the fire. Without looking at Baldwin, he beckoned.

The knight reckoned that he had come here because this was a private nook, where even the trusted servants could not hear them speak. 'Sire?'

'You have been very loyal. Most of those upon whom I have showered rewards and honours have already deserted me. My own household knights have failed to support me, and yet you have remained with me. That shows your nature, Sir Baldwin.'

'You have my oath, Your Highness.'

'I would ask one more favour of you, Sir Baldwin. Would you do my bidding?'

'If it is in my power, Sire.'

'It is only this: that you will serve and protect my good friend Sir Hugh le Despenser with the same loyalty you have given me.'

Baldwin stiffened. He could recall the pain and hurt in Simon's face as he described the way that the young Despenser had stolen his home in Lydford, the way that Despenser had attacked Simon's daughter as a means of blackmailing Simon into doing his bidding ... He shook his head. 'Sire, that is impossible.'

'You say it is not in your power?'

'I do not know. But I do know the harm that Despenser has

done to many, including you yourself and your realm. How could I serve the man who has done so much to ruin my King?'

'It is your King's express wish that you do so.'

'Then I shall of course try to help.'

'All I ask is that if all goes wrong, you do what you may to protect him.' The King looked up at Baldwin at last. His eyes were red-rimmed, and there were tears in them. 'Please, Sir Baldwin. It would make whatever comes to pass for me that much easier to bear, were I to know that good Sir Hugh was safe. I consider you the only man still loyal enough to me to undertake such a task. Will you do that for me, I beg?'

Before Baldwin could answer, the door opened and Sir Hugh himself entered with another page, Sir Ralph walking behind them.

'Sir Hugh, I am glad to see you again, my friend,' the King said a little formally.

'My liege, there is news,' Hugh said, his face working.

'Speak!'

Sir Ralph spoke quietly. 'It seems the castle at Bristol is fallen. A man has arrived to say that the castle was passed to the rebels yesterday. He saw the Duke of Aquitaine's banner over the gates.'

'He must be mistaken. My father would never surrender,' Sir Hugh declared. 'I will not believe it.'

'Sir Hugh, the feeling in the castle was surely quite devastated after the capitulation of the city,' Sir Ralph said. 'It is not to be wondered at, Your Highness, since the folk were standing against their Queen and your heir.'

'I should have disinherited the ungrateful wretch! How can my own son do this to me? I would not have dared to attempt such a grave offence against my father.' Edward shuddered.

'That is my greatest failing: sympathy to those weaker than me. I am too kindly to those who hardly merit it.'

'What are your orders, Sire?' Sir Hugh asked.

'Eh?' The King gazed at him for a moment as if he didn't recognise his own favourite.

'You will need to move away,' Baldwin said. 'You must go to a place of safety as soon as you may, Your Highness.'

'Safety?' the King repeated blankly, and then he bellowed the word, bringing a fist down onto the bench beside him with enough force to make the servants turn and stare. '*Safety?* And where shall I find this *safety* in my kingdom? Or anywhere? I may not travel to France, because the King would likely arrest me and give me to his sister, my wife, for her sport. To Scotland? Bruce would see me executed.'

'There is yet Ireland,' Sir Hugh le Despenser muttered. 'We can go there and raise another host to retake the country. At least we would be safe there.'

'Perhaps. For a while,' the King said heavily. His eyes dropped and his toe tapped on the floor as he considered. 'And then, what?'

'As I said, my lord. Raise an army, fight these rebels, remove them, and retake your throne,' Sir Hugh le Despenser said.

'You would have me wage war on my Queen, then, and my son? What then, Sir Hugh, when I have retaken my throne, and these rebels have been executed or imprisoned, and I have gained a new reputation for cruelty? What then? For as soon as I have seated my backside on my throne, you may be assured that the next plot to remove me will already have begun. There were hundreds who resisted last time, and after that battle I had many killed for their treachery. And when I won, it gave an impetus to these, who immediately sought to start anew where they had failed. If I win again, events will

319

repeat themselves. Must I always prepare for the next war with my barons?'

'Perhaps, yes, my lord,' Despenser said irritably. 'You must do something, though. You cannot stay here – it is too dangerous.'

'What is the point of continuously moving about the country?' the King retorted. 'All that happens is, our forces erode as the men desert us. I may as well wait here for them. I am sure my wife would not be so cruel as to—'

'A fig for your wife! The one you should fear is Sir Roger Mortimer,' Sir Hugh spat. 'He's the one you imprisoned in the Tower, he's the one who had his death warrant signed by you, Your Highness! Forget your Queen. She is a pretty face at the head of the Mortimer's force, but it is not she, nor yet your son, who directs them. It's Mortimer who tells them where to go, what to do, and who to kill!'

The King put a hand to his temple. 'Then prepare the men to leave this place. We shall ride to Caerphilly. At least we should find some peace there. Dear God, I hope so!'

CHAPTER THIRTY-THREE

Bristol

Simon, Hugh and Sir Charles crossed the town to return to the castle. On the way, they passed the execution ground where the headsman, liberally beslubbered with gore, was drinking from a great skin filled with wine, humming a tune with a slurred inflection. Sawdust had been liberally spread over the area to soak up the blood, and Earl Hugh's body was already being fought over by the dogs.

'It is a terrible thing to see a man brought so low,' Simon murmured as they passed.

Hugh grunted. He had detested the Despenser family since his wife's death, because it was Despenser's men who had killed her and her child, he believed. The shock of it had, if anything, turned him still more introverted and misathropic than before.

Sir Charles was not concentrating. 'Hmm? Yes. Not good to see that the highest in the land can be killed. Precedents like that should not be popularly displayed to the peasants. They may get all sorts of unwholesome ideas!'

Sir Charles was one of the new knights, a man who had lost his home and livelihood when Earl Thomas of Lancaster had been toppled from power and executed by his cousin, the King. That had been a terrible time, with many of the Earl's followers being taken and knights who had been loyal to him being forced to flee. Sir Charles was one of them. He had reached France, hoping to make his fortune in the tournaments, but later managed to win the trust of the King again, and had returned to favour. He had experienced the lowest fortune and the highest, and even now there was a measuring look in his eye as he glanced over the gibbet.

He looked at Simon. 'Where do you wish to go?'

'The knight described by the fosser sounds like the man who was so keen to throw open the gates of the city for Mortimer and the Queen: the Coroner, Sir Stephen Siward. Let's see if we can speak with him.'

It was easy enough to find the knight. He was lounging at a table at an inn not far from the one where Simon and Margaret had stayed on their first night here.

The impression Simon gained was entirely positive. Sir Stephen Siward was a large man, heavy and tall, and with black hair cut short, and with his piercing blue eyes in that round face, he looked the sort of man who would make excellent company around a table. 'So, you seek me?' he said amiably. 'What, will you join me in a cup or two of wine?'

Sir Charles agreed with alacrity, sitting on a bench, and Simon too was glad of the offer. Soon the patron had arrived with two flagons of wine and more cups, and all three could begin talking, while Hugh stood a short distance away like a guard, leaning on his staff.

'How may I help you?'

'Sir Stephen, this is nothing to do with the surrender of the city. This is about a woman who was killed here a little while ago.'

'I won't pretend I don't know who you're talking about,' the knight said. He frowned into his wine, then, tipping his head back, he emptied the cup. 'Poor Cecily. She was such an unfortunate woman. To escape one hideous attack, only to be slain in another.'

'You knew her well?' Simon asked.

'No. I thought you realised: I am Coroner here for the King. I cover a wide area, but I happened to be here in the city, fortunately, when Squire William went on his mad crusade of death. You know the story of him and his wife? Oh. Well, you know then, that he assaulted the Capons' house with a gang of men, slew the old doorman, then Capon, his wife and daughter, before finally dashing out the brains of the baby. A terrible revenge. There were – oh, I've lost count of them now – but many, many blade wounds on his wife's body. Poor girl – she was only eighteen when he killed her.'

Simon felt his belly tighten at the thought of such carnage. 'He was arrested?'

'Oh, yes. In little time. Everyone knew him, and poor Cecily was able to identify him and some of his henchmen once she recovered. It was enough for the jury. Besides, as she accused him, he tried to launch himself at her. It was hard enough in the first place to persuade him to come to the court, but then to try to attack Cecily just because she told what she witnessed . . . that was shameful.'

Sir Charles leaned on an elbow. 'Why would they leave her alive?'

'Well, when they took the baby from her, the horror made her faint – so perhaps they thought her dead?'

'Committed killers are rarely so careless,' Sir Charles said. Then: 'Why was the Squire not in gaol?'

'The King has issued a general pardon to those who will serve him. Squire William was more than happy to take that offer with both hands. I had heard he was going to join the King when His Highness arrived here – but his body was so mutilated and decomposed, I suppose he was killed before the King arrived.'

'Was there any sign as to who could have killed him?' Simon asked.

'I swear I do not know. I . . . But no.'

'Please?' Simon pressed him.

'It is probably nothing, but I did hear that there was a priest out there, not far from where the man's body was discovered. A fellow who recently arrived from Tewkesbury.'

'What of it?' Sir Charles said.

'Only this: young Petronilla ran away with her confessor, a young priest called Paul. Now I hear that a priest by that name has been given a living just far enough from here to be safe from people in the town, and far enough away from Squire William, too, generally. Unless . . .'

'You are speaking in riddles,' Sir Charles snapped.

'Am I? You must accept my apologies. All I meant to say was, that if this same Paul, who is some three to four leagues from Bristol, were to hear from some passing traveller that a woman called Capon, along with her father and mother and a little illegitimate baby, had been slain by her husband, and that the husband had been captured, but then freed under the King's order – well, if you were that priest, thinking it was your woman, your baby, what would you wish to do? Forgive – forget? Or waylay the Squire and hack off his head and disembowel him for the traitor he had shown himself to be?'

Simon pursed his lips in a whistle. 'That makes sense. What would your priest do then?'

'Return to his church as though nothing had happened. What

else would he do? There's nowhere for him to run to now, and if he is found, what can you or I do about his crimes? *Nothing*, for he has Benefit of Clergy! And I confess, I find that there is little merit in the idea of chasing him down and capturing him. What, would it bring back any of the dead? No, of course not. I think it would be better to leave him alone. There is enough to think about here, with the King and Queen's enmity.'

'True enough,' Sir Charles said. He made ready to stand.

'One thing, though,' Simon said. 'The dagger. Why throw that into Cecily's grave?'

'The dagger? What dagger?'

There was instantly a falseness in his tone, and as Simon looked at him, he saw that the man's eyes were averted. 'Sir Stephen, a man saw you throw the dagger into the woman's grave. Why did you do that?'

Sir Stephen looked away, over towards the castle's open gates, as though musing on the foolishness of life.

'I did not know Cecily, not until I had to go and view all the bodies at the Capon household, but I do distinctly recall the feeling of something akin to joy, to find one person who was still breathing in that slaughterhouse. She was a mere maidservant, but the fact that she survived seemed to me to be a good thing in its own right.'

He rubbed at his nose. 'So, you can understand how appalled I was to be called to her body when she was killed. In fact, I was so horrified, I asked Sir Charles here to go to it instead. I could not face the accusation in her eyes. To know that she had died as well . . . it felt as though I too had failed her.'

'And the dagger?'

Sir Stephen glanced at him as if startled. 'Oh, that. Well, the dagger was the property of Squire William de la Bar of Hanham. The husband of Petronilla, the man who killed her entire family.'

'Where did you get it?' Sir Charles asked with frank astonishment.

'From the man who found his body,' Sir Stephen said.

Simon put his head to one side as Sir Stephen spoke of the
dagger and of Robert Vyke finding it in the hole in the road. 'So
someone waylaid Squire William and killed him . . . and his
knife fell into a hole. None of that explains why you set the knife
in Cecily's grave.'

'Because I thought it would be better for her soul if the knife
that slew her mistress was with her. To show that in the end, right
did prevail. Her mistress was avenged.'

'Tell me,' Sir Charles said, as they walked away from the knight
once more, 'did that make any sense to you, because it made
very little sense to me.'

'I suppose there are some who believe that the weapon which
caused so much death could be a symbol of the maid's rising up
over the earthly horrors – or something,' Simon replied, 'but I
am fascinated by this. If the Squire was dead some days ago,
according to the knight's words, then he did *not* kill the maid.
And nor did the dagger.'

'In that case, we need to find out what happened to the Squire
as well, if we are to learn what happened to the woman.'

They were inside the gatehouse to the castle when Simon had
an idea. He led the way up to the first level, and along to the
Constable's chamber. Inside he found Sir Laurence Ashby.

'Yes?' the knight asked.

Simon bowed a little from respect. 'Sir Laurence, my apologies for troubling you about this again, but I have been ordered
to investigate the murder of the woman Cecily. Sir Roger himself demanded it.'

'I will help if I may,' Sir Laurence grunted.

'There are some interesting circumstances because of Squire William. Sir Stephen was holding inquest over him a little while before Cecily died. Can you tell me where the Coroner's rolls are kept? I would like to see the one concerning his inquest, and perhaps speak with the clerk involved.'

Sir Laurence ran a hand through his hair. 'I don't know myself, but my own clerk is bound to. If a mouse farts, he knows about it.'

He stood and walked with the men along the walls to a small, cell-like chamber set into the next tower. Here, David was sitting upon a stool and carefully ruling lines on a piece of perfect vellum.

Sir Laurence stood in the doorway and indicated the two men with him. 'David, do you know these men?'

'I know Sir Charles. You, sir, are a stranger to me.'

Simon nodded and introduced himself, saying that he was seeking the murderer of Cecily and explaining about their meeting with Sir Stephen. 'And so, if the dagger was there, and the Squire was killed already, I wish to learn who killed the Squire. Then, I can perhaps learn who killed Cecily. I do not see how these two, who must have been enemies, could have been struck down by the same man.'

David frowned. 'Well, for that, I will leave you to decide, master. I can at least take you to the Coroner's rolls, for they are stored here in the castle.'

They were taken down to the castle's courtyard, and then up into the main keep, in which there was an iron-barred door. David used a key on a thong about his neck to open it, and they were inside a small cellar which smelled mainly of rats and piss. Four great chests were inside, and the clerk walked straight to the third, unlocking the lid and lifting it.

'Here,' he said, 'are all the rolls for the last six years, when the

Justices last came to hold their eyre.[1] The latest ones are on top. Sir Stephen's clerk was captured by the Queen's men on his way here, but they did not molest him, and he was able to bring his rolls here without hindrance.'

'Good!' Simon said, looking through the various cylinders of parchment. Soon he found the one he was searching for, and eagerly unwrapped it. Reading through it, while David held a candle aloft to aid him, Simon frowned at the ecclesiastical language. It was many years since he had learned his letters in Crediton, and he had to work hard to make sense of the characters used here. They were more rounded than those to which he was accustomed. 'Dear Heaven!' he exclaimed.

'What is it?' Sir Charles asked.

'The man who found the body – *he* said he was held and looked after by a priest – a priest called Paul.'

'So?'

'Paul was the name of the priest who seduced the maid Petronilla and persuaded her to run away with him,' Simon reminded him. 'So this same man, whose love had been slaughtered by Squire William, was also the same one who rescued the man who found Squire William's body.'

'You mean, the priest could have killed the Squire?' Sir Charles said.

'No!' David protested. 'Father Paul is a good and generous-hearted soul – he would not go against the Holy Commandments and kill.'

'But he broke the sixth and eighth, did he not – and I think you will find any man can kill, given the right provocation,' Sir Charles said lightly.

'You do not know him. I do,' David said stoutly.

---

[1] Court

'Did you think he would take a man's wife and make him a cuckold?' Sir Charles asked.

'No, of course not!'

'Then perhaps I know his kind better than you,' Sir Charles said suavely.

Two Tuesdays before the Feast of St Martin[1]

Bristol Castle

'Master Bailiff, I hope I find you well?'

Sir Roger Mortimer strode into the hall like a man in a hurry to be off with his hounds. He reminded Simon of his old friend Bishop Walter II when he was younger – a strong, charismatic man, with an almost feral energy about him. Where Sir Roger went, a small group of others always followed. There was the pair of clerks, a priest, three men-at-arms, two messengers, and behind, Simon saw a familiar face.

He dropped to his knee, bowing his head, urgently motioning to Hugh to do the same.

'Master Puttock, please rise,' the Duke of Aquitaine said.

He was only fourteen, Simon reckoned, but from his looks and deportment, he could have been a great deal older.

'So, Master Puttock, I am very glad to meet with you again. You left France in a hurry.'

'I had to, my lord. I had a bond of honour to Bishop Walter.'

'Of course. It was a great shame that he died. You heard of that, of course?'

Simon nodded. It was odd – he could feel that thickening in his throat again at the mere thought of the Bishop's death. He

[1] 28 October 1326

had been snatched from his horse, along with his squires and servants, and had his head sawn off with a bread-knife in the middle of a London street. Barbaric! 'He was a good man. I know your mother had cause to—'

Sir Roger cleared his throat irritably. 'Duke, I think I should continue with my discussion. With your permission, my lord?'

The interruption made the Duke pale. He was unused to being treated like a boy. From the first weeks of his life, he had been the Earl of Chester, and he had maintained his own household for years already, and yet from the look in his eyes, Simon saw recognition of the limitations of his position. In the eyes of the world at large, Edward, Duke of Aquitaine and Earl of Chester, was the King's son and heir; but here, in this chamber, he knew he was at the mercy of Sir Roger Mortimer. The latter would allow him the feel the power of his position, but not to exercise it. For now, he was still a boy, and Sir Roger had assumed the role of Regent and adviser-in-chief.

The Duke nodded. 'Bailiff, I look forward to speaking to you soon. You will come and see me.'

'I am grateful, Your Highness,' Simon said, kneeling again as the King's son strode from the room.

'So, Master Puttock,' Sir Roger said, sitting at a bench. 'Tell me all.'

'Squire William is dead. He died some miles east of here. When we checked the Coroner's rolls, we learned that there is a priest not far from the scene who was the confessor who ran away with Squire William's wife. It is surely too great a coincidence that they could be in a similar area without the priest learning of it. If he heard that the woman he loved was dead . . .'

'It would be natural for him to seek revenge.'

'That was our thought.'

'And this first-finder discovered the knife and brought it here. That makes a coherent story, if nothing else.'

'Sir Stephen threw it in with the body because he felt it was proof that her death was avenged,' Simon said.

'Hardly. From what you say, the man was already long dead before this Cecily.'

'Yes. But that doesn't mean Sir Stephen didn't want to honour her.'

'It means we still have no idea why the woman died, and I do not like that,' Mortimer said. 'Find the priest. Question him, and return to tell me what he said.'

A clerk stepped forward with a board, on which were set parchments and ink and a reed. Mortimer picked up the reed and dipped it in the ink, scrawling his name on the papers. 'So much to do. So many men to speak with. So many to threaten. The King is in Wales, apparently. It's good. We had feared he could have made his way to Ireland. God is with us, though.'

'Sir Roger, I would be most grateful if I could leave the castle with my wife and child,' Simon said hesitantly.

'Of course you may. As soon as the matter in hand is settled. That is enough. Thank you, Bailiff. You may leave.'

CHAPTER THIRTY-FOUR

Near Caerphilly Castle

'You don't like me much, do you, Sir Baldwin?'

He turned to look at Roisea Redcliffe with an eyebrow raised enquiringly. They were jolting along in the King's column, heading almost due northwards, on the old road that took them up from Cardiff to Caerphilly. This castle was high in the hills, and had the advantage of providing them with a clear view of the land all about, but Baldwin could not help but think that the King would be better served by remaining near the sea, from where he could take ship either to another English port, or to Ireland. Coming inland here felt like the last march of a prisoner to his cell.

'My dear lady, I am sure that—'

'You never have liked me, have you? I thought at first it was just that you considered my husband and I were too foolish, or perhaps too parochial for your refined tastes. But it wasn't that, was it? It was simple dislike.'

'No,' Baldwin smiled. He jerked his head to Jack, signalling a need for privacy, and the lad obediently rode on a short distance in front, Wolf at his horse's heels. 'Madame, it was merely anxiety for my own wife, who is all alone many miles away.'

'No, I don't believe that. You simply didn't like me. And since my husband's death, you have liked me still less.'

'Why do you think that?'

'I have seen your looks of suspicion, Sir Baldwin. They are plain enough. But I swear to you, I did not hurt my husband. I woke to find the camp in turmoil, and then realised that my darling Thomas was dead. It was a terrible shock to me. To see his poor, dead body . . .'

It was a scene she would never be able to forget. The sight of her dying husband clutching at his chest, as though he could push back all that blood, as his face blanched, his lips grew grey, and his eyes sought hers desperately. She had knelt at his side, helpless, while his life was leaking from him. All she had known was the overwhelming sense of failure – she could do nothing to save him. And then he was gone.

Baldwin's words drew her mind from that terrible picture.

'The men who attacked us that day were the very same men who had tried to kill your husband on the road near Winchester when I was with him. I do not suspect you, Madame. Rather, I blame myself for not being there to help him.'

'What did they want?'

'I assumed they wished to find his purse or something else. Or perhaps they simply wanted to kill him. That is what they told me beforehand. I didn't believe them then – but maybe I was too mistrusting.'

'I do not see what else he could have had. There was only his purse.'

'You still have it?' Baldwin asked. 'May I see it?'

Roisea reached into the bag she had slung over her shoulder, brought out the leather purse and gave it to him. Baldwin had forgotten how heavy it was. He untied the thong that bound it, and lifted the lid.

It was an old purse, battered and worn on the outside – but inside, the lining could have been brand new. As he jolted along on his rounsey, Baldwin studied it with a frown. In the most part, the lining was sewn together with a plain dark thread. However, at the bottom of the purse, he could see a paler, creamy-coloured thread.

Working on impulse, he took his little eating knife from about his neck and used it to attack the thread. It was good, waxed linen, and he found it hard to cut, especially on horseback, but at last he managed it, and the lining came apart. Forcing a finger inside the little gap he had made, the knight found a strip of something, and managed to tease out the tiny shred of parchment.

'What is it?' Roisea asked, suddenly anxious at the sight of his face.

Baldwin could not answer for a moment. The crabbed, uneven writing on the scrap of parchment was too shocking.

Bristol Castle

Sir Laurence of Ashby was glad that he was not imprisoned immediately, although he knew that it could happen at any time. The Mortimer appeared content to have him remain here a little longer, and did not seem to fear that he might prove a danger to the Queen or her son.

And he was not, of course. He could no more hurt either of them than he could the King himself. It was galling to have failed to keep the King's castle for him, but equally impossible for any man of honour to have held it against the King's own wife and his heir.

Now that the castle was passed over to the men whom the Queen had installed, his main duty now, as he saw it, was to help the men of the garrison who had been arrested and were now held in little cells near the gates. It was cold in those chambers, and several of them were damp, which inevitably meant that the men within would succumb to illnesses. Sir Laurence saw to it that there was good pottage and broth taken to them to try to guard against the worst of the chills, and now, at last, he had an order for their release.

It was good to see the poor fellows stumbling out into the daylight. The weather was overcast, but at least it was dry today, and they could walk about on their stiff legs, blinking in the light without fearing the rain.

While he was there, a shout came from the gates, and a pair of riders cantered in. They rode past the guards, and then Sir Laurence saw that there were two bodies bound to a third horse. The beast was wild with the scent of blood, his eyes rolling, and he would scarce calm down long enough to allow the hostlers to grab his bridle and keep him steady, while others slashed the ropes holding the two corpses and lifted them down from the animal's back.

Sir Laurence strode across the yard. 'Take that brute away and calm him!' he bellowed, before turning his attention to the two bodies. 'Who are these?' he demanded.

One of the riders was a man he vaguely recognised as belonging to Mortimer. 'These two are known to my lord Mortimer. One was a trader he has used – Thomas Redcliffe – while the other was a page in the service of Sir Ralph of Evesham. They're both dead.'

'I can see that, you fool,' Sir Laurence snapped. 'Why? Did they get into a fight with each other?'

More horses were arriving with other men draped over them, and Sir Laurence stared at them in astonishment.

'What's all this?' Sir Roger Mortimer had arrived and was standing in the doorway of the hall, glowering into the courtyard at the huddle of men. 'Who are they?'

The man shouted out who the two were, and Sir Roger marched down the steps and crossed the yard. He pushed the bodies over with his boot, then shook his head thoughtfully. 'This man was known to me,' he said, reaching down to Thomas Redcliffe's belt. 'Who had his purse?'

'Not us, sir,' the man on the lead horse said. 'Could it have fallen from him while we rode here?'

'Where did you find them?' Sir Roger rapped out, his eyes going to the gate as though to hurry out even now.

'These two were by the ferry over the Severn, sir. They were lying almost *on* the ferry. These others were in a camp, and one in a forest.'

'Were these two alone?'

'No, there were other men there, but they managed to get on the ferry. They'd been going to take these two on board, I think, but us turning up stopped that.'

'This is important,' Sir Roger said. 'I want to know who was with these two, and who could have killed them. Especially this fellow, because he was robbed.'

'I don't know if it's right, sir, but I thought I heard someone calling out to "Sir Baldwin".'

'Really?' Sir Roger said. Baldwin was not an uncommon name, and he wondered which knight this could be. 'Search. Someone must have seen or heard something. If the worst comes to the worst, find a boat and go to ask the ferryman.'

The men glanced at each other, then nodded, before whirling their horses about and thundering out through the gate again.

Sir Roger Mortimer grunted to himself, and then caught sight of Sir Laurence. 'Yes?'

'You are very concerned about this one man?'

'I have known him for some years. He used to buy horses for me.' Then Mortimer continued quietly, 'He had something of value to me.'

Sir Laurence shrugged. It was none of his business.

'Sir Laurence, do you want something?'

Sir Roger Mortimer's eyes were on him now, slightly wide, unblinking, and in that moment, Sir Laurence knew real fear. This man was perfectly capable of killing in an instant.

'No, Sir Roger. I have work to do. Please call me if I can help you, though.'

There was no answer. He turned and walked back towards his chamber, and all the way he dreaded the blow that must come upon his hideously exposed back, until he had entered his chamber and closed the door behind him.

David was at his board writing. 'Are you all right, Sir Laurence? You look shaken.'

The knight eased himself into his chair. It creaked as he tilted it back and rested his boots upon the table-top.

'You know, David, I think there is something very odd about Sir Roger Mortimer,' he said in a low voice.

'I could have told you *that* a while ago,' David snorted.

'You are a most perspicacious fellow,' Sir Laurence said. 'And you have good contacts in the city, don't you?'

'What of it?'

Sir Laurence considered a moment. He had an urge to learn all he could about this friend of Sir Roger's.

'Find out all you can about a man called Thomas Redcliffe. But David?'

'Yes?'

'Your enquiries: make them with subtlety, old friend. We do not wish to arouse Sir Roger's ire.'

Riding to Marshfield

They had set off as soon as they had broken their fast, Simon and Sir Charles. Simon had not been content to leave his wife all alone in the castle, and insisted that Hugh remain with her. Hugh was only too pleased to be spared another journey on horseback, for although he had grown accustomed to this mode of travel of late, it was not with any enjoyment.

It was about noon when the pair reached the little vill where they had been told the body had been found. Simon and Sir Charles looked around for any signs of someone who could help them, but there was nobody to be seen. Eventually they rode up to the nearest cottage – a poor, dilapidated little hovel – and Simon dropped from his horse and rapped on the green, mossy timber of the door.

'What?' The door opened a short way, and the bearded face of Halt glared at them suspiciously. His looks were not improved by the scabs on his broken nose, nor the bruises.

Simon smiled winningly. 'I would like to speak to you.'

'Well, I don't want to speak to you—' His words were cut short by the penny spinning and catching the light as Simon tossed it in the air and caught it.

'There was a body found near here a few days ago,' Simon said. 'Do you know where?'

'Just over there.'

'Could you show us, please?'

Halt was keen to help. Crossing his garden to the roadway and taking Simon and Sir Charles up towards the little spinney, he showed them the hole in the hedge made by the jury as they had forced their way through.

'Do you know who the corpse was supposed to have been?' Simon asked.

'No. All the Coroner said was, it was the Squire from over Hanham way. That was all.'

'Did you know this Squire?'

'Me?' Halt shook his head. 'He was from miles away, master. I'd never seen him before.'

Simon went into the little wood and gazed about him. There was no lingering aura of evil, such as he might have expected. 'The body was here?'

'No, sir, it was on the ground over there, and this is where his head was stuck.'

'His head?' Sir Charles repeated, interested. 'You say he was beheaded?'

'Yes. As if he was a criminal – or a traitor.'

'To his wife, perhaps, as well as to his parents-in-law,' Simon murmured. He looked about him, and then walked out, back to the road. There was nothing to be seen there, and to stand gazing about the trees felt ghoulish.

Simon asked where the priest lived – some two miles further on – and the pair made their way onwards after Simon had paid the man his penny.

'I don't think much of the quality of the peasants about here,' Sir Charles said ruminatively.

'He was a poor example of a dull-witted serf,' Simon agreed with a chuckle. 'But look at this landscape, Sir Charles! Good, wholesome territory. Any man would grow strong and hearty in a place like this.'

'If you say so,' Sir Charles sighed.

In truth, it was a good day to be out riding. The sun was breaking through the clouds, and as it did so, the leaves and puddles appeared to be outlined in silver. There was the constant calling of birds in the trees and, disturbed by their passing, flies rose up in fine swarms of mist. Simon felt all the worries of the last days fall away from him. It seemed as though all the troubles in this worried land were for a little while dissipated, and while he remained here on his horse, the country, and he, were safe.

His mood stayed with him all the way to the little vill where the priest was living. And then all his euphoria was wiped away as he spoke to Father Paul.

CHAPTER THIRTY-FIVE

Bristol Castle

The castle was in uproar. Men ran about like headless chickens while Sir Stephen watched them from the comfort of an old bench, a jug of wine at his feet, a cup in his hand.

It was clear that the Queen and Mortimer were keen to be away from the place as soon as possible, although he would guess that the Queen's son was less enthusiastic about the prospect. It was not surprising. The lad must be wondering what on earth would happen to his beloved father, when the Mortimer caught up with him. Edward had, after all, tried to have Mortimer executed – and that was never a perfect basis on which to maintain a friendship.

The Queen's men were soon to be on the move, then. Well, so much the better. Sir Stephen did not enjoy being in the vicinity of so many men with weapons. He was happier when things were quieter, and he would be content to remain here for quite a while longer. It was a good city, he'd always thought, and now, with the place in Mortimer's hands as a result of his own hard efforts, he was better positioned than ever before.

Carts were brought, and the barrels from the undercrofts, so carefully stored against the day of the siege, were rolled out and loaded. There was little point in larger wagons for transport. The oxen to haul them were too slow, and the Queen and Mortimer had an urgent desire for speed. Besides, the roads west of here were deplorable. In Wales the land was rough and undercultivated. It would be better to have their goods brought on sumpter horses rather than these carts even, because roads were few and far between. There had been some communications built in the days of good King Edward I, the man who had done so much to pacify the unruly Welsh peasants, but not enough. All that effort to gather up food, he thought regretfully, only to see it removed in this way.

He heard steps behind him, and cast a glance over his shoulder. In a moment, he was on his feet. 'Sir Laurence. I wish you a good day.'

'Do you?' Sir Laurence said. 'Well, I wish *you* a slow death. You betrayed us all, especially your King.'

Sir Stephen gave a weary smile. 'Look about you, sir knight. Would the King have preferred to see one of his greater cities devastated, the buildings destroyed, the land laid waste? I think if he wishes to retain his crown, he will be glad of a few places like this left standing. He will need the money.'

'Money! What good is that to a man with no honour?'

'You press me hard, my friend,' Sir Stephen said. He spoke with a lazy drawl, but his hands moved to his belt and rested, thumbs hooked near the buckle.

'Why, would you like to fight now?' Sir Laurence said contemptuously. 'I will be happy to stand here and defend my honour. What of you, though? Is your honour worth the defence? Or can you no longer find it?'

Sir Stephen kept his eyes on Sir Laurence. 'I will fight you here and now, or at any other time and place of your choosing. I am no coward, and will show that my courage and honour are of the highest.'

'Your courage may be, but you have no honour in you, by my faith!' Sir Laurence spat. 'This city was given away by you, when you were sworn to help defend it. That you did so *proves* your unfaithfulness. I call on you now. Draw your sword, Sir Laurence!'

With a slither of steel, both men drew their weapons and crouched, Sir Laurence with his sword hanging in the true *guardant* – held with his fist above his head, the point aiming down and across his body towards Sir Stephen. The latter had his own weapon in the medium guard, his fist low at his belly, the blade pointing upwards, ready to rise and knock aside any attack. But before either man could make a move, there came a great bellow from the other side of the yard.

'You – stop that! Both of you, put up your swords!'

There was a moment in which the two knights stared at each other, and Sir Stephen saw Sir Laurence's eyes narrow as though preparing to launch himself forward, but even as the idea began to communicate itself to his legs and arm, a pair of spears intruded, and guards stepped between them both.

'Sires, I would be very glad if you would save this for another day,' a serious-looking man said. He was older than either knight, and not noble, but for all that, he had a firm quarter-staff grip on a lance, and he looked as though he not only knew how to use it, but would willingly do so.

A man with a sword stood little chance against a man with a staff. The reach of that pole gave him a great advantage, especially when it had a sharp tip. Sir Laurence gritted his teeth, but stood back, his sword at rest, but unsheathed. The tip of the lance came closer to Sir Stephen, who smiled politely at the intruders.

'Tell me,' he said pleasantly as he shoved his sword into the scabbard. 'What is your name, my friend?'

'I am Otho, sir.'

'And you think you have the right to stop two knights from fighting over a matter of honour?'

'Sire, I would not dare to stop a knight from doing what he wanted. But I was ordered to see to it that there was no brawling or fighting here today, and I obey Sir Roger's orders.'

'I see, Otho. Well, I wish you fortune. For if you try such a thing again, I think you may lose your head.'

'Sir Stephen, when would you like to meet again?' interrupted Sir Laurence.

'At the first opportunity, my friend. If we are to come to blows, it would be better to do so sooner rather than later, eh? Perhaps in the morning?'

Otho stood aside as Sir Roger stormed between the two. 'There will be no fighting in the morning. There will be no fighting whatsoever here, not while I'm in charge. Tomorrow, Sir Stephen, you will join me, as will you, Sir Laurence. We go to hunt the King, and if you think I will willingly permit you two to deprive me of one or both of you, you are mistaken. Sheath that weapon, Sir Laurence. Better! Now, shake hands, both of you, if you don't want to be gaoled and left here until I return.'

Sir Stephen smiled thinly, and held out his hand. Seeing Sir Laurence's reluctance, he smiled more broadly, until the two gripped each other's hands. But there was no peace in either man's eyes as they stared at each other.

The Coroner let go, and stepped back quickly. It was not unknown for a man to be held by the hand while his opponent drew a knife and stabbed him. But Sir Laurence was not made in that mould, clearly. He turned, bowed casually to Sir Roger, and walked away.

'You won't leave him in charge here, Sir Roger?' Sir Stephen asked.

'You think I'd leave a man who is still coming to terms with his betrayal of his loyalty to the King? If Sir Laurence was left here alone, he could easily lock the gates again, and hold out even with a smaller garrison. No, I won't let him out of my sight for a long while.'

'Would you let *me* guard it for you?'

Sir Roger turned and stared at him. 'You think I'm a fool? You were unfaithful to the King after you gave him your word. What could you possibly say to me that would let me trust you now? You, Sir Stephen, will also stay near me, where I can see you.'

Marshfield

The priest was a sad man, Simon thought. His face was weary, as though he had already seen too much suffering and was scarred forever. In his sorrow, the man reminded Simon of Baldwin when they had first met; there was the same sense of one who was marked by the way he had been hurt. And yet, whereas with Baldwin Simon had always had an appreciation of the steel beneath, this man did not give that same impresssion.

'You are Paul, Father?'

'Yes, my son. You are from Bristol? I have been expecting you.'

Simon and Sir Charles exchanged a look before they climbed down from their horses and lashed them to a tree nearby. The mounts immediately began cropping the grass.

'Father, you know why we're here?'

'Yes. But I know nothing about it.'

'What?'

'The murder of Squire William of Hanham. Oh, don't misunderstand me, I'd have killed him, gladly, and I would have confessed it with pride had you asked me – but I cannot take the credit for this death.'

'Perhaps you would like to tell us your story from the beginning,' Sir Charles said. Then: 'I don't suppose you have any wine here?'

The priest led them into the church. There was a bench cut into the wall at the back, and here Father Paul had already lighted a charcoal brazier. The warm glow of the coals was a delight in that chilly chamber, and the two guests sat with cups and a wineskin, while the priest stood, his hands over the warmth, his face contemplative.

'You must know my story, or you wouldn't be here,' he began. 'People say the cruellest things, though, and I would have you know that for my part, I adored that woman. It was more than flesh and blood could bear, to see her so foully beaten and abused. Poor Petronilla was a delicate, beautiful little thing, slender as a willow-wand, with a smile that could heat a room.'

'Aye,' Sir Charles said drily. '*And* she was married.'

'She was – but not by her own choice. Her father sold her. Yes, like a slave, he sold her. Squire William wanted money, and Arthur Capon wanted access to nobility. So Capon exchanged his daughter for the promise of high-born blood in his grandchildren's veins. She could suffer so long as his family was well positioned.

'Well, his daughter was a virtuous, honourable child. Fourteen years, she was, when the marriage took place. So young for a woman to be forced to a man's bed. Squire William was greatly pleased by her, and the dowry she brought with her, and paraded her whenever he had the opportunity. Before long, however, her parents visited, and arguments began. She told me about them. Her mother was unimpressed with the manner of the Squire's hospitality. She wanted better food – the cook, she said, was incapable, the house a mess; she hated hounds, and the Squire was a keen hunter; she hated noise, and the Squire was a loud kind of man. Wherever he went, there was much commotion.

'I think Mrs Capon was too set in her ways. As was Arthur, her husband. He wanted for nothing at his own home, and he expected the same attention to be lavished on him when he visited another house. But Squire William was not rich. He could ill afford all the luxuries which his father-in-law demanded. Their little jibes grew into arguments and then into hatred. Real, bitter hatred. And the Capons returned to Bristol.

'Arthur had a banker's mind. He was always thinking of the cost of everything. He thought he could upset his son-in-law best by removing any money he had already paid in dower. That was why he made the statement.' Father Paul sighed.

'Which statement was that?' Simon asked.

'He told the man that Petronilla was not their natural child.'

Sir Charles winced. 'Ouch! Was it true?'

'They swore it. She had been fostered from a whore, so they stated.'

'What happened?' Simon asked.

'As you would expect, Squire William was enraged. They threatened to pursue him through the courts for their money, because there was no need for them to pay for her, they said, since she was not of their blood. Meanwhile, *he* declared that since she was not theirs, he would keep her *and* their money, for if they had made the marriage vows with him in deceit, it was not his fault. He had married her in good faith, taking her dower in good faith. He would not give up the money. And it was then that he began to treat her really badly.

'You have to understand, I was watching this terrible situation develop. It took three years for matters to come to this pass, a slow but inevitable slide into misery and despair for all concerned. And yet only now did I become so close to her that she allowed me to see her pain. Until then she had held herself composed at all times. Her fortitude was astonishing. I think it was that which compelled me to love her. Anyway, as her confessor, I knew all, of course. All this is common knowledge now, so the secrecy of the confessional is not relevant. But when I saw how she was becoming bruised and injured, although I attempted to remonstrate with the Squire, he would not listen to me. Why should he? All that bastard cared about was money.'

Sir Charles shifted. 'So, what happened? You ran off with her, eh?'

'Only after a lot of soul-searching,' Paul said. He was very calm, and Simon guessed that to be able to unburden himself of the whole story was in its own way a relief. He continued: 'We ran away, yes. And yes, I was dreaming wildly of a new life with her. A life with rose petals carpeting the ground beneath our feet. We would live in a state of perpetual bliss, and our souls would become inextricably entwined. I was so innocent!

'At first, we were happy. But she was used to furs and pewter: I could offer only rough fustian and wood. We scraped along somehow for almost six weeks before we were captured and brought back to Bristol.'

He paused and smiled sadly. 'Six weeks. It could have been a lifetime. My happy Petronilla!'

'Her father was pleased to have her home?' Simon asked.

'It appeared that all was well. As I said, he was a money-man, and I swear he would have been happier to have the dower returned than his daughter. Still, he tolerated her. But then the truth of my love for her became obvious, and Petronilla was sent away to a nunnery. I had already been taken and held in the Bishop of Bath and Wells's gaol for almost a year, before I was released. That was when I heard I was the father of a little boy.'

'You are sure the child was yours?'

Paul shrugged. 'We were alone for almost six weeks. She had her natural blood in the first week after we ran away, but not again until Little Harry was born. He was my child.'

'And then?'

'Two and a half weeks ago I heard that they were all dead. Slaughtered in their hall by that wicked fiend, Squire William.' There were tears in Father Paul's eyes. 'So, do you wonder why I would willingly have killed him?'

Simon was watching him closely all the while. There was little doubt in his mind that, physically, the priest was nowhere strong enough to kill anyone, let alone a sturdy country squire.

'Who else could have wanted him to be killed?'

'I have no idea. Many, I expect, because he was a violent man. You know what these . . .' he glanced at Sir Charles before saying anything more derogatory about knights . . . 'rural Squires can be like,' he amended.

'Yes, indeed,' Simon grinned. Then a thought struck him. 'Do you know whether he was a loyal man to the King?'

'He was pardoned, wasn't he? And his men with him. I think that tells you what King Edward thought about his loyalty.'

'And yet he did not go to the King to support him.'

'Perhaps he died before he might do so,' Paul said.

'The man who found him . . .'

Paul winced. 'I still feel the shame of that. I saw the body in there, and saw the first finder with him, and I confess I panicked. I thought this fellow had killed Squire William, so I knocked him on the pate. But then I looked at the body, and realised that the man had been dead some while already, so the fellow I had struck down could not have been the murderer. However, I thought it better to say nothing. I put the poor fellow in a cart and took him home, and there I nursed him back to health. But

I denied seeing the dead body, or finding him there, or knocking him down. I did not want Squire William found.'

'Why?' Sir Charles demanded.

'Sir Knight, why do you think? Someone deliberately killed him near to my home in order to implicate me. If I had volunteered that kind of information, I could have been arrested again, sent back to gaol, and left to die unshriven.'

'Like him?'

'I feel pity for that. He deserved his chance – but he was long dead before I saw him.' Father Paul looked away from Simon, down at the ground. 'Perhaps he could have been brought to repent of his cruelty. I do know this: whatever his crimes, to kill him was wrong – as wrong as it was for him to murder Petronilla.'

And he began to weep. He was still weeping when Simon and Sir Charles left him, seated hunched over, arms around his legs, rocking silently in his grief, and when Simon glanced back and saw him, he had a hideous vision of himself doing the same thing, were someone to kill his beloved family.

It was enough to make his heart crack with dread.

CHAPTER THIRTY-SIX

Bristol Castle

'Sir Laurence! Wait, please!'

The knight turned at once, his heart still pounding painfully. Without the release of actual fighting, he felt weak, as though the explosion of rage that had flooded him had torn all energy from his soul. It was a huge relief to see that the person hailing him was David, his clerk.

'Yes, old friend?'

'Redcliffe, you remember? – you asked me to learn what I could. Good God, you look awful. Been back to the garderobes to get a whiff of the stench?'

'Not now, David.'

'Very well. The man you asked about was a merchant here in the city until he lost all his money. He was closed down some months ago. There were rumours that he was going to try to start again, but he had no money to begin.'

'I see.'

'There was a story I heard . . .'

'What?'

'Some say that he had been used by the King as a messenger, that he was especially trusted. He had been a purveyor of Spanish horses for the King, and used to take messages abroad for His Highness.'

Sir Laurence nodded, but he still felt numb and couldn't quite grasp the significance of this. 'What would that matter to Sir Roger, then?'

'There is one possibility, sir.' The clerk looked around cautiously before speaking. 'This man could have been suborned by Sir Roger. If he was truly a man with access to the King, he could, perhaps, have been sent to try to assassinate him . . .'

'No, surely not!'

Then Sir Laurence remembered the look on Sir Roger's face, and thought about the latter's strenuous efforts to be gone from here and chase after his quarry.

'David, you keep this to yourself. Don't mention it to anyone.'

Caerphilly Castle

In its own way, the note was thoroughly unremarkable. A short line it read simply: *This man has my confidence. Give him all help. Roger Mortimer.*

And yet nothing could have been more shocking to Sir Baldwin. This scrap of parchment was, in effect, a letter of safe-conduct for the man. A man who was supposed to be a loyal messenger to the King.

'I don't understand,' Roisea protested. 'How could he have something like this?'

It made no sense. Unless . . . 'Perhaps,' Baldwin said, 'Sir Roger Mortimer gave him free passage so that negotiations could continue?'

But he knew perfectly well that Sir Roger would be highly

unwilling to negotiate with the King. There could be no discussions about how to surrender. The whole process of war for Sir Roger Mortimer was concentrated on destroying the King, utterly.

'I don't think so,' Roisea said. 'Thomas was never that close to the King. He was a merchant, that was all.' Her face reflected her terror. 'How could he do this? He was a traitor, wasn't he? He must have been!'

Baldwin put a hand on hers. 'There is nothing to say that. One line on a strip of parchment like this is not proof.'

'What would the King say? Would *he* need a great deal of extra proof?' she said agitatedly. 'Destroy it! Please, Sir Baldwin, burn it!'

He took the strip and set it inside his chemise, passing her the purse again. 'You keep that, and I shall keep this for now. It is nothing to do with you, and if you are asked, say you have no idea about it. You have not seen it. You do not know anything about your husband's work.'

'So you think he was a traitor, too.'

'It is difficult to know what else to think,' the knight admitted.

Jack was nearby, and Baldwin lowered his voice so that only Roisea could hear him. 'Whatever your husband was trying to accomplish, it is too late now. He cannot be punished, and there is no point in making you suffer for his actions. So try to forget all about it, madame.'

She could not, of course. As Baldwin rode on, he could see the tears falling down her cheeks. This was the first time he had seen her weeping with such passion, he noted. The death of her husband had not affected her thus, but this discovery, which could potentially threaten her own safety, was different.

He put her from his mind. She was not important – but the note was. It showed that all he had done since meeting that evil, lying fool in Winchester had been based on deceit. He had diverted himself from his home in order to protect the man who was plotting to kill the King! Instead of bringing a messenger, he had brought an assassin. That was how he read the message, and he could see that Roisea thought the same. It was terrifying. But at least Thomas had been killed.

Which then brought another thought to his mind: if that man whom he had injured at Winchester, and then killed at the Severn, was actually determined to kill Thomas Redcliffe, then surely he had been ordered to do so by someone who was supporting the King and had learned something about the plot to hurt him. Which meant that Baldwin himself had tried to protect the assassin. If he had succeeded ... A shiver of dread went through his frame.

The castle was before them now, the great keep rising up to a monstrous height. With such a small force as this, it looked enormous. So many of the King's men had already disappeared, Baldwin wondered how long they could actually survive.

So long as he could keep silent about the note in his chemise, he would be safe. As soon as they arrived in the castle, he would seek a fire on which to burn it.

Bristol Castle

It was raining when they woke. It rained as they breakfasted; it rained as they packed their few belongings; it rained as they walked to their horses and saw them saddled and bridled; it rained as they mounted in the courtyard; it rained as they waited for the Queen and Mortimer to appear with the Duke of Aquitaine. The castle was an echoing chamber as heavy drops fell on helmets, armour, leather and the tiles of the roofs.

Simon wiped a hand over his face. 'This is going to be absolute misery,' he grunted.

At his side, Sir Charles, wearing a broad-brimmed hat that was already absorbing too much water, nodded. 'I can scarcely remember a storm like this. It is, indeed, very unpleasant.'

Simon waved to the group standing at the door. There, he saw Margaret and Peterkin, with Hugh and Rob behind them. It was a wrench to be going, but Sir Roger had flatly refused to countenance releasing him.

'I need you and every other spare man, Bailiff.'

'But I—'

'Will not be permitted to see the King by riding on ahead, Master Puttock. If you wish to do that, you will run the risk of your wife and child being kept here for a long time. I think that is plain enough.'

Sir Roger recollected something and lifted a hand to stay him.

'Master Puttock – I recall that you were in France with another man. A knight.'

'Sir Baldwin, you mean?'

'A little while ago, a horse dealer and confidential agent of mine was murdered on the banks of the Severn. Do you think you know anyone who could have been there? No? Interesting. Well, it shows how even my agents can be killed. The assassin was, I think, on his way to the King. You may try to do the same if I release you. So do I trust you? No. But this way, you come with me, and your wife and child remain here in Bristol as hostages. You will serve me until I release you, Master Puttock, and you will do so with all your heart.'

The scene came back to Simon out in the ward. He turned back to the gates as the first men began to leave. This was not what he had hoped for when he had prayed that Despenser might be removed from power. The man was a poison at the heart of government, and Simon had wanted to see him destroyed – but now that his replacement was here, Simon was beginning to wonder whether he was any better. Perhaps Mortimer would be powerful enough to make changes, but if the main difference was only a name, Simon was not sure that the fighting and deaths would be worth it.

'What did he say when you told him about the priest?' Sir Charles asked.

'Only that the man must have been lying. Who else had as strong a motive to kill Squire William as Father Paul? Sir Roger said he would have him arrested and brought here, but I think he has more on his mind than a mere churchman who may have committed homicide. There are murders all over the realm just now. Most will go unpunished.'

'I wonder how he will get all these men across the Severn,' Sir Charles said, glancing all around as they rode up the streets of Bristol towards the northernmost gate.

'I don't know, but if there is one thing that impresses me about this man, it is his ability to organise. He will surely have a plan.'

They spent the morning battling through torrential rain, heading north and east towards Gloucester. The river was too formidable a barrier, especially with this weather: there was no possibility of a crossing. In normal conditions, they might have made the city by nightfall, but with this downpour, that was out of the question.

'I wonder where we'll stay the night,' Simon said miserably. 'If this weather holds, we'll need real roofs over our heads.'

'I think you can dream of such things,' Sir Charles said, 'but do not expect your dreams to come true!'

Caerphilly Castle

He had not destroyed it.

The scrap of parchment was stored in his own purse for now, but Baldwin had changed his mind about burning it, for reasons he dared not consider too deeply. The main thing was, Roisea did not still carry it about her person. She was safe.

He had installed her in a house in the town itself. The castle was no place for a woman. Not now, with the garrison filling it.

Here, within Caerphilly Castle, there was an atmosphere of scarcely restrained panic amongst the men. Some were managing to hold themselves together; this was most apparent with the smaller, close-knit groups like Sir Ralph's men. Even though his squire, Bernard, was suffering from the wound he had received at the Severn, he and Alexander were entirely devoted and loyal to the King. The three would not falter, Baldwin saw, and he was impressed by their fortitude.

However, others were losing control. There were several cases of extreme drunkenness, especially amongst the peasants. The more that Baldwin saw of these poor fellows, the more obvious it was that they were formed for farming or other country pursuits, not for drawing steel and trying to hack at another man. Although two men did just that last night, picking a fight with each other, bickering and spitting insults until at last one drew a dagger, and the two began rolling about in the muck, trying to stab each other. Afterwards, only one was left alive. Not any longer. His body now moved with the wind outside the castle walls, his face swollen, tongue protruding, the rope tight about his throat.

Baldwin knew that the execution was necessary, for with so many men, all armed, it was essential that order was maintained. But it was shameful to see such a waste of young men. The fellows here were all terrified of Sir Roger Mortimer's men arriving, that was all. They knew they could expect little sympathy when Sir Roger demanded their surrender: there would be no quarter for any who refused. Thus it was that they retired to the buttery and undercrofts, seeking what solace they could in the wine and ale barrels. If the attack did not materialise for a couple of days, there would be no effective troops left, Baldwin considered. They would all be drunk or too hung-over to put up any resistance.

At least Caerphilly was one of the new design of castles: it required fewer men to defend it. There was no single keep as in castles of old. Instead there was a powerful curtain wall, strongly protected by a series of circular towers that allowed defenders to fire weapons at attackers below. There was a second wall, lower, but with similar defensive towers, and then beyond that a large artificial lake that encircled the whole castle. It lay in a wide, flat area with hills rising in the distance.

Baldwin could appreciate the location and the strength of the place. Originally it had been built for the Earl of Gloucester, and its construction had caused the wars in Wales. The Prince of Wales, Llywelyn ap Gruffydd, had deprecated the appearance of such a fortress in the middle of his realm, and eventually his resistance was to lead to Edward I's invasion with a huge force of fifteen thousaand men.

The castle remained, and when Despenser managed to acquire the lands, he took it over as well. It was now the strongest remaining fortress upon which the King could depend. After this place, there was nothing left. The men knew that, and drank to try to forget.

Baldwin was up at the battlements of the gatehouse when the rider appeared. He was rolling in his saddle with fatigue. The challenge was given and the gates finally opened, and the man trotted into the inner ward of the castle, having to be helped down from his horse as grooms held the reins.

'I have messages for the King,' he gasped.

The messenger was little more than a boy, Baldwin thought to himself.

As soon as the fellow had been taken into the main hall, he and all the knights and knights banneret were summoned to hear his words.

The fellow was kneeling on the ground when Baldwin entered. Sir Ralph and Bernard were standing opposite him, not far from the King, and as the men gradually filed into the chamber, Baldwin was struck by how even this room, small by the King's standards, did not seem to be filled. Those men left who were loyal to Edward were pitifully few.

The King himself glanced about him as the men of his household entered, and his face had taken on a tragic mask, as though he suddenly truly appreciated his predicament.

As he should, Baldwin said to himself. He felt betrayed by the King. His life had been one of service, and while he had occasionally sought to thwart Sir Hugh le Despenser, yet had he always been loyal to his monarch. Through all the tribulations of the last ten years, Baldwin had been determined to remain so. Yet on each occasion when it had been possible for the King to step back from the brink, he had pushed on. Now the last opportunities had been squandered, Baldwin felt, and while there might be a face-saving scheme that would allow the King to recover some of his royal dignity, it was not entirely up to Sir Roger Mortimer. The King simply lacked authority.

He caught the eye of Sir Ralph, and could tell that the other knight was sensing the same dejection. All the men in the room must be aware of it.

'Your Royal Highness, I bring very grave news,' the messenger began. He remained kneeling, his head towards the ground, as though it would protect him from the inevitable wrath.

'Speak. You need not fear in this room,' the King said. 'We are all understanding of your concern, my friend, but know that here we appreciate your courage in bringing us messages.'

'Do you have a message from my father?' Sir Hugh le Despenser blurted out. His fingernails were bitten so badly, Baldwin could see only a quarter inch of nail on each.

'My Lord Despenser, I am sorry. Your father was captured.' The messenger's voice was almost inaudible. 'He is dead.'

'My father? No, he cannot be dead,' Sir Hugh said. He was shaking his head, and now he put a forefinger into his mouth, raking the nail with his lower teeth. 'My father is an Earl. They wouldn't dare . . .'

'The garrison surrendered three days ago, my lord. Your father was executed the day before yesterday.'

The King swallowed and put a hand on Hugh's forearm to silence him. 'Mortimer and my son – where are they? At Bristol?'

'They were to leave Bristol yesterday, and make for Gloucester. They will, I think, be there tomorrow, and then I doubt me not that they will come here.'

'And what then?' the King said mildly. 'They plainly intend to see me dead. I can see no other outcome for me.'

There was a protest, a cry of 'No!' but it was a solitary one. The majority of men within the chamber were eyeing each other thoughtfully, and all were considering the same: would they be safer, were they to leave the King and join with Mortimer? One or two, like the Chancellor, Robert Baldock, and Edmund Fitzalan, the Earl of Arundel, could expect little in the way of magnanimity when they were paraded in front of Mortimer. After all, they had shown none to him.

'Come, what then? Is there any hope? Did you hear that they will send a man to negotiate with me?'

The messenger did not look up. Slowly he shook his head. 'I have heard nothing of that, my liege. All spoke of the Mortimer riding with his host to find you.'

'My friends,' Edward said, 'we are alone in this world. We have no means of escape. In truth, I fear I am the unhappiest King that ever ruled this sad kingdom. My doom is fast approaching.'

CHAPTER THIRTY-SEVEN

Two Thursdays before the Feast of St Martin[1]

Gloucester

Simon's worst fears were realised on the way to Gloucester. All the last day, they had plodded on in rain that seemed to fall more heavily the further north they travelled, and by the time they stopped for the night, all were entombed in misery. There was no way for the men to warm themselves or to dry their sodden clothing. The only thing that served to lighten Simon's spirits was the efficient foraging of the man Otho.

Otho reminded him of Hugh – but an older Hugh with a more pleasant attitude. As soon as the order was sent for the men to make camp, Otho and his companion, Herv, had headed off towards a small shaw. There, beyond the trees, Simon found them a short while later. Although there was no firewood or hot food, at least Simon and Sir Charles could settle down in the dry of the hovel.

[1] 30 October 1326

'How much further is it to the city?' Herv demanded as he tugged his boots from his feet and stared at the blisters. 'My boots may make it, but I don't know that me feet will.'

'Goose grease,' Otho said knowledgeably. 'That's what you need for them.'

'Oh. Good. Don't suppose you'd noticed, Sergeant, but there isn't any here.'

'No?' Otho reached into his pack and withdrew a wide-mouthed pot stoppered with a piece of cork. He opened it, and passed it over. 'Don't use too much. God knows when we'll find any more.'

Simon had closed his eyes soon afterwards. There was some bread and biscuits to eat, but he had little appetite. He was more interested in where they were going, and what he was expected to do. Mortimer had given him little idea what he intended to do with him, and Simon found it made him anxious. And yet, no matter what Mortimer intended, Simon was less afraid of him than he would have been of Despenser. The latter was a far more dangerous and unpredictable foe.

The next morning, thank the Lord, the skies were leaden but dry. They gathered up their belongings, and while Simon and Sir Charles saddled their rounseys, Otho made a little fire, enough to warm some water, into which he threw some chunks of dried bread to make a drink that, while fairly tasteless, was sustaining. They also had some cured sausage, too, which they chewed as they returned to the column, and joined in the general march northwards again.

It was when they had been travelling half the morning that a rider came down the line, seeking Simon, and asked him to go to speak with Roger Mortimer.

Simon bade Sir Charles godspeed, and cantered off to the front of the column.

Sir Roger was a different man from the fellow Simon had seen in France or even in Bristol. In France the last year, Sir Roger had been living under a shadow, aware that the King of England would stop at nothing to see him executed. He was living under the protection of the French King, but that support was liable to be removed at any time, since Charles was a fickle ally who would use any lever to try to unsettle his English neighbour, especially if it gave him a pretext for snatching of the English territories remaining in France. Guyenne and the rest of Aquitaine were enormously valuable lands.

The position of sitting between two powerful men meant that Roger Mortimer's life was always at risk. But now, he was once more a leader of men, with thousands behind him, ready and able to challenge King Edward and his right to rule. There was a feeling that Mortimer had God behind him, as if even He was distraught at how King Edward II had squandered all the good fortune with which he had been so liberally showered at birth.

'Master Bailiff. I hope you slept well?'

Simon drew in closer to the man. Sir Roger rode with a straight back, his left hand gripping the reins, his right resting on his thigh, while he surveyed the lands ahead. Simon thought he looked like an emperor, studying his next conquest. 'Very well, I thank you, sir.'

'Good. The hovel was comfortable, then.'

It was a comment designed to remind Simon that he was under constant surveillance. The Bailiff saw no need to respond.

'We should be in Gloucester soon. We shall not stop, but will continue on to Caerphilly. And there we shall encounter the King.'

'Good,' Simon said.

'After that, I may release you. There is much to do, to rebuild this country. Despenser has done so much harm, would you not agree?'

Simon cast a look at him. 'Sir Hugh le Despenser has persecuted me for the last year or more. He has threatened me, my family, and my livelihood. He has taken my home from me. You would find it hard to make any comment about him that I wouldn't personally consider too gentle.'

'You too?' Mortimer smiled. 'Still, I imagine he has not procured your death warrant, as he did for me. No matter. There is one thing, though. I told you a man of mine was found dead recently – a fellow called Thomas Redcliffe. He lay on the banks of the Severn. Are you sure you did not know of him?'

'No. He is not a man I have met,' Simon said.

'Others will know of him. I want to find out who killed him. There is a tale that there was a man there when his body was found – a knight called Sir Baldwin.'

Simon was taken aback. 'If you mean Sir Baldwin de Furnshill, he should be home again in Devon by now. Are you sure it was him? There are other knights who bear the same name.'

'Home again? Where was he?'

'He and I were in London with Bishop Stapledon, but Baldwin left before me, and he was intending to head straight back to Devon,' Simon said. 'He wanted to see his wife again, and make sure she was safe.'

'Perhaps so.'

'Who was this Redcliffe? Why should Baldwin seek his death?'

'As for that, I do not know,' Sir Roger said, but his eyes were thoughtful. 'Redcliffe was only a merchant, but he was a friend of mine, and I would not see him killed and not try to find the culprit.'

'Unless he tried to waylay Baldwin, I see no reason why he would want to kill the man.'

'You were in London, you say?'

'Yes.'

'How was it?'

'Very bad.'

Sir Roger gave him a quick look and nodded. 'I heard about Bishop Walter. I didn't owe him any gratitude, but I was sad to hear of his end.'

'I saw it,' Simon said. 'It was terrible. No man deserves that sort of a death.'

'All too many die for the wrong reasons. The kingdom deserves better than it has received in the last years,' Sir Roger said grimly. 'And I shall do all in my power to see that it does. From now on, there will be fairness and justice. No more of Despenser's thieving.'

'I see.'

His stoic response was enough to make Sir Roger grin. 'Come! You will find your life improved, too, when Despenser is gone. For now, though, we still have to capture him. That may take a little time.'

'What do you want of me?' Simon asked.

'You?'

'At first you wanted me to search for the killer of the woman Cecily. I learned all I could, but it wasn't that which you wanted.'

'What makes you say that?'

'You said you wanted to bring law and order to the city, that allowing her killer to go free would show people that anyone could break the law. But if you were serious, you would have left me there and given me more time to seek her murderer. And yet here I am, joining you on a hunt for the King.'

Mortimer smiled. 'So?'

'So you didn't have any real interest in finding the woman's killer.'

'I spoke to your friend Sir Charles, and he said something quite interesting. He suggested that the woman could have been killed by the same man who killed Squire William. Perhaps it was your priest.'

'Father Paul? It is highly unlikely. I didn't think he seemed guilty when I spoke to him, but I admit his cloth could have blinded me to his guilt.'

'So: you discovered the probable killer. And I can do nothing with him because he enjoys the Benefit of Clergy, and is secure from secular authority. Only the Church can arrest him and prosecute him. So if I go to him, what do I achieve? Instead of showing that no one is above the law, I wonderfully reinforce the view that a whole section of the community is precisely that. And not only will he not be punished, he will also very likely make others decide to take the law into their own hands. Which would mean you had forced me to incite other men to break the law. So a gang of men would go to this Father Paul's church, and slay him, and defile the church, and themselves in the process. And I suppose then I would be entitled to round up his killers and hang them. So some justice would finally have been done. Is that what you would like?'

Simon grimaced. 'I think I prefer my part of Devon and the laws I maintain there. It is easier than the judgement you display.'

'You are wise, my friend,' Sir Roger said. 'Now, you did ask what I wanted with you. Let me give you another riddle. I should like to learn who killed Thomas Redcliffe, the merchant I told you of. He was slain by the Severn. That is all. Find who it was, and I will set you free immediately.'

'With no body, without seeing the land? You think this is possible?'

'I don't know. I do know that it occupies my mind all the while. I would know who killed him – and *why*.'

Caerphilly Castle

The castle was quieter this morning.

Baldwin went out to the battlements and made a circuit of the walls, looking out over the encircling lands, trying to see the approach of Mortimer's army, but there was nothing in sight. Only the town and the spread of the valley all about, the hills far off. It was a beautiful sight, and a tormenting one. He was sure that Mortimer was out there, that he would appear soon. Until then, all they could do was wait.

'Sir Baldwin, a fine morning, is it not?'

'Sir Ralph,' Baldwin said. 'I wish you a good day, sir.'

'We can only hope,' the other knight replied. He cast an eye into the outer ward. 'Quiet today. All the men still sleeping off their drink.'

'I think so,' Baldwin agreed. 'It is alarming to see so many turn to ale for comfort. They are despairing of ever seeing their homes again, I think.'

'They are not alone,' Sir Ralph chuckled, but without humour. 'Still, if I could, I would not leave now. I owe much to the King and his patronage.'

Baldwin nodded. 'I have sworn loyalty. I would not willingly be forsworn.'

He mused on that strange aspect of his life, staring out at the hills to the east, his elbows on the battlements. When he had joined the Knights Templar, it had been in a spirit of humility and gratitude. He would have died at Acre when the Moors invaded the city, were it not for the Templars rescuing him. They put him on one of the last ships from the stricken city before the Temple was overrun, and it was to demonstrate his thanks that he took the three vows: poverty, chastity and obedience. They were the same oaths taken by monks through the centuries, and just because the Templars were formed to protect with all their strength the pilgrims who tried to make their way to the Holy Land, that did not change their monkish behaviour. Their Rule was as stringent as that of the Benedictines, or the Cistercians. In many ways, it was harsher.

But then the King of France demonstrated his vile greed, and persuaded the Pope to join with him. The two conspired to destroy the Templars, and arrested the entire Order throughout France on Friday 13 October 1307 – a date that would live on in infamy. Not since the false trial of Christ Himself had a more deplorable court submitted a more unjust act than that of the Pope when he later sought to destroy the Order utterly.

So Baldwin had been released from his vows. Not willingly, not by his choice, but irrevocably. Even when he married his wife, Jeanne, he found making the new vow, so entirely contrary to his existing oath of chastity, very difficult to speak. Perhaps he had now earned his freedom. He had, he hoped, lived a worthwhile life. Honour and truth had guided him on his journey, and if he were to die here in the service of the King, well, he could accept that he had to die at some time, just as all men must, and at least dying to protect his liege-lord would be honourable. He only prayed that his wife Jeanne would understand.

Sir Ralph was speaking. Baldwin cocked his head. 'I am sorry, I was wool-gathering. You said?'

'I was thinking aloud. I have no children, you see, so my lands will go to my brother, who has remained with Mortimer. We agreed that he should do so. That way, if one was found to have

369

acted as a traitor, at least the lands would remain in the family somehow. But I would not go to Mortimer in any case. The idea of tying my fortunes to an adventurer like him . . . no, treachery has never appealed to me.'

'Nor me,' Baldwin said. He looked out over the countryside again. 'They will come from there, I think.'

'Yes, although I do not know how Mortimer would attack a place like this.'

'It would be a lengthy siege,' Baldwin agreed. 'And he would have to accept heavy losses. The troops would freeze in winter; in summer they would soon succumb to fevers. And he would have the expense of paying them all, with so many mercenaries in his force. Add to that the fact that mining to destroy towers and walls would be impossible with these lakes, and the double circle of walls, and the assault would be enormously costly.'

Sir Ralph nodded grimly. 'I keep thinking about Bristol's collapse – the notion that Earl Hugh of Winchester surrendered the castle. That was a surprise. To do that, knowing that he must surely die – that speaks of courage.'

'You think he knew he would be killed? Perhaps he tried to sue for peace on terms which were later denied?' Baldwin said.

'I would say many things about Sir Roger Mortimer, but that he would knowingly lie and break an oath, I reject. He was always honourable until he was arrested by the King. Even now, I doubt he would be dishonourable to that extent. No, I would think that he rejected all applications for terms. Which adds to Earl Hugh's courage. He must have known he would enjoy no quarter if he submitted.'

'Indeed, if that is so, he acted with enormous bravery,' Baldwin said.

'I suppose he did so to protect the city from attack, and to spare the lives of all those in the castle.'

Baldwin nodded, and then found his gaze moving to the town at the feet of the castle as he considered how many men, women and children lived inside it. 'I wonder if his courage is shared by his son?' he thought aloud.

CHAPTER THIRTY-EIGHT

Two Fridays before the Feast of St Martin[1]

Caerphilly Castle

Baldwin stood in the deep recess of the doorway and stared out at the greyness. There was no possibility of seeing ten thousand men approaching in this. It was raining, with an all-encompassing fog.

He made his way out onto the slick stones of the walkway, careful not to come too close to the edge. It would be a demeaning end to slip from the wall here and tumble to his death in the inner ward. There was a hooded and cloaked figure up ahead, whom he assumed was Sir Ralph, and Baldwin put his head down and walked to him. 'Miserable weather again, sir.'

'Yes.'

Baldwin stopped in shock, then bowed low, about to drop to his knee. 'My lord, accept my apologies, I did not realise in this weather . . .'

[1] 31 October 1326

'Sir Baldwin, please. No one saw, no one can guess,' the King said. He sounded peevish from lack of sleep and from worry. Then he sighed. 'Please, Sir Knight, you and I, out here, are no more than two knights who have found a few moments in which to enjoy some leisure. Soon our leisure will be over. Please, humour me in this.'

'My lord, I can try,' Baldwin said.

'This castle was built by the Earl of Gloucester forty or more years ago. Strange – it was a cause of dispute with the Welsh even then. They stopped its construction a number of times. Of course, my father would not brook any obstruction to his plans, but he showed some patience, I believe. Even when the Welsh wouldn't come to pay homage to him in Westminster, my father journeyed all the way out to Gloucester so that Llywellyn didn't have to travel to London. That was when he broke with the Welsh, since Llywellyn did not deign to travel even that far. It was a humiliating insult. So my father returned, but this time with fifteen thousand spears behind him, and took the country.'

He was silent a few moments and then, when he spoke again, it was so mournfully that Baldwin felt a sympathetic lump in his throat.

'Have I truly been so foul as King that none will support me?'

'My liege, please!' Baldwin said. 'You know you have my sword at your side – *and* Sir Ralph's.'

'Yes. Two of the very best knights in my kingdom. And what will be your reward, eh? Death, I suppose – the same as awaits all the others who remain with me. My Chancellor, my closest adviser. All will die.'

Baldwin could not help but glance towards the town. 'And the people here, my lord. They will lose all.'

The King shook his head with an enormity of sadness. 'They called me the Prince of Wales. I suppose it is natural that I should fight my last battle with my people. But to cause so much hardship, so many deaths . . . better by far I should do something to prevent any more bloodshed.'

Baldwin said nothing. The King was staring out into the greyness with eyes shadowed by his hood. All Baldwin could see was a gaunt face, the beard sodden and thin, the cheeks sunken, the man's eyes gleaming with despair.

'My King, I wish I could do something to help,' Baldwin said quietly.

'My friend, there is nothing any man might do for me without *men*! That is what I need. I sent for them days ago. Messengers were on their way here before I even reached Gloucester, to Gruffydd Llwyd in the north, and to Rhys ap Gruffydd in the south, but neither has appeared. They were both loyal in the past – I don't understand why they have deserted me.'

'Perhaps they themselves have been attacked on the way here?' Baldwin suggested.

'Perhaps,' the King said, and sighed. 'It matters little. If no one comes soon, the castle will be overrun. I have demanded procurers to fetch all the food they can so that we can survive a lengthy siege here, but what is the point when there are no men to eat it? You know Bogo de Knoville? No? I pardoned him last year for supporting my enemies, in return for only a thousand Marks. He has served me well, and I agreed to rescind half the fine for his loyalty three weeks ago. For his efforts in the last week, I was to rescind the remaining half – and what has he done? He has ridden off with his men today. All of them. I fear he will join the Queen too.'

Baldwin winced. Bogo de Knoville had been the leader of the last significant force the King possessed here. Without him and his men, there was no possibility of surviving an attack even by a small force. They were stuck here, in one of the kingdom's strongest fortresses, and to leave would be near suicidal.

'And you know the worst, most galling fact?' the King asked quietly. 'Down in the undercrofts I have more than twenty thousand pounds in gold and silver. Enough money to arm all the men in Wales, if need be. Enough to reward all of them like princes, were they only to step forward. But no one comes! No one supports me any longer!'

Gloucester

Simon woke to the rattle of armour, the rasp of swords being sharpened, the tramp of boots and everywhere the squeak of harnesses and leather under strain.

Rubbing his eyes, he eased himself sideways from the bench on which he had slept, and sat for a while, hunched, running a hand through his hair and grumbling to himself. He had the beginnings of a sore throat that felt as though he had swallowed broken glass, and his head was heavy. To sniff made his skull ache.

'Awake, Bailiff?' Sir Charles enquired. He wandered over with a quart of ale and half a loaf of bread. 'Best ready yourself, I think. It's likely we'll be ordered to travel on soon.'

Simon groaned. 'I'm going to give up travelling when this is all over. Once I get home, I will stay there, I swear, and will never again try to take up arms or interest myself in any aspect of the realm. It's nothing to do with me. All it does is give me a headache and a chill.'

'Drink up. It's a good ale, this. I fetched it myself. Have you some of that smoked sausage still? I've lost mine.'

Simon searched for his pack, and found it near the wall where someone had kicked it. Inside was a small chunk of sausage, which he cut in two, giving half to Sir Charles. His own piece he sliced thinly, chewing each morsel one at a time. At least the strong garlic and salt soothed his throat a little. 'So what do we do today?'

'We'll ride to Hereford first, then on into Despenser lands. Wales – that's where the King is now. And I dare say he will be trying to raise an army.'

'With what?' Simon said sourly.

'Oh, he has money with him, and plate and gold. Despenser has plenty of coin of his own, too. You can be assured that where those two are, there is no shortage of money.'

'Wonderful! So I must continue on this mad rampage through the countryside in the hope of catching the King, when all I want to do is investigate the murder of the man as Sir Roger instructed me to, so I can release my family.'

'Simon, you are present at the scene of an adventure,' Sir Charles said, hurt. 'It is the kind of event that many would dream of experiencing.'

'I have a cold,' Simon reminded him, sipping some of the ale. He threw back his head and gargled with it. The ale soothed him for a moment or two, but then the glass renewed its attack, and his sinus was trickling into it too. It made him want to choke. 'All I want is some peace.'

But there was to be none that day. The column was soon mounted and off again, this time heading north and west to Hereford, as Sir Charles had told him.

At least with the weather improving a little through the day, Simon was able to study the men about him. He was surprised to see that Otho and Herv and their group were quite rare; the rest were mostly Hainaulters, with a number of French free-booters, and he could understand only a little of what they said. Even when he was speaking in his own fluent French, he received little more than expressions of bemusement and shrugs.

It was because of this that he and Sir Charles tended to remain with the men in Otho's little group.

'There was a hundred of us, nearly, when we set off,' Otho explained. 'But there was one got run down by a horse, one fell into a well in the dark, another slashed his leg and we had to leave him, two got fevers . . . There's scarce seventy of us now.'

'Who do you march with?' Simon asked.

'Our lord was with Leicester. He's a knight banneret called Sir Daniel of Henret. His is only a small manor, but he has a number of vills under his lordship.'

'So you were marching for . . .?'

'The King, until Leicester changed sides and moved to support the Queen. So now we have to be as loyal as possible to her.'

'An easier dedication, I suppose,' Simon said with a grin.

'It's all easy enough. We're just peasants, we do as we're commanded,' Otho said, but with a sidelong look that proved his seriousness was false.

'Masters, it is good to hear an English voice again,' Sir Laurence said, riding up alongside Sir Charles. 'Bailiff, good day to you, Sir Charles.'

'Are you finding it hard to converse with the men here?' Simon asked. 'I thought it was only me.'

'No, their speech is difficult for me as well,' Sir Laurence said. He lowered his voice. 'In truth, though, it is the company of Sir Stephen Siward which I find more unappealing.'

'Ah,' Sir Charles said.

'Well, you can hardly trust him, can you? The man is a disgrace to the Order of Chivalry. To have run out on us and given up the city to the Queen, in denial of all his oaths to the King, was a shameful act – the act of a man who has no sense of honour.'

Simon nodded. 'I too found it repellent. I just hope the bastard keeps away from me.'

Sir Charles shrugged like a confused Hainaulter. 'You have to admit, he probably saved all our lives. You may choose to dislike the man for a number of reasons, my friends, but do not lose sight of the fact that you are alive now due to his cowardice. I wouldn't consider it such a terrible fault!'

Sir Laurence smiled thinly. 'You are incorrigible, Sir Charles. Master Puttock, may I ask if it is true that you have been asked to investigate a homicide?'

'Yes, Sir Roger asked me to look at the death of a man called Thomas Redcliffe,' Simon said. 'Why?'

'I have no idea whether it is relevant, but he used to be a successful merchant who imported destriers and other horses for the King. The King used him as a confidential messenger occasionally into Aragon.'

'But Mortimer said he was a trusted friend of his!' Simon said, confused.

'Perhaps the man was a friend to *both* sides,' Sir Laurence considered. 'I thought you would be grateful to hear.'

'I am, and I thank you,' Simon said.

'Well,' Sir Charles breathed as Sir Laurence trotted away. 'So, was there anyone this merchant was not friendly with?'

Two Saturdays before the Feast of St Martin[1]

Caerphilly Castle

In the end, Baldwin was not sure whether it was compassion or the urge to flee that weighed most heavily in the balance.

[1] 1 November 1326

The King was almost silent the night before at the evening meal, and left soon after to return to his little portable altar, communing with God as best he might. After he left, the men in the hall were subdued. A couple grew quietly drunk in a corner, but even they were moderate in their language, and neither tried to draw steel. It was as though everyone in the castle realised that their situation had indeed grown hopeless since the departure of Bogo's men.

Sir Ralph was feeling the strain too, Baldwin saw. The lines at the sides of his mouth were graven more deeply, and there were bruises under his eyes. This was not mere tiredness from lack of sleep, it was the lassitude of a man who had been driven too far. While riding and preparing to fight, a man could retain a semblance of his former fortitude, but when those pursuits were removed and he was left to wait for an attack, even a knight would grow fretful.

Thus it was that the news that they were all to leave the castle came as a surprise – and a most welcome one.

The castle was to be left in the hands of Sir John Felton and Sir Hugh le Despenser's oldest son, Hugh, who was sixteen years old and would need Sir John's help. It was stocked with provisions enough to survive a siege lasting many weeks. All the King's unnecessary belongings, even his chamber book which recorded all his expenditure, were to remain, and he and a small force of men would make their way west to Neath via Margam. King Edward had a desperate hope that he might still meet with some of the men from North or South Wales, and enlist them in his support.

Only a small number of men were to join him – the remainder of his household knights, Despenser, Baldock and some few others. Their intention was to ride away at speed and outrun the slower host of Mortimer, which would almost certainly be hauling large weapons of war with them.

379

The King appeared in the inner ward when all the others were prepared and ready. At the steps to the hall, he went to the son of Sir Hugh le Despenser and Sir John Felton, offering his best wishes for their security and insisting that they held on to the castle and did not surrender it shamefully. Then he gave his thanks to all the men in the castle for protecting him so well, and reminding them that he was their lawful King, the one who had been anointed with God's holy oil.

With that, and as the men all shouted their approval, he strode to the mounting block and easily threw his leg over his horse. Always athletic, he looked like King Arthur now in his armour, and Baldwin, for all his usual cynicism, felt his heart thrill a little at the sight.

The King's standard-bearer hefted his great flag, and the King's banner opened out, displaying the royal arms of gules, three lions passant gardant in pale or, armed and langued azure. As soon as the bearer's horse began to move, a little wind caught the flag, and the lions rippled on the bright red material, their blue claws and tongues catching the light.

Baldwin waited in turn until he too was at the gate, and suddenly, as he rode beneath the massive gatehouse, he felt as though some of the worry of the last few days was at last dissipated. He looked across at Jack, who wore a fretful expression, as though wondering whether he would ever stop this aimless travelling about the country. Wolf was at his left foot, his allegiance apparently switched from Baldwin to the boy. And in the distance, Baldwin was sure that he could see a familiar slim figure: Roisea.

Yes, action was enough to remind him that he was a man, not a caged animal, and as his horse's hooves thundered over the timbers of the bridge across the moat, Baldwin could have sung for joy, just for the fact of being on horseback and free once more.

Over the bridge, Despenser paused and Baldwin saw him look back towards the castle. And in his eyes, Baldwin saw genuine tragedy.

Sir Hugh le Despenser knew he would never see his son again.

CHAPTER THIRTY-NINE

Two Sundays before the Feast of St Martin[1]

Hereford

After another long ride, they at last reached Hereford in the middle of the day, and Simon was pleased just to clamber down from his horse.

He had always prided himself on the fact that he was hardy, and that his common practice of riding each morning, and travelling over Dartmoor to his various duties, made him more resilient than most, but after riding for so long, since the middle of October, he was feeling more than worn: he felt bone weary.

It was not only him, either. As he dropped heavily from the saddle and looked about him, he saw that the others were in a similar state. Even Otho and Herv moved in a lacklustre manner with stiff legs and backs as they set about gathering firewood from some trees at the edge of the roadway. Sir Laurence too was saddlesore, climbing gingerly down from his mount. He had

---

[1] 2 November 1326

spent too long in the castle dealing with the administration of the place, and was unused to so much exercise, and it was clear that Sir Charles too was ready to drop.

Simon gathered up his few belongings and made a little pile along with Otho and Herv's packs, before seeing to his horse. The beast was already head down, cropping the grass at the side of the road, and it was difficult to undo the cinch of the saddle and remove the bridle. There were hostlers moving about, but Simon had no idea whether any would be prepared to help him, and it would have been a long job, had not Sir Charles's groom appeared. He took Simon's brushes and began to clean the beast. 'You go and sit, master. I'll see to this. Sir Charles insists.'

'I am most grateful,' Simon murmured, and stumped over to where the knight sat on a log. 'Thank you, Sir Charles,' he said, and eased himself down beside him.

'It did not look as though you were going to be able to stand much longer,' Sir Charles said with a feeble grin. 'I wasn't sure that I could, either.'

Simon took a look around to see if there was a tavern or inn where they could buy some meats or hot broth, but there was nothing nearby.

They were immediately outside the city of Hereford. Sir Roger Mortimer and the leading elements had already crossed the bridge over the Wye and entered, but the force was now so large that there was no space to accommodate so many, and it was clear that Simon and Sir Charles and the others would be forced to remain out here.

Hereford stood on low-lying ground. The River Wye was immediately in front of them, and it curved around, past the bridge and on. Where the river flowed, the town was well-pro-tected, Simon could see, but even where the river did not form a natural defence, the people had recently renewed a system of ditches. The soil in the ditches was dark and stood out clearly, and beyond them the city walls were tall and immensely strong, from the look of them, with a series of huge towers to give more opportunities for the defence to attack an enemy.

However, Simon was less interested in the city, and more keen on the direction he would be taking later. Off to the west he could see the hills rising, thickly wooded, through which he guessed he would have to ride soon, in order to seek the King. With his aching legs, that was a daunting sight.

'Do you think we'll have to go today?'

Sir Charles shook his head. 'I refuse to go anywhere before tomorrow. My backside has been flattened by the shape of that saddle, and I will ride no further until I have allowed it to recover a little. In any case, if we do try to press on at this rate, we will risk the lives of our horses.'

Simon had to agree with that. 'Have you been to Wales before?'

Sir Charles looked at him suspiciously. 'Not for a long time.'

'I just wondered. You see, I have never been there,' Simon explained, and a little of the tension in Sir Charles seemed to leave him.

'It is a hilly country, with many woods and copses, and a lot of rolling moorland. It is good land for farming sheep, but very wet at most times of the year.'

'How easy will it be to find them, do you think?'

Sir Charles gave a chuckle. 'If the King has managed to persuade anyone to fight for him, he will be very easy to find, but if, as I suspect, he is learning that he has no friends in Wales, it will be much harder, for he must know he is a wanted man: he will have to hide while we ride towards him.'

'And what then?' Simon said more quietly.

'Then? We find him and invite him to join us here for supper.'

'If he refuses?'

Sir Charles shrugged once more. 'Perhaps the Hainaulters won't understand him. They don't speak very good English or French, do they? They may just feel that it would be better to bring him here anyway so that he can be protected, eh?'

Simon was tempted to ask what they might do if the King refused their invitation, but there was a look in Sir Charles's eye that dissuaded him. The fact was, Sir Charles had been a mercenary for some years. He had suffered the loss of his lord, and had become a wandering exile for so long that it had coloured his entire outlook. The man probably had reserves of brutality that Simon could only guess at.

Otho and Herv had a fire ready, as did many others all along the roadway. Groups were huddling around them, feeding them with sticks and chatting in a subdued manner as they stared at the flames. Simon and Sir Charles sat with Otho and Herv, and before long they were joined by Sir Laurence and two grooms.

'Are you to come with us?' Simon asked Sir Laurence.

'Me?' Sir Laurence laughed. 'I don't think so. I gave my oath to the King. I would hold to that, and Sir Roger knows it.'

'I expect he will send a number of us to scout,' Sir Charles said. He squatted down nearer the fire, his cloak over his shoulders, holding his hands to the warmth. 'You, Bailiff, me, and one or two other knights. He will have to keep a guard here, and the Queen and Duke will need their own guards for their households, so he will not want to send too many.'

'He has plenty to keep here *and* to send off to fetch back the King,' Sir Laurence observed sourly. 'He is not short of men.'

Sir Charles glanced at him. 'I heard he will send Sir Stephen off so you and he don't come to blows again.'

'That would be sensible. If I see him again, I may kill him,' Sir Laurence said bluntly. 'I would have nothing to do with a man who was so false to his word.' He threw a look at Otho and Herv. 'It was your men there who stopped me.'

'Was this for surrendering the city?' Simon said.

'Yes. He is an evil man. A oath means nothing to him. You may believe that he will behave honourably, but unless there is money in it for him, your wishes will be misplaced.'

Sir Charles pulled a face. 'I know the chivalric ethos as well as any man, Sir Laurence, and I tried to live by it when I was servant to Earl Thomas of Lancaster. But when a man, even a knight, is forced to fend for himself, he will sometimes take a course he regrets.'

'My friend, I make no comment about you. I am sure you are an honourable knight,' Sir Laurence said. 'Sir Stephen, however, is avaricious – he wants money for its own sake. If he were not noble, I think he would have been happy as a moneylender, loaning money for interest like any other usurer.'

'Sometimes a man must borrow money,' Sir Charles argued.

'Yes, but there are some who use it despicably, especially those who should know better – such as Sir Stephen.'

'In what way?' Simon asked.

'In big cities like Bristol, where there are many merchants, you will always find one or two who need additional funds, and they go to moneylenders to raise the sums required. Sir Stephen used them too.'

'That is hardly his fault,' Simon said gently. 'If a man strikes hardship and needs money, you surely wouldn't blame him, would you?'

'No. But there are some who like to live an extravagant life, and when those men go to the moneylenders just to finance a new horse or their gambling, I can condemn them. It is wrong to try to improve your status by borrowing. A knight or a squire should enjoy his rewards as a loyal servant to his master. The feudal system works well for all. When a man decides to take money instead, he unsettles the whole system.'

'You say that Sir Stephen took money?'

'He gave away a city to his feudal lord's enemy,' Sir Laurence said uncompromisingly. 'And he enjoys ostentation. Do I know that he took money? No. But do I suspect it? Oh, yes. I would not trust that man within the reach of my sword. I would never allow him within my guard.'

Two Mondays before the Feast of St Martin[1]

Hereford

Simon checked the cinch and tugged at the straps holding on his blankets and clothing. Wrapped inside were some dried strips of meat, a few biscuits and a loaf of bread. He wore a new thick jack of padded material over his tunic, with a thinner fustian cotte over the top. A broad-brimmed hat kept his head warm and the worst of the rain from his eyes, while over his back he had a long cloak. The rent made by the felon who had chased his family just before he met Sir Charles had been sewn up. Swinging up on the beast's back, Simon saw that the men were gathering a short distance away, and he went over to join them.

Sir Charles sat easily on his mount. He wore a simple armour, light enough to allow him movement without being too tiring on a long ride. Sir Stephen Siward was nearby, astride a black destrier which, although it was no larger than Simon's rounsey, was spirited enough to keep the hostlers away. His flailing hooves spoke of his fighting temper.

There were a good number of Hainaulters and Frenchmen

[1] 3 November 1326

with them, but the majority were the men of Henry of Lancaster, and they were all keen to catch the King and his diminishing circle of supporters.

'Sir Charles!'

A short man with a gait like a barrel on a rolling ship swaggered up to the knight's horse and clouted him on the knee.

'Simon, this reprobate is Sir Giles of Langthwaite. An old friend of mine.'

'I knew this fellow before he could hold a sword,' the short man said, but by the grin he gave the other knight, Simon could see that he was fond of Sir Charles. 'So, sire, you are with us to hunt the King?'

'Aye,' Sir Charles nodded. 'And all his friends.'

'Yes. The King, Despenser, Arundel, Baldock and any others who ride with him. Well, we'll soon have 'em. Can't leave things as they are.'

Before long, the men had been arrayed in groups. The Earl of Lancaster's men were to the fore, with some Welsh behind them, and the Hainaulters brought up the rear. Simon and Sir Charles rode with Sir Stephen, not far behind the Earl himself.

'Sir Charles,' Simon said as they rode, 'the Earl of Lancaster was your master before, was he not?'

'That was Thomas of Lancaster, the Earl's brother, yes,' Sir Charles said.

Simon knew that Sir Charles had lost his home, position and status when his master had been executed. Because Earl Thomas had been judged a traitor, many of his servants were forced into hiding or exile. But even though the family of Lancaster had a stain on its reputation, clearly the King had seen fit to maintain the earldom and not simply destroy all memory as he had tried to do with the Earl himself.

'It was quite wrong,' Sir Stephen said. 'The Earl Thomas

was a decent man, and to treat him in such a manner was disgraceful.'

'You mean his execution?' Sir Charles said.

'Of course,' Sir Stephen said, his round face serious. 'The Earl was the King's own cousin, in God's name! That is taking ruthlessness a step too far. And as I said, the Earl was a good man. You know that there have been pilgrims to his grave? They say that astonishing miracles have been seen there.'

'Yes,' Sir Charles said languidly. 'They say as much at any church where they need money.'

'That is an appalling slur!'

'Yes. And it's true, as well.'

Simon had to look away before his amusement could be seen by Sir Stephen.

'What of you, master? Did you get to the truth of the murder of that woman in Bristol?'

Simon felt a quick shame. He had forgotten all about Cecily in her lone grave. The last days had been so filled with excitement and fear, that the poor woman was driven completely from his mind. 'No, I fear not. I learned about Squire William's death, though, and the priest you told me of – Father Paul, the man who ran away with Squire William's wife.'

'It was a terrible event, that,' Sir Stephen said. 'Dreadful to think a man like William could stoop to such a killing. But you haven't found whoever it was who killed the maid?'

'Cecily was killed without witnesses, it would seem,' Simon said. 'She died quickly, with the one stab, so that is good, but as to who did it – I do not know. Perhaps one of Sir William's men?'

'Not "Sir" William: he was only a Squire,' Sir Stephen said sharply.

'My apologies, Sir Stephen. I meant no offence,' Simon said

quickly. A prickly knight was not a pleasant companion. 'Squire William had several men with him when he stormed the banker's house, so perhaps it was one of them who slew Cecily, in revenge for her giving evidence against them.'

'Perhaps so. They would have been released as soon as he was, so they would have had the same opportunities. And while Squire William's home is some miles away from Bristol, and thus beyond Cecily's reach, his men would be more fearful of being denounced in the streets.'

Simon could not disagree with that. The men who had been paid by Squire William would already have a reputation, and if a woman was to point to them and accuse them of being the source of her fear, others in the street might decide to do her the honour of setting about them. It would be hardly surprising if one of the gang reckoned it would be better to kill her as well, before that happened.

'I wonder, Sir Stephen, why the men left Cecily alive in the first place? It makes no sense. They killed everyone else in the Capons' house, did they not? Did that not strike you as peculiar?' Simon asked.

Sir Stephen shrugged, but Sir Charles had been listening carefully. He now set his head to one side, his eyes narrowed as he said, 'You say that all in the house were killed bar one? That is indeed most peculiar, Bailiff. Was she hiding when they arrived?'

Simon looked at Sir Stephen, who stared into the middle distance, racking his brains.

'No,' he said at last. 'I recall that she had run out into the front court, where she was captured by the Squire himself, and there and then, he snatched the baby from her and dashed his head against a wall. I think that is what she said.'

'That was written in the Coroner's rolls,' agreed Simon. 'The Squire caught her outside – but then saw no need to hurt her.'

'I believe she collapsed, probably from fainting. You know what women can be like,' Sir Stephen said.

'So he thought she was dead anyway, you mean?' Simon said.

Sir Charles gave a harsh laugh. 'You believe a Squire would do that? Assume someone was dying when he had not even struck a single blow? No, more likely he'd have struck three times at a fallen body just to make sure. A man cannot take risks.'

'I see,' Simon said. In his mind's eye, he saw again Cecily's body, with the single stab wound. 'Would a knight have behaved in the same way, Sir Charles?'

'How do you mean?'

'Would a knight have stabbed many times, "just to make sure"?'

Sir Charles looked at him very directly. 'When we meet the King's men, and if any of them dare to stand against me, I will strike each of them precisely as many times as I can before they fall to the ground.'

'I was thinking of the woman. Cecily. Would you have struck at her more than once?'

'No, not more than once,' Sir Charles laughed. 'But that once would have taken off her head!'

CHAPTER FORTY

Thursday before the Feast of St Martin[1]

Neath Abbey

They arrived late in the afternoon, as the light was fading. This pleasant little abbey, all grey stone walls, but with some well-carved blocks of paler stone at the corners and towers to reinforce them, it was a pretty sight as they approached, and Baldwin had asked a man who seemed to know the place a little about it.

'Yes. It was built under a warrant from the King's father, Edward I, who always loved this area. Fortunately, it is one of the few places down here that wasn't attacked by the rebels.'

Baldwin nodded. In the short wars of the Marcher Lords against the overweening arrogance of Despenser, many of these little abbeys as well as castles and manors owned by Despenser were laid waste. The buildings were robbed of all their better fixtures and anything movable was stolen.

[1] 6 November 1326

They rode in through the gates, and Baldwin was glad enough to drop from his saddle. The journey had not been long, only eight miles or so, but with the cold weather, it was not pleasant to ride even that far.

They were all given a little time to take some refreshment and settle themselves in any spare corners they could find. Only the King's closest companions would share the hall, while he took a chamber set next to it, over a small storage room. The Abbot had offered his own chamber, but the King piously refused his generosity. 'This is your kingdom,' he had said with a small smile.

At the time it had sounded wondrously gallant, but Baldwin was sure that there were more prosaic reasons for his decision, such as the fact that the chamber the Abbot had was further from a room large enough to house all his guards, and the hall with its chamber was further from the abbey walls. Even now, tired and emotionally drained as he was, the King was careful about his safety.

The summons for Baldwin and Sir Ralph came as the two were sharing a mess with two others. Their meal, a bowl of good, nourishing broth, with some barley to thicken it, and a loaf of bread between them, was marvellously warming, and Baldwin could feel the heat distributing itself through his body. The call was doubly unwelcome, for it meant leaving the remains in the dish for the other men, but Edward's orders were impossible to ignore.

'You called for us, Your Royal Highness?' he enquired, after he and Sir Ralph had been permitted to stand again.

The King waved his servant away, and leaned back in his seat. He was pale and nervous, a tic twitching near his left eye. Behind him, Despenser said nothing, but chewed at his nails and lower lip all the while. Baldwin thought he seemed unaware of anything that was being said.

'Sir Baldwin, Sir Ralph, I wanted to ask you what you think we should do next,' the King said quietly. 'This is no longer a matter on which I can decide without suggestions from those whom I trust.'

'My firm belief is that you should cross the sea to Ireland,' Sir Ralph said. 'There is no other course open to you, my lord.'

'Sir Baldwin?'

'Your Royal Highness, I do not know this land or the best places in which to fight,' Baldwin replied. 'If I had seen a place better suited than Caerphilly, I would suggest you go there. As it is, I would seriously think about returning to the castle, for the reason that it's got excellent defences and a good store of food. Even with a great siege-train, Mortimer would find it an extraordinarily difficult fortress to demolish, and it would take him a long time. And in that time, perhaps, your people would remember that you are their King. Surely some would come, and perhaps raise the siege?'

'I like this advice better!' Edward said with a triumphant tone, shooting a look over his shoulder at Despenser. 'I would return with a sword in my hand, rather than scuttle off with my tail between my legs.'

'Your Highness,' Despenser began. His voice had become weaker, as though he was fading from the strain of the last months. 'If we had any additional men, Sir Baldwin's advice would make sense. However, we have to live with the position we find ourselves in now. How can we rush back to Caerphilly, now that the Mortimer and his men are no doubt already at its drawbridge? It is too late. The only choice is for you to do as Sir Ralph said, and head further west.'

'Run away to exile, then,' the King said flatly.

'There are times when a leader has to escape the traps set for him,' Despenser said. 'Even the Mortimer succeeded in that.'

'You want me to copy a traitor?' the King rasped suddenly.

'There is another aspect, Your Majesty,' Sir Ralph said in a placatory tone. 'If you keep heading west, you may come across more allies among your people in Wales. You have enough friends here. Many will come to your call.'

'Not *one* has come to my aid so far, and we have journeyed so far through the land already. How can I believe that there is a host of men waiting to support me when not a one has shown me his face, eh? Do you think me a fool who must be cosseted and lied to, in order that I may continue to believe? Believe in what? I don't believe that the country wants me, I don't believe that the realm will come to my banner any more. I have lost, lost all. But if I turn back and *fight*, then maybe the people will see that their King is resolute, and may come back to my standard.'

'Send men to the west, Your Majesty,' Sir Ralph urged him. 'Send to see whether they will come to your assistance, as they should, for they are all men of Despenser's lands.'

'They are my men, but I fear they do not want to obey their own lord,' Despenser said dully.

'Then we should ride and find a ship,' Sir Ralph said uncompromisingly. 'You must not be captured, my liege. Under no circumstances should we permit that to happen.'

'I . . . I do not think I should leave the kingdom. They already say I have deserted the realm – did you know that? The son of a whore has said that I have left England *extra regnum*, and that this is the reason why he is permitted to declare himself Regent. Have you heard such a thing before? He dares to do this, and I cannot prevent it because no one comes to my support!'

'My liege, *please*! He has done this already, so there is nothing to be changed by taking ship to Ireland. All you need do is collect a host of men from that land, and return and defeat these people. You have skill as a warrior – you showed that at

Boroughbridge when you defeated Earl Thomas of Lancaster. Fetch a host and then come back to retake your kingdom. As soon as the people see you with a force, they will flock to your banner. You only need those first few men with you to make it all a reality.'

'I do not know!' the King cried out.

To Baldwin, it felt like watching torture. The King had sunk in the last days until now he was a pale shadow of his former self. Despenser had gradually declined over the last year, the fear omni-present that soon he would be captured by the King's enemies and killed. Edward's fears were more for his friend than for himself, but whereas before he had always had a belief that at some point men would come to rescue him and Sir Hugh, it was growing clear that no such support existed, because Sir Hugh was detested by one and all.

Everybody knew that the reign of King Edward II was tee-tering on the cliffs, and ruin lay below. Not only for the King himself, but for all those who had remained loyal to him in recent years. There was certainty about the fate of Sir Hugh le Despenser should Mortimer or the Queen capture him, and a degree of equal certainty about many of Sir Hugh's servants; many of the King's other advisers could go the same route. It was not a consideration which gave anyone in the Abbey great comfort.

'Sir Hugh, what should I do?' the King said at last, turning in his seat and giving his friend a look in which Baldwin saw anguish and longing

'Send to find a ship,' Despenser said flatly.

'You think I should leave the kingdom?'

'You need to ask me that? We'll die if we remain here, my lord! We must get away while we still can.'

The King turned to face Baldwin and Sir Ralph. 'There,' he

said, and even as Baldwin watched, he looked as though he was shrivelling into himself, his skin going as grey as a corpse's, his hands suddenly clawlike as they gripped the chair's arms.

As he was dismissed from the company of the King and his adviser, Baldwin felt a pang of sympathy for both men. They were trapped in a cage which they had forged for themselves, and gradually the walls were contracting in upon them. Against his advice, the King had decided to flee the country.

But first they must find a ship to take them.

Sunday before the Feast of St Martin[1]

Hereford

The party straggled along back into Hereford, defeated by the weather and their failure to find anyone who would aid their search for the King.

They had been riding every day since their departure. Down to the coast, all along towards Cardiff and beyond, up to the manors of Sir Hugh le Despenser, visiting all the local magnates to ask who had seen the King or Despenser. All denied any knowledge. Nobody had seen either.

Simon found it soul-destroying to ride about the countryside convinced that the surly, ungracious folk who denied all knowledge of the King were lying; but as the grinning Sir Charles kept pointing out, although the Welsh might not want to surrender him, King Edward was hardly in receipt of their undying devotion, either. At least that meant there were no forces of knife-wielding Welshmen on their trail.

Sir Stephen and Sir Charles joined him.

[1] 9 November 1326

397

'That looks like a bush over that doorway,' Sir Stephen observed. 'Sir Charles, Bailiff, may I offer you a jug of something warming?'

'I'd be glad of it,' Simon said.

Sir Charles said nothing. He was already striding towards the alehouse.

Inside, there was no decoration, but the ale itself was tasty and strong, and the fire in the hearth was burning with a soft hissing sound, the coals warming both by their sight and their heat. Simon took a stool near the fire, thrusting his dagger in among the coals until it was glowing dully, and then used it to stir and heat his ale.

'Wales is a large country,' Sir Stephen remarked, as he sat on an up-ended barrel.

'Large enough to lose a hundred men,' Sir Charles agreed.

'I believed we would have caught him by now.'

'At least we have learned that he has left Caerphilly Castle,' Simon said. 'He won't have come this way, because the Severn will force him up towards Gloucester and that would be too dangerous. He wouldn't risk the lives of his men on a gamble like that.'

'Gamble?' Sir Stephen queried.

'To gamble on passing between the Mortimer's men,' Simon explained. 'He would be caught if he tried to head towards England.'

'What about the ferries?' Sir Charles said.

'I don't suppose they'll be working, not with Mortimer holding the eastern bank. And if a ship did sail, the King would be a fool to board it with the risk of capture on the other shore.'

'True enough. So you think he's gone farther west?'

'Yes. He'll be trying to take a ship to Ireland.' Sir Stephen sipped his ale disconsolately. 'Which means we'll be riding all the way to the arse of the country, I'll be bound. Right over to the Irish Sea. There's a lot of hills between here and there, and from what I've seen, every one has its own raincloud waiting for us.'

'We shall find him soon enough,' Simon said. He eased his shoulders with a grimace. 'That's better. I seem so tense.'

'It's the weather and all the riding,' Sir Charles said. 'Sleeping out in this poxy weather is no good for man or beast.'

Simon grunted and sniffed, but it was not only the residue of his cold, it was also the thought of his wife, back at Bristol, waiting and wondering what had happened to him. She would be suffering, he knew, petrified that he might be dead or injured. News would take time to get to Bristol, because all the messages were being concentrated on Mortimer – wherever *he* was.

They were all glad to buy some hot cakes and cheese, and sat about in comfort as they chewed, all too tired to talk. There was an easiness about all three now, which Simon found comforting. So often a knight would not deign to talk to those beneath his rank. There had been few indeed who would have spoken to Simon only a few years ago. It seemed as though that had changed when he first met Baldwin, and the new knight's respect had done much to change Simon's own attitude to other knights. There was something about his frankness and intelligent approach to people that set Sir Baldwin apart. And of course Simon had known Sir Charles for some years now, since his pilgrimage with Baldwin to Compostela and the great cathedral dedicated to St James, but it was good to see how even a man who hardly knew him, like Sir Stephen, could treat him almost as an equal.

As he was thinking how fortunate he was to have met these men and be spending time with them, he heard steps outside. A man-at-arms entered, gazing about him with a frown. Then: 'You! Are you Bailiff Puttock?'

Simon looked at the fellow. He was maybe three and twenty, with a thin, gangling frame, even with his armour. 'You wish for me?'

'No, Master Puttock, *I* do,' said the Duke of Aquitaine as he stepped into the room.

CHAPTER FORTY-ONE

The fire lighted the Duke's face as he sat. It gave him an other-worldly look, and not a pleasant one, with his cheeks illuminated but his eyes in inverted shadow like a demon. But the red light also showed the lines on his brow and at his cheeks. He was no longer a child.

Simon poured him ale from his own jug. 'Your Highness, I am sorry, I did not see you there.'

'No more should you have. I was hiding behind the door until I could be sure who was here with you. You trust those two – Sir Charles and Sir Stephen?'

The two knights had hurriedly made their apologies when it grew clear that the Duke wanted to speak with Simon alone.

'Yes, I think so. They have been honest with me, I believe. Sir Stephen is Coroner in Bristol, and Sir Charles is a good fellow.'

The Duke's mouth twitched upwards. 'You say that most grudgingly, but I trust your judgement. I have heard that you have not yet found my father. Is that true?'

Simon grunted. If he had, there was little chance that the discovery could have been kept secret. 'No. We have found no trace, but he was apparently at Caerphilly a while ago. A local told us that the King stayed there, but has separated his force, leaving a garrison behind while he has ridden westwards.'

'Where would he have gone?' the Duke said with a frown. He stared into the fire, considering, before nodding to himself. 'Neath. He always had a soft spot for the Abbey there. Assuredly, that is where he has gone. Poor Father. He will feel like the hart who hears the hounds upon all sides.'

'It must be a most uncomfortable situation for the King,' Simon agreed sadly.

'I feel as though I am a traitor to my own father,' the Duke said quietly, his voice scarcely more than a whisper.

'Your Highness, this is none of your making. Your father's adviser has set the realm against himself, personally, and that has made some of the barons react in this way, but it is no reflection on you.'

'You think so?'

Simon felt those eyes bore into him as though the Duke was trying to see into Simon's heart. But the Duke looked away after a moment, and spoke as though to himself.

'But they will see me here, and they will say, "The Duke is only a child. He cannot serve us." And they will look at my mother, and think, she is only a woman. But then they will look at Sir Roger Mortimer and tell each other, "He is a leader of men. He has power and authority; he understands others and how to reward them." So they will ignore me, and instead will cultivate their friendships with Sir Roger, for he is the strong man in the realm. My mother has no authority to compare with his. So, while I am here, Sir Roger will gain in power and influence. And my father: what will happen to him? A solitary figure without allies or friends, a shambling, shuffling figure of fun. The realm will laugh to see him because the kingdom does not fear him any longer. And what then? How will he be able to sit on his throne if no one looks up to him, respects him, *fears* him?'

'My lord, I do not know,' Simon replied. Now that the Duke spoke of it with such a depth of understanding, Simon realised that no matter what happened between Mortimer and the Despenser, the King himself would be in an intolerable position.

'You were asking about someone who was killed in Bristol the other day, I heard,' the Duke said after a few moments, changing the subject. 'A man?'

Simon sighed. 'I have been asked to enquire into so many deaths in recent weeks, it is hard to recall them all. First there was a poor maidservant in the city itself, and then a man who had been a merchant, put to death just outside the city. Sir Roger Mortimer seems to have an interest in all the people of the shire.'

'This merchant, what was his name?'

'Thomas Redcliffe.'

The Duke sat back and smiled at last with real feeling. '*He's* dead? Thank the good Lord.'

'Why?'

'He was an assassin, trying to kill my father.'

Vigil before the Feast of St Martin[1]

Neath Abbey

They had waited here for four whole days now, and there was still no news of a ship that could take them from Wales. It was making Baldwin feel half-crazed to think that all this while, Sir Roger Mortimer was preparing his men and getting ready to

---

[1] 10 November 1326

attack. Today, he had sent Jack off to ride his horse with Wolf to guard him. The boy was fretting at being kept here, too, and needed some fresh air and exercise for his muscles and his mind.

'We have to leave this place,' Baldwin said to Sir Ralph that morning as they walked about the Abbot's garden and orchard.

It was a scene of perfect tranquillity. The sky was clear, for once, and he could see the woods to the north where they covered the hills. Should the weather deteriorate, however, it would be impossible to spot an approaching force of men.

'The King is grown completely despondent,' Sir Ralph said. 'He has already resigned himself to capture, I think.'

'Which is all very well, except it means he is consigning all of us, his most loyal men, to destruction with him,' Baldwin said drily. He took a deep breath. All he could see in his mind's eye was his wife's face as she was told that he had been executed for his part in the flight of the king. 'Sir Ralph, we have to do something!' he went on. 'We can't just sit around, passively waiting for Sir Roger.'

'What do you propose we do?' There was an edge to Sir Ralph's voice which Baldwin had not heard before. 'We can flee farther to the west until we reach the sea, or we could try to work our way eastwards, through Sir Roger's men, hoping to get to the English countryside in one piece. Do you have any better ideas, Sir Baldwin? If so, please enlighten me!'

He watched as Baldwin shook his head, before continuing, 'I know, sir, that the situation is hopeless. Look at the men. They spend their time drinking and gambling. If Sir Roger appeared now, what could they do? Nothing. We are lost, my friend. There is no rescue for us.'

'Sir Ralph, Sir Baldwin . . .'

The knights heard the voice together, and turned to face the man who walked in leisurely fashion towards them. Even messengers had lost all sense of urgency now. This was a man Baldwin had seen before – a tall fellow called Giles. 'The King would see you both now, please.'

Hereford

Simon was ready to leave with the others at dawn. For once, he was glad to be out in the open air.

It was a fact that his interview with the Duke had not gone as well as he could have wished. Simon had had no idea what to say, nor how to react with him. All the while, he was aware that Duke Edward was restraining himself, watching his every word, wary of letting slip anything that could be construed as demeaning to his mother and Sir Roger Mortimer, while not wishing to be thought of as disloyal to his father. It was a tortuous path he trod.

And equally tortuous must be Simon's. It was wearying to talk while having to watch that by neither word nor expression did he dishonour any of them.

Yes, he told himself, looking back at the town in the murk as he trotted away, it was far better, and safer, to be in the saddle and having a clear, defined function to perform, rather than being cooped up inside those town walls. At least here a man could speak freely.

They had ridden a league or more when he found Sir Stephen close by.

'Master Puttock, I am glad that you are well. This riding to and fro is exhausting, is it not?'

Simon grinned, but he remembered Sir Laurence's scathing words about this man, and decided to be circumspect. 'Very tiring, Sir Stephen,' he said.

At least Sir Stephen didn't have too much in the way of wealth on display, unlike some other knights, who often seemed more prone to ostentation than a peacock. Simon detested all that dressing up in bright colours, the tight-fitting clothes, the emphasis on jewels and other fripperies. Sir Stephen's red tunic and parti-coloured hosen, and his thick cloak were all of good quality, but unlike Sir Laurence and others, he was not dripping in gold. His sword was simple and robust rather than decorative, and his hair was cropped short after the fashion of Edward I.

'You have had all your hair off,' Simon remarked.

Sir Stephen nodded. 'It seemed best while we were travelling. Do you have any idea where the King might be?'

'I wish I did,' Simon replied. 'I don't really know Wales, but what I have seen of it shows that a man could hide in the valleys for a year and a day if he wished to, and if the locals did not give him away – but as to whether our King would be happy to live in such a manner is another tale.'

'I doubt it. He enjoys his comforts, as does Sir Hugh le Despenser. The two would find life in a peasant's hut unendurable, to my thinking. They are not so hardy as some.'

Simon glanced at him. It sounded as though Sir Stephen was comparing their own relative positions. If so, he was honouring Simon more than he would have expected. 'And who do you consider so hardy?'

'You are a man of great resilience, master. I have seen that already. I think it is fair to say that I too have more capacity to endure hardship than many. Look at Sir Laurence, for example. To ride out in the rain like this would be a severe hardship to him. He needs his soft bed, his pewter and silver to dine from. Me, I have wooden trenchers, but prefer hard bread for my meats; I can drink wine, but am content with ale or cider. If there are good clothes which will keep me warm or dryer, I will buy them, but only because they serve a practical purpose. And look at my sword: it is simple, crafted of steel, with no decoration.

Then consider Sir Laurence, with his fripperies, his goblet, his sword with gilt over his cross, the velvet of the hilts, his long hair . . . Was there ever a knight who looked less suited to campaigning? Ha! I hope I will never grow so soft and determined to seek fashion.'

Simon was careful to indicate a certain disinterest in his tone. 'I believe Sir Laurence and you don't enjoy the closest of friendships?'

Sir Stephen laughed loudly. 'Closest? No! He and I have always been at odds; he dislikes me because he knows I eschew his life of ease. Oh, I don't hate him, but I do find his attitude . . . *inappropriate* for a knight. Always seeking the next reward is not good for a man whose duty should itself be adequate reward.'

'I don't quite follow.'

'Well, look at him,' Sir Stephen said. 'He's always buying new flamboyant clothes, and then there's his position in the castle at Bristol until Sir Roger took it. Sir Laurence was a close friend of Despenser, I think, and looked to him for his advancement. It is no surprise that he was so keen to hold the city, since to lose it would mean losing his status in the world, and much of his income too. A knight needs an income, of course, but he should be satisfied with the money he receives from his manor.'

'Was he not?'

'He used to go to usurers.'

There was a tightening of his lips at the word, Simon noticed. 'Which usurers are you thinking of?'

Sir Stephen looked at him with a slight frown on his face. 'I was the Coroner of the city, as you know. In that capacity, I would often learn things I was forced to keep silent about – but there is no concealing some facts. I dislike slandering the dead, you understand, but you are a Bailiff. You have seen how the world wags.'

'Capon was a usurer, you mean,' Simon said. 'I have heard it said before.'

Sir Stephen nodded primly. 'Occasionally I have had to make use of such people myself, so I shouldn't look down on others who do the same, but I do confess that I find the attitude of men such as Sir Laurence to be thoroughly disreputable. The man knew Capon's reputation, but still tried to profit by him.'

'In what manner?' Simon asked.

'Sir Laurence was in a position of authority, as Constable of the castle. If he was to need money in order to perform works, he could ask for the city to help – and certain men might find preferential treatment, were they to contribute to the financing of the projects. Capon used to win many of these arrangements, by which he grew more wealthy, as did the Constable.'

'I see,' Simon said. 'It is hard to understand how men can behave so shamelessly.'

Sir Stephen nodded.

'I suppose many men try to keep such dealings a secret, but news of that sort of fraud is bound to become clear in time,' Simon continued. 'It is like the man who tries to conceal his gambling from his wife – it never succeeds. Fraud is the same. You can steal for only so long, before the theft becomes plain. And then a man loses his honour and all.'

'Some men, Bailiff, are not as honourable as they pretend,' Sir Stephen said meaningfully.

Neath Abbey

The two walked into the King's chamber and knelt, but Edward irritably bade them come to him. 'There's no time for all that folderol now. I need your brains, not submission!'

Sir Ralph glanced at Baldwin, and the two strode to join the King.

He was sitting at a small table, studying parchments which held commands in crabbed handwriting. Behind him stood the Abbot and some other men whom Sir Ralph did not know, as well as Despenser.

'These are supposed to guarantee a man's life,' the King said, and he chuckled deep in his throat. 'Orders for safe passage. I wonder who would read them and obey them now?'

He leaned back in his chair and surveyed the two knights with half-lidded eyes, and it was then that Sir Ralph understood that the King was drunk. Heavily intoxicated, in fact.

The King smiled lazily. 'Well, there is no other way for it, sirs. We have played our best game, and we have lost. There is, apparently, no ship in the whole of Wales. All are off at sea, or safely harboured in towns where my enemies hold all power. There is nowhere for me to go to safety.'

Although his mouth was smiling, Sir Ralph was appalled to see a solitary tear form in his eye. It welled, and then, as the King blinked, it moved off, trickling down his cheek. That was the only sign of Edward's misery, and it was somehow more shocking than a fit of fury would have been. Just one single tear of despair. The King could not even summon the justifiable rage at the way that his subjects were ignoring his plight.

'My lord, do not send me from your side,' Sir Ralph said, and dropped to his knees. 'I have given you my pledge to live and die in your service. I will remain with you until the end.'

'Good sir, you are a true, honourable knight, I know that,' the King said. He smiled absently, and his eyes moved away to stare through the window. 'Very well then. Sir Baldwin, I have a task for you alone. You will travel with these men. I have issued safe-conducts for them all: for the Abbot of Neath, Rhys ap Gruffydd, Edward de Boun, Oliver de Burdegala and John de Harsyk. They are to act as my emissaries to Sir Roger and my wife. My lovely

Isabella. They will not allow all to go to ruin about our ears, or so we hope. You, Sir Baldwin, will travel with them, you will protect them as you can, and you will help to bring them back from the Mortimer with answers.'

'What answers do you seek?' Sir Baldwin asked.

King Edward answered flatly, 'Anything at all, Sir Baldwin. I am in no position to demand terms. I must *beg* for them.'

CHAPTER FORTY-TWO

It was already close to noon when Sir Baldwin and the men were horsed. There were ten horsemen, and the rest were on foot. Among the ambassadors he was surprised to see Robert Vyke, the messenger he had met at Cardiff.

'How is your leg?' he asked.

Robert Vyke smiled. 'Well enough for me to swing a sword, Sir Baldwin.'

'I am glad indeed to hear it. You are welcome with us.'

'I'm happy to be doing something, sir. I'm used to being off out and about, not staying indoors all the long day.'

Baldwin nodded, but his mind was already on other matters. He had taken his leave of Sir Ralph, and the two had clasped each other's hands before giving the other a short hug.

'Be careful,' Sir Ralph said. 'Be wary of ambushes and being hunted, my friend.'

'I shall,' Baldwin responded. 'And you be careful around the King and Despenser. Despenser is desperate and the King is desolate. Either could succumb to foolish suspicions or fancies. They could decide that someone here in their household has been spying, or that there is a traitor in their midst. Keep calm and ensure that they remain reasonable, so far as is possible.'

'I will,' Sir Ralph said. 'But Sir Baldwin, there is another thing. There are men with Mortimer who would benefit from the King's capture. Be careful of them.'

'There is a host to fear, then,' Baldwin said.

'Some are worse than others. Be on your guard.'

'I will.' Baldwin bade him farewell, and soon he and his little group were riding out of the Abbot's gates and down on the road towards Margam again.

Feast of St Martin[1]

Twenty miles west of Hereford

It was at noon that day, that Simon found an opportunity of speaking to Sir Charles.

The men had stopped to warm themselves, the weather having been so miserable all morning. Simon felt as though he would never be dry again. His clothing was sodden and clung to his back so closely he felt as if his chemise had been smeared with honey. It was a relief to loose his horse to crop the grass, while he pulled out his waxed purse from his breast.

His purse was the place where he routinely stored his tinder. Today he had a little roll of birch bark he had taken the previous night, along with some scraps of wool and some well-dried lichen, and fragments of charcloth[2]. All about were trees and he snapped off any dead twigs and branches that he could find. When he had enough for a small fire, he lit the charcloth,

[1] 11 November 1326

[2] material which has been semi-burned in a fire, like charcoal

blowing on it as he wrapped it about with tinder, and held the whole lot in a parcel of birch bark. Soon he had flames, and he could set it down, placing the dead twigs over the top. There was a great deal of spluttering and spitting, but before long the twigs were catching light too.

'You have spent a lot of time in the wilds, I see,' Sir Charles said as he joined Simon.

'You could have helped gather some sticks,' Simon remonstrated.

'Ah, but if I were to have done that, I would not have been able to collect this meat and bread,' Sir Charles said with a chuckle.

Simon was not unhappy with the trade. The dried meat was tough as leather, but it was filling to an empty belly.

'I spoke with Sir Stephen yesterday,' Simon said. 'He was most dismissive of Sir Laurence. What do you think of him?'

'Sir Laurence? About as honourable as they come. Why?'

'If Sir Stephen is to be believed, Sir Laurence was less so than you would think. He said that Sir Laurence was taking money in bribes, if I understood him aright. If there was work to be done at the castle, apparently he would give it to those who paid him most.'

'That's hardly unusual,' Sir Charles said with a shrug. 'It is the normal way of things.'

'Did he strike you as the sort of man who would live by profiting from usurers? That is what Sir Stephen intimated, and yet I would expect most knights to look down on those who make money that way.'

Sir Charles gave him a lazy smile, and Simon was reminded again that this man was not one to baulk at profit by any means. He had been forced to survive as a renegade for too many years when his lord had been executed.

'Simon, sometimes men are forced to do things they might regret, for reasons of survival.'

'I make no comment about that. I would probably do the same. But to ally himself to a usurer, surely would be demeaning to a man who did not go through the same trials as you, Sir Charles? This is a man copying Despenser, I suppose, making money from a merchant who was paying him a fee to recommend his loans. To me, Sir Laurence did not seem so bent on profit that he would do something like that.'

'Who is he supposed to have made money from?'

'The banker who died.'

'Capon, the man killed by Squire William?'

'Yes. Sir Stephen said that Sir Laurence was doing very well out of his relationship with Capon.'

'And then Capon died,' Sir Charles said thoughtfully. 'Did that happen recently?'

'I think it was as the Queen was invading the country.'

'If that is true, then he could have sought to prevent any discovery of his actions with Capon,' Sir Charles said. 'In God's name, it would be a bold act – but surely the Squire William was guilty, was he not?'

Simon stared into the flames. 'That is what all say,' he agreed. 'But I am fascinated by Sir Stephen's attitude yesterday. He was very definite about Sir Laurence's dealings with Capon.'

'I daresay the man Capon had similar business dealings with many men in the city,' Sir Charles said. 'And if with Sir Laurence as well, what of it?'

Simon agreed, and before long they were mounted and moving away again. But no matter how he tried to put it from his mind, the matter of Capon and Sir Laurence would keep intruding. Especially since Sir Laurence could have been present at the death of Cecily that night . . . And if the Constable had, in fact, had something to do with the removal of Capon, he would also have wished to silence Cecily, because she might have witnessed his murder of her master.

But no, that was ridiculous, he reminded himself. Cecily had been anxious because of the appearance of Squire William's men. Simon had heard that himself from Emma, her mistress.

Wednesday, Morrow of the Feast of St Martin[1]

Near Abergavenny

Simon and the Earl of Lancaster's men had been riding all that morning, and it was good when they reached a stream to be able to get off and stretch their legs. Sir Charles stood with Simon as their mounts drank from the little brook.

'The trouble with this land is that it is so perfect for ambushes,' Sir Charles said.

Simon had noticed that he kept his right hand free, ready to grab his sword, but as they were here with more than fifty men, all well-armed, the likelihood of an ambush against them was surely remote?

But a little of Sir Charles's wariness communicated itself to Simon and to the other men about. They kept together, and there was less chatter and joking than usual. When one man dropped his helmet with a clatter, more than one reached for a dagger or sword, and he was roundly cursed.

A short while after that, Simon saw one of the younger men freeze and stare ahead at the track. The lad had good hearing, because it was an age before Simon could discern anything, but suddenly, there it was: the irregular thud of hooves.

[1] 12 November 1326

Sir Charles sprang into his saddle, drawing his sword. '*Mount*! By Saint Loy! Mount!'

There was a general rush to horses, and the neighing of alarmed or excited beasts, and then the whole group was ready. Sir Charles grinned at Simon. 'Here we go – glory, or foolishness when we meet a farmer!' and spurred his horse on.

They rounded the next bend, and almost rode into Baldwin.

'Baldwin!' Simon burst out as he saw his old friend. 'What in God's name are you doing up here? Weren't you supposed to be home?'

'I could say the same to you,' Baldwin replied, delighted to see his old friend. 'You were on your way home, too. But where is Margaret – and Peterkin?'

Explaining to each other why they were here whiled away a large part of their journey, and they were already quite close to Hereford before Simon glanced behind him at the other men in the entourage.

'Baldwin, you know the King is lost, don't you?'

He nodded. 'It is clear enough that he cannot win. No one will go to his banner. Not now.'

'Then why will you not join us now? It would be a great deal safer.'

'I serve my King,' Baldwin said simply. 'I cannot turn from him now, just when he needs my support most.'

'Sir Baldwin,' Sir Charles said, riding up alongside him. 'I do appreciate your loyalty, but there is another consideration in all this. I do not wish to have to kill you when we finally catch up with him. If you are there to defend him, we shall have to draw steel.'

'I would regret that too,' Baldwin said. 'Let us hope that it does not come to that, for I would hate to have to kill *you*, Sir Charles.'

416

First Thursday after the Feast of St Martin[1]

Hereford

The Duke heard of the arrival of the contingent of men from the Earl of Lancaster's host when he was at his table with his clerks, and immediately took up his sword and hurried from the chamber, down the passageway towards the hall of the castle where Sir Roger Mortimer was directing the efforts to find the King, stopping only when he reached the doors with the men-at-arms on either side.

This was a quiet hall usually. There were plenty of painted decorations on all the walls, and a set of hangings on one that showed a scene from the life of King Arthur. It was a picture that had caught the Duke's imagination the first time he had seen it, and he thought how marvellous it would be, to recreate a little of the magic of King Arthur's time here in England again. Not that it was likely to happen in his lifetime, he thought. His father's decline in authority and his uncle's rise to power in France both militated against any such possibility.

By now, Duke Edward could hear the raised voices inside. They were enough to make him stop dead. Standing here outside the closed doors, he was unsure whether he was right to try to enter. He was not a king, he was only the son of a King. Duke he might be, but only in name. If he were to upset the Mortimer . . .

It was that thought which made him set his shoulders. His chin rose. For the last years, his father had not dared to upset Despenser, as though Despenser himself had some superiority even over Edward. He did not. He was a servant, nothing more. And nor was Mortimer more important than any other.

[1] 13 November 1326

He too was a servant, whereas Duke Edward would one day be King.

He stepped forward, thrusting with both hands at the doors. They creaked, but then opened wide, one slamming against the wall on his left, and all the men in the room were silenced as the Duke entered, slowly tugging at the fingers of his gloves to pull them free, gazing about at the men inside, nodding shortly to Sir Roger Mortimer, then bowing more graciously to his mother.

'I fear someone forgot to ask me to attend,' he said, striding over the floor to the long table which had been placed in the middle of the room. This was where Mortimer had been sitting, and the knight bowed and vacated the space.

The Duke sat and looked about him. He beckoned the steward and took a goblet from him, sipping as he studied the faces of their visitors. 'Sir Baldwin, you are welcome. Sirs all, please, be seated. Abbot, I hope you are in good health?'

He knew them all. Some of them perhaps better even than Sir Roger.

'My lord Duke,' Mortimer said after a moment, 'these good men have come from your father to ask for terms.'

'How is my father?' He addressed this to the Abbot, a slender old monk with the face of a wizened apple, wrinkled and leathery.

'He is well, my lord. Although it is no surprise to learn that he is very sad at the disloyalty of his subjects.'

'His behaviour towards his subjects has been the cause of their discontent,' Sir Roger grated. 'You will remember that.'

'Sir Roger, please,' the Duke said sharply. 'We are talking about my father. My lord Abbot, please tell him that I am sorry that affairs have come to this.'

'He asks what you intend for him and for his household,' the Abbot said. There was a light in his eyes as he looked at the

Duke, the light of hope. He had been thinking that he would be forced to negotiate with Sir Roger, but now that the Duke was here as well, surely the negotiations would go more easily.

'I intend nothing that—' Duke Edward began, but Sir Roger Mortimer spoke over him.

'He must surrender, along with all his household, and depend upon the kindness which we shall show. He can expect no more.'

'Sir Roger,' the Duke said admonishingly, his anger growing. 'I would prefer to speak to the Abbot alone.'

'My lord, I will not permit that. You are not of an age to govern nor to make terms. This is man's business.'

'I remind you, I am Duke of Aquitaine. I will be King after my father.'

'But for now, your mother negotiates. I am her mouthpiece,' Sir Roger said blandly. Turning to the Abbot again, he raised his eyebrows enquiringly. 'Well?'

'My lord, your King wishes for assurances.'

'There can be none. If he and his household surrender themselves and their arms, they can expect more leniency. That is all.'

'It is to be expected, Sir Roger,' the Abbot said, speaking so forcefully he almost spat the words, 'that a man of the King's stature could expect assurances of safety. That the bodies of his comrades and servants will also be protected by you.'

'In God's name, Sir Abbot! This is a man suing for peace because he has run out of space to run to! He cannot expect more, and he will receive no more than this. We do not make war on the King, we seek only to punish Despenser for the manifest offences which he has committed upon the weary English. He will come and surrender with all his men, or he will be captured with them all. Do not try my patience with these petty demands. You may leave!'

The Abbot was shocked at the outburst. His mouth fell open,

and he threw a look at the Duke as though pleading with him to intervene, but Edward could think of nothing to say. He felt as though he must weep if he so much as opened his mouth. For all the trappings of power that were outwardly his, he possessed nothing compared with the stern authority of Sir Roger. In the face of the man's martial confidence, Edward was reduced to a child. He looked away.

'Then, Sir Roger, there is little more to be said,' the Abbot murmured. He bowed, then turned and began to head towards the door, his companions walking with him, but when he arrived at the doors, he stopped and looked back at the Duke. 'Do you have a message for your father, my lord?'

Sir Roger snapped, 'Yes, that he should surrender and stop any more of this waste and nonsense!'

'And tell him I love him, please, my lord Abbot,' the Duke said coldly, without looking at the knight.

CHAPTER FORTY-THREE

Simon had been waiting outside with Jack and Wolf, whittling a stick into a point, and when the men appeared in the doorway, he looked up at Baldwin. 'Well?'

Baldwin smiled, but his eyes showed how troubled he felt. 'We are not to have any terms, it would seem. Our friend Sir Roger had already decided that the King is to be shown how low he has sunk in the estimation of the barons and people of the realm. There is no hope.'

'What do you mean?' Simon said. 'Surely if he surrenders, he—'

'The King cannot surrender, Simon. If he does, Sir Hugh will be executed, and the King will not have that. So instead he will defy Sir Roger, and that means that this will drag on a little longer. And what then? Who can tell.'

Simon clasped Baldwin's hand, and the two men were silent for a moment. There seemed nothing to be said. They released each other and stood a pace apart, but it felt as though they were on opposite sides of a great river. Words could not bridge that gap. It was too profound.

'Baldwin, be careful, my friend.'

'You too, Simon,' the knight responded. And then he tried a grin, and marched on, punching Simon's shoulder with his fist in a rare display of affection.

Simon was walking to his horse when Wolf rose and lumbered across the area. Soon he was sitting, panting happily while being petted by a tallish man with a stained and filthy bandage bound about his lower shin. As Simon wandered past, he saw the man Herv Tyrel. He was with Otho, talking animatedly with the fellow stroking Wolf.

There was a shout. The King's ambassadors were already preparing to leave, and Simon ran to his horse as Baldwin swung his leg over his own mount. Simon had his foot in the stirrup and was in the saddle before the Abbot had ordered his men to ride on. Sir Stephen had heard of the rapid departure of the men, and joined Simon now. 'Are you intending to ride with them?'

'Yes, I—'

'Best to leave them, friend. They're riding to the King. If you go too, they may think you're trying to follow them – that you're a spy. Wait a little. We will ride to the Earl of Lancaster's men together.'

Simon nodded slowly, his eyes on the backs of the men as they rode out from the gates. One of them, he saw, was the man who had been with Wolf. He was a short way from Baldwin, who turned once, and stared at Simon as though in an effort to remember his old friend, and then they were gone.

*

First Saturday after the Feast of St Martin[1]

Neath Abbey

King Edward heard the group of men ride into the court. There was little doubt that it was them. Few enough men were coming and going from Neath Abbey at this time. Even those who had been bringing food in, demanding the most exorbitant sums in return, had dried to a trickle now they believed that the King would not be here much longer. No one wanted to be found there when Mortimer arrived.

He felt a fleeting urge to leap up and run to the men, to learn what they had managed to negotiate, but that would have been unseemly. Instead he motioned to his steward and tried to ask him to fetch Sir Hugh, but when he opened his mouth, no words would come. The steward gazed at him uncomprehendingly, as the King forced himself to relax, while his heart thundered. This terror of the future was unbecoming of a King. 'Please. Sir Hugh. Bring him.'

It was the strain. The fear of the unknown was gnawing at them all, and the King was feeling it more than any.

It was a huge relief to hear the quiet steps and the quickly-closing door behind him. He recognised those footsteps.

'Sire.'

'Sir Hugh, we will soon know,' the King said fondly. He knew that his favourite would not be permitted to live, if Sir Roger had his way. The Abbot had been instructed to tell Mortimer that if there was to be a surrender, the King desired safe passage for Sir Hugh and his other companions. King Edward II would hardly be expected to submit to the wholesale slaughter of his house-hold. It was too ridiculous. And Sir Roger knew it. He would

[1] 15 November 1326

understand that there were limits, and would agree to perhaps hold Sir Hugh in the Tower where the King could visit him. Better that than exile. The thought of his friend being driven from his side for life was unendurable.

There they were! The envoys were approaching at last. King Edward put his hand out to Sir Hugh, and the two exchanged a quick look, before Sir Hugh took his hand away gently, and stood with his bitten nails concealed behind his back.

The Abbot and the others strode in, a herald preceding them. All bowed and knelt before their King, who motioned to them to rise. 'Come, friends! No need for this today. Tell me, what is it to be? Do we agree to surrender, then? Is there safe passage and honour for us all?'

'Your Royal Highness,' the Abbot said, and there was a broken note in his voice. 'I am truly sorry. We did all we could to secure some assurances.'

'So, what are you saying?' the King enquired, smiling still. 'Please, do not keep me in suspense. What was his answer?'

There was a moment's silence, and then Sir Baldwin stepped forward and bowed. 'Your Highness, he refused all suggestions. He rejected your proposals and demands your unconditional surrender. There are no terms, no assurances, no guarantees.'

The King's smile remained by an extreme effort of his will. 'I see,' he said. There was a horrible clenching in his breast that felt as though his heart was being squeezed, and his scalp tightened as though someone had grabbed it at the back of his skull and was dragging it over his head. 'So, that is it, then? There is no more?'

'Your son, my liege, he told us to tell you he loves you.'

'Oh. He *loves* me. That is good,' the King said. His breathing was more laboured now, and his chest rose and fell too quickly. 'I . . .' he began, then had to cough and clear his throat forcefully.

'I am a little surprised by your news. Is there no hope of magnanimity?'

'None,' the Abbot said.

'Then ... then we must decide what to do,' the King said helplessly, looking about him like a man thrown into a room he did not recognise.

'Sire, there is only one thing we may do,' Sir Hugh said urgently. 'We have to leave this place and ride, fast, away.'

'To where?' the King demanded.

'To Caerphilly,' Despenser said, and to Baldwin's surprise, his tone was almost pleading. 'I was wrong to argue against it. We cannot find a ship now, but at the castle we could hold out for weeks, perhaps months. We have more men, and provisions. We should be secure for a while.'

The King looked up at him with a smile. 'And it would allow you to see your son, my lord. Very well. If we remain here,' he told the abbot, 'we would run the risk of demolishing your lovely Abbey, my friend, and I would not see it thrown into ruin. It is no place for a battle.'

He stood, a little shakily. 'My friends, I thank you all for your forbearance and loyal service. I think now we should ride to Caerphilly, where we can take our places in the last, sad days. What comes after, God only knows.'

First Sunday after the Feast of St Martin[1]

Neath Abbey

That morning was heavy with rain. Even as they prepared themselves in the courtyard near the cloisters, the men were drenched.

---

[1] 16 November 1326

Baldwin was wearing his armour with more discomfort than he could recall at any other time. At least on duty in Acre, he had been younger, and there was no rain to contend with. It had been more a case of worrying about sand getting in under the throat and at the back of the neck – because even a small amount of rough sand between aketon and skin was enough to create a bloody sore in half a day. Today, though, the collar of his pair of plates kept touching his bare throat – and it felt as if his flesh must freeze to the metal each time. His clothes beneath were already clammy and damp, and the coldness of the metal was transmitted perfectly through the wet clothing, which meant that the ride today was going to be deeply uncomfortable as well as dangerous.

He wasn't scared. Baldwin was too experienced a warrior to feel fear, but he did have misgivings about setting off now, when they had been away from Caerphilly for so long. He only prayed that the castle was not already besieged. He wondered how Roisea would cope, if so. She was a lovely-looking woman – the sort who could all too easily become the target of men-at-arms with time on their hands.

They mounted, and Jack whistled to Wolf, who was idling away his time near the midden heap over at the wall's edge. The mastiff came at a wary trot when he heard the summons, think-ing he might be scolded for rooting about in the rubbish.

When all were mounted, the King at last appeared in the door-way. Over his left shoulder, Baldwin saw Sir Hugh le Despenser, looking pale and fretful, his hands worrying at his face as though he was scratching at an itch near his mouth. Beside him stood Baldock. He was in little better state than Despenser.

'My friends,' the King called, and his voice was firm, if not so loud as once it had been. 'There can be little doubt that there is no time for us to lose. You know that we cannot find a ship to take us to safety in Ireland, and no matter how we try, the rest of my people seem reluctant to come and help me wrest my kingdom from traitors and thieves!' He stopped, took a deep breath, and continued more calmly again, 'And so, we must ride. We go to Caerphilly. I do not doubt that it is strong enough to survive the worst onslaught that the foul Mortimer can throw at it.'

He looked around at all the knights and servants who stood watching, listening carefully. Baldwin glanced about him too, and saw so many taut, pale faces that it was brought home to him again just how dire their situation had become. No one there believed that the King could escape capture, and that would mean many of the men here would suffer the indignity of arrest and of gaol, of possible forfeiture of lands and goods, the disinheritance of their children, or even death. They all knew the position. And there was little that could be done to save themselves.

'Friends, I call you, because you *are* all my friends. You have stayed with me through all the recent turbulence which has so shaken my reign. I love you for the courage you have displayed, for the conviction in the rightness of my position that you have shown me. I honour all of you. But it is time, for some, to leave. Any man among you who decides he does not want to come to share my fate, I release from my service. I do not demand that you join me in this dark time. Better that any who feel they have fulfilled the duty which honour has demanded, should leave now.'

Baldwin watched, and suddenly felt a warmth flushing at his eyes. He was forced to wipe at them with a gloved hand as he realised that not a man was moving. All the knights, men-at-arms and servants were determined to remain with the King, no matter what his fate. He saw Robert Vyke not far away, and the man was weeping, his head bowed, but when he looked up and caught Baldwin's eye, there was no embarrassment. He was crying with pride, not fear.

The King looked about him with a look of mild bafflement on his face. 'Are you all moon-struck? My friends, I am most humbled by your support. I will do all I may to protect you as you have served me. Thank you. Thank you all.'

He strode down the steps and climbed upon his destrier, sitting with a rigidly straight back. His herald mounted too, and set the King's banner in its rest, and when Sir Hugh and all the others were sitting in their saddles, Edward nodded, and the whole cavalcade moved off and through the gates.

But not many saw, as Baldwin did, the tears that poured down the King's face as he rode from the yard to the fate which no one could foresee.

Near Llanharry

Simon had already been riding for three hours that morning, and he regretted it immensely.

From dawn, there had been a torrential downpour that seemed to pause occasionally only in order for it to continue its onslaught with renewed vigour. It felt as though the deluge was battering their very souls. The misery of staggering on under that terrible wall of water sapped their energy and it was only by an enormous effort of will that the footsoldiers were able to tramp onwards. Among the Hainaulters, Simon heard many men swearing bitterly in French and other, incomprehensible tongues. For himself, he was too depleted to bother swearing.

Then the clouds cleared again, and he wiped his face on his sleeve before staring about. There were trees on his right, then a clearing off to the left, with pasture or common land ahead. Just more of what they were used to.

'Enjoying the ride, Bailiff?' enquired Sir Charles.

'Loving every minute of it,' Simon muttered.

'I do not think,' Sir Stephen said with deliberation, 'that I have ever been quite this wet before in my life. Nay, not even in a bath – for then at least my head has remained dry. This,' he continued, tugging his felt hat from his head and slapping it on his thigh, making it instantly shapeless, 'this, is sheer, unadulterated wretchedness.'

They were riding a short distance behind Earl Henry of Lancaster; the Earl and his household knights rode in an armoured group bunched together as though they were clustered under a shelter.

And then Simon sat up, staring ahead, just as the rain began to pound at the land all around them again.

'What is it?' Sir Charles asked quickly.

'I thought I saw something,' Simon said. But he did not add the words that sprang to his lips: Baldwin's dog Wolf.

CHAPTER FORTY-FOUR

There were so few men left that Baldwin despaired.

Along with the King there was Despenser, of course, and Robert Baldock, the King's Chancellor. Apart from them, there were only the retainers, including Simon of Reading, who had shown himself to be devoted to Sir Hugh. John Beck, John Blunt, John Smale, Tom Whyther and Richard Holden were all there, with Sir Ralph and his two, and the cautious Robert Vyke, who rode like a sack of turnips but had proved himself to be honourable and true to his word. There were some fifteen other servants and men-at-arms, most of them riding dazed, like men in a dream. The King's Steward in particular looked as if he had suddenly aged twenty years.

He had never believed that this could truly happen, Baldwin thought. He had spent his life in service to this King, expecting to work until the King pensioned him off, buying him a corrody in a priory or abbey, where he would be housed, fed and clothed, and now it seemed certain that his dreams of ending his work at last and finding rest were flown. If the King were forced from his throne by Sir Roger, there would be nothing for his steward or for any others.

For his part, Baldwin only hoped that they were safe from Mortimer's men. They must be all about Wales now, he was sure. They would have set off in pursuit as soon as they could when the Abbot and the other negotiators rode out of Hereford.

He cast an eye about him, wondering where Wolf could have got to. The damned brute was always wandering off, following his nose. He wasn't down by Jack this time. It was only when he peered ahead, over the King's shoulder, that he thought he saw Wolf in between squalls.

And then he caught sight of the men.

'Your Highness! Ambush! Turn about, turn about!' he cried.

Simon felt his stomach lurch as he recognised the great black dog with the white muzzle and breast, the brown cheeks and eyebrows. He blinked away the rain, but suddenly it was over, and there was a patch of clearness – and all the men saw the King and his entourage immediately before them.

No one spoke for a second. The King gaped, his horse pawing at the soil, and Earl Henry and his men were equally nonplussed for a moment, until there was a shout from the rear of the King's men, and with a thrill Simon recognised Baldwin's voice; and then all was thundering hooves as the Earl's men set their horses at the King, and shrieks filled the air, while swords slithered from their scabbards and the horses lowered their heads to pound onwards.

Simon found his own mount plunging on ahead, as it careered after the Earl's group. It was clear that the King's men were forming a line to hold their enemies at bay. Simon recognised a few faces here and there, but even though they wielded their swords bravely enough, there were too few, far too few to hold back so large a force. The Earl's men went through them in no time, and Simon felt a fleeting sadness to see the King's own steward hacked across the neck and shoulder. He fell back in a fountain of blood, and Simon saw his body in the mud at the side of the road as he rode past, blinking and mouth moving, but making no sound as he died.

Then they were past, and up ahead Simon saw the King and Despenser, along with two knights. He crouched lower, to keep up with the others.

To the loud blaring of horns from his pursuers, the King rode with a mad determination. He would not allow himself to be caught, especially not by Lancaster. He had seen Lancaster's brother executed for his treachery, and the thought of being in Earl Henry's custody was not to be borne. He spurred his mount onwards, lashing at his charger's flanks with the rein-ends, teeth clenched, his muscles tensed against the threat of an arrow in the back.

There was none. He rode on, around the first curve of the roadway, the cold rain slapping him in the face like small icicles, his horse lurching and slipping in the mud, almost throwing him at one point. Beside him, his face set in an expression of horror, rode Sir Hugh.

He couldn't let them take Hugh! Hugh was his only friend in this repugnant world. All the friends he had were always snatched from him. It was so cruel, he could weep, but there was no time for tears. He had to stay on horseback, keep on riding, *escape* with Hugh. He couldn't submit, not now!

A shout, a flurry of noise to his right, and he saw a group of fresh riders pelting towards him through the thin woods. The leader was a knight, but that was all he saw before he spurred his brute to greater efforts, and pointed his charger towards a gap in a hedge a short way ahead. Two paces, a bunching of muscles, and he was in the air, over the hedge, twigs and thorns snatching at his shins and thighs, then . . . *down* on the ground once more, and thundering over the turf towards the opposite side of a good-sized pasture, sheep scattering in terror as he came. And when he cast a wild eye over his shoulder, he saw Sir Ralph and Sir Baldwin behind him, Sir Ralph's squire near him, but the second one was gone. His horse was still there, galloping with rolling, terrified eyes and a great smear of blood and gore over his saddle and flank from the blow that had killed his rider.

'How many more?' he asked himself.

Baldwin saw Sir Ralph gauging the distance ahead, then they were both in the air, their beasts leaping high over the hedge and down onto the soft soil the other side. There was a broad expanse of pasture in front of them, leading down to a small rivulet which Baldwin saw sweeping across from the left, and he hoped to Heaven that the King wouldn't be foolish enough to head for that, because the ground nearby would likely be boggy and dangerous for their mounts.

He saw that Alexander's horse had lost its rider, and he winced at the thought of yet another man dead, but before he could think more, he saw Wolf, who was galloping as fast as his heavy frame would allow, his tongue dangling free as he gazed up at his master in consternation.

But just as Baldwin saw his mastiff, he became aware of the man riding towards Wolf with a spear ready to spit him. Without thinking, Baldwin turned and rode for the attacker.

Wolf had no idea what his master was doing, but in his hound-like conviction of original canine sin, he stopped and cringed, thinking Baldwin was about to clout him. During that pause, he spotted the rapidly approaching horse and, yelping, shot across in front of Baldwin, startling the pursuer's horse and making it stop so sharply that the rider was hurled over its head to the ground.

Baldwin was already spurring his horse onwards, back to the King and his companions, but even as he did so, he saw that it was too late.

Although the main force of men was still behind Baldwin, there was a second party in front, waiting patiently, while a third, smaller group had appeared at the other side of the brook. There would be no escape that way. And when Baldwin cast a look to the right, he saw that any exit from this pasturage was obstructed by the thickly laid thorn hedge which surrounded it.

It would be for the King to decide what they must do. Before he could be cut off from them, Baldwin rode at the gallop to join the King and the others.

Simon was a little behind the group, delayed by his shock at the sight of Wolf when the others were already whooping onwards.

He urged his rounsey on, and soon was galloping off after the others. He saw them all leaping over the hedge; where there had been a narrow gap, now there was a ragged tear, and the men were piling through, their horses whinnying with fear and excitement. Simon was the last man to go, and he felt no concern at taking it at the gallop. All the others were already throwing up clods of grass at the other side, and he had to duck to avoid one large lump of earth, and then he felt the huge muscles bunch and thrust, and he was shoved against the high cantle at the rear of his saddle and using his legs to haul himself upright, filled with the thrill of the chase.

There was a flash of red on his right, and his horse shied in mid-leap, trying to swing to the left; Simon found himself lurching, thrown first right, then left – and then he was out of his saddle. There was a moment of vague surprise as he realised that he was flying through the air, with his left foot caught in the stirrup . . . and then the stirrup leather tightened, jerking him in mid-air, only to slam him hard to the ground. His head bounced up, and his blurred vision caught sight of a horse and rider clad in red just before his body crashed to earth again. He felt the stones, twigs and thorns shred his clothes and rip into his flesh as his mount thundered on, and then something hit his head with a crunch that drove all pain, all fear and meaning from his mind – and he was engulfed by night.

Sir Charles had landed well, and as soon as he was at the other side of the hedge, he whipped and spurred his mount after the others, but even as he leaned down over his horse's neck and felt the mane slap damply against his cheeks, he cast a quick look to his side, looking for Simon. Nothing. He shot a glance backwards and saw the horse trying to follow; it looked odd somehow – and he suddenly realised there was no rider on it.

'God damn the fellow!' he muttered, and pulled on the reins. His great horse pounded back, and that was when he saw Simon being dragged along by his leg. Sir Charles slapped his beast's rump hard to make him hurry on, and was soon able to turn level with Simon's horse. Calming him, Sir Charles grabbed at the reins. He had to do so twice before he managed to catch them, and then he pulled on both sets of reins to slow both horses; his own and Simon's. It was hard work, and Simon's horse snorted and tried to pull his head free, his eyes terrified, forgetting all his training and becoming almost a wild animal.

Sir Charles stood up in his stirrups, then sat down and hauled, and gradually both horses slowed, then stopped, and as soon as they were still, Sir Charles was out of his saddle and down beside his friend's body. He saw that the stirrup was caught about Simon's foot, twisting the whole of his leg, and without ado, drew his dagger and cut the leather. Simon's leg dropped instantly, and he groaned.

Rolling him over gently, Sir Charles saw how his back had been lacerated, and winced at the sight.

'My friend, you need help – badly!'

The King reined in his horse and stared at the men confronting him. There were thirty or so in this motley band. Ten on horseback, and those on foot already had their polearms, braced.

There were men in front, men behind, and a party over the brook. 'Sir Hugh!' he cried in desperation, and he saw Hugh turn to him. Under his helmet, Despenser's handsome face was twisted with anguish.

'My King!' he shouted, and for a moment King Edward thought his friend might throw himself on the spears of the schiltrom before them, but then he bent his head and covered his face. There was no spirit left in him to fight further.

And that was it, King Edward thought. They were all too worn with trying to gather a force to defend his reign, with hiding and running again. A month and a half of trying to avert disaster – and it had all been in vain.

Sir Ralph rode up to him, with Sir Baldwin close by.

'Your Royal Highness, we are ready to die for you,' Sir Ralph said quietly. 'Command us.'

The King looked at them both, at their resolute expressions. 'Sirs, there is no point. Fighting will avail us nothing. How many more must die?'

He saw behind Sir Baldwin the armour and face of Earl Henry of Lancaster, and walked his horse to the man.

'Earl. I submit.'

Llantrisant Castle

Simon was able to do little more than cling to his horse for the journey to Llantrisant, and he was fortunate that Sir Charles rode at his side all the way, for he was continually passing out and at peril of toppling off.

They rode into the castle before dusk, and the whole party entered the hall together, Sir Charles and Sir Stephen assisting Simon to walk. As soon as he was set down on a bench, he turned, leaned his shoulder against the wall, and began to snore.

It was only a small castle, this. It had been Sir Hugh le Despenser's for some little while, but now it had been taken over by Mortimer's men, and the place was filled with men-at-arms and their weapons. The King and Sir Hugh looked about them in astonishment to see how many men there were crammed into the place as they were taken up into the hall. While the King was given due honour, and many men tried to encourage him, Sir Hugh was set in a corner and left to his own devices. Food was brought, good simple fare, set out on wooden trenchers, but neither man appeared to have any appetite.

Sir Charles stayed with Simon for the most part of the evening, and when he saw Sir Baldwin and Sir Ralph, he beckoned them.

'What happened to him?' Baldwin said in a hushed tone.

'Fell from his horse and got dragged over the ground. His back is in a bad state,' Sir Charles commented.

'He needs a physician,' Baldwin muttered.

'I will see what may be done,' Sir Charles said. 'There should be someone with leeching skills.'

'I am most grateful,' Baldwin said, sitting at Simon's side.

Sir Ralph looked at him with some surprise. 'You know this man?'

'He may not look like much just now,' Baldwin said, 'but he is a good man, a good friend.'

Baldwin remained with Simon as Sir Ralph walked away to sit with the rest of the men held captive. Some saw Baldwin sitting quietly at Simon's side, but most ignored him. There appeared to be a feeling of anti-climax now that they had the King in the hall with them. A few stood aimlessly with sheathed swords near Edward, as though to reinforce the fact that he was captive, but for the most part, men idled about the place, unsure what to do with him.

That changed as it grew dark. There was a rattle of hooves in the ward, then loud bellowed commands, and a short while later, three men marched inside, closely followed by Henry of Lancaster. He strode in without looking to either side, going straight to the King, and standing at his side without kneeling. It was a while before he appeared to make a decision, and he dropped quickly to one knee, then stood again, his short demonstration of respect complete.

'Your Majesty,' he said, 'I am glad to have you safe in my custody. You will consider yourself my guest, and I will ensure your protection. Is there anything you require?'

'I have all I need.'

'You will be gracious enough to tell me or my men if you require anything else. Tomorrow we shall set off for Monmouth, thence we shall travel to Hereford, where we shall meet your wife and your son. I fear that the accommodation here will be stretched to its limits, but I can at least provide you with the solar block, if you wish some solitude.'

'No. I will remain here with my men.'

'Very well. I will leave a guard here for your safety, and hope that you rest well, my lord.'

The King nodded. His reverse of fortunes, while expected,

had still come as an appalling shock, and he glanced at Sir Hugh as though expecting his friend to chastise those who had taken him and now held him in this demeaning way. But Sir Hugh had nothing to say.

As the Earl made to walk from the room, he said, 'Sir Baldwin! I hope you are well?'

'As well as a prisoner may be,' he answered. He held no malice for those who had caught him, only trepidation. All could be executed for remaining at the King's side, if Mortimer wanted. It was a distressing situation, but not so worrying as the thought of how Jeanne would survive without him. His only consolation was that Edgar, his Sergeant from his Templar days, was still with her and would ensure her safety, if it were humanly possible. 'Thank you for not binding us.'

'There is no need with honourable men. Is that the Bailiff? Was he with you?'

'No, my lord. The good Bailiff was with your men, but when your fellows charged through the hedge, he was knocked from his saddle and dragged along by his mount. His back is sorely lacerated. Sir Charles of Lancaster has gone to fetch a leech for him, and I will stay at his side, if my captor will allow it.'

'For my part, Sir Baldwin, if you give me your parole not to try to escape, that will be good enough for me.'

'I so swear.'

'I will have wine brought for you both. I hope he will recover. Is there anything else I can do for you?'

Baldwin saw that Sir Charles was returning with a fretful-looking cleric hurrying along behind him. 'Only that you tell your men that if the clerk asks for hot water, or anything else they might have here for treatment of wounds, that they fetch it for him. I am worried that Simon is sleeping. A man with a broken head will sometimes sleep and snore, and I fear his injuries may be worse than I realised.'

'I'll tell them. You make sure that he recovers.'

The clerk stood at Simon's side, gauging his injuries, but when he tried to cut away the clothing to look at Simon's back, the Bailiff suddenly woke, staring about him in a state of shock. 'Settle yourself, my son,' the priest said, wincing at the sight of his back. 'This will take time.'

CHAPTER FORTY-FIVE

It took an age to clean Simon's back. The priest had a bowl which the guards filled with hot water, and in that he steeped rose petals and lavender, using it on a clean linen strip to wash the damaged skin. There were so many thorn splinters and bloody gashes there that he could only dab gently, while Simon hissed and muttered. He seemed very drowsy still, and Baldwin felt sure that Simon must have hurt his head badly. The wound resembled one that a mace or cudgel could produce, and Baldwin knew that on occasion a man would die from such a blow even when there was no sign of blood or broken bone, and he worried more now for Simon than he did for himself.

Sir Ralph had assisted, and now that the clerk had completed cleaning and salving and binding Simon's wounds, he advised the two to go and rest themselves, for they could do no more to help Simon now. His health was in the hands of God.

Reluctantly, Baldwin walked away, while the clerk pulled a blanket up over Simon's poor back and settled at his side.

'At least he's stopped that snoring,' Baldwin sighed. 'It worried me to hear that.'

'Yes, I've known men snore like that, and vomit,' Sir Ralph agreed. Both had seen enough men die in such a manner for them not to need to discuss it further.

Robert Vyke was sitting a short way away with Wolf, stroking the great mastiff's head. He looked up as the two approached.

'Do not worry,' Baldwin said, for Vyke looked terrified, as though he could be punished for making a fuss of his dog. 'Wolf enjoys attention.'

'He is a handsome animal.'

'You like such brutes?' Baldwin said. He could not deny his own affection for the dog, but it always rather surprised him to see others who had the same feeling. 'I bought him from a Bishop who detested him. He would keep beating and kicking poor Wolf, wouldn't he, fellow?'

'I dislike cruelty to dogs.'

'I know I distrust those who would use such behaviour. A good dog is a wonderful thing,' Baldwin said. He was suddenly struck with the thought that if he were to die, Wolf would have no master. Perhaps, if Simon was well enough, he could take Wolf back to Jeanne.

It was his last thought as he settled himself later – that he had so many people and animals dependent upon him. It left him feeling feeble. At this precise moment, was unable to support anyone.

He had nothing left he could give.

*

First Monday after the Feast of St Martin[1]

Llantrisant Castle

The Earl of Lancaster was as good as his word the next day. Baldwin was woken by a servant to tell him that a light cart had been procured for 'the good Bailiff', and would he be ready to travel with the rest of the men?

Simon did look a little better. His eyes opened when Baldwin sat beside him, although the right one was bruised and bloody, and had swelled alarmingly.

'I imagine I am a pretty sight?' he croaked.

Baldwin chuckled. 'It is good to see you in your usual humour, Simon. I think it is fair to say that Margaret would find it hard to recognise you.'

'Aye, well, she may desire a new man, of course,' Simon said with a grunt of pain as he tried to ease himself upright.

'I would take your movements cautiously for now,' Baldwin said. 'Your back is a mass of scabs.'

'I'm not surprised. I feel as though someone's thrown me into a bear pit for the fun of watching me be torn apart.'

Baldwin said, 'If not for this good priest, you would feel greatly worse.'

'I thank you, Father.'

The priest yawned expansively. 'I am glad I have provided some service to you, my son.' But soon he made his apologies, and hurried off to his chapel to hold services for those who wished to pray and confess.

The two old friends chatted quietly for a while, about the small matters which both felt comfortable discussing, nothing to do with their arrival at that place, nor what might happen to

---

[1] 17 November 1326

Baldwin once they had returned to England. His future was uncertain, and both knew it.

In the clear morning, they were herded outside, and mounted their horses. Simon was helped to the back of a cart, but looking at the worm-infested wood and the wheels with their worn and rusted tyres, he shook his head firmly. 'No. I'm not travelling on that. Bring me my horse.'

It took some little time to get going. A number of men were injured from the fighting the day before; they lay in three carts, moaning piteously at every rut and pothole.

The rain of the day before had given way to a steady drizzle now, and more than one man was shivering with an ague as they marched or walked their horses.

Simon did not feel too bad. His head still hurt abominably, but apart from an occasional desire to vomit, which he reckoned was as much due to the poor food he had eaten yesterday as to any injury, he felt well enough in himself. A spare chemise and jack had been found for him, and his cloak, mercifully, had not been too badly torn during his terrible dragging, but the stitches where the earlier damage had been mended were now ripped a second time. His leg was extremely painful where the muscles had torn, but his back was surprisingly good, provided he did not try to move too suddenly and reopen the scabs that dotted it. The cold seemed to soothe it.

It was not like him to have fallen in such a manner, he mused. His horse was usually so reliable. And then he had a sudden memory of redness flashing across in front of him . . . It was almost as if a man had been there – but that was ridiculous.

'Are you all right, Simon?'

'Talk to me, Baldwin,' Simon said thickly. 'Every so often I get this urge to puke, and I'd appreciate some distraction. How did you get here?'

Baldwin whistled to Wolf, who was padding along behind the

horses of Robert Vyke and Herv Tyrel with a hopeful air, watching as the two shared some dried meat.

'There is not much to tell,' Baldwin began. He told Simon of his fast journey across the South of England, intending to get to Furnshill before war could reach it, and how he met with Redcliffe. 'It was clear enough that the man was in danger.'

'I know that name,' Simon said with a frown. It took him a long time to recall where he had heard it. 'Oh, I'm a fool. He's dead, of course!'

'Yes, I had to leave his body at the banks of the Severn,' Baldwin said.

'He was intending to murder the King, so the Duke of Aquitaine thought,' Simon said.

Baldwin nodded. 'Yes – and I sought to protect him. If I had succeeded, he would have killed our King.'

'Who discovered him?' Simon asked, remembering Sir Roger Mortimer's interest. 'Was it you?'

'No. The man who tried to kill him at Winchester managed to reach him in the end,' Baldwin said, and explained about the bearded killer.

Simon closed his eyes as a wave of nausea washed through his belly, and he shuddered with the taste of bile in his throat. 'I think, my friend,' he said very quietly, 'you managed to kill the Duke of Aquitaine's man. He sent a fellow called Sam Fletcher to kill the man Redcliffe before he could get to the King.'

Baldwin screwed up his face into a grimace of anguish. 'Ach! And I thought at the time I was only protecting a messenger for the King.'

'Best to keep quiet about it, I think,' Simon said weakly.

'There is one thing,' Baldwin said, and he pulled out the note of safe-conduct which he had found in Redcliffe's purse. 'I still have this.'

'Keep it safe, my friend,' Simon advised, reading the somewhat bedraggled sliver of parchment. The ink had begun to smudge in places, but it was still legible. 'You never know when it may come in useful.'

Second Friday after the Feast of St Martin[1]

On the road to Hereford

After three days in the saddle, Simon's back was giving him less pain. He winced at regular intervals as a sudden lurch of his mount jolted his leg, but at least his head and neck were healing.

The aim had been for them to ride to Monmouth first, and thence to Hereford, but progress was slow. With all the injured men, they were only managing a scant three leagues a day, and the Earl of Lancaster was to get back to Sir Roger Mortimer and the Queen.

Baldwin understood their urgency, but could hardly share it. He did not know how he would be received when they reached Mortimer.

The King was obviously deeply troubled, and whereas Baldwin had the companionship of Simon, Jack, and even Robert Vyke and his ever-present Wolf, the king had no one to comfort him. His oldest servant had died in the battle trying to protect him, and Despenser was a spent force.

It was strange to see the Despenser now. He rode loosely, as though he was drugged or filled with burned wine[2], and his eyes glittered. He looked about him menacingly, as though storing up a memory of each and every face in order to ensure that all were

[1] 21 November 1326
[2] medieval term for brandy

captured and tortured when he had an opportunity, and Baldwin wondered if his mind was unbalanced. He must surely have realised that there would be no escape for him.

In those periods when he was able to speak rationally, Despenser was coldly polite, but for the most part he would say nothing, not even to the King who had risked so much and had now lost all on his behalf.

He must be fearful, Baldwin thought, and this appeared to be confirmed by the fact that he refused all food. Nothing had passed his lips since Llantrisant, and he was showing signs of deterioration. His eyes, Baldwin saw, were growing yellow instead of white, and his face was sinking in upon itself.

Sir Hugh had made the decision to starve himself, Baldwin reckoned. Perhaps that was not a bad idea. Sir Roger Mortimer would want him to be executed in public, in the most humiliating manner – probably by having him dragged all the way to London so that the mob could jeer at the sight of their hated oppressor. But if he drank nothing and ate nothing, Despenser would never reach London.

Perhaps, Baldwin wondered, that was a reason for the Earl's haste? He wanted Despenser to be delivered alive so that he could be punished for the sport of Mortimer and Sir Hugh's many enemies. It would not please Sir Roger Mortimer to be cheated of his revenge.

So on they trotted and ambled, a small force guarding the two men who until the last month had been the most powerful beings in the whole country, and who were now little more than wraiths, their energy and souls sucked clean from their bodies.

Baldwin pondered on this thought. And wondered what would happen to him.

CHAPTER FORTY-SIX

Second Sunday after the Feast of St Martin[1]

Outside Hereford

Robert Vyke dropped a crust of bread for Wolf as the great mastiff lumbered along beside him, and when he looked up, he saw Otho and Herv riding nearby.

'Not far now,' Otho muttered. He was not comfortable on horseback, and his body lurched from side to side in the saddle.

Robert Vyke smiled, but his heart was not in it. There was no telling what would happen to him when they arrived. When captured, if you were rich and important, you would be ransomed and your life saved; but if you were a simple peasant from another lord's host, you ran the risk of being slain out of hand. He had a nasty suspicion that his own fate could follow that path.

'You look like you've swallowed a wasp,' Otho said after contemplating him for a moment or two. 'What's wrong?'

'Nothing. I just don't want to get to Hereford that soon.'

---

[1] 23 November 1326

'Your leg all right?'

'Yes. It's no trouble now,' he said, flexing it to show.

'You'll live.'

Robert Vyke shot him a look. 'What?'

Otho shrugged. 'Your leg, I meant. Why?'

'What's the chance of me living, though? They will want to make a show of those who supported the King, won't they? And I was with him when our master went over to the Queen. I'm a traitor to my own master.'

'You didn't do that on purpose,' Herv objected.

'Doesn't matter, does it? Not to a knight or a lord. They just look at me and see a peasant who can't be trusted.'

Otho sucked at his front teeth. 'I think you're missing something here, Rob. If this was the other way round, and the King was waiting for you to be brought to him, maybe you'd be right. But I reckon the one who's worried most now is that one there.' He pointed at Despenser. 'You really think so?' asked Vyke, cheering up.

'Yeah. He's shit scared.' Otho studied the man for a while, and then spat. 'Nah, you'll be fine Rob. They'll hardly even notice you.'

Second Monday after the Feast of St Martin[1]

Hereford

They reached the city in the middle of the morning. Trotting down towards the gate, Baldwin saw a party of men riding out to meet them. If he could, he would have turned his horse and galloped away.

'What is all that lot?' Simon asked, gazing ahead with his eyes narrowed.

[1] 24 November 1326

'Looks like Sir Thomas Wake at the head,' Baldwin said. 'I know him – he's a good man. The others, I don't know.'

They were soon to find out. As their party reached the gates, there was a flurry of activity. Three men came and took hold of Despenser's horse. He was forced to dismount, and while four men rode to the King and took him into the city at a brisk trot, Despenser had the tunic ripped from his back and chest, and was forced to stand still while a fresh tunic was placed over his head.

'What's that?' Simon asked, peering. His eyes had not recovered their full vigour yet, and trying to focus from here was giving him a fresh headache.

'They have made a tunic with his arms reversed,' Baldwin said, his voice hushed. 'His arms are destroyed.'

'Oh?' Simon said.

'Yes. "Oh". It means his place in the nobility will cease to exist,' Baldwin said.

Simon nodded, and then, 'What now?'

'They are writing on him,' Baldwin said. It was impossible to hear what was being said, but someone had tied his wrists, and now men with reeds and inks were scrawling all over Despenser's back, sometimes straying onto his neck and bare shoulders, while the man stood whey-faced and uncommunicative. Around him was a growing crowd who taunted him and laughed. Then a crown of green nettles was brought and rammed on his head. That brought on a reaction: he writhed with pain as the stings burned his brow and temples.

He was not alone. Baldock also had his tunic cut from him, and naked, he was clothed in his own arms reversed, with his own crown of nettles shoved hard over his brow. Despenser's herald, Simon of Reading, was given a banner, but he refused to accept it, his face showing his revulsion.

'It's got Despenser's arms reversed, too,' Baldwin answered before Simon could ask.

It did not work. Simon of Reading was forced to take up the banner, and then Despenser was given a miserable hack to ride into the town. It was mangy, thin and spavined, and looked as though it could scarcely bear his weight, but then Simon of Reading was beaten and prodded with swords until he led the way into the city, Baldock and Despenser following.

Simon and Baldwin could hear the crowds inside the city. There was jeering, cat-calling, and rotten fruit was thrown, and eggs, at the unfortunate trio. For the most part, when Baldwin caught glimpses of him, Despenser was sitting stiff-backed on his nag – oblivious, apparently, to the missiles and taunts.

There was a justifiable hatred of this man, but Baldwin felt alarmed at the way that the people of the town were respond-ing to him, this despot who only weeks ago would have had them trembling with terror by merely looking at them. Now, in the hour of his downfall, they were happy to throw all caution to the winds and shame him for their pleasure. It was foul to witness, and Baldwin wondered if Mortimer realised that this crowd, which was learning to insult its betters with impunity, could all too easily turn on him as well, given the opportunity. To see women screeching abuse, their children joining in, and men with their faces twisted with loathing, was not an edify-ing sight.

They were taken to the market square. This was where judge-ment was to be declared.

The names of the judges were read. The Earl of Lancaster was there, and the Earl of Kent, and Thomas Wake, as well as the other man from the gate, Jean de Hainault, and, of course, Sir Roger Mortimer. Set slightly aside, sat Queen Isabella and her son, the Duke of Aquitaine.

Despenser was commanded to be silent. There was to be no defence to the clear and manifest crimes of which he was accused. No man was asked to speak for him, and instead a series of charges were read out to the suddenly quiet market square.

Baldwin found himself distracted by the gaily-coloured flags which fluttered about in the breeze. He thought how festive the square looked, as if it was a holiday, so wonderfully at odds with the terrible scene now playing out in front of him. The silence, apart from the wind and the voice relentlessly reading the charges, gave a feeling of unreality. Looking up, in a window in a tower overlooking the square, he saw a face wearing a rictus of perfect horror.

'The King!' he whispered.

King Edward II stared down at the square and felt his breast and belly melt in fear.

They wouldn't, they *couldn't* kill his Hugh, his lovely Hugh. The man was not guilty of these crimes they were inexorably listing. They were saying that Hugh had left Isabella, his Queen, alone at Tynemouth when the Scottish were attacking. That was *unfair*! Sir Hugh had tried to reach her, but he couldn't because of the numbers of Scots in the area. And she had escaped anyway, climbing aboard a ship at the last minute. He craned to listen. What was that? That he had granted the Earldom of Winchester to his father? That wasn't his doing, it was the King's action! What now? That he had stopped the King from travelling to France to pay homage for Aquitaine, to the detriment of the kingdom? Ridiculous No! No! This was a travesty!

Down there in the square he could see poor Hugh, standing so still and calm, like a saint before his martyrdom. Like Christ

Himself with his shameful crown while the hideous wretches all about him revelled in his pain.

Then the words he had been dreading came up to him. There was not even a pause to give the pretence that Sir Hugh was being judged. Instead, they went straight to the judgement from reading the list of charges. He was to be hanged, drawn, castrated, quartered, and his rank and nobility would die with him.

No, no, no, no . . .

Baldwin heard the last words: *'Go to your fate, traitor, tyrant, renegade; go to your own justice, traitor, evil man, criminal!'*

All Baldwin could see was the King's face. The expression on his drawn features tore into the knight's heart. He had sworn to aid Sir Hugh if the King could not, and now he was forced to witness and do nothing. It felt shameful.

Despenser was no longer a knight. Stripped of rank and chivalry, he was pushed and beaten to a sledge, where he was forced to lie, his hands tied to the topmost rail, and four horses dragged him over the cobbles, bumping and rattling, past people who spat and laughed at his anguish.

All were to follow. Baldwin was drawn along with the others as the crowd surged after him, and he noticed that guards were all watching him and the other men from the King's last servants as though they were expected to launch themselves at Sir Hugh and Simon of Reading in an attempt to rescue them. There was no chance of that.

They went along the lanes, winding this way and that until they were by the castle walls.

Baldwin saw it all. Hugh was cut from the hurdle and stripped beside a fire, then with his hands still bound, he was helped up the ladder to the scaffold, the rope fitted about his neck, and hanged from a gallows high up until he was almost dead, face swollen, eyes popping, legs thrashing. When his struggling slowed, he was cut down and bound to a ladder. Water dashed in his face to revive him, and then he was castrated, the executioner throwing the offending parts into the flames, before slicing into his belly and, while Despenser's mouth worked, the man dragged out his intestines, bundling them into a heap and burning them too.

There were taunts and laughter as the executioner reached in with his knife and cut out Despenser's heart. When that too was on the fire, he took up a bright new cleaver to finish his butchery.

It was enough for Baldwin. This was bloody revenge, not justice. The entire realm wanted to know that Sir Hugh le Despenser was not merely dead, but defiled for all to see. His head would be sent to London, his quarters to major cities so that all would see the punishment meted out to those who sought to destabilise the kingdom. He felt sickened.

'What of me?' he said to Simon.

'You won't be harmed,' Simon reassure him. 'They have their figurehead. They don't need you.'

Baldwin felt shaky and befouled, as though he had been an active participant, not a mere witness. This was too much like the deaths of so many of his friends in Paris and all over France: Templars who were tortured and then burned at the stake for refusing to confess to crimes they had not committed.

'Poor England,' was all he said.

Simon managed to force a way through the press as people edged closer to the guards standing with polearms held across their chests, keeping them all back as the executioner continued his grisly work. His cleaver could be heard clearly, each blow striking wetly as it sheared through bone. Simon of Reading was already dangling limply from a rope, the life throttled from him, but Baldock had been rescued and whisked away. Some weeks afterwards, Simon heard that it was Bishop Orleton who rescued him, only to have him gaoled later for his 'offences'. But the London mob would later find him and drag him from his gaol cell to murder him in the street.

Baldwin walked away with Simon, still feeling that strange sensation, as though his soul was separating from his body. 'I do not know what is to happen to me,' he said, when they were some distance from the execution. He felt a total alienation from the world, as though he was merely waiting in a queue for the executioner to take him in his turn.

'Baldwin, you are safe.'

The knight ignored him, saying, 'There was no need to kill Reading. You saw him hang just now, Simon. Why?'

'He was too close to Despenser,' Simon said. 'I've heard he was insulting to the Queen, too. I think she wanted her revenge.'

'Perhaps,' Baldwin said wearily. 'Perhaps so.'

'Come, my friend, you need a good jug of wine, and so do I.'

'I rather think that this once, a pint of wine would be an excellent idea,' Baldwin admitted.

Soon they were standing in a loud chamber with a jug each, trying to avoid being jostled by the happy revellers who were celebrating the death of a tyrant.

Simon and Baldwin drank in silence. Baldwin was moody, not at all himself. In all the years Simon had known him, Baldwin had never been morose, but today he seemed to have convinced himself that he was shortly to be arrested and killed.

To try to draw him from the bleak shell into which he had retreated, Simon began to tell him of Cecily and the murder of the Capon family by Squire William. It was not, perhaps, the happiest of tales, but there was one message that Simon thought relevant for his friend.

'So the Squire received a pardon, as did his men,' he finished at last.

'Only to die at the hands of a village priest,' Baldwin noted.

'But they were able to return to their homes,' Simon pointed out. 'And so will you.'

Robert Vyke had felt a profound terror strike him at the sight of the man's butchered quarters. The naked body had been man-handled like a hog's, the eviscerated torso separated from the hips, then held up and accurately separated with a series of blows straight down the middle of the spine; and finally the legs were separated by five firm cuts at the groin which slashed through the bone with ease. The pieces were all to be left in tar to seal them so that they would survive for years on display.

It was enough to turn a man's stomach, to see such brutality.

'Will they do that to me?' he asked in a whimper.

'Why'd they make the effort?' Otho said, but Robert scarcely heard his joke.

'They're going to do him next, aren't they?' he said fearfully, pointing to the body swinging overhead. Simon of Reading's face was a purple mask, and the rope was stained red where his fingernails had tried to pull it from his neck as he rose in the air.

'Nah,' Otho said, and spat into the road. 'He's already dead. No point. Anyway, he's not important enough. You got any idea how much it costs to get an executioner to joint a man? It don't come cheap.'

'What will they do to us, then?' Robert shuddered.

'Probably forget you exist,' Otho said patiently. 'Look, that sort of death is for the nobles and high-born. Not for the likes of you and me, Rob. Now, I'd suggest you stay with me and Herv for the next few days. We'll look after you.'

'How can you?'

'By saying you've been with us all this while. Right?'

'What, pretend I wasn't there?'

'Who will say you were?'

'There were all the knights . . . the king . . . Despenser . . .'

'The knights, believe me, have more to think about than whether you were there with them or not. The King's off tomorrow, so I've heard. They're going to take him somewhere else so he can't escape. And the Despenser's not really a problem to you now, is he?'

'What about the others, though? I can't just walk away.'

'Course you can! No one's holding you, Rob. Wake up, man! You've been with me and Herv all the while, right? All the way from Bristol.'

Robert nodded, and would have felt reassured, but for the man who at that moment turned and recognised him.

'Why, if it isn't the injured messenger – the man we sent to the King. Have you only just returned, then?'

'Sir Stephen,' Robert said, his heart sinking to his shabby leathern boots.

CHAPTER FORTY-SEVEN

Baldwin was feeling a great deal better as they drained their drinks. The talk with Simon had brought a measure of calmness. It was good just to be with a friend again. He let his hand fall to his side, resting on Wolf's great head.

'What will happen now, do you think?' he said.

'You, a knight, ask me, a mere yeoman, what *I* think is going to happen?' Simon said with a laugh.

'You have been with the people who have won the dispute,' Baldwin reminded him. 'I come from the losing side.'

'Well, I do not know,' Simon said. 'I simply hope we may soon be permitted to leave this place and return homewards.'

'I could wish for nothing more,' Baldwin agreed. 'However, I fear that there may be a desire on Sir Roger's part to prevent my leaving any time soon.'

'This is ridiculous!' Simon said. 'You have served the Queen, and the Duke her son, and even Mortimer himself in the past. Why shouldn't we see one of them and ask that you be released?'

'I should like to think that I could be trusted.'

'Then let's go and see the Duke. We can ask him for permission to leave. There can be no need for us to be held here any longer.'

The room to which they were conducted was a small chamber a little away from the hall, and here they were told to sit and wait.

Simon and Baldwin looked at each other, both of them feeling the boldness caused by their wine fade away.

Baldwin could feel that strange hollowness in his belly again. There were noises of festivity coming from the hall – singing, clattering of dishes and cheering, as though this was a warrior's hall from King Arthur's day. It was a strange counterpoint to the helplessness Baldwin felt.

There was the sound of marching. Soon, two men walked in and stood at either side of the door, before the figure of the Duke appeared.

Baldwin and Simon both knelt and bowed their heads.

'Sir Baldwin, please, and Bailiff, stand. There is no need for this.'

'My lord, I need to apologise,' Baldwin began, but the Duke shook his head emphatically.

'No, Sir Baldwin, you do not. You have served my father well, and you deserve to be honoured for that. You performed your duty admirably, and I am very grateful to you for it.'

Baldwin bowed his head again, and suddenly felt as weak as a new-born calf. 'Thank you, my lord.'

'And you, too, Master Puttock,' the Duke continued. 'I would have you rewarded for your service – but I fear that the strings to the realm's purse are closely bound as yet.'

'I'm content if you are happy with the service I have performed, my lord,' Simon said.

'How could I not be?' Duke Edward smiled.

'Simon has told me of your agent, Sam Fletcher,' Baldwin said hesitantly. 'I must apologise, Your Highness. I thought he was trying to kill the King's own messenger. Redcliffe had told me he was the King's man and I saw no reason to disbelieve him. And when your man tried to kill him . . .'

'It is understandable,' Duke Edward said, saddened. 'I trusted Fletcher entirely. He was a good man, and decent. Very loyal.'

'You should know that he and his party succeeded in killing Redcliffe,' Baldwin said.

'I am glad of that, at least,' the Duke replied.

Simon cleared his throat. 'But you should also know that Sir Roger has been asking who killed Redcliffe. He asked me to investigate personally.'

'What will you tell him?'

'I don't know what to tell him,' Simon admitted.

The Duke grunted. 'Then tell him that it was a band of men from Hainault. They saw Sir Baldwin here, and gave chase, killing a man from the party.'

'It was two they killed,' Baldwin said. 'And they injured Sir Ralph's squire too.'

'So much the better. There are witnesses to the deaths. You did not kill Redcliffe, after all, did you, Sir Baldwin?'

'No. It was one of the men with your fellow Fletcher.'

'Then there is nothing for you to fear. I will tell Sir Roger that you have investigated the affair, Master Puttock, and that you should be permitted to return home now.'

'I am most grateful to you, your lordship,' Simon breathed.

There was a great bellow of laughter from the hall, and the Duke's face stiffened. 'They executed Despenser today, and those laughing in there all witnessed his awful end. I confess, I find my appetite is somewhat curtailed.'

A step at the door heralded the arrival of Sir Roger Mortimer.

'Your Highness, you should be in there and celebrating. Oh, you have guests, I see.'

The Duke's chin rose slightly in defiance. 'These friends are here to tell us of the death of a man.'

Simon hurriedly spoke. 'Sir Roger, you asked me to find out what happened to Redcliffe. Well, Sir Baldwin here was present when he was killed.'

'Speak!' Sir Roger said.

Baldwin told the story as briefly as he could, without embellishment. 'I had no idea who the men were who attacked us,' he finished. 'I can only think that they were men from your host – perhaps Hainaulters? Certainly the man I killed was not dressed as one of your regular men, but he and the others appeared set upon stopping us from escaping.'

Mortimer nodded slowly, then shot a look at the Duke and at Simon. 'This all true?'

'I believe it,' Simon said.

'Then there's nothing more to be said.'

'Are we released, then?' Simon asked hopefully. 'Can we return to our homes? I want to see my wife and make sure that she is safe and—'

'Soon, I would think,' Sir Roger said. 'For now, there is still much to be done. You may wait here until you are told you may go.'

'I have already thanked Sir Baldwin for his service and assured him that he is free of any stain on his character,' the Duke said.

'He was with the Despenser when we caught him,' Sir Roger said.

'I was never a companion or ally of Despenser,' Baldwin said coldly. 'I *am* a loyal servant of the King, however.'

'Do you mean you would serve his interests?' Sir Roger said.

'Absolutely,' Baldwin said, feeling his belly churn at this statement. He had no idea how Sir Roger would respond to such a declaration. 'I made him my oath of allegiance. I honour that vow.'

'Good. So you should,' Sir Roger said. He pursed his lips. 'Come, Sir Baldwin, I believe you are a fair and reasonable man. Come with me, both of you, and share in the festivities. There is no reason for any of us to feel rancour towards each other, this day of all days.'

Sir Laurence was forced to fix a smile upon his face and raise his mazer to his neighbour as another toast was given in honour of the brave men of Hainault, as their leader, Jean, stood, braying with delight.

The hall was filled with shouting, joyous men. At the head table, Jean de Hainault sat with Sir Roger Mortimer and the Queen, while her son had been sitting near her at the end of the table. The rest of the hall was given over to merrymaking knights, squires and men-at-arms, all engaged in mutual congratulation at their part in the destruction of the King. Drinking vessels were all raised periodically in toasts, while men staggered from one table to another, as drunk as a peasant at a midsummer's feast.

It was revolting to be forced to witness this, Sir Laurence thought. To listen to the paeans offered to these grubby mercenaries, one would think that they were the epitome of all that was chivalrous and honourable, when in reality they were nothing more than paid servants without even the merit of having given an oath. He sipped his wine, feeling the desolation of loneliness in this hall filled with happiness, and offered up his own prayer for the King, his master.

'Sir Laurence, I hope I find you well?'

He looked up. 'Master Puttock. You survived the capture of the King, then.'

'Only by the merest margin, I fear,' Simon said. His head injury was making him feel unwell, and he motioned to the bench. 'May I join you?'

'Of course.'

'Do you know Sir Baldwin de Furnshill?'

'I believe we have met.'

The two knights nodded amicably enough, and Sir Laurence moved along his bench to make space for the other two.

'You were hurt in the action?' Sir Laurence asked.

Simon winced. 'I fell after a jump, and was caught in my stirrup and dragged a distance. I'm lucky to look this well.'

Sir Laurence whistled. 'I had a friend who died in such a manner. You are fortunate.'

'Yes. Thank God. Sir Charles was there,' Simon said. 'He saved my life.'

'Oh,' Sir Laurence said.

'You do not like him?' Baldwin enquired.

'I mistrust those who will seek mercenary reward,' Sir Laurence said. 'In my youth, all men gave their oaths and were rewarded from their lords' largesse. Now, apparently, a man's body and soul are likewise for sale.'

'Sir Charles was forced into it,' Simon said protectively. 'And surely, if you feel like that, you would not wish to go to a banker and make money from your position.'

'No. I would not wish to do so, and would not do so in practice.'

'Really?'

Sir Laurence glanced at Simon with some surprise. 'Yes. Why?'

'I've heard it said that you yourself were involved with

projects in Bristol, and that you were close to Arthur Capon,' Simon said.

'Whoever said such a thing was lying to you!' Sir Laurence snapped. 'I scarcely knew Capon – and never had any dealings with him. I saw my position there at Bristol as a position of trust, not a venture from which to gain profit. And in any case, I have no need of money. My manors bring in plenty each year, unlike those of others.'

'Of whom do you speak?'

This was Sir Baldwin, and there was a curious intensity about him as he asked the question.

'I was thinking of no one in particular,' he answered. 'But if you must have an example, I would say that the best is a man your companion here knows only too well. I am sure that it's the reason why he sold the city and castle of Bristol.'

'Sir Stephen, you mean?' Simon said.

'Yes. It is no secret that his manors have failed him, and that he cannot maintain the standard of expenditure that once he managed. There was a time when he was among the wealthiest in the land; now he is almost penniless. He needed money desperately badly, and I am sure he was counting on the gratitude of Mortimer when he opened the city gates.'

Second Tuesday after the Feast of St Martin[1]

Hereford
The next morning, Simon and Baldwin sat down to breakfast together in a small building near the hall. It was cold, but was at least quieter than the main hall, where many of the men had not

[1] 25 November 1326

bothered to sleep, and instead continued drinking through the night.

'Interesting that Sir Laurence denied anything to do with the moneylender,' Baldwin said. 'From all you said before, I had thought that he would be a more vain, self-conscious man.'

'Me, too' Simon thoughtfully kicked a pebble from under the table and watched it roll across the floor to strike the wall. 'If he is right, Sir Stephen is more likely to have seen Capon, but then Sir Stephen is the man he most detests in the world, because he surrendered the city at Bristol, and directly led to Sir Laurence being forced to give up the castle as well.'

'Well, all I know is that I shall be inordinately glad to be home again,' Baldwin said as he drank a little of the weak ale. He bit into a crust of bread and pulled a face. 'Dear Heaven! Someone made this from a piece of moorstone, not flour.'

Simon smiled as he chewed at his own. 'Anyway, surely it's a fact that the men who killed Capon weren't motivated by money.'

'No, not if you are right,' Baldwin agreed. 'That was a matter of a simple family dispute. There are enough cases of men who kill their wives, whether by accident or intentionally.'

'Yes, although it's rarer for them to kill their parents as well,' Simon said.

'True enough. But not unknown,' Baldwin shrugged.

They finished their meals in comparative silence. Only when they were done did Baldwin look across at his friend with a pensive frown.

'Simon, did Sir Roger actually say that we could leave now? I am not sure that he did, and yet that was the implication, was it not?'

'So far as I could tell,' Simon said.

'Perhaps,' Baldwin said, 'we should ask for a letter of safe-conduct for ourselves, just to make sure.'

Simon agreed, and soon they presented themselves to the clerks who were serving Sir Roger in a chamber in the castle's keep.

'Safe-conduct? Why would you need them?' the harassed senior clerk demanded. 'If you are attached to remain here, remain here. If you haven't been taken, then go, if you want. It's nothing to do with me, but if you think I have the time to get my boys here,' he waved his hand, taking in the seven middle-aged clerks behind him in a belligerent sweep, 'to write foolish notes for all and sundry, you have another think coming!'

'I am Sir Bald—'

'You could be the Holy Father from Avignon, and I'd give you the same answer. I have suddenly discovered that I am the senior clerk to the King, the Queen, their son and heir, and the kingdom, as well as Sir Roger Mortimer, so begone. Now!'

And to their surprise, Simon and Baldwin found themselves pushed unceremoniously from the hall.

'That cheeky . . .' Simon said, and would have returned into the chamber, had Baldwin not taken his arm and begun to laugh.

Simon glared at him, until Baldwin's mirth communicated itself to him, and soon the two men were helpless, Simon leaning against the wall, while Baldwin wept with the tears falling down his cheeks, while he held his stomach to try to stop the pain of so much amusement.

'What is the matter with you two?' the clerk demanded, throwing the door open. 'If you don't bugger off, I'll call the guards to have you arrested immediately. Did you hear me? I'll have you arrested, I said!'

Simon tried to hold his gaze, determined but the sheer incoherent fury on the clerk's face forced him to turn away and face the wall, his whole body jerking with the gales of laughter that enveloped him.

'You must be moon-struck. Madmen the pair of you,' the clerk sniffed disdainfully, and then, unsure that they were not deriving much of their delight from his own discomfiture, he slammed the door again.

'Simon, Simon,' Baldwin protested weakly, 'my belly aches so much!'

Simon sniggered again, wiping at his eyes. 'I think we are safe to leave, don't you?'

'First, old friend, I think I need another pot of wine!'

CHAPTER FORTY-EIGHT

Simon and Baldwin made their way back to the tavern they had attended the day before.

It was open today, and quite well-filled, but Baldwin was able to forge a path to the plank set on two barrels that served as a counter, and the two of them were soon gripping large jugs of wine, leaning against a wall while they discussed matters of less importance than their safety.

And Baldwin felt as though this was truly a wonderful, safe day. Over the last few days, he had feared that at any moment he might be arrested and raised to a gallows, kicking his heels in a scaffold's dance while the crowds laughed and jeered. To go from those nightmare visions to this peacefulness seemed little short of a miracle.

Preparing his soul for death had been a hideous strain, he realised, because now that the fear was gone, he was aware of a ridiculous feeling of freshness and gaiety. It was as though he had been reborn, and with the feeling came a flood of gratitude and joy that he had never known quite so poignantly before.

He could not keep the broad smile from his face.

468

'You look like you've just been given the whole of Devon-shire for your own hunt,' Simon commented.

'I feel as though I've been given the whole of Devon and Corn-wall as my plaything,' Baldwin countered. 'The relief is intense.'

Simon tapped his jug with his own. The pots met with a dull tone, and then both men drank deeply again.

'You know, Baldwin, all I want now is to return to Bristol and see my wife and child.'

'And I to get home once more,' Baldwin agreed. 'So you don't intend to do more about the dead maid Cecily when you get to Bristol, eh?'

'What more could I hope to learn?' Simon said. 'All the while I was thinking of her, it was really my own neck I was consid-ering. I thought that Mortimer would see me arrested if he didn't see me working. But I spoke to the maid's mistress, then her lover, the priest, and learned all I could about Squire William's inquest. There was little more I could do.'

'Did you speak to those who were said to have attacked her with this Squire?'

'No. But she must have been shocked to see them, I suppose,' Simon said.

Baldwin nodded. 'Well, if she saw them go into the Capons' house and slaughter all inside, including her charge, it would be hardly surprising if it almost turned her mad.'

'Indeed. She must have felt greatly threatened.'

'And, if you are right, at least one went on to murder again. Not that it would be very sensible for them to kill her,' he added with a frown.

'Because they would be laying themselves open to another arrest.'

'Yes. And so to kill her was madness, unless she posed a novel threat to them,' Baldwin said.

'She saw them; she pointed them out.'

'You think one of them killed her for revenge? Foolish, but you can never tell why a man draws his dagger. Perhaps he was drunk. Or it was someone who sought to rape her? Was she a comely woman?'

Simon drew down the corners of his mouth and shrugged. 'You know what a dead woman looks like, Baldwin. When dead, they are mere husks. There is nothing to show what sparks they used to hold in their eyes, how they would wriggle their back-sides to tease a man, or how they could torment with their bawdy speech, is there? And even the plainest-looking wench can be attractive when she is talking about something that excites her.'

'True. So perhaps it was rape, perhaps it was not. Poor woman.'

'Admittedly there was no actual sign of rape,' Simon remembered. 'Sir Charles and I did look, but there was no bruising or blood. You know, where she would have . . .' He did not need to finish. Baldwin knew perfectly well that Simon had always been affected with a curious reluctance to study dead bodies from close quarters, a trait that Baldwin found either touching or intensely irritating. Today, it was irrelevant to him. He was in too good a mood.

'Well, if she was not raped, you are led straight to the obvious conclusion that she was killed as a result of her evidence. The Squire or his men did it.'

'Not the Squire,' Simon told him. 'I believe he was dead already.'

'So, one of his acolytes,' Baldwin said. 'A common enough tale, if depressing nonetheless. But . . .'

Simon had seen that far-away look in his friend's eyes before. Something had occurred to him. 'Yes?'

'Well, a man who was that vicious – would he not gain more

pleasure from tormenting her than killing her? If bent on revenge, he could have watched for her daily, welcomed her loudly in the street, perhaps pressed near to her? All would drive the woman half-mad with terror, knowing that the men who had slaughtered her mistress and family were close. The satisfaction of that would be pleasing to most of the felons I have known.'

'She didn't panic,' Simon said without thinking.

Baldwin's eyebrows shot up. 'What makes you say that?'

'No knife-cuts on either hand.'

'Are you sure?' Baldwin frowned, and now Simon saw that all thought of his escape from Hereford was flown. 'No marks at all?'

'No.'

'Was she slain in a frenzy? How many stab wounds were there?'

'Only the one. She was stabbed straight to the heart.'

Baldwin let out his breath in a little sigh. 'Well, if you are right about that, it sounds a great deal more like a tormented woman who stabbed herself to death.'

Simon shook his head. 'No, Baldwin. If she had, the knife would have still been with her.' Then the smile froze on his face.

Baldwin set his head to one side. 'What is it?'

'The knight . . .' Simon said. 'Sir Stephen was there the next day, and threw a knife into her grave. That knife could have been the one that killed her. He was there, and he threw the knife in after her!'

'But what possible reason could he have had for killing her, when he was the Coroner for the city?'

Simon chewed at his lip. 'I don't know, Baldwin. But perhaps he knows something about her death he hasn't told me yet.'

*

It did not take long to find Sir Stephen. He was out in the castle ward, drinking a pot of wine.

'Sir Stephen. I am happy to see you, sir,' Simon greeted him. 'I feared you might have been hurt.'

'What, in the battle, you mean? No, I was fortunate. The fight was almost over when I reached the King. But you have been injured, as I can see.'

'I had a tumble from my horse,' Simon admitted.

'You are fortunate to be alive. It could have been deadly to fall in that mêlée.'

'Sir Stephen, you do not know my friend Sir Baldwin de Furnshill, do you?'

'Sir Baldwin, God's blessings on you.'

'And on you,' Baldwin said. 'Simon has been telling me of the terrible murders in Bristol. I have an interest in such matters. He said you investigated the Capon murders?'

'Yes. An awful affair. Arthur Capon was a good man.'

'You knew him well?'

'He was known about the city,' Sir Stephen said.

'And then their maid was killed in her turn, I believe?'

'A great shame. Her killers must have been out for revenge.'

'Have you ever seen a woman killed as punishment or in rage with one simple blow to the heart?' Baldwin said.

'Why not? I know little of such things.'

'But you are Coroner in Bristol?'

'I was.'

'Then surely you will have seen dead women many times. Raped, slain, and left?'

'Oh, perhaps a few . . .'

Baldwin was frowning with disbelief. 'And you think such a woman would be found with no defensive marks on her hands, slain with one single blow, and unraped?'

'It is possible.'

'And then, when she was being buried, you threw a knife in with her.'

'That damned knife again.' Sir Stephen looked annoyed. 'It was the knife Squire William probably used to kill her mistress. I had seen it on the man often enough. Many recognised it.'

'I may tell you, sir, that I am convinced the poor child was killed by her own hand. She had one blow to her heart: that is often the sort of wound a woman will give herself to end her life.'

'Oh?'

'So, please, you must not think that we are trying to entrap you over this,' Baldwin said earnestly. 'I just wanted to know why a knight would have thrown that dagger in the grave with her.'

'It was because the dagger was the one that Squire William always carried about his person. That is all. It seemed fitting that it should be taken with her. A deodand for the dead.'

'I see. Yes. But there is one thing that confuses me, Sir Stephen. If, as I think, the woman died by her own hand, there was no dagger with her. So someone took it.'

'And?'

'You grew to know her, I suppose, in your duties as Coroner. It must have been very hard for you, and dreadful for her – to relive the murders in front of the jury, I mean.'

'Yes.'

'So if you came upon her later, and saw that she had committed suicide, it would be natural for you to take away the dagger so that people would think she had been killed by another, so that she would not be refused a Christian burial as a self-murderer.'

Sir Stephen licked his lips. 'True, but . . .'

'You see, Simon told me you were not there at the scene. You asked Sir Charles of Lancaster to investigate the murder, didn't you?'

'Yes. It was a difficult time. There was much to be done.'

'Yes, of course,' Baldwin smiled. 'And it could have been . . . embarrassing, if you had been seen leaving that alley the night she was killed. Better to keep it secret. You saw her die, you took her knife, and arranged for another, less experienced in work as Coroner, to deal with her body, returning the knife to her when she was buried, yes?' Then Baldwin gave a little frown again.

'When I saw the dagger, I recognised it at once. It was the dagger Squire William de Bar had owned. Obviously poor Cecily was deeply distressed by the killings, and I thought she would appreciate the dagger as proof that Squire William would not be able to harm her. But she killed herself with it.'

'I see. So you gave it away? That was most generous.'

'A man may show largesse, even to a poor maid.'

'It is possible, yes,' Baldwin said. 'So, you gave her the dagger, and she killed herself with it. And afterwards you took it from her to protect her memory and in order to falsely allow the Church to believe that she had not, in fact, taken her own life.'

'Yes.'

'Well, let us draw a veil over matters, then,' Baldwin said. 'Although giving her the weapon that was responsible for her mistress's death and her own might be considered a gift in bad taste, when you threw it into her grave.'

'You may think so.'

'I do. Tell me: why were you talking to her in that alley?'

'What?' Sir Stephen snapped. His stance changed subtly. 'I have endured your questions, Sir Baldwin. Now I ask you: what do you mean by this?'

'I mean nothing, my dear Sir Stephen. I merely try to isolate the truth from all the hints and vague glimmerings which I hear. It is my hobby. A harmless pastime.'

'You have heard all I wish to say.'

'I see. So why were you in the alley with her?'

'I told you. I will say no more. Good morrow, sir.'

'Because I was saying to my friend here that her death was inexplicable. And the more I consider it, the more significant I find it.'

'What does that mean?'

'Just this. She killed herself with the very weapon that had ended her mistress's life. That suggests to me that there was some conjunction of actions in her mind.'

'What are you trying to say?'

'Oh, that she felt guilt for the death of her mistress, perhaps?'

'Sir Baldwin, are you raving?' Sir Stephen said impatiently. 'This makes no sense! Why would she be willing to see her mistress killed?'

'The reasons for the murder of a master or mistress are manifold,' Baldwin said. His mind suddenly flashed to the face of Sir Roger Mortimer and the King. 'Sometimes, it is because of a slight or perceived insult. Sometimes because of a real threat. Sometimes it is money that is the spur. So many reasons.'

'Well, if you are right, the money did her little good, did it?'

'True enough. Perhaps it was not just money, though. As I said, some will harm their masters or mistresses for less.'

'Eh? This is nonsense!' Sir Stephen said. 'If you are trying to accuse me of something, say so and be done. Otherwise, leave me alone.' He threw his hands up in the air and stormed away.

'Simon,' Baldwin said, 'I am rarely convinced of guilt, but just occasionally, I can see it staring me in the face. And today, it was in his eyes.'

'You mean he killed her?'

'Yes. Which may mean that the whole story has been concocted. Simon, walk with me. I must discuss this with you again.'

As they walked along the road, Baldwin mused over the death of this woman Cecily whom he had never met, never seen, killed because of a murder in which she had no involvement except as a witness. Anger pulsated through him as he thought that the man who could do that to her deserved the most vicious death the law could impose.

He recalled that Sir Hugh le Despenser was supposed to have tortured a poor widow to death. A Madame Baret had been caught by him, and tortured to agree to give up her dower and the lands belonging to her dead husband. This was one of the accusations levelled at him yesterday during his mock trial. And yet this maid Cecily had died for even less reason.

There were some boats drifting down the river, and Simon and Baldwin stopped to watch them for a while.

'This all makes no sense to me,' Baldwin said. 'Why should that knight suddenly lose his temper like that, unless he thought we were coming close to the truth?'

'Well, there is one explanation,' Simon said. 'If he was entirely innocent, and did as he said, and tried to hide her self-murder, surely he would grow peevish at being asked if he was responsible for her death?'

'Yes. But did you not notice, Simon – he grew most unsettled when I suggested that she might have had some feelings of guilt from the murders of her mistress and the other Capons. When I said it, I was thinking that she could have felt bad to have survived the killings – I did myself when I was rescued from Acre, and it was the guilt as well as the gratitude that made me join the

Knights Templar. But I think he took a different meaning. He thought I meant she was guilty of complicity . . . and then I thought, what if she were? Consider, Simon,' Sir Baldwin went on. 'If she had been guilty of such a crime, what could have motivated it?'

'Money? Sex? Hatred? Jealousy?' Simon guessed. 'But from what I heard of her, when her family was killed, she was left wandering the streets until Emma gave her a position. So financial gain is unlikely.'

'Sex is always a possibility. If she and Sir Stephen had been lovers, that would explain his mood,' Baldwin said.

'Hatred of her mistress seems unlikely,' Simon said. 'I have heard nothing from anyone that suggested she was anything other than a happy, loyal servant. And as for jealousy – well, again, surely there would have been hints if she were jealous.'

Baldwin rubbed his face. 'Ach, maybe I am being too sensitive. The maid showed no signs of disloyalty, as you say. What is there to suggest that she was anything other than a loyal member of the household? A guess; an intuition. Nothing more.'

'Except the fact that of them all, only she survived,' Simon said. 'Although they did kill other servants, I can think of one very good reason to spare her. If she had been an accomplice, at the inquest, she could have pointed out the guilty ones, Baldwin. The only person who could identify the felons was Cecily herself. Without her there were no witnesses.'

'So if a man arranged for the murders, he had his accomplice in the house to point to Squire William, and at the inquest she did her job.'

'And later,' Simon breathed, 'she saw some of the men released from gaol and *that* was why she was so overwhelmed with fear – because she knew that they would kill her for bearing false witness.'

'And the man she ran to was Sir Stephen, who laughed at her, or maybe just told her it was her problem. He would have nothing to do with it. And so she killed herself in front of him.'

'Why? Despair?' Simon wondered.

'Or in the hope that someone would have seen the two together, and accuse him of her death?' Baldwin said.

'So why did she help see the Capons killed?' Simon asked.

'I would wager that, since it cannot have been for money, it was for love.'

'Love for whom?' Simon said.

Baldwin frowned. 'You don't realise yet? Love for Sir Stephen.'

They made their way around the moat, back towards the castle. It was close to the gate, under a low roofway that served to protect a cart, that Baldwin saw his mastiff, and then spotted Jack. He smiled at the fellow, and was about to wave when he saw something behind Jack, a shape in the shadows of a doorway.

'Simon? Look, behind Jack. Can you see that man who seems to be trying to hide?'

Simon peered out, and nodded. 'Oh, don't worry about him, Baldwin. He's the man who advised me to meet the fosser who saw Sir Stephen throw the dagger in the grave. He has been with me ever since.'

'Oh,' Baldwin said, and the two walked out into the open. Then, as some drizzle began to fall, Baldwin pulled at his cloak's hood to cover his head. As he did so, he saw the man in the shadows make an urgent gesture, and all his years of training made Baldwin step back again, just in time to avoid the dagger that was thrust forward, almost scarring his breast. He grabbed the wrist with both hands and wrenched it. The man grunted in pain, and Baldwin swung the fellow around in an arc, over his right thigh, to fall on the ground. Instantly he planted his boot on the man's chin while hauling hard on the knife-hand. 'Simon!'

Simon sprang to Baldwin's aid. Then he felt a snatch at his own cloak, and heard the slithering of cloth being cut by a razor-sharp blade. Spinning on his heel, he came face to face with Robert Vyke, who had a knife in his hand.

CHAPTER FORTY-NINE

'What in God's name are you doing?' Simon shouted in fury, looking down. 'Not my cloak *again*! Do you know how much this cloak cost me?' And then he realised that the dagger had not been wielded in jest. 'Put that knife away, fellow, or I'll rip out your liver and feed it to the hound!'

Baldwin looked up at Simon with exasperation. 'Simon, he's a footpad. For the love of the Blessed Virgin, just prick him with your sword and be done with it.' He set his jaw and stared down at the writhing face under his boot. 'Let go of the dagger, you fool, if you don't want me to break your arm.'

Otho stared up at him with a look of disdain, but the relentless pressure on his outstretched arm was too much. 'A' right!' he grunted, and released the blade.

Simon was still glaring at Robert Vyke. 'What is the matter with you, man? Put the blade away or I'll have to do as my friend suggests. Dear Christ in Heaven, look what you've done to my cloak! You will buy me a fresh one before the day's out, I warn you.'

'Vyke,' Baldwin said patiently, 'drop the dagger or sheathe it.

I care little which you do, but if you continue to hold it like that, I will cut your wrist from your arm.'

Robert Vyke had been in battles now. He had fought alongside the King against knights and squires, and he had not died, but that had been a confused mêlée, a mad, slashing battle. If he had been an assassin, he would have killed Simon already, before Baldwin and Otho had come to blows, but it was something he could not do. He couldn't just stab a man in the back. He closed his eyes, swore to himself and stepped away, thrusting the knife back in its sheath. 'I couldn't do it.'

'Do what?' Simon demanded.

'Kill you.'

Simon's face twisted with incomprehension. 'Why would you want to do that? What have I done to you?'

'Not me. Not us. It's what you've told Sir Stephen Siward,' Robert said. 'He told us.'

Baldwin took his boot away. It left a raw patch on Otho's jawline. 'Told you what?'

'That you two were going to have me arrested – because I'd been with the King. I didn't want to believe it, but he said you were going to stop me leaving the town, that I'd have to kill you to leave here.'

Baldwin looked at him, then at the crowd gathering in the road, the three faces peering out from the tavern itself, the shock on young Jack's face, and at Wolf's bared teeth as he loomed over the now alarmed Otho. 'You really thought you could murder two grown men in broad daylight and escape?' he asked, and shook his head at their folly.

The day had started so well, too, and now he was forced to run; it was enough to make a man spit blood!

Sir Stephen Siward finished rolling his blanket, swung his

pack over his back, and hurried through the door. The garrison accommodation here was fairly modern, a chamber set above a large hall, where the men could rest in their spare time. Leaving by the door, he gazed about him sharply, before quickly going down the stairs and out to the inner ward. His horse was already waiting, and a hostler with the patient look of a cow chewing the cud, stood holding the reins while Sir Stephen bound his belongings to the saddle. There was a packhorse, but he would leave that for now. Perhaps he could send a message for his servants later, to have them follow him. Perhaps. For now, the only thing of which he was certain was that he should be away from here as quickly as possible.

And then he saw them. 'Damn their cods!' he swore viciously under his breath as the Bailiff and that damned knight from the ditches of Devon walked in through the doors. He moved around behind his horse as the two entered the ward and crossed to the stairs which led up to the hall, and then he swiftly mounted, snatched the reins up, spurred his beast, and was off, across the ward and out through the first gates.

They were doddypolls, the pair of them. Unandgitfull[1], buzzards. Why they had to chase him down, pursuing him for no purpose, he had no idea, but he was not going to make their capture of him any the easier, if he could help it.

Lashing his horse's flanks, he spurred the beast on, past the last gate to the castle and out into the busy streets. Here he must bellow and roar to have people move from his path. He did not want to hit someone, since it would hold him up, perhaps even injure his horse. A hog stood in the middle of the road, snuffling amid the faeces and garbage of the kennel, but he merely aimed his horse at it and leaped over, the horseshoes striking sparks

---

[1] dim, dickheads

from the cobbles where he landed. There was a pair of men chatting in the road, but they bolted when he came past although, from the shriek, one was caught by a flailing hoof.

It did not affect his mount. The beast thundered on, blowing heavily through nostrils that were opened wide, chest filling and emptying, and Sir Stephen felt sure that they would escape. Those two mopish fog-brains would find it hard to have a horse mounted with speed, and by the time they had, he would be a league away.

He hurtled down the last stretch to the bridge, and was over it in an echoing hammer of boards. And then he was onto the softer, safer road surface, and here he gave a loud cry of exultation, lashing his mount to greater efforts as he took the road south.

Simon heard the rattle of hooves and went to the door just as the knight shot out through the gates.

'Baldwin! He's gone!' he shouted, and then ran out, down the stairs, bellowing as he went, 'My horse! The bay rounsey, and Sir Baldwin's too, saddle them now! *Now*!'

Gripping his sword, he pelted over the ward, and then watched keenly while two hostlers hastened to his horse, four others standing and gaping. 'In the King's name! Fetch Sir Baldwin's horse and saddle him!'

Baldwin was at his side now, swearing as he stared at the gate whence Sir Stephen had escaped. 'We should have realised he might do that,' he muttered.

Even as he spoke, Otho and Robert ran in, Herv panting a short way behind them. Otho ran past Baldwin, calling, 'We saw the bastard. We'll come with you.'

'I don't think we need *your* help,' Simon said pointedly.

Otho looked at him. 'Really? We have more need to catch him

and prove we're not felons than you, Master Bailiff. We're coming.'

Simon was not prepared to argue. As he stood irritably tapping his foot on the ground, waiting for his horse, Otho and the others grabbed their own horses from the stable, saddled and bridled them in little time, and were ready to mount almost before Simon and Baldwin.

Shoving his foot in the stirrup, Simon sprang up, calling, 'Which way did he go, did you see?'

'Towards the river, I think. Down to the south,' Otho shouted back, and was already moving off before Simon had his other, sore foot firmly located.

Baldwin was away, and Simon after him, wincing, with Robert and Herv in their wake.

The town was full, and it was terrifying to rush headlong down the narrow alleys and streets towards the bridge, with men and women scattering and shouting, one hurling imprecations, another a stone, which fortunately missed. Then they were into the darkness between some hugely tall houses, and Simon heard the dread call of *'Gardez l'eau!'* but a concerted roar from him, and from Otho, who appeared to have heard as well, prevented the chamber-pot from being emptied over them. Instead a shocked maid stared out at them as the five men pounded down the cobbles, and out into a broader thoroughfare, where they all turned left towards the bridge. Simon felt his mount slip a little, a rear hoof sliding on a smooth cobble, and then there was a shout behind him. He daren't throw a look over his shoulder yet, but when he did, he saw Robert and Herv still on horseback, and thanked his stars that no one had fallen. Behind them, Wolf pelted along on his great paws, tongue hanging out.

Over the bridge, and he felt the thrill of the open country fill his heart and belly with fire. Here there was no need to ride so cautiously. They could all go at full speed. And with luck, since they had no heavy packs, and Sir Stephen was carrying all his belongings, they should be able to overtake him.

They did not pause until they came to a small bridge, where the hoofprints of a single horse stood out clearly. Simon reined in briefly to glance down. The prints were very distinct: one of the shoes, he saw, was cracked and should be replaced. He only hoped it would break and make the horse slow, but then he was riding on again, bending low as he let the horse have its head. The knight would surely not be able to keep on forcing the pace like this. He would have to slow before too long, or risk killing his beast.

Rushing past a little village, Simon saw that the land rose from here. And suddenly he saw Sir Stephen! Up ahead, on the brow of the next hill, perhaps a third of a league away, was a man on a large horse, who stopped and stared back.

'It's him!' Simon roared, and lashed his mount again, all thoughts of care for his own beast suddenly flown.

'I see him,' Baldwin shouted back, urging on his horse.

Trees whipped past, and the wind snatched and tugged at Simon's shredded cloak. The hood billowed out like a sack, and every so often he pulled at it ineffectually. It was freezing, too; the wind reached in through the gaps, chilling his spine all the way down to his buttocks. Every part of him throbbed and ached, burned or froze, and he hoped that the knight would soon be forced to slow his mad onward rush.

And then they were down a hill, fording a rushing torrent, splashing their legs and gasping with the icy water, and then up the other side into a small wood and thence past another hamlet, where the road split. Baldwin and Otho pointed where the hoofprints had gone – and there was Sir Stephen, up ahead, lashing and spurring his poor mount with abandon, a scant 150 yards away, and riding over the crest of a ridge.

It was enough to make them forget the cold, forget their tortured muscles, and think only of their prey. As soon as they reached the top, they hurtled down the other side like hounds seeing a hare.

Sir Stephen could not escape them – that was clear. He had forced his horse to go too far, too fast, and now the brute was winded.

They reached him as the horse gave up the ghost, and Simon rode around to block his path, his sword out and ready. 'Sir, stop. If you flog your horse any further, you will have to walk back with us.'

'Damn your soul, Bailiff!' Sir Stephen spat.

'Others have suggested that,' Simon said easily.

It was late that afternoon when they all returned to the city. Sir Stephen had been silent for almost the whole journey, but as they reached Hereford and rode over the bridge, he gestured at a tavern. 'You will question me anyway: is there any reason why we could not do so over a pot of wine?'

'There is no reason to avoid wine,' Baldwin agreed.

Soon they were all inside the tavern, in a small chamber which had a charcoal brazier to warm them, and jugs of wine set out on a tray with a mazer each.

'Killed? What is that supposed to mean?' Sir Stephen said as Baldwin questioned him.

'You asked those three men to kill us, we know,' Baldwin smiled. 'Your attempt failed, although you owe Simon a new cloak for his trouble. Why did you want us dead?'

'Because you had decided I was guilty,' Sir Stephen said. 'I wanted to remove you, Puttock, ever since you mentioned my guilt.'

Simon drew a face. 'What?'

'On the way back with the King's men, you said something about bad debts, and gambling. I knew what you were getting at.'

'Well, I don't,' Simon said. 'Do you mean when I spoke of the Capons?'

'Yes. You clearly knew about my debts. That was why I tried to kill you – at the hedge. I saw you were at the back of the column, so I rode across to make your horse shy. I'd hoped you'd break your neck, but oh no, you managed to live, and told this knight.'

'Of the murder of the Capons,' Baldwin interjected. 'I believe Cecily was lying when she declared that Squire William had been there and killed the Capons. I think it was you, with your accomplices, who carried out the murderous deed, because Capon was a moneylender,' Baldwin said, 'and you owed him money. Lots of it. So you lured the maid Cecily into helping you. You swore no one would be hurt, and she was shocked when your men went into the house and slaughtered all inside. Perhaps she said then that she wanted nothing more to do with it? I see by your expression that I am right.'

'She told me that she'd sworn to protect the babe, and as the child couldn't bear witness against me or my men, so he should live. But I didn't want some bratchet growing into a vengeful youth and hunting me, so I had him killed, just in case.'

'I see. And then, of course, you persuaded her that she was as guilty as any, and if she wanted to live, she must point her finger at the ones whom all would believe were guilty: Squire William and his men. Which was why you allowed her to live, of course.'

'Oh, good. Very good. What else?'

'This knife which you threw into Cecily's grave. A good, golden hilt, with some jewels . . .'

'That was mine! *I* found it!' Robert declared. He drank deeply from his mazer. 'I found it in the road near the body of the Squire. And then *he* killed the maid with it.'

'That's a lie! I didn't kill her. You'd take a peasant's word instead of a knight's?'

Baldwin motioned to Robert Vyke. 'Continue. How did you find the knife?'

'I fell, you see,' Robert Vyke said, and explained about the pothole and the dagger in the bottom. 'When Sir Stephen here saw it, he bought it from me.'

'You bought it,' Baldwin said, 'and then threw it into the grave with her? Why?'

'You ask a lot of questions, Sir Knight, but I fear I have no desire to make your task easier.'

'Really?' Baldwin said. 'Then you will answer to the court. I will have you held for the next Court of Gaol Delivery. And then you will, in all probability, hang.'

'Damn you. Damn your offspring, your hounds and your home! You have nothing, and you will not keep me here. I am a knight, damn you!'

'You are being held here under my authority as Keeper of the King's Peace,' Baldwin said. 'And I will convey you to the castle, where you can be questioned by the local Justices.'

'You will find no one who will stand against me,' Sir Stephen said. 'I will be free as quickly as – nay, quicker than – Squire William.'

'The King does not need you now,' Baldwin said mildly. 'He has other affairs to concern him than a knight who committed murder. Especially one who killed a man who was going to fight for him. One who surrendered a city of his.'

Sir Stephen turned, only to find that Herv and Otho were both blocking his escape. 'Get out of my way, churls, or I'll cut you down,' he hissed.

'By the devil's ballocks, you have a nerve,' Simon said, as he put his hand on his sword. 'I declare, if you try to draw a sword, man, I'll knock your pate so hard, you'll not wake until Christmas!'

Sir Stephen looked at him, and then drew his dagger and lunged.

Baldwin gasped as the blade passed by Simon's breast, missing him by a cat's whisker, and then Sir Stephen continued, toppling to the ground, while Simon stared down at the body before him.

Otho weighed the stone in his hand. 'I didn't hit him too hard,' he said apologetically. 'But I've wanted to knock down a knight for a good long while now. It's satisfying.'

CHAPTER FIFTY

Third Wednesday after the Feast of St Martin[1]

Hereford

The Duke of Aquitaine stood as the two men walked into the hall, and waited as they made their way to him.

It was an old chamber, and smoke from the fires had marked the beams with soot, blackening the rafters and staining all the thatch that lay above. There was a comforting smell about the place, a smell redolent of ale, of dried hams and bacon, and of the pleasures of eating and drinking with family and friends during a long cold winter's evening. The fire was lighted now, and the well-dried wood was burning brightly, sending occasional sparks flying up into the air, where they mingled with the very fine smoke a little higher. Later, as the chamber warmed more, the smoke would dissipate and the air would be cleaner. For the young Duke, this chamber smelled of happiness.

And he detested it.

[1] 26 November 1326

This was the room he had been in when they had come to tell him that his father had been caught. Caught and brought here like a felon, all power, authority and honour stripped from him like so many garments. If they could go against God's holy law and do that to one king, they could do it to any.

'Sir Baldwin, I am glad to see you well,' he said, forcing a smile as the two men reached him. 'Master Puttock, your head is recovered?'

'Almost, Your Highness,' Simon answered. 'My back will be sore for a while, though.'

'You are lucky. Such a fall could have been fatal.'

'It was intended to be,' Baldwin said. 'Fortunately, Sir Charles saw his danger and saved him. Otherwise he would be dead. And all because Sir Stephen attempted to see him thrown.'

'He tried this?' Duke Edward said.

'He has admitted it. He regrets very much, so he says, that his plan failed. Apparently he felt anxious that Simon was coming too close to his secret, and wanted to remove a possible threat.'

'So many are dead because of him. What did he hope to achieve?'

Simon answered him. 'The man Capon had been a money-lender. I should have realised it before. So many told me, and Baldwin too, of people who had been to Capon to borrow, and who had suffered for their pains, that I should have taken note. But I failed, I fear, because all told me of the death of Squire William's wife, and the focus of us all was on his unique cruelty.'

'So was he not so bad as he was painted?'

'Oh, yes. He was a most unpleasant man, by all accounts. But this crime was not his. I am quite sure that the murder of Capon and his family and servants was committed by Sir Stephen, purely in order to conceal a large debt he had accumulated. He

had no means of repaying it, so he sought to kill the money-
lender who wanted it returned. Redcliffe had told Baldwin about
the methods he employed. He was no kindly, amiable merchant,
any more than Squire William was a warm-hearted nobleman.
Their behaviour towards Petronilla, Capon's daughter, shows
that. Both sought to take what they wanted, and when thwarted,
were equally resolute in seeking revenge.'

'Why would Cecily have agreed to help Sir Stephen?'

Baldwin answered. 'Sir Stephen has already told us that she
was exceedingly upset to have been sent away from her mistress's
side by her new employer Squire William. Suddenly, Cecily was
thrown back on the charity of Capon – except that Capon was not
sympathetic. He was about to evict her from his house, when
Petronilla returned with her lover, and needed a maid again. And
then, presumably, Capon found it convenient to keep Cecily on
as a dry-nurse. The experience had scared Cecily, and she wanted
revenge on Capon. The thought of helping someone to rob him
was appealing; Sir Stephen vows that she had no idea that Capon
was to die. She must live, so that there was a witness to declare
that it was Squire William, and she played her part well. William
was accused, arrested, and found guilty.'

'But then,' Simon continued for him, 'the Squire and his men
were released. Learning of this, Sir Stephen ambushed Squire
William on his way home, slew him, and pointed the blame at
the priest. He even disembowelled and beheaded him, making it
look like an act of revenge for his woman and child. And then
Cecily saw the other men in the city.'

'Which made her fear for her life,' the Duke said.

'Sir Stephen said that, in fact, Squire William's men were very
unlikely to risk committing a crime when they had just been pardoned for one of which they were innocent. True, they had been
wrongly accused and it is not surprising that she feared they

would seek to punish her for her false witness. However, Sir Stephen laughed at her. He held out the dagger, I think to threaten her, and she took it and killed herself. He couldn't remain there with her, so he took back his dagger and ran. And in case someone had seen him there, and would remember, he refused to return, instead asking Sir Charles to hold the inquest in his place.'

'Where is he now?'

'In your gaol at the castle, my lord,' Simon said. 'But I think he should be sent back to Bristol to be tried there. If I may suggest it, Sir Laurence would be an excellent guard to take him. He would like to return to his city, I am sure.'

'Yes. Certainly,' the Duke said.

There was a little additional business. He had letters to be taken to Bristol, and Simon and Baldwin asked for safe-conducts signed in his name for their journey, for the roads were still hazardous. Soon their business was over, and he took their farewells, offering them 'Godspeed' on their way.

'You go home now?' he said.

Baldwin bared his teeth in a smile. 'I have not seen my daughter or son in months, Your Highness. I am desperate to see them, and my wife.'

'Me as well,' Simon said. 'My daughter is a mother now, in Exeter, and my wife and son are incarcerated in Bristol. I would ask one last boon.'

When they left him, the Duke wandered over to the large table where his clerk sat, and leafed idly through the parchments on the desk.

Two men, he thought. Two men with wives and families whom they adored. Their children would never know how terrible it felt – the wrenching guilt of a son who was the source of contention between his parents.

For Duke Edward, the future King of England, such a peaceful, amiable family existence would never be his lot – and it made him heartsick, to think of the comparison between his life and that of Baldwin and Simon's sons.

Otho said guiltily as Simon walked up to him. 'I am sorry, sir, that we—'

'You more than made up for your foolishness with your excellent service capturing the murderer,' Baldwin said. He held out his hand, and Otho looked from Simon to him, before grasping it.

'Robert Vyke, how is your leg now?' Baldwin asked.

'Not too bad, Sir Knight. Only hurts a little when I use it.'

'You should be well enough for the journey home, then?'

'He'll last it,' Otho said. 'I'll kick his backside if he doesn't. He failed me on the way here; he won't fail again on the way home if he knows what's good for him.'

Robert Vyke gave a smile, but it was thin and his anxiety was plain to both Baldwin and Simon.

'What's wrong?' Simon asked. 'You look as though you've been sentenced to death.'

Otho answered. 'He's terrified he'll be caught by someone who saw him when he was with the King's men. He thinks his life is in danger still because he stayed with the King and didn't come to Sir Roger Mortimer's side.'

Baldwin remembered that feeling all too clearly. He could recall how he had felt smothered by the increasing fear, wondering how he would be treated, expecting to be slain in his turn. 'Vyke,' he said. 'Take this.' He reached into his purse and took out the small scrap of parchment he had taken from Redcliffe, now stained and blotted. 'This is a safe conduct for any man. It will guarantee your safety.'

Robert Vyke gaped, and took the note with many bows of his

head and expressions of gratitude, but Baldwin waved them away.
'You behaved honourably enough, man. Get you home to your
wife and forget war. Let us hope we may all forget this sadness.'

The men took their leave of each other. At the stables, Jack
was waiting with Wolf. The dog was sitting, leaning against him
comfortably while the lad tickled his ears. A short way off, Sir
Ralph stood watching an armourer running his sword over a
spinning stone, the sparks flying in showers for a yard or more.

'So, Sir Baldwin, you are leaving already?'

'I think the sooner I am away from here and heading towards
my home, the better,' Baldwin said. 'I am grateful to you for
your companionship, Sir Ralph.'

'As to that, it was my pleasure,' Sir Ralph said, taking the
sword and peering down the length of the blade with a critical
eye. 'A little more, man. I am only glad that we had just the one
fight, and that neither of us was hurt.'

'Yes. Although others were,' Baldwin said soberly.

Sir Ralph shrugged. 'Men live, men die, every day. Some die
in a battle. If not, they would have died some other way – fallen
into a well or tumbled into a river when drunk, and drowned.
The main thing is, we survived. And now Despenser is gone, life
will be incomparably better for all of us.'

'Yes,' Baldwin said. One image had remained with him from
the last weeks: that of King Edward's face, watching from a high
window as his most beloved friend was accused and judged and
then executed.

He would never forget that face.

Worcester Castle

He didn't even know where this place was. They had stopped so
often in the days since his capture to allow him some peace, that
now he was entirely confused as to where they were.

Edward II, King of England, sat at the window and stared out from eyes ravaged by weeping. It was a vaguely familiar landscape, but he didn't care. If he had been here, Sir Hugh would have commented on it, would have known where they were.

It was enough to bring on the desperate sobbing again.

'Dear God!' he wept. 'Why have you done this to gentle Hugh?'

Not for the first time, God had decided to punish His poor servant Edward.

'I will never have another friend,' he declared, and put his hands to his face. All whom he loved were taken from him. His Piers, captured and murdered by his enemies; now Hugh too. Was there no compassion in God for a simple man who enjoyed the companionship of a few special friends? All he had ever sought to do was to maintain his realm, protect his people and his friends, and rule wisely. The fact that others did not approve of his pleasures was not his fault. He was the *King*, he should be permitted the pastimes he desired. Swimming was no sin, neither was hedging with the peasants on his estates; if the lords and barons disliked such activities, they could avoid them – but for him, they were necessary distractions from the strains and stresses of royal life. Could God truly seek to punish him for that?

But he knew it was more than just that. It was his intimate relationships with Piers and Hugh that had led to God's aversion. Yet why punish only *them*, and leave him alone? He would have preferred to be taken with them. There was no point in life now. Not with his wife become his enemy, and adulterously engaging with the arch-traitor Mortimer. Even his own *son* had deserted him. All the kingdom was against him. Only a tiny number of men had been there with him at the end. All others had fled.

So now here he was: alone. Without host, without castles, without hope.

He could never know happiness again.

Third Friday after the Feast of St Martin[1]

Bristol

Roisea Redcliffe walked into her house with a feeling of mild curiosity; she wanted to see if there was anything in there that could remind her of her darling Thomas.

The fool! Thinking he could renew their fortunes by killing the King. Oh, that would have been a magnificent act, that would. What had he imagined he would do? Just draw a dagger and stab him during a meeting? And what would have happened then? Succeed or fail, the first thing would have been that the King's men would have slain *him* – and Roisea too, since she would have been assumed to be guilty by association.

She walked through to the hall. The place had been stripped of anything valuable by the men who had encircled the city. The house had been used as quarters. The hallings she was so proud of were gone. Her cushions, the decorative candle-holders, the little crucifix from its niche by the fire – all had disappeared – and in their place were bones, filth, and excrement. The bed-room, she was sure, would be as bad, and when she walked through to the solar, she had to leave in a hurry. From the stench, this whole area had been used as a privy.

Outside, she sat on the step and put her head in her hands, thinking furiously. There was no money, nothing to sell, and she had not eaten for a day.

[1] 28 November 1326

Then she stood and eyed her horse. It was a good beast, and would bring in some welcome money. That was first: sell the horse and use some of the payment to buy food. And then she would have to clean the house.

That would keep her busy for a while. And meantime, she would have to work out how to make some money.

She looked over at the horse again. He was a well-bred beast, worth several pounds, if she was careful about where she sold him. And then she remembered a man Thomas had used, over towards Berkeley, who could usually be relied upon to sell beasts for a reasonable sum. In recent times the horses all about Bristol had been depleted, but with luck the Queen's men would not have gone so far as Berkeley. Perhaps she could use the money she made to buy some more horses, bring them here and sell them on to make a little profit, and fund another trade.

Whatever else happened, Roisea was determined that she would not lose her house. She would somehow keep it all together. And if it took time, so be it. She had time and enough to spare.

Bristol Castle

Margaret heard the crying in the darkness, and rose, shivering, to go to Peterkin. There was no candle, and she drew on a robe, trying to find her slippers with her feet to save them from the cold stone floor.

'Hush, my love,' she cooed, picking up her son from his small bed and hugging him tightly. 'Hush!'

She began to rock him with the automatic maternal movement which was second nature to her, almost asleep herself. It was hard to imagine what the world was like outside. All was dark, all was grim. There was no happiness left in her, since her husband had been taken from her.

Simon. She thought of his calm grey eyes, his kind smile, his companionship. In the last weeks she had felt so entirely alone, it had been like living in a cage. All the guards about the castle stared at her suspiciously, while the servants and maids who had been here before the capture of the castle, avoided eye-contact with all, in case they were suspected of some offence. Only one guard eyed her differently from those who seemed to think she was about to poison the entire garrison, and Meg found his attentions even harder to bear, as he licked his lips lasciviously whenever he saw her glance in his direction.

In the front of her tunic, under her chemise, she had taken to wearing her little sheath knife. She swore that if the man came within a foot or two, she would kill him before he could touch her body.

She rocked Peterkin.

In her mind it was summertime in the woods up behind her home, just after the last bluebells were dying away, and the little star-flowers were sprinkled over the grass under the trees. There was the scent of rich soil, the smell of cattle and sheep on the air, and the sound of Simon walking beside her as they tramped down to the stream at the bottom of the second pasture. He would unstopper the wine skin, and both would drink before they lay in the grasses together. She would sleep then, with the sun on her body, his kiss on her lips.

And then she woke. The sun was streaming in from the window in the southern wall, Peterkin was yawning and stretching his little arms, and Simon was over her, grinning wolfishly as he leaned forward to kiss her again.

'Morning, wench!' he said.

Baldwin watched as a hostler began to rub down his horse, making sure that the fellow knew his business, before following Jack and Wolf into the inn itself.

It was so deeply engrained in him from his earliest days as a Knight Templar that a knight should always see to the needs of his mounts first, that even at a good inn like this, and even when he had his own servant to keep watch over the beasts, he still preferred to see to their welfare himself.

Jack was standing at the fire already, a quiet figure with large, anxious eyes, and Baldwin pursed his lips at the sight of the lad. 'Are you ailing?' he asked.

Jack stared at the flames. 'I wanted to do right and help protect the King, but all we did came to naught, Sir Baldwin.'

'It did, I fear. But that is how life is sometimes, lad. We did our best, and no man can ask more.'

'I had thought that to fight would be glorious. In Normandy in the summer, I was brave enough.'

'You were.'

Jack looked at him. 'I thought that the most honourable thing would be to serve my King – but he was caught anyway, and so many men have died.'

'Men die all the time, Jack,' Baldwin said quietly, repeating Sir Ralph's words. 'It is not the dying that matters, it is how the man lived.'

'But think of the men at the river's side, when poor Master Redcliffe was killed. He died, and so did those who attacked us. Then Sir Ralph's servants, both there at the river, and later, when the Mortimer's men caught up with us. They didn't deserve to die there. It was all wrong!' The boy's eyes were full of tears now.

Baldwin held his hands to the fire. His feet were frozen, and his hands felt so cold they could crack like icicles. 'But Sir Ralph's men were proud to have served him, and they died doing their duty,' he said patiently. 'No man enjoys dying, just as only a fool enjoys taking life. There is no merit in killing, but there is great merit in dying honourably, for a good cause, and being remembered for that. The men with Sir Ralph will always be remembered by him, and honoured for their courage.'

'It is not as I expected.'

Baldwin gave him a long look. 'Did you think to learn that you were glorious just because you fought on one side rather than another?'

'No. But I had hoped I would at least show some courage. Instead, I found myself petrified. And not just because I feared death – but because I feared that I might have to kill.'

'That is good,' Baldwin said, and his eyes returned to stare at the fire. 'Because the first man you kill, Jack, will stay in your mind forever. If you must kill, kill swiftly and for a good reason. Because I swear this: if you kill a man for the wrong reasons, your soul will be tormented all your life.'

Jack's tone was hushed. 'Are you speaking of yourself? Have you regretted killing a man?'

Baldwin smiled. 'No, Jack. I was a warrior, and helped defend the Kingdom of Jerusalem as I might, but without success. The kingdom failed. I have killed several men, but always only when I thought it necessary. Never from a frivolous motive. No, I was thinking of others.'

In particular, he was thinking of Sir Hugh le Despenser, and his mean butchering at Hereford. And it made him think too of Sir Roger Mortimer, the man who had caused Sir Hugh's execution.

One who could act with such casual savagery was not the sort of man to rule the realm, he thought.

'Come! Let us discard these solemn thoughts, Jack,' he said. 'Soon we shall be at my home, and you will be welcome to remain there with my family if you wish. There is peace in the land now, and with God's help you will never need to confront your fears of warfare again.'

Baldwin hoped that was true. But as he thought of the King, now the prisoner of his wife, his son, and Sir Roger Mortimer, he was aware of a grim certainty.

The kingdom would not know peace until the throne was occupied properly once more.

Lane near Devizes

The way here was muddy and thick, with stones of different sizes. Walerand the tranter had thought that his new cart would fit perfectly, but now, several hundred yards down the lane, he realised that he was unable to continue. He got down and thrashed the pony a few times to work off the worst of his rage, but it didn't achieve anything.

Edging his way past, he saw that one of the wheels had become clogged with nettles and old brambles. The wheel had fallen through icy mud into a deep rut that ran close to the wall where the weeds grew, and now the wheel's hub was jammed against the wall itself, firmly fixed in place. He set his jaw. He would somehow have to push the cart away from the wall to free the hub, but doubted he would be able to move it on his own.

'You need help, friend?'

'What do you think?' Walerand said rudely, looking up to see an older man gazing down at him. 'The cart's stuck here, and it's so tangled up, I can't move it forward or back. Can you give me a hand?'

'Cost you a shilling.'

'What?' Walerand exploded. 'I only want you to help push it, not build me a ruddy new one!'

'A shilling if you want me to help.'

'Six pennies.'

'Two shillings.'

Walerand put his head to one side. 'What? You said one!'

'You argued. If you try that again, it'll go up again.'

'All right, all right. Two it is.'

'Show us your money then.'

'Eh?'

'You heard.'

Walerand looked at the cart, then at the man again. Two shillings! But God alone knew when someone else was likely to come by here, and he'd never be able to pull the damn thing free on his own. He'd have to empty the cart, take the pony from the traces and tie her up, then cut out the weeds and move the empty cart, before setting the pony back, refilling the cart ... Reluctantly he pulled two shillings from his purse and held them out.

The old man took the coins and studied them carefully, before pushing them into his purse. Then he climbed down from his horse and studied the cart's wheel. 'You've got it jammed in there.'

'Thanks for the information – I'd never have guessed,' Walerand said sarcastically. 'Put your shoulder to the wheel.'

It took five minutes of grunting effort before they could move the cart away from the wall and heave it out of the rut.

'That's the problem with lanes like this,' the old man panted. 'Get your wheels stuck in a rut and you've had it.'

'Aye. Well, friend, I thank you for your help,' Walerand said, wiping sweat from his brow. He jerked at the pony's halter and teased it onwards.

The old man remounted his horse and stared after him thoughtfully, before riding back the way he had come.

Walerand found the inn at the edge of the next wood, not far from a little ford. There was a patch of scrubby grass, and he left the pony there, nibbling, before stalking inside and ordering himself a pint of strong ale. He sat down at a bench, and drank thirstily, stretching his boots towards the roaring fire. The weather was that cold, it was a wretched time of year for a man to continue with his travels. His passage here had been long, too. At least four-and-twenty miles today. Christ's cods, but it would be good to get back to Farnham and rest awhile, he thought, bending his right leg and feeling the tightness of his calf.

There was a rattle at the old door, and it creaked open to show the man he had met on the trail. Walerand did not greet him. The fellow had taken him like a cutpurse. Two shillings! Daylight robbery. It would be tempting to hold a knife to his throat and take his money back. In fact, it was more than tempting, it was a damned good idea.

With that thought, he set his cup on the floor, and was about to rise, when a second man entered, glanced about him, and followed Walerand's two-shilling helper to the bar in the corner.

Too late. Walerand pulled a face and settled back down on his bench. He should have jumped the bastard as soon as he walked in. The two seemed to know each other. Talking together now, they were, and he strained an ear to see if they spoke of anything useful.

Another man walked in, but this one didn't join the other two as they chatted. He stood staring down at Walerand.

'What?' the tranter demanded. 'Who you gawping at, you prickle? Stare somewhere else!'

The man smiled, and there was something about him that stirred Walerand's memory.

'Walerand, I note you have a new pony.'

'How do you know my name?'

'A gull never forgets the thief.'

'Who are you?'

'He's forgotten me, Otho,' the man called out.

The older one was leaning on the bar, his pot of ale in his hand. 'Forgotten you, Robert?' he said pleasantly. 'No, I reckon he remembers you. He was upset that day, though, don't forget. He'd just seen his horse die.'

Walerand felt the memory like a kick in his flank. He saw the cart, the filthy, rainswept roadway, and a man shouting at him for thrashing his pony. And he distinctly recalled hitting the fellow over the head and taking his dagger.

'Oh, master, yes, I remember now,' he said silkily. 'I am glad you made it to safety – but I did all I could to help you.'

'You struck me down and broke my head!'

'Not I.'

Robert sucked at his bottom lip. 'Very well friend, I think I should take your dagger now, to repay me for your theft.'

'I stole nothing. You can go to hell with my blessings!'

'I want compensation for the theft of my dagger, or you'll find bad luck will befall you.'

He had moved away from the door towards Walerand, and the latter saw his chance. Quickly flinging his ale in the man's face, he darted out. It was fortunate that he had possessed the good sense to leave his pony in the traces. It was the work of a moment to jerk the pony's head around, and whip her into movement. He would keep tight hold of his whip, he decided, and if the arses came close, he'd cut them about the face. They wouldn't get him that easily.

The cart rumbled and squeaked more than usual. It needed grease on the hub, he reckoned, and the pony neighed and complained, but then the thing was moving . . . and then he heard a rending sound, and the cart lurched. A huge splinter of wood sprang from the wheel, and as he watched with appalled eyes, the whole carriage began to tilt over, the bed moving, and then the wheel fell to pieces. The cart collapsed and shed its load, a bale ripping open on a broken spoke, and all the rest of his goods tumbling out on the muddy roadway.

'God's ballocks!' And in the doorway, he saw the three men peering out and grinning at him.

Robert Vyke raised his pot in a mocking toast. 'Oh, you can keep the dagger,' he said. 'My new one's got a good enough blade. Shame about your cart, though. Looks like the wheel's broken.'

And as they watched his crestfallen expression, they began to laugh.

ABOUT THE AUTHOR

Michael Jecks gave up a career in the computer industry to concentrate on writing and the study of medieval history, especially that of Devon and Cornwall. A regular speaker at library and literary events, he is a past Chairman of the Crime Writers Association and judges awards for the CWA and other literary groups.

Michael lives with his wife, children and dogs in northern Dartmoor.